Love Endures All Things

KATHLEEN HOWELL YOUNG

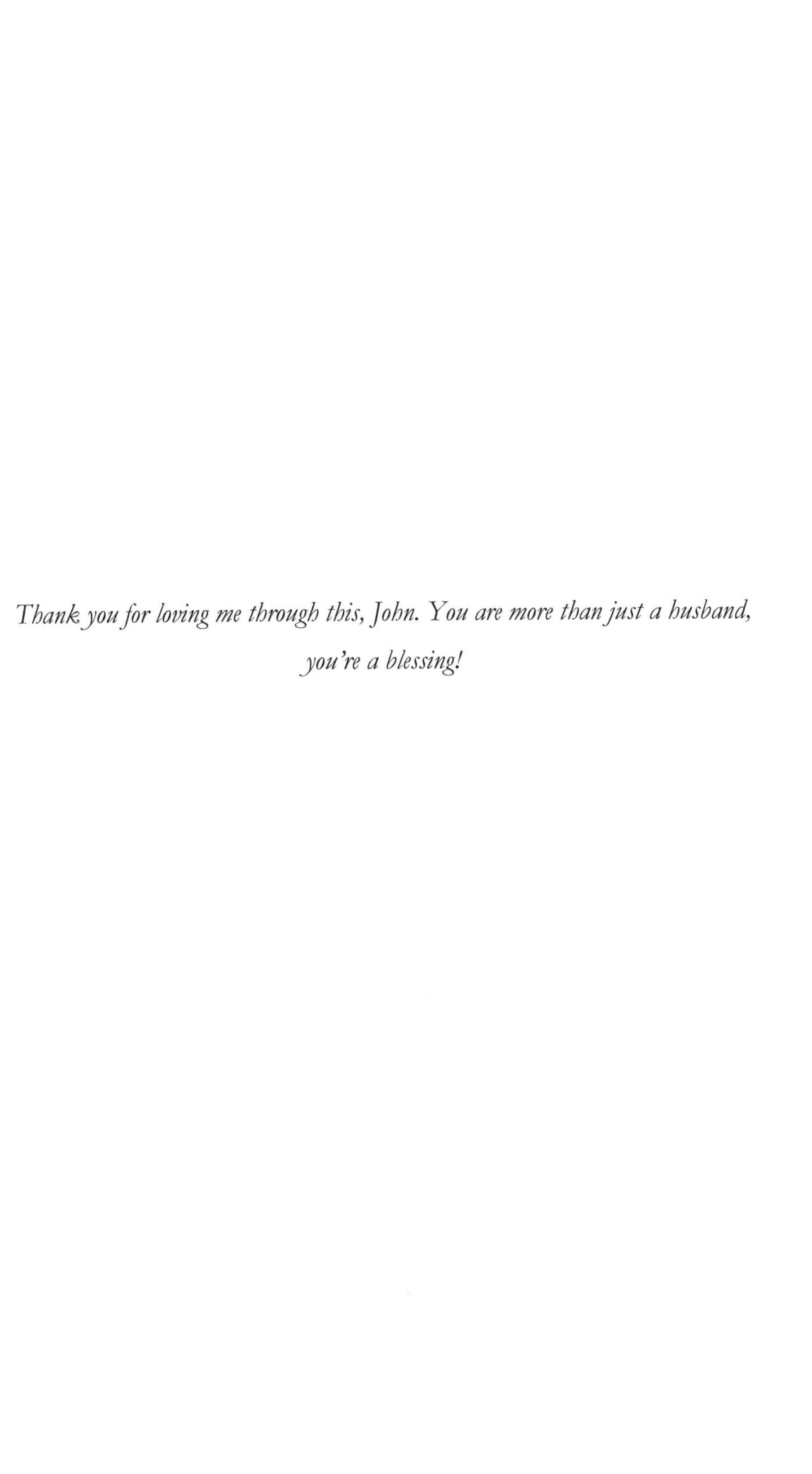

Thank you for loving me through this, John. You are more than just a husband, you're a blessing!

Acknowledgement

Peggy, it's amazing that one friend telling another of a story in her head would lead to a book, but it happened because of your insistence. Thank you for listening that night and for insisting I get to know your sister who pushed me to the finish line.

L.B. Brookes, it's been years of Zoom meetings, phone calls, texts, and lunches but we both got to publish our works! Love you.

Table of Contents

Late Night Meeting

Isabelle pulled her bedroom door closed as slowly as she could, turning back the glass knob just as cautiously to lessen the dreaded clicking sound. Holding the knob tightly, she twisted her body around and leaned against it. She felt her knuckles dig into the base of her spine as she looked to her left. *The moon is bright tonight.* She thought. However, the glow of it stopped abruptly at the top of the front staircase. It offered nothing to the long hallway before her that led past the other bedrooms to the back stairwell.

Her mind raced with worrying thoughts. *My heart is beating so loudly that it will wake them all. I need to get downstairs straight away.*

She weakened her grip as she arched her back and pulled away barely a half step. Indecision about which way to go kept her tethered to the door. All the while, she was reassuring herself. *I'm doing a good thing. I'm doing what's best for her.*

The hallway's darkness was unrelenting, and it looked like it could swallow a person whole. She could barely make out the mahogany table she knew was just a few feet away. The Ming vase her husband thought was "another expensive and useless trinket" reflected very little. The moon's rays could not reach around the hallway hidden from the front entrance's ten-foot window.

Not wanting to take a chance to turn on the lights made the decision easy. She would take the front stairwell. *Good heavens. The back stairwell squeaks louder than my old bones do, and that's enough to wake up the entire household.* She was exaggerating, of course. Constantly feeling older than her actual years in a wishful sense that time would pass more quickly.

Her hand slipped off the doorknob. Turning left, she descended the front stairwell, hesitating on the third step. As she often did, she imagined the old shack she was raised in would fit nicely within the front foyer below.

Isabelle had the kind of memory that never faded. She remembered everything with unwavering detail. While many who knew her considered it a gift, Isabelle called it a curse. For it meant that time would never heal the pain she endured. Those bruises, the fear, and the anxiety she had suffered in that shack remained in a constant loop she lived with again and again.

Those broken shutters, peeling paint, and dirty, cracked windows were forever ingrained in her memory. And it was just the kind of broken dwelling she feared for her daughter's future. *Is it so horrible to want more for her? Is it so terrible to want her to have what she has here?*

The moon's light offered clear passage down the large foyer and the grand hallway. Her eyes were drawn to the light reflection on the gilded frames that adorned the walls. She felt the eyes of the portraits following and judging her as she made her way past the sitting room, library, and her husband's office, finally reaching the kitchen.

Isabelle pushed the small button atop the stove, illuminating the crud-covered lightbulb. Giving off only enough glow, she read the clock. *Eleven o'clock – exactly. He should be here.* She complained and went to the bay window. Her searching gaze slowly scanned as much as she could of the few pristine acres behind the house until they met the woods.

Nothing.

Isabel focused quickly on the cement steps just outside the back door. *Tsk! He's late.*

Returning to the dimly lit stove, she put a small pot on medium heat. Filling the pot halfway with milk, she noticed the uncontrollable quivery of her hands. The milk inside swished back and forth until a drip landed on the burner and sizzled.

Isabel sat at the servant's dinner table and stared out the window at nothing in particular. *I'm doing a good thing. I am. I'm doing a good thing.*

Standing up to stir the milk, she tested it with her finger. She poured some into her favorite porcelain flowered teacup and returned to the table.

Isabelle allowed her eyes to blur and her thoughts to wander back to when she was her daughter's age. She drifted back to the day the church doors flung open to an almost empty room of pews.

She could envision her husband as if it were yesterday, standing tall and looking handsome, waiting for her at the altar. It was the first time she had ever laid eyes on him, and for that split moment, she forgot the anger that had overwhelmed her.

Less than a week before, her father had told her she was getting married. Not asked her – but told her.

<u>Eighteen years ago</u>:

"William who?" Isabelle had asked.

"Harrington. I'm sure he's a nice enough boy." Isabelle's father replied. "His father said his son had seen ye and your friends at the plaza."

"I don't remember ever meeting him."

"I didn't say ye did. His son only knew your first name when he had to give one."

"'Had' to give one?" Isabelle's jaw gaped open after asking.

He cleared his throat, sounding like a half-cough. "All I'm say'n is when he was asked who he wanted to marry; he picked you."

Her father stood tall and unyieldingly thin. Meals had been an inconvenience between his drinking and chain-smoking, neither of which played a positive role in his disposition.

Isabelle shook her head in disbelief. "Well, I...I don't want..."

"Bloody hell, girl. I ain't ask'n ya what ya want!" His quick temper snapped at no surprise to her. He stepped closer, towering over her small frame. "You're wed'n date is May 15th at 2:00 pm at St. Joseph's church." He spoke in a slow, darkly calculated tone.

Isabelle stepped back a bit and let his statement take hold. "Wedding date? May…May 15ᵗʰ is THIS coming Saturday!" Sweat formed on Isabelle's brow. Searching her father's face, she waited for the rare drunken smile when he would tease her. **Please, God, let this just be another one of his cruel jokes.**

No smile appeared as he lit a cigarette and asked, "How much will ye be need'n for a white dress?" His hand waved up and down as if painting an imaginary dress on her as smoke wandered aimlessly around them. "Ye won't be need'n one of those fancy, flow'n kind."

Tears welled up in Isabelle's eyes, silently pleading with every expression and gesture of her being. **Oh God, he's not slurring his words or swaying. Is he not drunk? Would he play such a game sober?**

She knew the answer when he threw her a few pounds for the dress, money she usually would have had to beg for.

"Why, father?" The tears were now flowing freely down her cheek.

His head tilted up, and his mouth mimicked a fish as the smoke rings floated weightlessly. Finally, he lowered his head again and blew the big finale of dark air directly at her before answering. "His father made an offer I couldn't refuse." With that, he turned about and strolled off.

She couldn't comprehend the words immediately and kept repeating them until she fell to her knees with the answer. **Offer? Did he sell me? Oh, good Lord, he sold me like a WHORE!**

<u>Present:</u>

Jolted. Coming out of her daze, she mindlessly wiped away the fresh tears that memory had caused. Her eyes focused on the dark figure out the window.

She turned on the outside light above the narrow, wooden door, causing the young man to step backward into the cover of night.

Isabelle opened it slowly, feeling the bite of the cold air. She stood staring directly at him. When he didn't move, she whispered loudly, "Well?"

"Mrs. Harrington?" His Irish accent made her wince as if it pierced her ears.

"I haven't time to play games with you, boy," she snapped.

"Yes, ma'am." He straightened his jacket, coming closer to the light.

Isabelle inspected him with the same look of disgust she gave most people she didn't feel the need to impress. "Are you sure you know him well enough?"

He nodded, "Yeah. He and his buddy live in my build'n. I hang with him most days."

"Good. You will get half our agreed amount now and the remainder when he's gone." Her hand reached out, holding a white envelope. He snatched it from her grip before she could blink and started counting it immediately.

She never took her eyes off him while she counted the fingers on her right hand by blindly feeling them with her left. Assured all her fingers were still attached, she took a deep breath and regained her attitude. "Are you paying attention, boy?"

He looked up with a satisfied grin, oblivious to her demeanor, as he stuffed the envelope into his side pocket.

Her words came hard and fast now. "You need to convince him that it will impress me. Point out how many men in my own family have done it. Most importantly, make sure he does it soon. I want him gone by the end of the month."

Just then, Isabelle's head snapped to the right, and she looked back into the house. She turned back to him with furrowed brows, "Well—go on then." With the flick of her wrist, he chased the dark while she closed her door to it.

Isabelle was shaking and could feel the burning heat rising in her cheeks. She decided to sit and finish her milk before returning to bed.

Just as Isabelle landed in her chair, she heard a thunderous creaking sound and then, "Mother?" Her daughter, Alexandra, fell backward into the darkness of the rear stairwell.

"Good Lord, child. What are you doing up so late?"

Alexandra pulled her robe tightly around her. "I…I… was thinking the same as you, it seems. I couldn't sleep and thought some warm milk would help."

"Sit down—I made a bit more than I took." Isabelle took a deep breath in hopes of steadying her hands. As she poured another teacup full of warm milk, she asked, "So, what did you do locked up in your room all evening?"

"I finally finished a book I'd started last week. What did you and Father do?" Alexandra knew the answer, but asking allowed her to survive her delusion of normalcy. However, reality always came crashing in - always in her mother's voice.

"I don't know what your father does closed up in that office other than smoking those smelly cigars." Isabelle laid the saucer and cup on the table before her daughter and slowly lowered herself back into her chair. "I, of course, was productive and paid the bills, decided on the menus for this week, and answered correspondence."

CREAK.

Isabelle just about jumped out of her skin at the sound while Alexandra concentrated more intently on her milk.

"What in heavens was that?" Isabelle started to get up from the table but was stopped by a gentle hand.

"Mother, you know the noises those stairs make. They're just settling in for the night."

Isabelle's body seemed to relax back into her chair before taking the last sip of her milk. "Finish up. It's late, and we should get turned in."

"You go on. I still have some left, and I'm in no hurry to toss and turn again for a while."

Her mother nodded in understanding, and Alexandra watched as she stood up, placed her cup in the sink, and grabbed the soap to wash it out along with the pot she'd used. "Please don't forget to wash your cup. You know how I am if I know there's a mess somewhere."

"I will, I promise," Alexandra replied. *Heaven forbid she allow the maids to do their jobs.*

Isabelle went toward the back stairs.

Alexandra avoided looking at her as she spoke, slowly lifting her cup for another sip. "Those stairs are very noisy. We're liable to wake up Bobby and Father."

Isabelle gave an agreeing nod. "I'll just go around the way I came from the front. Good night, sweetheart."

"Good night, Mum."

Alexandra listened carefully until she was sure her mother was well on her way back to her room. She turned to the blackness of the stairwell. "Come on. She's gone." She had to laugh at the glowing smile that seemed to be floating in the darkness, unattached like a Cheshire cat. Finally, the moonlight revealed their secret and showed the handsome blonde-haired, blue-eyed man.

His heavy Irish tongue rang through his whisper. "Your mum doesn't sound so bad. I think she'd like me. I's tempted to come down and join ye."

"Oh Erin, if you had, I'm not sure who would have killed you first: her or Me. Now, go!"

Erin's Plan

"Good even'n, ladies." Erin spun with panache. He was giving the sisters a full view. Stopping, he tipped his cap. After hearing their usual girlish giggles, he returned his cap to his head, winking. "Out here drive'n the young lads wild, are ye?" Their giggles were faster and higher pitched this time. So, he put his hand to his chest as if protecting his heart while he walked backward, finally turning to continue home.

Anna was seventy-six years old, and her sister was seventy-two. They loved to sit out front of their flat to see the young crowd that emerged after five o'clock. Erin was one of their favorite people to watch. He was young and handsome with an unbridled energy they could scarcely recall having back in their day. It also didn't bother them one bit that he was an insatiable flirt.

The ladies barely noticed when Erin's roommate, Jonathan, had walked by an hour earlier.

Jonathan returned home from work to take a nap on the couch. He wasn't sleeping, though, since a spider had crawled out from under the table on the far side of the room. He was alert and awake, staring in awe at the tiny creature. The similarities to another annoyance in his life didn't escape him. This spider was colorless, average in size, yet demanded his attention all too often.

How long has IT been living here at my expense? He wondered, smiling.

The spider moved again, abruptly to the left. Jonathan's eyes were still fixated, powerless to let it be and not watch over it, anxiously awaiting…

SPLAT!

Jumping off the couch, almost involuntarily, Jonathan watched as his shorter, pale, blonde-haired friend, Erin, slammed his shoe against the floor. "Obnoxious little buggers, aren't they? So, ya ready to go? I don't want'a leave Alexandra wait'n on me," Erin said, heading for the door.

"C'mon, c'mon, let's go. Ooh, wait." Erin turned back and rushed into Jonathan's room, grabbing a shirt from his closet. "Thanks, man. You don't mind, do ya?" Of course, he had already discarded his shirt on the floor in the hall. With both arms in Jonathan's nicely pressed shirt, he fastened the buttons and ran toward the door, practically flying down the stairs.

Jonathan thought Erin looked silly since his shirt was at least a full size too large for his average-sized friend. The shirt's length proved an issue while trying to tuck it in, rushing down the stairs to the exit.

As both men reached the front steps of their building across from the Billsworth Café, they watched the luxury cars approach and the beautiful people get out. They also saw their fellow working-class people walking up to the same door from the south.

The café, positioned in the middle of Hobb Street, sat on the imaginary line separating the wealthy from the working class.

One block north stood rows of stores that sold shoes for the price of a small car.

Going one block south sat homeless people, seeking warmth in the steam rising from street vents.

Jonathan and Erin considered this café their favorite place to eat. They—meaning Jonathan—could afford the food while mingling with the wealthier clientele they wished someday to be.

Tonight, they entered with the crowd and found a table, waiting for one of those beautiful people—Erin's love, Alexandra.

Ordering them both an ale, Jonathan asked, "Why were ya so late get'n back to the flat tonight?"

Erin sat back, tapping his fingers on the table rapidly. "I did it! I signed up!"

Jonathan's jaw dropped. "Have ya lost yer mind? I thought we would discuss this before you got yourself locked in."

"Ah, ya worry too much, ole friend."

Jonathan felt an immediate but familiar anxiety stirring within him. He'd known Erin all his life, born in the same hospital only a month apart. Erin's mother always said they seemed to complement each other well.

Erin was the more egotistic and energetic, almost childlike in his attitude toward life. And Jonathan…well, Jonathan was a strong, confident, and reliable bloke whom Erin knew how to manipulate.

Feeling his face getting hotter, Jonathan said, "You and your bright ideas! It never ends with ya and only seems to be get'n worse! In just the past few years, I've paid off your illegal gambling debts, been forced into a bar fight, invested in two of your 'get rich quick' schemes, and had to console countless girls you've left behind. And now this? I can't get you out of this, Erin."

Sitting up, Erin rested his chest against the table. "Oh, please, you loved win'n that money back at the blackjack tables, count'n cards like ya do. Beating the crud out of Roger Pierson put ye on a high for weeks. Plus, ye didn't lose anything in those schemes. Ye made back every cent with your business savvy. Oh, and let's not forget Sara O'Hara."

Erin sat back with a smug look now because Jonathan had a crush on Sara throughout school. After Erin broke up with her, Jonathan 'consoled' her right into bed.

Jonathan's shoulders curled toward the table, and the color ran from his face. "You're right. I'm not angry 'bout it all, but your latest scheme has me scared. I have always figured that God put ya on this earth to keep me on my toes, Erin. But I'm no ballerina. I want to feel my heels hit the ground every once in a while."

Picturing his large friend as a ballerina, Erin chuckled. "Ye thought me crazy when I suggested moving to England when we turned eighteen, and look at ya now! That bright idea has paid off quite nicely for ya, hasn't it? We've been here for, what, a little more than a year? And you've already been promoted twice."

"Three times, as of today," Jonathan admitted quietly.

Erin rolled his eyes. "Yer the only man I know that gets embarrassed by success."

"It's not that…it's just that I know you've been having a tough go of it here. I don't want it to seem like…well-"

"Like you're rub'n salt in a wound?" Erin said with amusement in his voice.

Jonathan nodded his head, pursing his lips.

Erin took another chug of his drink. "Like I've already said, ya worry too much ole'friend."

The two young men sat with their thoughts for a bit amongst the crowd of patrons. Erin stared at his beer mug, but his eyes began to blur.

Despite not having a job or the cash benefits that come with one, nothing stopped Erin from enchanting the ladies. They'd moved into the area less than a week before when he found Alexandra in the same café.

Thinking back to that night, Erin remembered being very aware that he hadn't been the only one watching Alexandra:

Erin approached her while amongst her friends and asked her to dance.

"Dance? In a café?" she replied in her strong English accent. Her friends started laughing, but before she could turn away, he took her hand in his and held it to his chest.

"Hold on to my heart for a moment, would ya?" His other arm wrapped around her tiny waist, swaying her around with perfect control. The song on the speakers could hardly be heard, so he sang the words loudly (occasionally on key).

The café was thick with patrons, but everyone was so amused they pushed closer and made room for them to move about. And when he finished his song, he ended with a big finale dip as the entire room clapped and whistled.

Yes, he had won her over that night, but more amazingly, she seemed to enchant him just the same. Alexandra had a way of drawing attention without any effort. Most flocked to her because of her natural beauty and upbeat personality. Others enjoyed her wit and ability to entertain while describing even the most mundane experiences.

He was truly in awe of her, and she knew it every time their eyes met.

Erin got a devilish grin, "I wonder if Alexandra got locked away in her room again?"

Jonathan, pointing a finger, "The answer is no, don't ask!"

"Aw c'mon, it's not that bad."

"Not for you! I'm tired of being your human ladder so you can reach her balcony," Jonathan complained.

"Stop whining. I'd do it for you if I could."

"Yeah, sure you would." Jonathan gave Erin a more severe look. "Hope you two are being careful."

"Ye-ye, although a bun in the oven might do us good. Then her mum would have to let us marry." Erin focused on the café door, eager to see his girlfriend.

Both men were unaware that Alexandra was still struggling to escape.

Alexandra's Escape

Alexandra stood behind the open bathroom door with her feet turned out like the 'first position' of a ballerina's pose. She was no dancer, though, so it was most uncomfortable.

Nevertheless, she remained as still as the wall behind her while her mother called her name. She held her breath when she heard the footsteps halt on the other side of the opened door. The light flickered on and off again.

"Alexandra? Are you home, Alexandra?" Isabelle called, her voice fading as she walked down the hall.

Her mother wasn't as fast as she once was, so Alexandra headed for the back stairs while her mother descended the front. Knowing she could reach the bottom floor first, Alexandra moved swiftly and quietly. With her shoes in hand, she remembered to skip the third from the last step, avoiding its give-away squeak.

She crossed the kitchen and went out the back door. Once outside, she slipped her shoes on and ran around the side of the house, slapping the old maple tree as she zig-zagged her way through the thick trees and darted across the front lawn to the parked car waiting for her.

Her best friend, Claire, kept the motor running, and when Alexandra was safe inside, she took off for the main road leading into town.

"Mothers on a rampage today," Alexandra said as she fussed to untwist her skirt.

Claire slammed her hands on the steering wheel. "You must get out of that house and away from that crazy, overbearing, control freak of a woman. Are you aware that your mother has been inquiring after Samuel Bristle?"

"Why on earth would she be asking around about that old fool? He's almost 30."

"For YOU!" Claire turned away from the road to glare at her friend.

"Me? Whaaa-"

"You're 17, and your coming-out party is only a few months away. That old fart is wealthy, and no doubt your mother believes you can overlook the age difference. Oh Lord, and it wouldn't end there, would it? You'd also have to overlook his crater face, public flatulence, and eww-"

"Smell!" They finished together. Glancing at each other, they giggled.

Yet, Alexandra shrugged her shoulders with a smile. "Well, I needn't be concerned with her plans any longer. When I turn 18, Erin is going to marry me."

Claire raised her eyebrows. "Umm- I love Erin. You know I do, but how does he plan to support a wife? He hasn't held a steady job since he and Jonathan got here. Now, Jonathan, mmm—there's a catch."

Alexandra's eyes widened, and her mouth gaped open at hearing her friend's flirtatious thoughts. "Jonathan's nice but a bit intimidating, don't you think? I'd swear his shoulders are as broad as I am tall! He could crush me with one arm tied behind his back."

"Yumm…exactly!" Claire made a dreamy look at the road ahead.

"Oh, good heavens. Stop pretending you'd leave Jarred for Jonathan Yule or anyone else," Alexandra said before smirking and rolling her eyes.

Claire's face morphed into an exaggerated pout. "Must you ruin all my fun?"

With as much sympathy as she could conjure through her smile, Alexandra said, "Sorry, love."

With a quick shrug, Claire announced, "I'm over it!" Claire's large smile returned. "But you still haven't told me how you and Erin intend to survive."

"I'm not sure, but he says he has a brilliant plan and will surprise me tonight."

Turning onto Hobb Street, the girls could see that the Café was crowded when they parked out front.

Inside the café, Erin had to practically stand beside his chair to see beyond the crowd and keep an eye on the entrance.

Jonathan was red in the cheeks, trying to keep Erin's attention. "This scheme won't work. Alexandra's mother will never accept you as a suitor. It won't matter what title you hope to bring home. You'll still be an Irish sewer rat in her eyes."

"Hush. I don't want you ruining the surprise." Erin could see Alexandra just on the other side of the glass doors. He unintentionally pushed his chair from the adrenaline rush that put him on his toes and stiffened his joints.

Alexandra entered the café, and her eyes scanned the crowd until it caught those of her lover. She rose to her tippy-toes and took a deep breath with a huge smile.

The sight of her was lost for a moment when she landed back on her heels and started making her way through the patrons. She was revealed by the last few who moved to allow her the final few steps to their table.

Erin, still standing, greeted her, "Good even'n, beautiful. Care to dance?" They both giggled while he bent down to the petite woman with a kiss.

"Good heavens, love. You need a haircut." She smiled as she reached up and moved his blonde curls with her fingers. "I can barely see your baby blues."

Standing at average height, 5' 8", Erin still towered over Alexander at 5' 2".

Although short in stature, she had a figure that was curvy precisely where men like Erin—appreciated it most.

Alexandra remained focused on her lover but addressed them both, "Claire says hello to both of you, but she had to run to meet up with Jarred. I made her late again." Finally, she stole her attention away from Erin long enough to greet his friend. "Good evening, Jonathan. How are you?"

Jonathan found her smile contagious. "Very well, thank you. And you?"

"Wonderful, although a bit chilled. Oh, congratulations! Steve Quinn told me about your latest promotion. At this rate, I suspect you'll own the company within the next year or so."

That comment caused the three of them to chuckle at the thought.

Jonathan was almost 6' 4" tall and had a thick Irish accent like Erin. He, too, bent down to kiss Alexandra, landing on her cheek. "Wouldn't that be a hoot, owning my own business?"

He then whispered loudly, "I could finally afford Erin." Causing Alexandra to giggle.

Erin pushed between them, pretending not to have heard the comment. "Break it up. Aw, break it up, you two."

Alexandra found Jonathan overwhelming. He had a huge build, dark hair, and dark brown eyes, and he was usually quiet and reserved. This was very unlike Erin, who was always the life of the party.

Nevertheless, she decided to like Jonathan because she knew his level-headedness was likely the only reason her crazy Erin had survived life thus far.

Erin slammed his frosted mug down, causing his beer to spill over onto the table. Sitting up straight, puffing his chest out, and taking a deep breath, he exclaimed, "I've joined the armed forces!"

Alexandra's head whipped around to face him. Her smile is gone. "Oh, good heavens, you did what?"

Sitting with his shoulders back and chest inflated, Erin repeated, "I've joined the armed forces. I report tomorrow morn'n."

"Why? Why would you choose to leave me?" Alexandra's eyes were wide with shock.

"So, we can marry someday with your family's bless'n. I figure if I work hard, I'll move up quickly in the ranks until I've reached a suitable level to impress your mum. Most of the men in her family served."

Alexandra's eyes squinted a bit, and her chin pulled back toward her neck. "I doubt it, but how would you know that?"

"Ummm- I heard it somewhere- but never mind that. The idea is to impress her."

Sinking into her chair, Alexandra stared at the floor. "Oh no, Erin, that's impossible." Looking up at him again, she said, "No one can impress my mother, not even me!"

Jonathan leaned in with both elbows on the table. "I tried to tell him, Alex, but it's like talking to a brick wall," he interjected.

"Ye know she hates being called Alex," Erin snapped at Jonathan with piercing cold eyes.

Alexandra shook her head wildly, causing her hair to come out of the barrettes. "Don't try to change the subject!"

"I'm not." Erin leaned over to place his hands in her lap. "I think this plan will work. I'll come back in a spiffy uniform with some title, like Captain Connolly. That'll have to impress your mum."

Ignoring him, Alexandra spoke her thoughts aloud. "Is it possible for you to get out of this? Tell them you changed your mind. Or maybe a medical condition—we could tell them-"

"He's mentally insane," Jonathan muttered under his breath. He already knew the answer to her question, dreading her reaction.

Erin's chest seemed to deflate, and his shoulders dropped forward. He sat back with such force that it caused the back legs of his chair to screech against the floor. "No, I can't. You two need to have more faith in me."

"It's not a lack of faith, Erin!" Her lips quivered a bit as she spoke. "I turn 18 in only a few months, and you won't be here to marry me." She slumped back in her chair and sighed heavily. "Do you know that my mother has already decided who she intends to stick me with?" Alexandra put her head in her hand and her elbow on the table to support it. "Oh God, it's awful."

"I'll be back for leave by then." Erin reached over and took hold of her hand. "If she doesn't approve, then I'll come for ya, and we'll elope as planned." His hand squeezed hers. He said in a higher voice, "I'll have a steady income too!"

Alexandra lifted her head and gazed at the ceiling. After a few moments, her eyes found his, and a small smile appeared. "But I still hate knowing you will be away for so long."

It won't matter beating him up about it now—he's locked in, Jonathan thought to himself. So, instead, he bought another round of drinks. "What's done is done. We need to do what you often say, Alex...andra. We need to love him through it."

Jonathan held up his mug with his arm out forward, giving Alexandra a smile and a wink. "Here's to the future, Captain Connolly."

Erin and Alexandra lifted their drinks to his toast and tapped their glasses together.

After taking a swig of his ale, Erin whispered, "How long do we have before ya have to sneak back?"

Alexandra leaned closer to him and whispered back, "I don't intend to let you go until I must. When do you leave?"

"Early in the morn'n."

Alexandra sat up straight, "Then I'll sneak home shortly after that."

"Now, that's how ye love someone through it," Erin replied, causing even Alexandra to giggle.

When they returned to the flat, Jonathan lay in bed listening to the occasional sounds from Erin's room. *Alexandra is beautiful,* he thought to himself. *And there will no doubt be numerous suitors the moment Erin is gone. What the hell difference does impressing her mother make? What a bloody fool! I'd never take the chance at leave'n her behind.*

The following day, Erin woke Jonathan up when he entered his room. It seemed like only seconds since Jonathan had closed his eyes.

"Hold this, would ya? Don't think we'll be wear'n watches and don't want it get'n stolen."

Jonathan's father gifted both boys a watch when they graduated high school. Not knowing his own father, Erin cherished the gift and had pride in the symbol the watch represented. Jonathan's father had two sons, one of his blood and one of his heart. The watch was also the only thing Erin owned that was worth anything.

Jonathan and Alexandra stood on the sidewalk looking pale while Erin stepped onto the bus with only a few other young males. They looked about Erin's age and, at this early hour, maybe headed to the same destination.

Once on, Erin immediately sat by a window, stuck his head out, and stole one more glance at the woman he loved. He called out to her, "I'll be back, and you'll be proud, beautiful!" The tall building behind them made Alexandra look tinier, and even Jonathan seemed small.

Alexandra struggled to force a smile through her tears and looked up at his window. Her last words were a choked whisper, "I love you." Just then, the bus pulled away, and Alexandra took a step forward with her arm stretched out as if she could catch it before she broke down into full sobs.

Jonathan hesitated and, with stiff movements, put his arm around her, patting her on the back. "It's all right; he'll be back before we know it."

But Jonathan felt the pain, too. He wouldn't see Erin tomorrow for the first time since they were born.

Alexandra's Surprise

Alexandra pushed herself away from the cold porcelain and sat on the tiled floor with her back against the wall. Her chest was heaving while her left hand slid down over her stomach as if it could calm the storm inside. Suddenly, she heard footsteps. *Oh God, here she comes.* She focused on the knob, realizing she hadn't the time to lock the door behind her.

She sat and watched helplessly as the doorknob turned and the door swung open to reveal her mother. Isabelle's perfectly primped hair and smart shirt tucked into a straight, long brown skirt didn't match the downturned corners of her mouth and the narrowed eyes on the old woman's face.

Isabelle stepped closer, stopped, and placed her hands on her hips to look down at Alexandra. "How far along are you?"

"How far along?"

"The pregnancy!" her mother barked.

Alexandra's mouth gaped open, and her eyes wide. She shook her head slightly. "I'm not pregnant. What makes you think I'm pregnant?"

"Don't play games with me, girl. You have been either eating, sleeping, or vomiting. You're pregnant."

There was no use denying it. Alexandra's mind was a whirlwind of thoughts. *Oh God, Erin is gone. I'm only seventeen. I'll be well more than a month along before he returns to marry me…*

As she left, Isabelle turned back toward the hall, saying, "I'll make a call, and we'll have it taken care of."

"Mother?!" Alexandra called after her. "What do you mean 'taken care of?'"

Her mother never answered. She didn't have to. Alexandra knew exactly what she meant, and the very thought of it made her reach for the porcelain again and hold on tight as her body convulsed.

When Alexandra returned to her room, she fell to her knees, placed her elbows on her bed, and slapped her hands together. "Please, God, I know you work in mysterious ways, and I need you to work for me now. Please help me save this baby."

No more than an hour later, Isabelle stood at the ready inside the front door as it slowly opened.

Returning home from work, William Harrington barely had a foot in the door when his wife announced, "Our daughter is pregnant!"

Every muscle in William's body tensed as he shuffled sideways past her to get fully into the foyer. He placed his briefcase on the floor and started taking off his coat to give to the waiting house manager without losing eye contact with his wife. He couldn't help but notice how sharp his wife looked this evening. *It's the same shapely figure after so many years.*

William finally asked, "The Irish fellow?"

Isabelle snapped back, "It's irrelevant who!" She folded her arms in front of her to signal that her solution was not up for negotiation. "I'm making the arrangements to rid her of it as soon as possible."

"Rid her of it? That 'it' is our grandchild." William replied incredulously. *She was happiest when the children were little; wouldn't a grandchild to spoil be a good thing?* he thought.

Isabel's fists opened and rose, landing on each side of her waist. "I've worked too hard to gain this family the respect it deserves in the community. I'll be dammed before I allow her to destroy it with the embarrassment of a bastard child."

William took a deep breath and stood as tall as he could, towering over her. "Now look here, Isabelle, you can NOT force her to abort it. Young girls are having kids out of wedlock all the time now. It's not unusual anymore. We're not living in the 1950s, for heaven's sake!"

Isabel didn't back down but stepped closer to her husband and looked into his eyes. She replied in a cold, steely voice, "It may not be unusual with the lower classes, but it is still frowned upon at our level. Besides, she's only seventeen. I can still make her do as I please for at least a few more months."

William's entire body seemed to deflate. His shoulders dropped forward, and his hands raised together as if ready to pray. He pleaded, "Izzy, be reasonable."

She stepped closer, bumping him a little while she screamed, "Don't call me that!" A pursed-lip smile then appeared across her lips.

She thinks she won, but not today, he thought. William never budged and stood defiant, yelling back even more loudly. "SHE'S MY DAUGHTER TOO! I have just as much say in the matter!"

Isabelle stepped back, mouth open, eyes wildly searching for his weakness to shine through.

You won't break me tonight, Izzy, he thought while bending down to reclaim his briefcase. He stomped hard but quickly and took his small victory to his study.

William's heart was pounding in his chest and just about beat out of his skin when he entered the room and almost tripped over his son, Robert. "Good God, boy, what are you doing crouched there like that?"

William's son, Robert, was the younger of the two children, only 11 years old. The boy, though, took after his father in his love of maths and playing chess. He took after his mother, though, with thick blonde locks and below-average height.

Alexandra always described Robert, whom she called Bobby, as a fragile soul. He would agree to anything that would bring peace and calm. The young boy avoided conflict like the plague.

Bobby rose and peeked out the doorway to ensure his mother had gone. Turning back to his father, he asked, "Why can't she marry Erin? She loves him."

William closed his eyes and let out a long sigh. "I can't marry her off to a man without a proper job." He put his briefcase next to his mahogany desk and reached to turn on the TV.

"But he does. He joined the armed forces. Alexandra told me he left weeks ago," Bobby pleaded.

William raised an eyebrow and took a moment before answering. "Maybe there is hope then." He gave Bobby a wink and headed toward his couch.

"Can I stay in here with you, father?"

"Have you been home with your mum all day?"

"Yes," Bobby replied dryly.

"Then close the door, son, and make yourself comfortable."

The closed door, however, did nothing to protect them from Isabelle's ranting.

Isabelle retreated toward the office suite she made from two of the servant quarters – after having her house manager shift the two maids to a smaller guest room. "How dare he," she yelled for whoever could hear her. "How dare he step up now and try to take the parenting role. I raised these kids, and I built our reputation in society."

The staff scattered, and her voice became more distant until William and Robert could no longer hear her. That doesn't mean she stopped, though.

When Isabelle reached her office, she picked up the phone and began to dial. "He can have all the 'say' he wants after it's over."

Meanwhile, Alexandra, who had been in the kitchen when her father was confronted, finally felt safe making her way toward his office. She knocked lightly.

"Yes?" He called from within.

"Father? May I-"

The door opened, and his arms did, too. "Come here, honey." William hugged her while manipulating her into the office to kick the door closed again.

Alexandra became emotional at the kindness but choked out, "I'm so sorry. I'm so sorry, father."

"Oh, honey, calm down. It's not the end of the world," William replied while patting her back. Pulling away a little to look her in the eye, he said, "So tell me about this young fellow. Robert says he joined the armed services?"

Alexandra took a deep breath and let it out slowly. "He left a few weeks ago. Erin thought you and Mum would approve of him if he had steady employment."

"I definitely think better of him for it," William replied with a smile. "Are the two of you writing often? Does he know about your condition?"

"Not really. I have only received one letter since he left. His brother, Jonathan, says he has only gotten one letter, and I don't want to tell him in writing. I know he'll be happy, but I really want to tell him in person."

William turned and coaxed her to the couch to sit with Bobby. "I can understand that." After retaking his seat at his desk, he looked at her with a serious expression. "Your mother intends to take you to a doctor that will abort it. Is that what you want?"

"No, father, no."

"Then you must refuse to go. Don't allow her to convince you that it's for a checkup. I'll plan for you to get to a doctor we can trust, okay?"

"Thank you, Father," Alexandra replied, following it with a sigh of relief.

"How did you get pregnant?" Bobby asked.

Alexandra gave him a pursed-lipped smile. "By doing something I should have waited until marriage to do. You'll understand soon enough."

The three sat quietly, pretending to pay attention to the TV. Alexandra had another worry she was afraid to mention and quietly gathered confidence.

"Dad?" Alexandra asked.

"Yes, honey?"

"If I do have the baby, do you think I'll be able to homeschool it like Mum did with us?"

William puffed on his cigar and waved his hand to stop the smoke from wafting to the kids. He placed it in the ashtray, "Most of your mother's friends sent their children to the prestigious boarding school in town. She will probably insist you do the same."

"Why didn't she send us? If she didn't send us, then why should I have to send mine?" Alexandra protested.

"She was different then and didn't want to let you out of her sight. I'm afraid she may feel differently about yours, though. She-"

"That isn't fair," Alexandra cut him off. "Besides, Erin and I can't afford it."

"You know as well as I do, she'll pay for it." William put his hand up to stop her from protesting again. "If she does, the school is only an hour away. You wouldn't have to wait for holidays to go visit."

Sign Here, Please

"Sign here, please," said the delivery man.

Jonathan took the clipboard and signed his name as he had done 14 times that day. He handed it back to the courier and accepted the package.

He opened it to find more contract paperwork to be checked and filed. After retrieving the larger folder for the corresponding project from the filing cabinet in his office, he laid it on his desk and got to work.

Numbers were his specialty. He loved them and had always assumed he would be an accountant, but no one was looking for another accountant. Insurance required much more reading, but the numbers were just as fun. More importantly, they were almost always looking for new agents.

Considering the hour, that would probably be the last delivery today, but Jonathan was in no hurry to get home. Erin made every day an adventure, always thinking up some crazy new scheme. Always ready for a party or figuring out a way to get one started. Without Erin, Jonathan's days were work, shower, eat and sleep. He didn't treat a Saturday or Sunday any differently than Monday or Tuesday.

The only people Jonathan knew around here were Alexandra, Claire, and Jarred. Jarred was in law school, and Alexandra was never around. When he saw Claire, she explained that Alexandra couldn't escape her mother and other idle chit-chats. She also never invited him to meet her other friends at the café, so he would eat alone or take it back to the flat.

Tonight, the security guard gave Jonathan the usual look while checking his watch. The unspoken signal was to remind Jonathan he had overstayed his welcome and to get out. Security couldn't secure the floor until he did, so Jonathan packed his things and headed home. He started the four-block walk back to the flat, all uphill.

"Good evening." Jonathan tipped his hat a bit to the two women sitting out front but kept moving until he reached his building. He could hear one of the old women trying to whisper to the other, who was obviously hard of hearing.

"He's handsome too, but I miss his flirtatious friend with the golden locks."

Jonathan couldn't help but smile at the thought of Erin strutting his stuff for two women in their 70s. Did Erin have any boundaries? He wondered. *One more week- just one more week- and Erin comes home. I hope he stops here before meet'n up with Alex. They'll close themselves off for who knows how long.*

Since Erin left, he had only seen Alexandra once in passing. Both asked if the other had heard anything from Erin. Both only had one letter to speak of. Alexandra did mention the care package she'd sent him with all the candy and books he could share with his new 'brothers' but seemed disappointed he hadn't written since getting it.

One more week, he thought again. *I should do what Alex did and make sure I get to shop'n, so we'll have all his favorites.*

Jonathan was deep in thought about his grocery list as he made his way up the stairs to his flat. As he approached his door, a man was in the hall.

"Are you Jonathan Yule?" said the man.

"I am," Jon answered while fumbling for his keys to the door.

"I have a letter for you, sir. Please sign here." He handed over a clipboard, and Jonathan quickly found the next blank line to sign his name.

Jonathan took the yellow envelope inside, kicked off his shoes, and ripped it open as he sat down. After noticing the formality and the official military letterhead, his chest deflated, and his back curved as if the bones had given way. His hand raised to catch his head, which became too heavy for his neck to hold. His eyes blurred after reading the first few sentences, which began with, "We regret to inform you…"

Jonathan held the letter away, down between his knees with eyes closed, trying to catch his breath. *Oh my God, Erin's gone – he's gone.*

He regained his breath and wiped away the tears, causing his fingers to slide across the letter and reveal a second page. There was a personal note from Erin's commanding officer along with the formal, probably generic letter he had received. The officer explained the incident in more detail, like a friend might tell a friend. *No doubt Erin charmed all his officers into liking him,* Jonathan thought.

The letter read:

Dear Jonathan,

It hasn't been confirmed, but I believe one of the soldiers must have been sneaking a smoke after lights-out when the fire started. I saw Erin escape it with my own eyes and then watched him run back in to answer the calls of another soldier still trapped. Within seconds, the fire grew too hot, too fast to save either of them.

After everything he has told us of you and Alexandra, I know this is as devastating to you as it is to all the men here. Please know that we would have stopped him if we could have.

He was a good friend to his brothers and a brave man.

Sincerely,

Col. Roger J. Shea

Jonathan sat back, breathing in short, fast spurts. He could visualize the scene in his head; *I couldn't have stopped him, even if I had been there.* John wiped his eyes again; *I couldn't have stopped him. Erin always lived like he was indestructible. Damn him.*

The letters were dropped on the table while Jonathan got up and pulled a few beers out. He opened one and started to drink it down so quickly as if he were empty. He slammed the finished bottle down and picked up the second, removing the cap.

Allowing his eyes to wander over the letters again, the familiar name jumped out at him, *Alexandra*. He bent over like he'd been punched in the stomach. *Oh God, give me strength. I'll have to tell her.*

Jonathan put the bottle to his lips again and gulped it down. Without throwing the empties away, he retrieved two more.

The Moment Of Truth

After a sleepless night, Jonathan dressed in his best suit to walk the four miles from town to the Harrington mansion and finally approached the door. In a groggy state, he had gone through numerous versions of how he would break the news to her, all of which caused him to lose his composure. His eyes and cheeks were raw from wiping away the tears.

The large front door opened slowly, and a man dressed in a black suit looked at him curiously. He asked slowly, monotone, "How may I help you, sir?"

Jonathan's voice cracked as he asked, "M..may I speak with Alex…andra please?"

Jonathan was escorted down the hall and into a large, spacious room. It had two sitting areas: one at the far end by the fireplace and another just inside the door.

Although the area in front of the fireplace looked much more comfortable and relaxing, he was directed to sit in stiffer-looking chairs surrounded by dark wooded tables with delicate porcelain figurines. The room seemed as tall as it was long, with drapes that hung from ceiling to floor.

A chill ran down his spine as he heard heels clicking outside the room. When Alexandra entered the drawing room, Jonathan wondered if she already knew.

Alexandra was exceptionally pale and looked tired. Her eyes had dark circles around them, and she was moving slower than her usual bouncy self. When her eyes focused on him, she picked up her pace and greeted him with a smile.

Alexandra started peppering him with questions: "When is he coming home for leave? Is it soon? I thought the initial camp was supposed to be six weeks."

Jonathan didn't answer, so she stepped back. "Jonathan?"

His throat closed, and he was unable to answer her. The tension grew as he tried to swallow down the emotion, and Alexandra retook the step she'd lost.

"Jonathan, what's wrong? Jonathan. Please. Speak to me."

Jonathan choked on the words. "Erin, he's…gone. There was an accident…"

He almost missed catching her as she fell but was able to coax her petite body onto the chair nearby and knelt in front of her. Tears were running down her face, but her head swung back and forth fiercely as if she was trying to shake out what she had heard. A strange panic was in the air as he felt her limbs become stiff.

Her head stopped, and she looked at him expressionless as if she had not the energy even to open her eyes much wider than droopy slits. "I'm pregnant." She spoke before her head dropped again. Her tears were no longer separated but a flow of constant water down her cheek.

He reached his arms around her and pulled her forward to lay her head on his shoulder.

Alexandra lifted both arms up and around his neck. She couldn't let go. The man she once found overwhelming was now an immense cave of protection. The muscular arms she once joked could crush her were now the equivalent of a warm blanket.

Alexandra spoke her words into his neck. "My mother is aware and has already demanded that I abort the child."

Jonathan pulled away to look at her. The motion caused her to lift her head and her hands to slide down from his shoulders to the front of his chest. "No, you can't," he said.

Alexandra sighed through her labored breathing, "I don't want to, but I'm too young and unwed. Mother keeps saying I'll disgrace the family if I let it grow." Shaking her head slightly again, she said,

"I don't care about the disgrace, but without a husband, I know my child won't have a chance here. If I have it, she'll send it off."

John arched his back, "This is unacceptable. You can't kill Erin's only child." His words hung between them for a moment before they fell into each other again at the painful realization of his statement.

Erin had always spoken of having a large family. "I want enough of them to use almost every letter in the alphabet name'n all," he had often said.

Of course, Jonathan couldn't resist teasing him at the time. "You must learn how the alphabet works, so let the wife name'm. I would hate to hear ya call out for the first three of your children, 'Hey A, B, and C, com'ere!'"

The memory brought tears to his eyes, a small smile to his lips along with the answer to his prayers. "Alexandra, would'ja consider marry'n a poor bloke like me to save the child?"

"Yes. I would do anything, but Mother would never agree to it."

She didn't even hesitate, he thought. "Does yer father have any say at all over what happens to ya?"

"He has come to my rescue many times and doesn't want me to abort it either," Alexandra replied somberly. "But my father hides from her as much we do."

Jonathan, feeling a purpose now, became very calm. "Do you know where he hides? Can I go to him?"

"His company office mostly. His office is probably the best place to talk to him out of earshot of my mother." Alexandra gave Jonathan directions to her father's office building on Torrington Avenue but continued to shake her head.

Jonathan looked at her inquisitively. "You're not helping my confidence shake'n yer head like that."

"This is a terrible way to feel, but I'm full of hate and angry as hell. I hate my mother for causing this and Erin for not including me in his decision. His 'brilliant' idea to make getting married possible was like all his others." She looked at Jonathan with pleading eyes. "Why didn't he tell me first before signing on? Why would he go and do such a stupid thing?" Alexandra balled up her fists and shook them in the air.

Jonathan's lips came together like a straight line, and he nodded. "He lived like every day was a new adventure. He never feared that tomorrow wouldn't come. But let's be fair, Alex, that was part of his charm."

"What is this?" Isabelle asked as she entered the room.

"He was just leaving," Alexandra said, standing up and prompting Jonathan to rise to his feet.

Jonathan held out his hand to Isabelle, but she didn't take it. She looked at it and then at him again, rolling her eyes.

He lowered his hand, nodded, and in a less than sincere voice, said, "It's nice to meet ya too."

"I'll walk you out," Alexandra said while pushing him.

"Wait. Why were you kneeling in front of my daughter, boy?" Isabelle asked.

"We lost a mutual friend and were comforting one another," Jonathan replied.

"You're Irish," Isabelle stated bluntly.

"Yes," he replied. Jonathan stepped closer to her, towering over her.

Isabelle took a small step back. "I thought we finally got you out of our hair when you joined the armed forces."

Alexandra let out a gasp.

"Wrong Irishman," Jonathan answered again, but now with the same scowl on his face that she had on hers.

Alexandra pulled on his jacket, physically pleading with him to follow. They left Isabelle behind while they made their way to the front door.

"She's a charmer, huh?" Jonathan said as the door opened and he stepped out.

Alexandra had a look of embarrassment, "Sorry about that. Call me tomorrow?"

"Yeah, talk to you tomorrow." Jonathan turned and started the four-mile walk back to his flat. He could feel the anger pulsing through his veins. *Arrogant, English snob. What a bitch!*

He stopped at a store for more brew and the café to pick up something to eat but took it to his flat. Before eating, he called the office to let them know he would need another day off without giving a reason. They didn't ask, though. It was the first time he had asked for any time off, so they assumed it was necessary.

The long walk did nothing to help dispel his anger. He kept seeing Isabelle's face and hearing the disgust in her voice when she noted he was Irish. His anger would only be interrupted by the reality of his loss. He would see something of Erin's, or an old memory would haunt him. The emotional rollercoaster was exhausting but only afforded him a short nap before another sleepless night.

Meeting William Harrington

Jonathan got a cab and went to the Harrington Inc. office building the following day. He could see the money invested in the marble floors and gold fixtures as he made his way to the front reception desk. "Mr. William Harrington's office?"

"One moment, please," the attractive redhead said before calling someone. She held the receiver away and covered it with her other hand. "Mr. Yule?"

"Um, yes, I am," Jonathan replied.

"Okay, I'll send him right up," she said before hanging up the call. "Mr. Yule, Mr. Harrington's office is on the seventh floor. They're expecting you."

How much did she tell him last night? He wondered on his way to the elevators.

When the doors to the lift opened to the seventh floor, a woman who looked to be in her late fifties but dressed very sharply met him. "Mr. Yule?" she asked.

"Yes," he replied.

"Follow me, please." She walked to the end of the hall, knocked on a door, and opened it. She then stepped aside and motioned for Jonathan to enter.

Walking into the office, he stared at the empty seat behind the large mahogany desk. He could feel his heartbeat at the tips of his fingers. *What am I doing?*

"Over here, boy." William Harrington sat in a cozier area facing out the window. The chairs were oversized in build, padded heavily, and covered in leather. They were like the set he saw at the house near the fireplace.

William gestured to Jonathan to sit in the chair on the other side of a small table. "Can I get you something to drink?"

"No sir, I'm fine." Jonathan took his seat and took a deep breath. "I need to speak to you about Alex…Ale…Alexandra, Sir."

"Yes, yes. I understand you have an idea of what should be done?" William asked.

"Allow me to marry her, sir. If we marry right away, maybe no one will suspect a thing when the child arrives."

William was now inspecting Jonathan's suit. "Can you afford to take on a family?"

Jonathan tugged at the front of his jacket to straighten it out as he does in the mirror. "Not in the manner she's accustomed to, but your daughter understands that. She wants…well, sir, we both want the child to live, and she's ready to accept living on my means."

William already felt sure of the answer to his next question, considering this young man was willing to marry his daughter to save the life of a friend's child. "Can I trust you will treat her well?" he asked.

Jonathan responded a bit more enthusiastically than he'd intended. "Yes! I'll keep working hard to ease the burden and be good to them, I promise."

William's shoulders dropped as if the world had been lifted from them. "Well then, you will need to give me a day to inform my wife, who won't be happy. Worse yet, she'll never like you." He leaned closer like he had a secret to tell. "But have no fear of it, son…she doesn't like most folks, me included."

Jonathan was curious about the statement, which put a wry smile on Mr. Harrington's lips but didn't respond.

Wishing that William himself could be saved from his wife, he saw this as an opportunity for his daughter to finally escape. Jonathan Yule looked like an intelligent, sturdy enough gentleman to care for her, and he was willing to trust in God to make it so.

His mind wandered back while he lit his cigar.

As a young man, William was in awe of Isabel. She was beautiful, seemed confident and intelligent, and commanded attention everywhere she went. Her clothing, although old and faded, made no difference. She could have worn a potato sack and made it look good. William used to follow her and her friends to the plaza to watch her, never having the nerve to approach and introduce himself.

He will never forget the night he spoke her name to his father. They had been sitting and having dinner. William's father had boasted about how he had figured out another man's price.

"What do you mean, father? What price?"

"Everyone has a price they'll sell their soul for, son. You can get anything you want if you figure out what it is and pay for it. Richard Stark's price was getting his daughter a better doctor to oversee her leukemia. It was a proud and admirable price—but still a price."

William's father read his facial expression and asked, "You don't believe me? Aha – tell me something you want from someone you think will be difficult about it."

"I don't know…" William looked down at his food and pushed his fork around.

"Come on. There must be something. Anything. Just give me an example."

William could feel his father's eyes burning into the top of his head and knew he was not going to let this go. Before he could come up with an idea, his father asked, "You need to be thinking of marriage soon. Anyone you're interested in but don't think you could get?"

William looked up with his mouth gaping open.

"Ah…who is she? Do we know her?"

With a shy smile, William looked down again. "I only know her first name is Isabelle. I followed her home once. She lives down on East Blossom Street."

"Well, that sounds easy enough. East Blossom Street doesn't have any wealthy men on it. Their price is probably monetary, which is the easiest price." His father said with renewed excitement.

Late the next day, William's father was blunt: "Your wedding date has been arranged and set for Saturday."

"My wedding day?!"

"I told you, son, everyone has a price. Her father is a gambling man with a taste for whisky. I didn't have to promise much more than a free month's worth of both."

As was usually the case, his father dismissed his questions with a hearty laugh. "We will need to get you a tuxedo, boy. I'll have one of the maids go with you."

The deal was made, and the wedding date approached before William could fully comprehend his fate.

Nevertheless, Isabelle never faltered once married, and he thought she was a good wife overall. She gave him two beautiful children, ran a tight ship at home, and, with her good sense, aided him in building his empire of wealth that far outweighed his father's.

He never understood her, though. She could have such moments of kindness and, in a crowd, look at him as if he were the only person in the room. But lately, Isabelle spent most of her days being angry, controlling, demeaning, and unbearable. If she hated me, why did she go through with the wedding? *He wondered for the 100th time.*

When their children were little, Isabelle was doting and loveable. She was so happy then. Everything about her glowed, *he thought.*

It wasn't until the children were old enough to rebel—to think for themselves—that she seemed to lose her way. And now he had to tell her she'd lost control of Alexandra completely.

Jonathan cleared his throat loudly, reminding William he was still there.

"Sorry, son. I got lost in my thoughts." William put his cigar in the tray and stood up. "Second thought: I'll rip the band-aid off immediately and tell her tonight. Alexandra can update you on the when and where."

"Thank you, sir." Jonathan put his hand out, and William shook it.

Once alone in his office, he couldn't think of much else. Before William knew it, his secretary was saying good night and leaving. *I suppose it's time. The sooner, the better,* he thought.

William returned home and confronted Isabelle immediately. "Jonathan Yule has asked for Alexandra's hand in marriage."

"Who in the hell is that?" Isabelle asked.

"He is the best friend of the boy that died. Alexandra has agreed to the marriage, and they have my blessing."

"Another Irishman, no doubt. Well, they don't have my blessing," she snapped back.

William arched his back. "They don't need your blessing."

Isabelle stepped back, her mouth gaping open while her assistant walked behind her.

"The ceremony will be private and quick here at the house." Looking over Isabelle's shoulder at her assistant, he said, "Make the arrangements." Before either could respond, he walked away and closed his office door behind him.

Isabelle stormed through the house like a mad woman, talking to herself for all the staff to hear. "'Make the arrangements,' he says. That son of a bitch wasn't comforting her; he was exploiting an opportunity. 'Make the arrangements?' Oh, I'll plan a wedding ceremony they'll not soon forget!"

A Funeral And A Wedding

Isabelle waited at the front door on this Saturday morning while her family was getting dressed and ready to leave for Erin's funeral. Isabelle had no intention of joining them but had some news she was anxious to tell them before they left.

Alexandra was the first to descend the stairs. "Are you coming with us, Mum?"

"No, honey, but I'll be busy planning a luncheon when you all return. Please invite your young man back to the house," Isabelle smiled.

"Claire and Jarred will be there. Is it okay if they come back with us?" Alexandra asked, returning the smile.

"Of course," Isabelle replied.

She's finally accepted the situation, Alexandra thought. "Do I look okay, Mum?" She straightened the skirt a bit of the knee-length black dress.

"Yes, that dress still fits you well. I told you it's important to always have a black dress in your wardrobe." Isabelle looked kindly while thinking, *but it won't for long. A pregnancy distorts your figure and will age her.* The light in her eyes seemed to fade just as Alexandra's father and brother joined her to head out.

Once the door closed behind them, William asked, "What was your mother saying?"

"She planned a luncheon for after the funeral. I was surprised, but I think it's lovely of her," Alexandra replied.

William drove and took a left out of the driveway.

"Father, where are we going? The cemetery-"

"To pick up Jonathan. I called him last night to tell him what I had done and agreed I would pick him up this morning to save him the six-mile walk." William replied.

"What have you done?" Alexandra asked.

William cleared his throat. "As I explained to Jonathan, I respect how hard he is working, but I know how young he is and how hard an unexpected expense like this can be. Jonathan chose a great casket. I know it was more than he could afford, but it wasn't Harrington standard."

"Oh father, Erin was like a brother to Jonathan."

"I upgraded it and paid for a fuller package with flowers and a proper headstone," William replied.

Alexandra thought for a moment before finally asking,   "Was Jonathan offended?"

"At first, but we spoke for quite a while. I explained that Erin is the father of my first grandchild, so he is as much family as Jonathan will be after you marry. He seemed appreciative that I would give his friend the respect I would to a family member."

The sentiment made Alexandra break down. She put a hand on her father's arm, giving it a loving squeeze of appreciation.

"Jonathan still insisted on paying for the original. I only paid the difference," William said as he reached with his left hand to touch hers.

Alexandra had been touched when her father insisted Erin be buried in the family cemetery, but this filled her heart. Her lover would be laid to rest with the dignity she believed he deserved.

There was no viewing due to the damage done to Erin in the fire, but Jonathan found an Irish priest willing to do a short prayer service at the grave site. When that was over, Jonathan stood where the priest had been.

After taking a deep breath, he began. "Blood is not the only thing that makes someone your brother. The love you share makes you family, and that family is always your home. Erin was my brother." Jonathan let out a strange sound before breaking down into full-hearted sobs.

Jonathan did the best he could to compose himself before he leaned over and touched his brother's casket and whispered, "I'm sorry, man. I'll protect her and your baby. I'll protect'm, I promise. We're gonna miss you."

Alexandra wanted to say something but couldn't compose herself enough. After standing there for minutes, they started to lower the casket, and Alexandra fell to her knees. Jonathan and her father both grabbed her arms to help her stand. William motioned Jonathan to start back to the car.

Jonathan and Alexandra joined Claire and Jarred to ride back together. They returned just before William and Bobby caught up with them, entering the Harrington house. Their moods were as dark as their funeral clothing.

Isabelle, dressed in a shimmering silver suit, summoned them to the kitchen after gathering in the foyer.

The priest stood near the sink and greeted them individually as they entered. William's reaction was instant. "Isabelle! Today? Here in the kitchen, right next to the loo?"

Isabelle smiled, tilted her head a bit, and batted her eyes. "Let us not forget her condition and how convenient it may be if the morning sickness kicks in." She then picked up a small flower bouquet and handed it to Alexandra.

Alexandra looked at the flowers and thought, *why wouldn't she give me flowers for the grave BEFORE we went?*

William's anger overtook his good sense. With a sharp flick of the wrist, he motioned for the priest to follow him. "We'll do it in the library."

William led the way and opened the library door. He stood just inside, waiting until the priest and the kids entered. When Isabelle approached the doorway, he shut it in front of her with a strong thrust.

Alexandra looked at the flowers, realizing what her mother had planned. She dropped them on the table and turned to the sound of the slamming door.

Everyone else looked back at the door and then at William.

"Father?" Alexandra put her hand on his arm.

After kissing her forehead, he said, "You needn't the stress of her today."

The priest, Jonathan, and Bobby allowed their shoulders to fall relaxed while simultaneously exhaling.

The air seemed lighter, their spirits a bit higher, and the sunlight coming through the windows warmed them despite the largeness of the open room.

"I'm surprised she thought of flowers," Alexandra said to Claire.

"Well, let's hope she didn't think of rice. Those can hurt when hurled at you," Claire chuckled.

"I'm sorry, but we should get this done," William said.

Jonathan and Alexandra awkwardly made their way toward the priest and stood waiting.

The priest was a family friend, so he was kind enough to keep the ceremony short and straightforward, reaching the defining moment quickly. "I now pronounce you husband and wife. You may kiss the bride."

Alexandra tensed a bit when Jonathan bent down toward her, but a smile overtook her lips when he - in a familiar fashion - respectfully kissed her cheek.

Claire stepped up and hugged Alexandra. "I happen to have my camera with me. Let me get a snapshot of you two." She then manipulated Alexandra to stand closer to Jonathan and face her. She aimed them to get some of the gardens out the window in the picture.

William also wanted a picture of himself with them and then with Bobby included in the group before offering to take a few of Claire and Alexandra. Jarred joined them and insisted Jonathan do the same for one last snapshot.

Jonathan's new father-in-law approached and shook his hand. "She's my little girl, and that's my grandchild," William said. His eyebrows raised, and he gave the handshake a firm thrust. "I trust you will take good care of them, son. Of course, when you need help-"

"We'll be fine, Sir. Thank you," Jonathan replied.

Bobby hugged his sister. Alexandra pulled away and held his face in her hands. "I love you, Bobby. I'll always be here for you, okay?"

After the hugs and handshakes were over, the moment came when they all looked back at the door. Deep breaths without exhalation could be heard throughout the room, but no one moved toward it.

William shook his head with a wry smile and said, "It's the only way out, I'm afraid."

"I'll go first!" Bobby tried to walk taller than his 4' 9" stance with his chest out and head high, but the priest stopped him, placing a hand on his shoulder.

"We appreciate your bravery, young man, but I think it would be safest if I led the way." Father Reissman straightened his collar with a shaky left hand while slowly opening the door with his right. To his relief, there was nothing but a large envelope on the floor in the hallway with Alexandra's name on it. He picked it up and handed it back before walking on. Bobby handed it back to Alexandra and followed the priest out.

She stopped in the hallway and broke the seal. Upon opening the envelope, she pulled out a picture of a large home surrounded by a great deal of property that seemed to wrap halfway around a body of water. Attached are two plane tickets and a short but direct note:

The home is waiting for you in Springfield, Maine, AMERICA. The distance will allow me to save the family from embarrassment and say that your husband had a prestigious opportunity awaiting him there.

Leaving immediately will hide the early arrival of the child.

Alexandra's head whipped around as she watched and hoped to control her father's reaction, as she knew he'd been reading it over her shoulder. To her surprise, she found a calmer, more peaceful look on his face than the stiff jaw and tight, wrinkled brow he'd displayed since leaving the kitchen.

William gave a half-smile of satisfaction before directing his words at them both: "I think the distance could only be to your advantage." Then he held out his hand again to Jonathan, shaking it firmly, and bent to kiss Alexandra on the cheek. Before pulling away, he whispered, "I'll start you off proper until Jonathan can get on his feet, love." Then he stood straight and remarked, "Hmmm, now I'll have a getaway spot to visit often." And with that, he turned and disappeared down the hall, a light skip in his step.

Alexandra turned to Jonathan, and they stared at one another blankly.

"America," he said dryly.

America

The home they had been exiled to and the vast surrounding property proved breathtaking. From the road, it looked like the house was built at the top of a large hill. However, when you entered the front door and walked straight through to the glass doors that aligned the back of the room, you quickly realized it looked out over a lake and a picturesque view.

The house was unique, and its designer used everything to his advantage. The wall protrudes out on the left just before you reach the glass doors, but if you pull at the corner trim, a hidden door opens to reveal a staircase. On your descent, there's a laundry room halfway down before you reach the ground floor and the tiny nook that fits only a small couch. Sitting there, you can look out the sliding glass doors to the beach.

The house was built on top of and down the side of a cliff, which curved like a half-moon. It met a steep, tree-covered hill just before it reached the water at the opposite end of the house. That curve in the cliff created a private beach.

Alex and Jonathan worked tediously cleaning up the house. It had obviously been vacant for a long time and had multiple layers of dust buildup. Even with all the cleaning supplies and a new vacuum, they had to put some old furniture out for trash. They salvaged what they could of the old, torn, fabric-covered couches and chairs that someone had been good enough to throw sheets over.

After making the house livable, John headed out first thing Monday morning to look for work.

"Jonathan?" Alex called out after hearing the door slam shut.

"Ye, it's me." John walked in with his head down and slowly took off his jacket. His shoulders were curled forward, his back hunched over, and he didn't make eye contact when Alex stepped out of the kitchen. "Nothing this morning unless I want to be a bag boy at our grocer."

"Cheer up, love. It's only the first day." Alex said, trying to comfort the deflated man she watched sit on the couch, throwing his head back with his eyes closed.

He was quiet and barely made eye contact with Alex when he returned for dinner that night.

The following day, Alex made him a hearty breakfast of eggs, ham, chopped potatoes, and toast before seeing him off again. She was very surprised not to see him again at lunch. The sandwich she had made him was eventually wrapped and returned to the refrigerator.

It was 4:45 pm when Alex heard a clammer coming up the front steps.

"Alex?!" Jonathan called out as he swung the front door open into the narrow entryway.

"Jonathan?" Alexandra came quickly from the kitchen with a wooden stirring spoon and a towel wrapped around her slightly thickening waist. "Are you alright? What's happened?"

"I found a job!" Jonathan's open-mouthed smile was as wide as his face.

A sigh escaped through her smile. "That was quick."

"It's about a block further than the grocery store we walk to."

Alex had never seen Jonathan so excitable and couldn't resist getting caught up in it. "Oh, Jonathan, that's wonderful!"

Jonathan tossed a folder of papers on the small table just inside the door. "I wasn't the only one there—about three others went in before me. None of them spent more than fifteen minutes getting interviewed. But not me! Once he invited me in, he didn't want to let me go. He also offered to help us get nationalized. The company will sponsor me."

His hands flailed with each word he spoke, and his cheeks reddened. As he approached Alex, he put his hands firmly on her shoulders. "The owner is a fellow Irishman!" He then kissed her forehead as if it were the most natural thing and immediately returned his eyes to hers. "He offered me the job straight away, and then we spent the next hour talking about home."

Alex was giggling. It was a welcome change from the awkward silence they usually shared. "Could you calm yourself enough to sit for dinner?"

He put his nose to the air. "Mm, smells delicious—I'm starv'n." He followed her into the kitchen, recounting everything from the interview while she set the table, served the meal, and ate.

Jonathan suddenly puts his fork down without reservation and announces, "My boss came to America for a beautiful woman, too!"

Alexandra's reddened cheeks and nervous giggle went unnoticed as he picked his fork back up while he explained how his boss' American-born wife had been transferred to Dublin for a year. His boss then followed her home to America.

"Aw, and I guess I should stop calling ya Alex."

"I've grown used to it. I don't mind."

"Yeah, but my boss kept referr'n to ya as my 'significant other' until I realized and explained that it was short for Alexandra." He explained as he waited for Alex to comprehend.

Her nose wrinkled for a moment until suddenly, her eyes got wide. "He thought you were gay?" They both laughed. "How very accepting of him. I like him already."

By the end of dinner, his recanting of the day had been exhausted.

Not wanting it to end, Alexandra kept asking questions that led them to personal memories of family, growing up, and even their future dreams.

Jonathan never read the paper that night, and Alex left her sewing unattended as they talked away the evening. He was in the middle of the couch while she sat beside him, almost close enough to be touching, with her legs curled up sideways to face him.

She can make even the simplest stories intriguing. Jonathan thought while Alexandra went on about a party she and Claire had attended. *And she is so incredibly beautiful. How did I get so blessed?*

It was getting late, and they knew they needed to turn in, but they both walked slowly while they continued their conversation. Another 15 minutes passed outside his bedroom door before they finally retreated to their rooms.

Alexandra awoke in such high spirits the following day she called home to her brother Bobby.

A familiar man's dry voice answered. "Hello?"

"This is Alexandra, and I would like to speak to my brother Bobby."

"One moment, please."

Alexandra could hear some whispering, but it wasn't clear enough to make out any words.

"Mrs. Yule?"

"Mrs.-?" After the formal address, she smiled before acknowledging she was Mrs. Yule, "Yes?"

"I'm afraid he is unable to come to the phone at the moment. Good day."

"Wait! Are you going to tell him I called?" Alexandra asked.

After a brief silence. "No. Your mother has asked that you not call the house phone in the future. If you need to contact them, please call her office."

Before Alexandra could argue, she heard the *'click.'*

AArrrr! *That bitch!* Alexandra immediately dialed her mother's office and did not hide her temper when it was answered. "How dare you stop me from speaking to my brother!"

"Adjust your attitude, young lady," Isabelle replied calmly.

"I want to speak to Bobby."

Isabelle took a deep, very loud breath. "It is not good for him to hear from you so often. He mopes around after your calls. I am glad you called, though. I have researched and found America has a few promising boarding schools in Massachusetts and Vermont."

"I am not sending my kid off to a boarding school, mother," Alexandra barked.

Isabelle ignored her, continuing, "I know you didn't marry well, so I expect to pay for it. I don't want my grandchild to grow up stupid." Isabelle replied.

"Like your daughter? The daughter YOU homeschooled?"

Silence.

Alexandra tried again. "I want to speak to my brother."

"Try again next week." *Click*

Babies & Romance

Alexandra and Jonathan fell into a nice routine for the next three months. She made him breakfast before he went to work. She cleaned, did laundry, ate lunch, walked, and then wrote in her journal until she fell asleep. She never napped long, so Jonathan always came home to a delicious, hot meal for dinner.

They would spend the evening talking or singing while Jonathan played the old, somewhat out-of-tune piano until it was time to turn into their separate rooms. He didn't mind that the piano was a little out of tune because Alex's vocals never were.

She had also decided to shorten his name and started to address him as Jon. He didn't seem to notice at first but later explained that his boss had shortened it before the end of his interview and introduced him to the staff as Jon.

Alexandra's belly grew -- fast. Jonathan's boss had warned him of the mood swings she would suffer and taught him a few tricks. His first piece of advice was to "call home before leaving work. If her craving is strong, it'll save you another trip out later."

There was one scenario, however, for which his boss had no advice.

"Slow down, Jon." Alexandria had been breathing hard since getting out of the taxi, trying to keep up with him.

"Sorry, I was rushing ahead to get the door for you," Jonathan said. Today was the day they would get a sneak peek of the baby at the Imaging Center. Her doctor insisted she get an ultrasound.

Alex stopped just inside the door. "Jon?"

"Yes, you okay?" he asked as he returned to her.

Alex whispered, "Did I wear matching shoes?"

Jonathan laughed out loud. He quickly peered down, lowered his voice, and answered, "Yes, they match, beautiful."

After a long sigh, she continued to the front window to sign in and sat in the waiting room. Not that she didn't trust her husband, but she leaned back and lifted one leg to see her shoe before doing the same to see the other.

She noticed Jon watching, "The shoes feel differently on my feet. I thought for sure I'd worn two different kinds."

"Mrs. Yule?" The nurse called from a door opening.

"Yes." Jonathan got up quickly and helped Alex stand.

They were led to a room with a bed and a computer next to it. The nurse handed Alex a gown and told her to wear it so it opened to the front. Jon turned his back to give her privacy, but he helped her get up on the dark pink cushioned bed once she had it on.

The technician then laid another folded paper over her lower half before opening the gown to expose her belly. The jelly they put on her stomach was cold, but the specialist rubbed a significant tool with a flat end. Then the specialist looked at the monitor, and her hand slowed with the device. She moved it precisely with purpose, stopping and clicking on the computer keyboard every 5 or 10 seconds. This continued for about 15 minutes before Jon and Alex couldn't stand it.

"Does the baby look healthy?" Alex asked while gripping Jon's hand tighter.

"They look fine. This'll take longer than usual, though. I have to measure both of them," the specialist said matter-of-factly.

"They? Both?" Jon let go of Alex and walked around to see the monitor. However, nothing on the screen made sense to him— nothing but a blur of black and gray shapes.

"If you want to step back over with your wife, I can turn the monitor so you both can see," the young woman said.

Jon made his way back around to Alex's side as the monitor was turned to their advantage. Neither of them could make hide nor hair of what they were looking at until suddenly, the specialist moved the wand on her belly, clicked a few keys, and they both held their breath.

"There are two of them!" Alex exclaimed.

"Oh my God! Two!" Jon said excitedly. Then, as his mind raced, he repeated it slower, quieter, "Oh…my…God…two."

As soon as they had returned home, Alexandra wrote a letter to Claire and included one about the twins for her to pass on to Bobby. She also planned to call her father at his office with the news, allowing him to pass it on to her mother.

"Hello, I would like to speak to my father. It's Alexandra."

"Hello, Alexandra. One moment," came the reply.

After a few clicking sounds, she heard, "Alexandra?"

"Dad! I have very exciting news. I'm having twins!"

William chuckled quickly before asking, "Am I having granddaughters or grandsons?"

"Granddaughters. Oh, Dad, you should see me. I'm as big as a house."

"It just so happens I may see you very soon. I planned a trip for all of us to see you, but your mother has decided she can't go."

"That's wonderful! You and Bobby can stay here; there's plenty of room," Alexandra replied purposely, ignoring that her mother wouldn't join them.

"Only me, I'm afraid. Your mother says that Bobby can't miss his extracurricular activities right now. He has a chess match competition coming up."

"She's determined to keep Bobby from me. Honestly, I don't understand it."

"I know it's disappointing. Can I still come and see you?" William asked.

"Of course! When are you coming?"

"As soon as I can get a flight. Is that too soon?"

"No, of course not. Oh, my goodness, I'm so excited. You are staying here, and I won't take no for an answer. Oh, Daddy, I can't wait to see you."

"Same here. I'll have to get back to you with the details. My assistant is making all the arrangements for me."

"As long as her arrangements don't include a hotel. I'll be hurt if you don't stay here. Oh, I can't wait to tell Jon."

"I hope he is just as excited," William said with a chuckle. "Okay, I'm going to let you three go." He waited for Alexandra to catch on, which she did with a giggle. "I love you, honey. See you soon."

"Love!" Alexandra replied before they hung up.

Alexandra's thoughts were racing. *I need to clean the room, make the bed, and make a grocery list. What else, what else?* She could not stop smiling and suddenly found the energy she had lacked with the added pounds. The room at the other end of the balcony would be next to her own, but they were slowly fixing it up for the nursery. *I'll fix up the room under the balcony to save him the stairs.*

Although she knew the room was clean, she stripped the bed to rewash the linens and started dusting and scrubbing the bathroom. Jon and Alex would often use that bathroom rather than the one at the far end of the kitchen.

When she was done, she picked the phone up again and dialed.

"Hello Agnes, may I please speak to my husband?"

"Hello, Alex. One moment," said his assistant.

"Alex? You okay?" Jon asked.

"Yes. Please take me to the library this weekend. I need to find a recipe book that has my father's favorites. He's coming to visit next week, and I want-"

"Your father is coming?"

"Yes! He's looking for the next flight out. Of course, my mother won't be joining him and won't allow him to bring Bobby. But I insisted he stay with us, and I want to make all his favorites while he's here."

"I have a better idea," Jon replied.

"What?" Alex asked.

"You could sit down, relax, and call the local restaurants to see which ones make his favorites. All that standing at the oven can't be good for ya. I've been say'n I could bring dinner home on my way from work."

"Oh, Jon, I really want to cook for him," Alex whined.

"Then let's compromise. We plan most dinners for me to bring home, but you make him your veal parmesan and rosemary chicken. Ya also have to let me keep helping with breakfast in the morn'n. Deal?"

"Deal," she replied. "I'll see you later. Love."

"Bye." *Click*

Just as Alex hung up, the phone rang. "Hello?"

"Alexandra, I have some news," her father said immediately. Before she could ask, he continued. "Your mother has arranged for Bobby to get to his commitments so she could join me."

Silence.

"Honey? Are you-"

"Yes, I'm here. Sorry, I was so excited about a relaxing visit," Alexandra replied.

"And a nice escape for me, so I understand. Would you rather I cancel-"

"No! No, please don't cancel your trip. It doesn't change how excited I am to see you."

"Okay, but I should add a hotel to our plans. You'll need some reprieve."

"Can't she stay at the hotel, and you stay here?" Alexandra said with a little chuckle.

"I wish," her father replied.

William And Izzy Visit

"Have they called to say they landed?" Jon asked as he entered the house.

Alexandra was sitting on the couch, reading a book, "Yes. They said they were going to go straight to the hotel. My mother said she had jetlag and didn't want to come tonight."

Jon had dropped his things just inside the door and made his way around to her. "I'm sorry, Alex. Did ya go to a lot of trouble for dinner?"

"Nope. I know my mother too well," she replied with a smile. "I did make hot roast beef sandwiches. Do you want me to put some French fries in the oven or just chips?" Alexandra started getting up, but Jon stopped her.

"I'll just have chips with it. Should I make you one?" he asked, looking at her.

Alexandra tilted her head back and just gave him a big smile.

Jon took that as a yes and went to the kitchen, but later realized she would need to eat it at the table, so she got off the couch and started walking toward the kitchen. She was about to enter the kitchen when she heard a knock at the front door. She opened the door, the view led to her eyes widening and a big smile appeared on her face.

"Father? Oh, my goodness, you came after all!" Alex yelled in excitement as they collapsed into a hug. When she pulled away and noticed the door shut behind him, "You're alone?"

"She fell asleep, so I left a note," William replied in almost a whisper. He sounded like he was still scared of waking her up despite being miles away.

"Well, come in, come in." Alex led him into the open area. "Have you eaten? I didn't make anything fancy tonight, just hot sandwiches."

Jon recognized the voice and made his way to the open area to welcome William, "Mr. Harrington," Jon said, holding his hand out.

William took his hand and shook it. "Please call me William if you aren't comfortable with Dad."

"Thank you, William. Can I make you a sandwich? We have plenty," Jon said.

"If there's enough, I would love to join you." William followed them into the kitchen, and they all made their sandwiches from the meat in the crockpot and sat down.

William looked in awe at the main room and now at the kitchen. *This is a beautiful house. I can't believe Izzy never told me about it before.* He carried his plated sandwich to the kitchen table, noticing the pretty cloth table cover. *The kids have made this house a real home.*

"You must be exhausted after that flight," Alex commented.

"It was more relaxing than you would suspect. Your mother was very tense but quiet," William replied.

"I must be honest; I'm not looking forward to seeing her. So, before she makes me miserable, I want you to know I'm really happy. Jon has been wonderful, and I'm loving this property," Alex told her father.

"It's lovely here, and your daughter is a master chef. I think I've put on at least 10 pounds," Jon added.

William replied, "Practice reverse psychology."

"What?" Alex asked with a crooked brow, confused about what he meant by that.

"If you talk about how beautiful it is, how much you love the property, and how happy you are-" William started.

"Mum will want to take it all away. This was supposed to be a punishment, not a reward," Alex finished her father's sentence, saying more to Jon than in reply to her father.

Jon gave her an understanding smile and nodded, "So, we talk about how the house is too big, too much to maintain, and the water is causing too much moisture. Is that the idea?"

"Yes. The moisture is giving us headaches, and the animals on the property make it too scary to walk far," Alex replied with a chuckle.

"The sign of a good marriage is teamwork," William snickered, followed by sitting up straight and putting his sandwich down on the plate. "I hope you don't take this the wrong way, Jon, because I know you're a proud man, but I insist you accept this." William reached into his jacket's upper left pocket and pulled out a check.

"Sir, it's really not necessary-" Jon started.

"I know. Alex told me about your new job and how simply the two of you have been living, which is great. I'm sure you're saving quite a bit on your own, but if my wife sniffs out any chance that you two are doing well, I fear what she'll do. This house belongs to her. I wasn't even aware she had purchased it."

"But sir, really-"

"It's William, and I insist. If my wife never kicks you out, then imagine what you could do for the babies with it. Please, Jon, this is more for my peace of mind than anything else."

Jon finally agreed and accepted the check, which he put in his wallet.

"Tell me about yourself, Jon. Where are you from?" William asked, picking his sandwich back up.

"Kilgarven, Mayo Ireland, sir. Sorry, William. My parents have lived there all their lives. Erin's Mum, too."

"So, you aren't brothers?" William asked.

"Not really, although we were raised like brothers. His Mum had moved in with my parents when she got pregnant. We grew up thinking we had two Mums and one Da. I think people whispered about that arrangement, but it wasn't like that," Jon said nervously.

"Do they know where you are now?"

"Yeah, I was on the phone with them a few times after Erin's passing. They were supposed to be at the funeral but, due to unforeseen circumstances, didn't show up until the day after. Alex met'm before we left for America."

Alex put her hands on her chest, covering her heart. "Oh, father, it was so bitter-sweet. They were crushed about the loss of Erin but told me so many wonderful stories about him. When Jon told them about my condition and what we had done, Erin's mother gave us her blessing. She was so sweet and insisted we call her granny from then on."

"I'm so sorry I did not get the opportunity to meet them. We could have waited to have the wedding ceremony. It may have been a more festive affair with them in it." William replied.

"I agree. Mum would have focused on impressing them rather than torturing us," Alex said.

William placed his hands on the table with one last potato chip left on his plate and looked at the couple.

"Well, if it's okay, I'm going to step outside and enjoy a cigar. I haven't had one since we left." William stood up, took his plate to the sink, and put the last potato chip in his mouth.

"I'll get that, Daddy; go enjoy your cigar."

Jon also got up, took his plate to the kitchen counter, and pulled the crockpot's power plug out of the wall so it would cool down. The inside dish was separate, so he removed it with the lid and put it in the refrigerator. He wrapped up the chips and put them back in the cupboard when he heard the front door opening again. "Too cold out there?" Jon asked.

"No," came the short answer from a familiar voice that made Jon's skin tingle.

"Mother? I thought you were sleeping back at the hotel?" Alex stopped scraping crumbs from the tablecloth as Isabelle entered the kitchen.

"Can you believe your father left me alone in a strange place?" Isabelle asked.

Jon and Alex just gave each other a look of 'yes,' but both chose not to respond.

"Are you hungry? The roast beef is still hot. Would you like to make a sandwich?" Jon asked her with a forced smile on his face.

"No, thank you. If I get hungry, I'll eat something more appropriate at the hotel."

Alexandra left the scraper on the kitchen table and moved toward her mother. "Well, let's go out to the living room and sit. Can I get you a drink, Mother?"

"A glass of water would be fine, but please finish cleaning the kitchen before I feel I have to."

"We will. I have iced tea; would you rather-"

"A glass of water would be fine," Isabelle said again as she walked to the open room to find a seat.

Jon reached for a glass and started to fill it while Alex finished scraping the table. He grabbed a few ice cubes to add to the drink.

Alex whispered as she took the glass from him, "Did you see how excited she was to see me?"

Jon held her shoulder gently to reassure her as they went out to sit with Isabelle. They chose the couch on the opposite side, across from her.

"How was your flight?" Jon asked.

Isabelle took a few sips of the water before putting it down. Ignoring the question Jon asked and said, "Alexandra, I would like the two of us to spend tomorrow together."

"What would you like to do? There's a shopping mall not far from here," Alex replied.

"If we have time, we should stop and find you some proper maternity clothes. You look silly," Isabelle stated.

"I know. Jon keeps trying to get me to the mall, but I haven't felt like shopping. He did pick me up a few things I planned to wear tomorrow when I thought I would see you. Tonight was a bit of a surprise."

"You knew our flight plans," Isabelle barked back.

"Yes, I did. I also knew you would find an excuse not to come tonight. Father's visit forced your hand, though, didn't it?" Alex replied with a small smirk and a song in her voice.

Just then, William came back into the house. His entrance stole Jon and Alex's attention, but Isabelle lifted her glass again for a few more sips. He sat beside Isabelle and gave his daughter wide eyes as if he knew he had interrupted something.

"Mother was just telling me that she wanted to spend tomorrow with me but hasn't told me what we would be doing yet." All eyes turned to Isabelle, waiting for her answer.

"Be ready early, by 7:00 am. I have already ordered a car service to pick us both up. Now let's talk about you. Are you finding my property enjoyable? You seem to have adequate space here."

Now, on the spot, Alexandra couldn't pretend she didn't love the house and property, but she knew saying as much would make her mother reconsider allowing them to stay. Not being able to complain about it caused an internal fight.

Looking at Alex, confused about what to say, Jon finally spoke up. "Of course, we're appreciative for having a place to get a start from, but it seems to be adding more difficulties than a solution. We'll probably suffer from lung issues after all the dust we breathed in trying to clean this place up. Had anyone occupied this house before us?"

"The architect who built it died before finishing, so I got it for a steal. But no, I haven't had occupants before you. Thank you for cleaning it up; now it is renter-ready." Isabelle said now with a little song in her own voice.

"Then I suppose we should give you the list of items you would need to update before legally being allowed to rent it out." Alexandra's voice replied with new confidence. "Let's begin with the thousands of dollars in plumbing costs, thousands more in flooring in case you didn't notice, the kitchen has floorboards we can't trust putting furniture on, and then there's those water leaks. I would happily make you a list and schedule an inspector to take a look."

Alex had found her voice. Her old fears of her mother, gone. She no longer cared if her mother kicked her out of the house. She was determined to be happy with whatever she had here in America, thousands of miles away from the old woman.

"Well, I'm exhausted enough that I think I can finally sleep. I told the car service to pick me up at 6:30 p.m.," William said, breaking the conversation between the mother and daughter. Looking at his watch and then at Isabelle, he asked, "Should we head back?"

"Yes. Remember, Alexandra, 7:00 a.m." Isabelle and William stood up, and Jon and Alex followed them to find the car service just pulling in.

A Trip To School

The car service arrived at 7:00 am as promised, but of course, her mother was not in it. Alexandra didn't expect she would be and was fully prepared to sit and wait at the hotel while her mother took her sweet time getting ready. She had brought a puzzle book to work in that fit nicely in her oversized purse. Also in it were a few snacks and a bottle of water.

Alexandra entered the hotel and had them call up to her mother and then asked for directions to her room. She didn't go to it but only wanted to figure out where her mother would be coming from. She decided to sit in the most hidden section of the breakfast area, forcing her mother to look for her when she finally came down.

Sitting down and laying her purse on the table, she ran her hand over her unborn babies. *May you never grow to resent me.*

Her mother's heels clicking toward the front door were unmistakable. Alexandra's hand ran over her stomach with more vigor as she giggled to herself. As the clicking sound returned, she quickly pulled out the puzzle book and pencil to look busy.

Finally, after hearing her make a few rounds of the sitting area, Isabelle found her daughter.

"Alexandra." Isabelle stood over her with her hands on her hips. "Let's go."

"I'll just be a minute, mother." Alexandra then slowly put her book back in her bag, then her pencil, before heading in the opposite direction.

"Where are you going, girl?" Isabelle asked, frowning.

Alexandra replied over her shoulder as she never slowed her pace, "To the loo. Since you won't tell me where we're going, I have no idea when I'll get another chance."

Isabelle sighed in displeasure, looking at Alex.

A full 10 minutes later, they were finally in the car and on their way.

"So, can you finally tell me where we're going, mother?"

"North Bridgeton," Isabelle replied.

"What is in North Bridgeton?"

"A proper boarding school for your children."

"I haven't even given birth, and you are-"

"It is never too early to start planning, Alexandra. There are others to look at; I'm only helping you tour the first one."

They sat quietly for a few minutes until Alexandra broke out in a giggle.

"What is so funny?"

"Oh, nothing," Alexandra replied before laughing harder.

Isabelle's every muscle tightened as she turned to look at her daughter. "What is wrong with you, girl?"

With a huge smile, Alexandra said, "Nothing is wrong with me. I am a happily married woman with twins on the way. Two babies that you will have no control over, no say over. It must drive you crazy." Alexandra replied with more laughter before she sat back and relaxed. "I can still enjoy the beautiful drive despite this wasted trip."

Alexandra stared out the window. *How is it that I used to love being with my mother? I would follow her all day after my lessons. She would supervise the kitchen staff, which I guess they didn't appreciate, but I learned so much from them. I learned how to clean a house properly and how the maids laundered our clothes. All during that time.* Alex's eyes were a blur while she tried to remember where things went wrong.

Giving up, she focused again on the beautiful scenery whirling by, wondering how much fun Jon and her father must be having.

"Where are we off to, son?" William asked as he got into the awaiting car service.

"I don't play golf, although I would be willing to try my best if you'd prefer. But ya may spend most of the time watching me chase my ball or even my club." The two men chuckled at the thought of it. "Instead, I thought we could shoot. There's a gun range that will rent us guns to use."

"Guns?"

"We're in America," Jon replied with a smile.

"I have never shot a firearm. My father used to hunt with his buddies but never included me," William said, unable to hide his excitement.

Agreeing, they made their way to the gun range. When they arrived, they had to take safety and proper protocols training. Both men listened intently but were still required to be with an experienced staff member since neither was a licensed gun owner nor a trained NRA member.

William rented a long shotgun, and Jon a handgun. They figured they could each take turns with both.

They were entering the booth, and Jon carefully loaded the pistol. The instructor had to remind him only once to keep his finger away from the trigger until he was ready to aim and shoot at the target.

The sound shocked them both despite the protective headsets, but Jon found it exhilarating. When he finished his rounds, William took over the pistol and reloaded it.

"Where do ya think the ladies are today? Did Isabelle ever let ya in on the secret?" Jon asked as William reloaded.

"To see a boarding school just a few hours away," William said as he put the last bullet in. He lifted the pistol and then lowered it again, chuckling. He placed it back down and turned around to Jon, whose jaw was visibly tight. "I bet you'll see a face on your targets today."

Jon's jaw relaxed as he realized the inference and tried to smile in return. But yes, he would be visualizing Isabelle's face today. His blood boiled, feeling like his wife had been tricked into doing something he knew she was against. They had looked at the schools in the area and were happy with the options close to home.

William shot the pistol, and it shook him. He wasn't expecting a kickback from such a small weapon. The incessant shake of his hand made hitting the target where he wanted almost impossible.

"It has a real kick, doesn't it," Jon said as William finally put it back down.

"My hands are shaking," William replied, with concern on his face.

"Well, shake it off ole'man. We each have a few more loads to shoot before we get to the rifle range."

After both shot off two more clips each, they compared targets while walking to the rifle range.

"You okay?" William asked.

"I'm just worrying about Alex. She suspected she was being tricked but didn't know how."

"Alexandra has had to survive her mother for 18 years. She's a clever girl. She'll find her way around it, and her positive thinking will protect her," William said as he touched Jon's shoulder giving him confidence.

Jon smiled bravely and nodded, "I hate seeing it though."

"You were very rude and quite the embarrassment," Isabelle said as they made their way out to the car.

"I wasn't rude; I was honest. It's sad you don't know the difference, mother."

As Alexandra gently entered the vehicle, Isabelle kept at her.

"I have already made it clear that I would be paying for them to attend."

"And I have already made it clear that I will not send my babies off to a boarding school," Alex replied.

"You are being rude again."

"I am being honest again. Not agreeing with you is not being rude. These are my children, and they are my responsibility. I will decide how they are educated. Did your parents make your decisions when we were born?" Alex asked.

"My mother died before I knew her, and my father sold me off to your father." Isabelle looked over at her daughter before saying with arrogance in her voice, "Their opinions were irrelevant."

Alex looked at her mother with sympathy but took a deep breath in and said, "And so is yours."

Birth

As the weeks went on, Jonathan had to bring more dinners home since Alex wasn't able to cook. The more significantly Alex's stomach grew, the more quickly she became tired. It was a hormonal roller coaster ride, but both of them survived it until Alex gave birth to two identical, healthy baby girls that May.

Alex watched intently as Jonathan picked one up and told him, "She looks even tinier in your monster hands."

Jonathan looked up with a smile and a tear, on the verge of escaping. "I can see a bit of Erin in them already. Look at their eyes."

"So, are we agreed then on naming them Erin Kathleen and Kathleen Erin?"

"Indeed," he replied, never lifting his eyes off the child. Erin's Mum will appreciate you using her name, even with the more English spelling.

"Have you sent out the birth announcement I gave you?" Alex asked.

Finally giving Alex eye contact, he nodded, "Yes, Claire called, but no word yet from your Mum, and she's still not taking my calls." Jon got a nervous look at what he knew was coming next.

"Has my father called?" she asked.

"No." Looking down at the small creature in his arms, he thought, *how do I tell her his number is no longer in service?*

A few days later, Jonathan brought Alex and their daughters, Erin and Kathleen, home from the hospital. Jonathan put both baby carriers inside the circle of couches in the great room. He headed back out to get the mail while Alexandra kicked off her shoes and nudged them under the table by the front window. As she leafed through the mail that she had missed while in the hospital, Jon came rushing back in.

"Alex? There's a letter from your mother." Jon held the letter in front of Alex while going through the others.

"Ooooh—she must have received the baby pictures!" She took it and tore it open eagerly as Jonathan entered the kitchen. He stopped dead in his tracks when he heard Alex scream, "How could she?!"

Running back into the living room, he found Alexandra on her knees, sobbing, the letter crumpled in her fist. She looked up slowly and choked out, "My father, he's had a heart attack."

"Is he okay?" Jonathan asked, coming closer to her with his eyes wide open.

"He's dead," she said bluntly.

Jonathan knelt before her and put his hands on hers. "Oh, Alex, I'm so sorry. I'll make arrangements straight away to be there."

"There's no point in going back. She buried him two weeks ago." Her eyes were drowning in tears, her mouth gaped open, and her head slowly shaking from one side to the other.

Jonathan picked her up and carried her to bed and watched the girls while Alexandra caught up on some sleep. She didn't get much in the hospital, wanting to dote on the girls rather than trust the nurses.

A few days passed before Jon asked her the question he'd been meaning to ask, "Have you spoken to your mother?"

"No!" Alex looked at him with crinkled brows. "Why would I bother? She won't care that she stole my chance to say goodbye."

Alexandra looked down at little Erin, who was starting to fuss. She began to rock her gently before quietly adding, "And it would just allow her to remind me of what an embarrassment I've become and how disappointed she is in me." Alex let her face drop to look at the floor. "Not to leave out what a waste of life I've proved to be."

"Oh, good heavens, woman, your mother would never say such a thing," Jon said, gently placing his hand on her back.

Alex blinked away the tears that now filled her eyes. "On more than one occasion."

Good Lord, how could any mother be so cruel? Alex is too bright and beautiful. Jonathan thought while taking a deep breath to relax his anger. "Well, she'd feel foolish if she saw you with the girls and could see what a wonderful mother and wife you are."

Alex gave him a half-hearted smile of appreciation.

Jonathan rubbed his stomach and continued, "And if I could send her some of your cook'n, she would be on the next plane here."

Her smile was genuine as she wiped her eyes, "Thank you, but another visit would be the last thing we need right now."

He wiped his hand across his brow. "Shew." He exaggerated the gesture with every muscle in his body, giving her reason to laugh. Jon found the only time he had to cheer her up was when the subject of her mother arose. He decided he would try to avoid the subject in the future, trying his best never to bring a tear to Alex's eyes.

Jonathan continued to work hard and long hours but doted on his wife and babies as much as possible. He found that the identical twin girls looked less like his brother Erin and more like their mother every passing day.

As their daughters became livelier, so did the fondness between Alex and Jonathan. They found their conversations came easily, their interests were similar, and their sense of humor was the same. They could connect without even trying.

One day, Alex commented, "You know why Erin and I got along so well and why he loved me so much?" After waiting a moment to see his curiosity peek, she looked Jon in the eyes and said, "Because I'm the female version of you, I suspect."

The girls were seven months old when Jonathan arrived home from work, grateful it was a Friday. He was surprised when he came upon the site of Alex sprawled out on the floor just inside the sitting area. Erin and Kathleen were strapped perfectly content in their bouncy chairs, cooing at each other.

"Alex? Alex?" When she didn't answer, Jonathan knelt beside her, sliding the back of his fingers down her cheek. Her eyes opened slowly. "Are you alright? Did'ja faint?"

Her lips came together in a smile, giggling under her breath, "No, I was exercising – couldn't you tell?"

Laughing together now, they rose to their feet. "I remember doing at least one sit-up before dozing off." Her giggle became a gasp suddenly, "Oh, Jon—dinner!"

He caught her arm before she could head into the kitchen. "Don't panic; dinner will be ready in about an hour."

"You've already started it?" she asked, confused at the statement.

"Well, no. I figure, after getting to the restaurant, being seated, and ordering, we should be eating in about an hour."

Alex returned his wry smile with a look of guilt. "I feel horrible putting you to that expense."

"But doesn't the thought of getting out…the change of scenery…excite you a little?" He asked, smiling back at her, "besides, we barely spent what your father had sent us, and we're building even larger savings from my paychecks. The money is ours, not mine alone."

Her smile stretched from ear to ear. "I'll need to get a quick shower." She started for the staircase.

"Ah, no doubt!" He called after her. "You must have worked up quite a sweat doing that…sit-up."

Alex turned back only long enough to purse her lips and squint her eyes at him.

Jonathan looked down at Kathleen and saw her face puffy and red. Her mouth became crooked as she stiffened up. "Aw, you doing that to punish me for teasing your mum?" He went looking for a clean diaper while she finished the dirty deed.

A while later, Alex returned to find Jonathan playing with the babies on his lap. "Tease me all you want about my workouts, but…" Then she stopped, put her hands on her hips, and bent her knee.

Jonathan steadied the girls against his chest, turning them to face out, and they both stared at their mother.

"Wow! No more wearing of my shirts then?"

"No. That was my real workout today—I gave the girls a fashion show. I was so excited. I think I tried on every piece of clothing I own."

"Wish I'd been here." His eyes were searching everything but her eyes.

Alex couldn't help blushing when he flirted with her, and she's been blushing a lot lately.

She bundled the twins up for the long walk, and they each carried one out. Jon followed Alex, carrying Kathleen out, and almost knocked them over before realizing she had stopped to stare at the old, beaten-up car in the driveway. "Who's here?"

Jonathan made his way past them and opened the front passenger-side door. "Your chariot awaits you, me'lady."

"That's your car?" Alex still hadn't moved toward it.

"I've been using my lunch hours to learn how they drive on the wrong side of the road here." Jon held the door open for her with a wide, proud smile on his face.

After strapping the baby carriers in the back, Alex climbed into the front for the short ride to the restaurant. It had been a small adventure. "I can't stand sitting here and not having a steering wheel in front of me," Alex said, wincing every time they passed another vehicle.

When they finally arrived, the restaurant looked crowded, with patrons doubling around the large bar in the middle. The lighting was dim, with a romantic glow from the candles on each table. Finally, the hostess came to escort them to a booth.

"Well, don't I feel lucky this evening," Jonathan said as they passed the bar.

"Why?" she asked.

"All eyes are on you, my dear."

Alex rolled her eyes, "It's the girls—people love babies."

"I beg to differ. Those men at the bar probably aren't even aware you're carrying a baby. If that was it, wouldn't I be getting looks? I'm carrying a baby."

Alex blushed and gave him a playful punch in the arm, letting out a laugh.

They sat in a booth that fit the baby carriers sideways beside them. She was about to feed Erin a bottle when Jonathan stopped her. He opened the menu, laying it in front of her. "You really should look at the menu first and figure out what you want first."

She stared at the menu for a few minutes, picked up Erin, and fed her.

"Do you know what you want?" He asked.

"I'll just have whatever you're having."

"Alex, stop worrying about the prices and get what you want."

"We like the same things. Just get me whatever you want. I'm sure I'll like it." She said, looking at Erin as she fed on the bottle, "speaking of money, though, I should start looking for a job myself."

"Who would look after the girls?" Jonathan sat forward, arms on the table and chest against it.

Alex put the bottle on the table and sat Erin up to pat her back. "Maybe I could find something that would allow me to work from home."

"Is there something you want to buy?" Jon inquired.

"No," Alex answered.

"Then there's no sense in taking time away from them."

"Jonathan, if I don't get on my own two feet, you'll never be rid of me." She finished with a wry smile, but instead of the usual flirtatious response, her heart sank when she looked at him.

Jon said nothing at first, looking down at the silverware he now fiddled with. Then said after a small sigh, "I've been feeling guilty."

Alexandra's eyes curled in curiosity. "Guilty? Why?"

"For living Erin's life. I married the beautiful woman he found and got to father the children he dreamed of."

Alex waited until Jonathan finally returned her gaze. "It's not his life you're living. He's gone." She took a deep breath and gave him a soft look. "You could have wished me luck and walked off that day, but you didn't. You stayed, and together, we made a life-changing decision in a moment—and that's the life we're living."

"So, I shouldn't feel guilty for enjoying it?" Jonathan asked.

"No. Nor do I want you to grow resentful of having to carry the burden."

"I don't feel burdened. I feel exhilarated by all of it."

"I know." She gave him a wide-eyed smile. "I've been drawing strength from you. All of this was very scary to me, but you make it seem so easy and stay so calm."

"Well, I'm nervous tonight."

"About what?" she asked.

"About you wanting to get free of me. I didn't realize this was a temporary solution for you."

"That's not what I meant." She stared off in thought for a moment and then looked at him eye to eye. "We never had a plan. We wanted to save the pregnancy, and we have. I didn't know…I…I wasn't sure…"

Jonathan put his hands flat on the table. "You have my heart, Alex. It's up to you what you do with it."

Just then, the waitress approached to take their orders, leaving them bread to start with.

Jonathan sat back and concentrated on cutting them each a piece. He broke the awkward silence by talking about work. They kept the conversation light throughout dinner.

They decided against dessert and returned home in time to put the girls down for the night. Jonathan quietly exited the girl's room, going over to his door, but stopped and watched as Alex came out to the hallway.

Alex looked over and smiled. She approached him, put her hands on his hips, and said, "Thank you for a lovely dinner." Then, holding on to him for balance, she lifted herself to her tippy toes to kiss him on the cheek.

Jonathan didn't turn his head and only offered her his lips. She stopped less than an inch away.

He held his breath and leaned in. The kiss was soft and slow, and when it ended, they just stared into one another's eyes for a moment.

Alex broke into a soft smile. "Would you like to continue this here, or…" She raised her eyebrow and glanced at his open door.

Jonathan's arm slid down to her lower back, guiding her in, closing the door behind them.

Alex woke up happy the following day despite getting even less sleep than usual. She knew she'd have to get clever before she could return to a whole night's sleep.

She had to learn some tricks to raise the twin girls. Before Kathleen could climb out of her crib, she kept Alex up 18 hours daily. Her baby girl only slept five hours at night and only about an hour in the afternoon. They quickly separated the girls into two rooms so Kathleen wouldn't keep Erin awake.

Fortunately, Kathleen learned to climb out by the time she was one year old and could keep herself content with toys, allowing her mother to sleep. That's when Alex started leaving a bottle full of ice and a chew cookie on a dish for Kathleen to wake up to. She figured that would hold her off until everyone else was ready for breakfast. She was now getting another three hours in the morning.

Nighttime was a challenge, too. She found that Kathleen didn't fall asleep until around 1:00 a.m. Alex put bells on the outside of Kathleen's door so she'd know if she tried to leave the room. Otherwise, she would be left to play when the family went to bed. Alex had Jon disassemble the crib, and they laid the mattress directly on the floor.

Kathleen's sleeping habits only worsened over the years. Five hours shrunk to four- and the hour nap shrunk to maybe 30 minutes on a good day.

Dear Claire

Dearest Claire,

Thank you so much for getting my letters and pictures to Bobby and for mailing his replies. I understand it is becoming increasingly difficult for you to connect with him due to my mother's overbearing, watchful eye. Nonetheless, we are both eternally grateful for your efforts.

Jonathan agrees that we should rescue him the day he comes of age. Of course, that is still years away. Worse still, I think my mother is already aware of my plans. I wrote to her asking if Bobby could come and stay with us for the summer, but she never wrote back and has never returned any of my calls. Bobby wrote that she never mentioned the idea to him even though my letter arrived and he saw her open it.

Never mind my woes; you have more important things to worry about. Your wedding invitation is beautiful and has taken its rightful place in my photo album. I'm grateful you sent it even though you knew we couldn't attend. I hope you'll be just as kind with pictures of the event.

I can't believe almost five years have passed, and your Jarred has graduated from law school. Remember, though, you need to keep his confidence level up if he's going to do well as a lawyer. Simply put, let him win a few arguments between you occasionally.

Jonathan has already reached top management in his small company, which is growing quickly. He is always talking about the new staff he's had to hire.

The answer to your last question is no. I haven't learned to drive here, and I have no intention of trying. What little time I spend in the car with Jonathan is mostly with my eyes closed. Having the cars passing us on the wrong side makes me feel woozy. Although I do miss the freedom, the ability would give me.

You asked about more children. We would love more children, but it hasn't happened yet. It's odd how I could get pregnant when I was trying so hard to be careful and can't get pregnant when I desperately want to. The girls would love a little sister or brother.

Erin's imagination is remarkable, and she shows her ability to entertain herself by playing pretend with her dolls. I call Kathleen 'my shadow'. She does everything I do, including writing. She writes the most fantastic stories! She learns so quickly and is unrelenting in her thirst for knowledge.

I'm already conjuring up an argument for Jonathan to allow me to home-school them. I would hate to have a school that has to accommodate so many, slow her down, or kill her spirit for learning. Of course, it makes it nearly impossible for them to make friends. Our property here is much too large, and the surrounding neighborhoods are across a dangerous, four-lane road, so I can't allow them to wander off. Without school friends, I'll have to find another way to remedy that.

Until then, Kathleen and I spend a great deal of time together cooking, cleaning, doing her studies, and playing. She insists on helping me with all my chores. When she isn't with me, I read mostly, and she either reads or writes. She loves to write out on the beach or inside the glass doors that lead to it when it's raining.

Erin keeps herself busy until Jonathan returns home. She then becomes his shadow. Jonathan calls her "Princess"- so much so that I think she truly believes she is one. I've told him to be careful, or he'll create a monster if he continues to spoil her as he does.

Oh Claire, I miss you terribly. I wish I could be there by your side on your big day, but I'm confident it'll be a beautiful event.

Love,

Alexandra

Education

"Jonathan, the girls, Kathleen especially, are well past where most six-year-olds are educationally, and they're only four. Kathleen learns so quickly—how will a school accommodate her?" Alex asked Jon, concerned.

Jonathan smiled and thought, *it's sweet the way she asks me as if I'm going to have a say in the matter.* "I'm not sure, dear; what do you propose we do?"

"Home school the girls, of course. I've already been doing so, although not on an official curriculum. Oh, Jon, I know I can do it, and it would allow them to learn at their own pace."

It was a rare occasion that Jonathan didn't submit to her wishes, and this would not be one of those rare occasions. "Kathleen would do well at school, but they would not likely accommodate her need for a nap. Unless she learns to get more sleep at night, I don't see her growing out of that need," Jon added.

"Oh, you're right! I hadn't even thought of that." Alexandra responded.

In response to this conversation, Jon immediately visited the library and found the necessary books and teaching aids for her to use. When Alexandra received the books, she believed it was a great help since now she can form a proper curriculum. She didn't waste any time and started straight away.

Kathleen and Erin kept her mother quite busy, especially Kathleen. Alex and Jon could not believe how quickly they soaked up information and how hungry Kathleen was to learn more. She was reading and writing her own stories before she turned five and seemed to have a natural talent for making her imaginary worlds come to life.

A few months into their program, Alexandra told her husband one night at dinner, "Very soon, I'll be learning along with her as we go through the instructional books. She is so far ahead of Erin it's hard to keep things straight."

Erin was not quite as enthusiastic about her lessons. Although she was bright and learned quickly, she was never as hungry for them as her sister was.

One morning, Alexandra woke Erin and headed downstairs. "Are you ready to start your lessons?"

Erin rubbed her sleepy eyes. "No."

"Finally!" Kathleen replied, looking up from her workbook. "I started without you." I read the instruction book and have been practicing the next maths lesson.

Alex just nodded with approval. "Okay, I'll get Erin started on hers and then come check on you."

Kathleen and Erin locked eyes and gave each other dirty looks, scrunching their faces and noses before returning to their lessons. They sat at the opposite ends of a small table next to the piano. Kathleen chose the spot in front of the glass doors to look out at the water when she needed a moment to think.

Once Alex went over the lesson and explained to Erin how it worked, she gave her the practice book to work on. She then made her way to check on Kathleen.

"What is this?" Alex asked her.

"It's called Calculus," Kathleen answered her.

"That's it, Kathleen, you are officially on your own. That is beyond what I learned in my schooling." Alex claimed, scratching the back of her head in confusion.

"Want me to show you?" Kathleen said in a high voice with a smile.

"I appreciate the offer, but I think I'll take this moment to keep the laundry going."

Alexandra left the girls and went through the hidden door to the laundry room. Shortly after she left, Erin moaned.

"What's wrong, Erin?" Kathleen asked.

"This isn't working."

Kathleen got up, walked along the table, and looked over Erin's shoulder. "If you write out your work, you can follow it. You did it correctly until you had to move on to the next number. Once you divide that, write it out so you can keep going. "

"Mummy can help me. Go sit down!" Erin yelled.

Kathleen put her hands on her hips and, in a very dismissive voice, said, "Okay. If you want your lessons to take longer, wait for her." She started back to her seat until she heard Erin groan, "Fine."

When Alexandra returned, the girls were quietly working, so she opened her book, sat on the couch, and read.

"Mum?" Kathleen called.

"Yes, dear? Are you finished with your work?"

Kathleen grabbed her practice books and walked over to Alex. "Yes. I've done three practice sections on the maths. Can I start reading the History books Da got from the library?"

"We normally do science before I let you disappear with the next history books."

"I told you, Mum, I started without you. I already did my science and Theology."

"Okay then, go ahead. What's the next history subject?" Alex asked because she hadn't kept up with Kathleen due to the attention Erin required. "Is it the American Revolution?"

"Oh no, I did that already. I also read a lot about the Civil War. I found President Lincoln interesting, so now I'm reading about all the American presidents.

"Have you already done your reports on both of those?" Alex asked.

"They're in your bin, Mum," Kathleen replied glumly.

Alex jumped up, realizing her bin was full of work to check. She only pretends to check the classes where Kathleen has surpassed her knowledge, but she loves Kathleen's written reports.

Alex put the pile on the coffee table in front of her, pulled out the first report, and started reading when Kathleen walked past her into the kitchen. She heard her daughter scream a short time later and rushed to run in.

"What happened? Are you okay?" Alex asked as she heard the splash sound under her feet. "Oh, honey, what happened?"

"I wanted a glass of milk," Kathleen replied with tears in her eyes. She was on the floor with a kitchen towel, trying to soak up the spill. When the towel absorbed all it could, she would ring it out in the sink before starting again. "I'm so sorry for the mess. I'm so sorry, Mummy."

Alex bent down, carefully keeping her feet out of the puddle of milk. "Relax, honey. Haven't you ever heard the phrase, don't cry over spilled milk?"

"But the mess. It's everywhere," Kathleen replied, tears dripping off her cheeks.

"A mess is not the end of the world. We can get this little spill cleaned up. Please relax, baby." Alex noticed that Kathleen wasn't satisfied even after cleaning up the floor. Her daughter had to rewash the floor and the legs of each chair before she insisted on getting the towels through the laundry.

Neatness was something Alex was strong about, but now she worried she had gone too far with her 'shadow.' She was bothered by watching her daughter stress so much over what she believed was a minor spill.

Once the laundry was running, Kathleen grabbed her pencil and her new notebook that she had just gotten for her sixth birthday and took them to the beach to write. Writing stories relaxed her.

She had only just stepped out beyond the glass doors when she saw someone making their way down the steep hill across the beach. Kathleen stopped from closing the door behind her and instead placed her things inside before sliding it shut. She started walking across and made her way over to him as he landed on the sand.

He was much taller than her, and his sandy-brown, curly hair hung over his eyes. He had to keep pushing it out of the way to see.

"Who are you?" Kathleen asked.

"I'm Batman!" He waved a stick like a sword at something imaginary, "I'm chasing the Joker before he can poison all the people of Gotham City." Then, with a look of seriousness, he asked in his strange American accent, "Who are you gonna be?"

Kathleen didn't have a TV in her home and had never seen a comic book, so although she thought Batman's name was odd, she assumed it to be his real one. With so little understanding, she answered, "Kathleen."

With the introductions over, their adventure quickly began. Kathleen followed his lead and helped him chase the bad guys. She got so caught up in it that she pretended to be captured and waited for her new friend to save her life. In her strong English accent, she exclaimed, "Batman, save me!" After cutting the air with a stick and battling invisible men, he grabbed her arm and ran with her to safety. By the end of the day, they were both the heroes of Gotham City.

Batman climbed back up the hill before Kathleen turned to run into the house to find her Mum. "Mummy? Mum?"

"Yes?" Alex exited the kitchen, wiping her hands on a dish towel.

"I made a friend today. His name is Batman."

"That's lovely, but how did you meet him?" Alex asked her, curious about the encounter.

"He came down the hill, and he wasn't scared at all! He said he would come back tomorrow. Is that okay?"

"How old is this new friend?" Alexandra asked more seriously, being concerned.

"He looks close to my age – a little older, I think. I didn't ask."

"Yes, of course. Although he's welcome to use the front door if he likes." Alex said with a smile.

"I'll tell him tomorrow. Can we make cookies tonight? I'm sure he'd like cookies."

The next day, Batman turned down the invitation to use the front door. "There's no fun that way," he said.

However, Kathleen's new friend loved the cookies and became a regular visitor.

Batman Returns

Kathleen usually waited every day just inside the glass doors for her friend, who would return to play new adventures for a few hours. She was amazed by his clever imagination with the characters he would create. There was the Joker, the Riddler, and even a Cat Woman. He had asked if she wanted to be Cat Woman, but she liked being Kathleen.

When Batman made his way down to the beach today, however, a little earlier than usual, he was surprised to see Kathleen playing with dolls. "Hey, why not my usual welcome? Don't you want me to save you today?" he chuckled as he walked toward her.

Erin looked up at him, and her face turned crooked. Before she could reply, they heard, "Batman! Save meeeee!" Kathleen ran out, asking, "What's the adventure today, Batman?"

Now Batman had a crooked face while his head swung back and forth between the two girls.

"That's my sister, Erin," Kathleen said with a slight scowl.

"You're twins?" Batman asked.

Erin's voice had more scowl in it when she answered him first. "Yes, Sir Obvious, we're twins. How clever of you to notice."

Batman's face tightened, but Kathleen answered. "And that's how NOT to make friends." She giggled, looking at Batman, who was now smiling back at her. "Let's play." Looking back at Erin, Kathleen called out, "Erin, if you want to stay, you can be the ugly villain we torture and kill in the end!"

They giggled while Erin scooped up her dolls and made her way back inside.

Batman noticed the few differences between them. Kathleen wore pants without shoes, while her sister wore a frilly dress with matching frilly socks. She kept her shoes on despite the sand. Erin also pulled her hair back neatly into two ponytails while Kathleen's curly blonde locks were down and free.

"Your teachers will have to put you in separate classrooms when school starts," Batman said.

"You go to a school?" Kathleen asked.

"Yeah, of course. I'm starting the third grade this year," he replied as they walked.

"Third grade?" Kathleen's eyebrows almost met when she scrunched her face. "I wonder what grade I'm in."

"Didn't you do Kindergarten? How old are you? Batman asked.

"I'm six," Kathleen replied.

"Then you should be in the first grade this year. You'll learn how to read and write with all the letters you learned in kindergarten," he informed.

"I can already read and write. What else do they teach in first grade?" She asked.

"Science, history and math." Batman listed.

"I'm finishing calculus in Maths. History is my favorite, though. We've read a lot about British history, but we're learning all about American history now. We've read books about the Revolutionary War up through the Civil War. I'm reading about the presidents now. Today, I started reading about our sixth president, John Quincy Adams."

"Where do you go to school? They make you study during the summer?" Batman asked.

"We usually do our lessons in the sitting room, but sometimes Mum lets us go out on the patio if it's not too windy." Kathleen then pointed up above them to the back of the house.

Batman could see that they had a railing up there that led to the cliff's edge, but he couldn't see the patio area from down on the beach. "You go to school here? At home?" he asked, confused about what she meant.

The look on his face made her answer a little sheepishly, "Yes. Where do you do your studies?"

"I go to Holy Angels School. It's a catholic school." Batman said.

"I was baptized there! Well, we were baptized there," Kathleen said, remembering her sister. "We go to morning mass there on Sundays."

"My family goes to the 10:30 am mass, and I've never seen you," Batman said.

"We go to the 7:30 am," she replied.

"That's too early," he scoffed. "I like to sleep in on weekends."

They continued with their game, but Kathleen kept thinking about the conversation she had had with Batman.

When Batman left, Kathleen ran inside to tell her Mum about their latest adventure. Her mother was making meatballs, and Kathleen immediately washed her hands and started to help while she talked.

Erin entered the kitchen with her favorite doll. "Who was that stupid boy? Mum, did you know Kathleen was playing with a stupid boy?"

"He's not stupid!" Kathleen barked.

"No fighting, girls," their mother said. "Erin, have you cleaned your room today?"

"It's not that bad," Erin said, looking back at her doll.

"Get!" Alexandra stood and pointed out of the kitchen.

Erin turned around and stomped out of the kitchen as loudly as possible.

"Erin! Come back here." Alex called.

Erin returned with a pouty look. Knowing what her mother was about to say, saying it before her, "I know, walk like a lady." After receiving a nod of approval from her mother, she headed back to her room much more quietly.

When the meatballs were finished and put in the oven, Kathleen excused herself, went straight to Erin's room, and entered without knocking. She couldn't stand knowing there was a room with things out of place. As usual, the room was messy, with toys and clothes strewn about the floor while Erin played with her dolls on the bed.

Erin looked up but said nothing. She knew if she did, Kathleen would stop cleaning up her mess and leave. However, after a rude look from Kathleen, Erin slowly slid off the bed and started to pick up. It was worth the small effort, knowing her sister worked at three times her pace and would have it done soon.

After Kathleen had hung the last dress in the closet, they heard the front door open downstairs.

"Da is home!" Erin exclaimed, running out of the room.

Kathleen looked around to ensure everything in the room was in proper order before making her way downstairs. *Mum will need the table set before dinner,* she thought.

Jonathan was sitting in his big chair with Erin on his knee, telling him about the "stupid boy" she saw. When Kathleen didn't hear her father correct Erin for calling Batman stupid, she continued past without a word.

Jonathan wasn't surprised. Kathleen didn't always bother to welcome him home with the same excitement Erin showed. He was blissfully unaware she was angry at him, though. He found Kathleen hard to read, whereas Erin was always bubbly and telling him her every thought.

He loved that Alex was enjoying her time home-schooling the girls, but now Kathleen is starting to challenge his political beliefs at dinner. She is so good at debating, and Alex is always in her corner. He wonders how Erin gets through the day with them. She always seems starved for his attention when he gets home.

When they sat down for dinner, Jonathan looked at his daughter, who sat furthest away from him, "So Kathleen, I hear you have a new friend."

"He's not new, and he's not stupid," Kathleen said, looking at Erin.

"I'm sure he isn't stupid," Jon started. "Does he come every day?"

"Yes he does, but he goes to school, so he won't be coming until after. He also said he has T-ball practice some days."

"Well, maybe we could go see a game one day," Jonathan said, noticing her wide smile. "How old is your friend?"

"I didn't ask him, but he said he is starting the third grade. He said I would be in the first grade, but I have already learned everything he said they teach in the first grade." Kathleen looked at her mother, asking the much-awaited question, "Mum, what grade am I in?"

"I'm not sure sweetheart. I think you are well past those lower grades, though. I never attended a university, but you have already learned what I did in high school." Alex and Jon gave each other a look with their eyebrows raised.

Erin smiled before saying, "He is stupid then." She laughed while Kathleen's face burned hot.

"Batman is not stupid, but maybe you are! In fact, why are you laughing, Erin? You aren't anywhere near my lessons either!" Kathleen pursed her lips, staring hard at her sister, who quickly lost her sense of humor.

"That's enough, ladies," Jon stopped the argument.

Later that evening, when Jon and Alex were alone, he mentioned their savings. "Your father was very kind when we were sent to America. The money he gave to help us get started was incredibly generous."

"I know. We have so much left; I keep expecting my mother to demand it back," Alex replied, changing into her night clothes.

"I've been thinking, Alex, since we don't pay a mortgage or rent and live so simply, maybe we can use it to set up a trust for the girls.

We already have an additional nest egg from my earnings." Jon pulled back the covers to climb into bed and watched his wife do the same.

"I think that's a great idea. What do you suggest, when they turn 18?" Alex asked.

"Oh no, I think they should have to wait longer than that unless we both die, of course."

"Oh, Jon, I don't think that's fair to Kathleen. We may have to investigate university for her very soon – I'm serious – very soon. So, although I can see Erin waiting till after 18, I disagree with making Kathleen wait. Maybe we say they must use it for university before receiving the remainder."

"Agreed. Unless, of course, we both die in any form of accident, and then they should have the full amount when they become legal age, regardless of education."

Alex laid back and pulled the covers up before adding one last comment. "They may need it if my mother evicts them after my death. I think I'm the only reason we're still living in this house. She's probably afraid I would go home to England."

Jon got under the covers and rolled over to Alex, putting an arm across the front of her. "I'll follow you wherever you go."

The comment brought a smile to her lips before he leaned down to kiss them.

Princess

"Princess! Princess?!" Jonathan yelled out to the beach.

It was Saturday, and after hearing yelling, both Batman and Kathleen stopped playing to look back at the glass doors where her father stood.

"Do you want to invite your friend in for some lunch?" Jon said, asking them to come in with a beckoning sign.

Kathleen turned to Batman with a broad smile and questioning eyes.

"Sure, I can eat," Batman said smiling back.

While they started toward the house, Batman kept hearing *'princess'* in his thoughts.

They sat at the kitchen table while Kathleen placed plates in front of them. Alex filled glasses for each with ice water and sat down with them.

"Is she really a princess?" Batman blurted out to the table, looking at the family in confusion.

Jon was quick to reply with a proud smile, "They are. They are both my princesses". Before Jon took another bite of his sandwich, he asked, "Are you really a superhero?"

"He is my hero!" Kathleen said with a smile. "I got stuck in that prickly bush, and he broke every branch away, one by one, to save me. I only got a few cuts falling into it, but no cuts getting out."

Just then, the phone rang. "I'll get it." Jonathan wiped his mouth and stood up immediately, heading into the other room. "Hello? Yes, it is. Oh, Bobby, Alex will be so excited! One moment."

Alexandra was already there and grabbed the phone out of his hand. "Bobby? Oh, my goodness…it's so good to hear your voice!"

There was a slight pause and Alex's eyes widened a little, "I'm sorry, Bobby. Are you okay?" Her voice lost the excitement and now took a more concerning tone, "Who's with you while she's there?" After another short pause, "Well, yes, I care that she's in the hospital because that means you're alone."

Alex bit her lip while Jon stood there watching her. "I didn't ask why she's in there because she isn't my concern; you are. Maybe we should plan for you to come stay with us for a while."

Jon could hear the girls arguing in the kitchen and returned to their company to quiet them down.

Alex returned to the kitchen shortly after that. "Bobby wants me to call my mother; she's in the hospital."

"What happened? Is she okay?" Jon asked, concerned.

"They found cancer, and she's having the lump removed," Alex responded with less concern.

"Alex, we can get you a flight home if you need to."

"Only if I can take the girls with me," she replied. "I would like Bobby to meet them, and I don't know what you would do with the girls otherwise."

"We can afford that. Maybe the four of us should go." Jon said with a bit of excitement in his voice.

Alex went back into the other room to make the call in private. When it was picked up, she asked, "Mother?"

"Who…Alexandra?" Isabelle asked from the other side.

"Yes. Bobby called, he said that you were in the hospital." Alex couldn't say anything insincere, like, *and I was worried* because she wasn't.

Isabelle felt the tension. "Bobby should not have bothered you. It was a small lump, and they removed it already."

"When will you be going home?" Alex asked trying to carry the conversation.

"Later today," Isabelle answered, not giving Alex much to speak about.

"If it would be helpful, Bobby could come for a visit so you would…"

Isabelle cut her off, "That won't be necessary. Thank you for calling, but the doctor will be coming in soon. Good day." *Click*

Alex hung the phone up so hard it could be heard all the way in the kitchen. She picked it back up and ignored Jon in the doorway. "Bobby? I did as you asked and regret it!"

Alex listened intently before answering, "And I wish you would give up on her and come here. You're old enough now. She has no power over you," she pleaded.

After listening again, Alex replied somberly, "I'll have to take your word for it, Bobby. I don't think I'll ever see that side of her. The bitch hung up on me. I called as you asked me to, and she hung up on me!"

There was silence for a full 30 seconds. Alex tried to turn the conversation positive. "I have a life here, and I am loving it. I wish you could meet my girls, Bobby. I do hope you'll consider coming to see us."

Alex stood still, listening again, and a smile came over her face. "I love you too. Goodbye."

"Mum, you okay?" Kathleen asked when her parents returned to the kitchen.

"Yes, I'm fine. It's just family stuff." Alex reminded her girls, "You know what I've always said about family, right? You never give up on them. Only love can endure all the ups and downs and allow forgiveness in the end."

Kathleen and Erin agreed somewhat begrudgingly before finishing their lunch.

After lunch, Kathleen and Batman went back outside. They were going down the hidden stairwell when Batman explained, "Sorry I was so late today. My friends and I played dodgeball this morning until Ray got hurt."

"Your friends?" Kathleen asked as they walked.

"Yeah, well, none of them are allowed to cross the highway. I've told them all about you, though." Batman replied, looking down and watching his step.

"Then tell me about them." Kathleen sat down in the sand with her back to the cliff.

Batman also sat down but started piling up the sand in front of him while he talked. "My buddy Jeff is my best friend," he told her. "He's a troublemaker," Batman continues, "our mothers had been best friends growing up."

"Jessica is a girl that doesn't act girly. She's a lot like you, never wears a dress, but her pants aren't even as nice as yours."

"My mother makes our clothes. So, who else lives in your neighborhood?" Kathleen asked excitedly.

"There's Joey. He's a bully, but not to me because I'm bigger than him, and we're friends."

"Would he bully me?"

"No. Not if I tell him not to."

Kathleen gave him a quick smile. "Who else?"

"We let a nerd named Ray hang with us sometimes. He isn't very good at sports and gets hurt a lot."

"What's a nerd?"

"Ya know, a geeky kid. He's always reading and stuff."

"Oh." *Reading is geeky and makes you a nerd?* Kathleen thought to herself.

Kathleen started using their names repeatedly in all the stories she wrote. Batman, of course, was always the main character who saved the day. Sometimes, in her stories, his friends helped them save the world, but in others, she would make Joey and Jeff villains who tormented her hero.

She never shared the stories with her friend. Being considered a 'nerd' did not sound pleasing to her.

In her eyes, Batman was handsome. She loved the sandy, brown curls that hung over his light blue eyes that shined against his dark skin. He was tall and strong enough to pick her up when she hung on the cliff, pretending to be captured.

That day, Batman's visit ended with bad news. As he headed back toward the hill to leave, he stopped and looked back at Kathleen. "I won't be seeing you all week."

"Why?" she asked with turned-down brows.

"We're going to visit my grandmother in Rehoboth beach. We leave early tomorrow morning."

"When will you return?"

"Next week. We're only staying until Saturday and then driving home Sunday."

Kathleen's entire body seemed to deflate.

Batman saw it and said, "Be ready to tell me how you defeated the bad guys when I return. And remember, never show your weakness to those villains; they'll eat it up like dogs!" With that, he turned and climbed the hill.

Noticeably Tired

"You look beautiful, princess," Jon said to Erin as she twisted to show off the new dress her mum had made her. This one was yellow with white lace at the belt and trim. The skirt was gathered, so it fanned out when she turned.

"Did your Mum make you one, Kathleen?" Jon asked.

"I hope not," Kathleen replied, looking at Erin.

Erin stepped between them, "Where is Mummy? I want her to do my hair."

"She's napping, princess. Can I help?"

"I can do it. Where are your hair bands?" Kathleen said while making her way to the couch.

Erin started for her room when Kathleen reminded her, "And bring your brush!"

Jon watched as Kathleen sat on the end of the couch, and Erin returned to sit on the floor before her.

"I want ponytails," Erin demanded. So, Kathleen split her hair down the middle, brushed one side, and banded it before doing the other.

"It's nice to watch you two get along," Jon commented, as his eyes shined bright looking at them. Erin got up to check it in a mirror.

"She pulled my hair too hard and probably didn't do them straight," Erin snapped.

With a smile, Kathleen rolled her eyes at her father.

"That was nice of you to do," he said, returning Kathleen's look.

"If I didn't, she would have driven us crazy until Mum got up." Kathleen stood up, "Are you hungry? I could make the hot roast beef sandwiches."

Jon stood from the couch, "Or I could be the parent today, and you could be the seven-year-old. As it should be."

"Or not," she replied dryly. She stopped, turned back to look at him, and put her hands on her hips. "Do you know how to make the gravy?"

"Ummm." He finally ended with a closed-lipped smile.

Kathleen giggled. "You can still be the parent while your seven-year-old makes you lunch."

"You even mock me like your mother," Jon said, which caused them both to giggle. Jon looked at her and asked, "You and Erin always seem to get along when we have singalongs at night. Why can't you two get along like that more often?"

"We sound good together, but it's probably our only shared interest. We're too different, Da." Kathleen headed toward the kitchen again but stopped before entering. She looked back at him, "Mum has been taking a lot of naps lately."

He caught up and put a hand on her shoulder, and they entered the kitchen together. "I'm sure she's fine. Now teach me how to make the gravy so I can play the parent part next time."

Jon's smile was glowing. He has been patiently waiting for Alex to tell him she is pregnant. *She's probably planning some unique way to announce it to all of us.*

Alex eventually got up and made dinner that night without any significant announcements. They did a few songs at the piano before it was time for the girls to retire to their rooms.

Alex took the girls to Erin's room for their bedtime story that night. "Erin, it's your turn to choose the book."

"Peter Rabbit!" she exclaimed. Erin jumped up on the bed but left space between her and her sister for their Mum to sit.

"Erin, Mum already read that book," Kathleen complained.

"It's my turn, and I want Peter Rabbit," Erin whined.

Alex fumbled through her bookshelf, "Okay, but where is it?"

Erin shrunk a bit on the bed and didn't answer.

"Erin, where is it? I can't find anything in this mess." Alex kept shuffling and straightening the books as she searched.

"Good grief, I'll read it to you." Kathleen sighed, sat back on the bed, and started reciting the book, word for word. Not only did she know it by heart after only having her mother read it once, but she also brought the story to life.

Erin listened in awe, hanging on to her sister's every word.

Alex, too, and she had let Kathleen recite all 31 pages before realizing the time. "Thank you, Kathleen. Now, it's time for bed."

Alex tucked Erin into bed and sent Kathleen to her room with a kiss on the forehead before telling Jon what had happened.

"She wasn't just summarizing the story?" he asked.

"No. I didn't have the book in front of me, but I would swear she didn't miss a word. The Tales of Peter Rabbit was my favorite book series when I was little."

Finally, Jon let out a harsh, fast sigh, "Are you pregnant?"

"Wha…No. I started 'hell week' this morning." Alexandra took off her socks and started to unbutton her dress. "That's probably why I'm so tired today."

Jon's tone was soft but direct. "It's not just today. Kathleen told me you've been sleeping on the couch during their lessons. She's been teaching Erin for months." He looked at her in concern.

Alex's eyes filled with tears, and she stopped undressing. She sat on the edge of the bed, "I don't know why, but I'm always tired. I have less and less energy every day, and I would swear I just had hell week just over a week ago."

Jon sat beside her and placed his hand on her back, "I'll call the doctor and make you an appointment. Tomorrow, first thing."

Jon did as he promised, which led to additional appointments and numerous tests. Finally, the results were in, and they needed to consult with the doctor to learn what they had found.

"Will I be getting a shot this visit, Mum?" Erin asked from the back seat of the car.

"Oh no, princess. This visit is for your father and me to see the doctor. Did you bring your doll? Kathleen, your notebook and pencil to keep busy?"

"Yes." They replied in unison.

When the nurse called to escort them back to the doctor's office, Alexandra and Jonathan left the girls in the waiting room to play and write. They took the two seats in front of the large desk and waited.

"Mr. and Mrs. Yule, I'm Dr. Paul Oscar. Thank you for coming."

Jonathan stood up and shook his hand as Dr. Oscar went from the door behind them to the desk they were facing. "Should we be worried?" he asked, half smiling.

Dr. Oscar continued to his chair behind the desk without answering. He placed a folder down and opened it, leafing through the pages. When he stopped, he put his hands together and gave them a sympathetic look. He took a deep, uneasy breath. "I'm sorry, but I'm afraid it's cancer."

Jonathan dropped back into his chair hard as his breath got heavier.

"I'm afraid it's been spreading for a while and is now inoperable. Chemotherapy and radiation may help extend life a little, but most likely not much."

A strange sound came from Alex as she grasped Jonathan's hand tight. He held her close, losing control of his own emotions, shaking with sobs. His eyes were closed, and tears were falling into her hair while he laid his lips on the top of her head.

Alex finally choked out the question on both of their minds. "How much…time do I have left?"

The doctor was red in the face and fidgeted in his seat. He cleared his throat, "Maybe six months."

Alex put her head back against her husband's chest and, pulling at his shirt, cried aloud. "Oh God, how could you? The girls are only seven. Why take me now? Why now?"

They sat crying in the office long after the doctor walked out.

Jonathan, desperate to keep his family together, did all he could to convince Alex to fight the cancer and give her and himself hope, "There must be something we can do. The girls and I need you."

The kind words brought more tears to Alex's eyes. But she choked out, "They've only given me six months to live, and I won't spend them in the hospital. Not when I could spend them at home, soaking up every last moment with my girls."

Jonathan slipped out of the chair and fell to his knees in front of her, putting his head on her lap.

Alex stroked his hair. "You are a great father, and I trust you to raise them well."

It had been over an hour, and Erin was getting restless. Kathleen did her best to keep Erin happy, making up stories for her dolls to act out. Finally, their parents came to retrieve them.

Kathleen listened to her parents' sniffles while Erin was oblivious, complaining she was hungry. "I promise to make you something as soon as we return home," Kathleen told her.

Before Erin could protest, Kathleen held a finger up to her lips and gave Erin a stern look. Her sister looked at her and didn't say another word.

The remainder of the car ride was quiet, with only the occasional sniffling sounds her parents made. When they reached the house, Kathleen made Erin lunch and immediately went to the little room overlooking the beach. It had a small couch where she would sit and write while she waited for Batman to appear on the hill.

She had her notebook and pencil on her lap. Usually, the words came easily, but she couldn't write one today. Thinking about her parents made her muscles tense. She worried about what made them so sad.

Tap, Tap.

The sound surprised Kathleen and caused her to jerk in her seat. Her pencil fell to the floor, but she caught the notebook before she looked up and saw her Batman.

He was laughing when she slid the door open. "I don't think I've ever made it over here before you came running out."

Kathleen gave an embarrassed giggle, and the two walked to the water's edge. She put her feet in and felt the cold. Batman bent down to grab a few stones to skip on the water.

"Batman?" Kathleen looked at him with a side glance.

"Yeah?" He bent down again, grabbing more stones to skip.

"Do you love me?" she asked straight up.

Batman's face turned red as he rolled his eyes. "What? You're a girrrrl."

Kathleen's face scrunched, and her jaw tightened. She took a deep breath, looked straight at him, and in her strong English accent, said, "Well, I love you, and I'm going to love you forever." She quickly crossed her arms in front of her and turned back to face the water.

"Whatever." He tried to dismiss it but was glad she turned away and missed the uncontrollable smile that came across his lips.

They didn't have their usual adventures that day. They skipped stones, mostly with Batman teaching her how.

Shortly after Batman headed home, Kathleen's parents called her into the living room. She noticed their eyes looked tired, and their smiles were forced.

Jonathan started. "Sweethearts, Mommy is sick."

Kathleen looked at her mother, who was now crying again, and she climbed into her lap. "It's okay, Mummy, you'll get better." Erin followed by climbing into her father's.

"No, sweetie, I won't." Alex was having trouble talking—her throat was closing up. "I'm getting ready to go to heav-" She cleared her throat, "heaven…"

Kathleen knew what that was and didn't like the idea at all. "I don't want you to."

"God has…" Jonathan choked up and couldn't continue.

Alexandra finished, "decided that I'm ready to be an angel and can watch over you from there."

The four of them sat and cried together, Kathleen on her mother's lap, her head on her shoulder, while Alex wrapped her arms around her and rocked her softly.

"Why does God need to take you away?" Kathleen whined.

"He needs angels and thinks I would be a good one." Alexandra kissed her on the top of her head again before saying, "Your father can handle things here, on earth. He'll take good care of you."

Without raising her head from her mother's shoulder, Kathleen looked at her Da. She watched as he hugged Erin harder and kissed her head. A long, drawn-out kiss, never looking over at Kathleen to give her the reassurance she so desperately needed.

Alexandra Finds Peace

As the weeks turned into months, Alex grew sicker. She slept later in the morning and took more naps throughout the day. The chores she had once done daily became a struggle for her.

Kathleen, who had always helped her mother, started doing the chores alone. She was always the first one up, so she would quietly collect everyone's laundry. The clothes were usually clean, dried, and folded before anyone else awoke.

When Erin came down, Kathleen would do her hair, make breakfast and lunch, and plan dinner. She also taught Erin to run her own baths and stayed on her about her room.

Kathleen always found time to play with Batman and only hinted about her mother's condition but never told him everything.

The nurses who eventually came to care for her mother were amazed to see such a tiny girl offer them coffee. They were even more impressed to watch them do their studies.

Erin didn't fight Kathleen's help while she set up her lessons, and she didn't fight her sister when Kathleen asked her to clean her room because Kathleen always did it with her. They still squabbled over a few things, but the fighting had become minimal. Kathleen kept busy while Erin stayed out of her way.

Kathleen ran the house in her parent's absence. Her mother was very sick, and her father had to continue working. She also insisted on knowing every detail about her mother's care. She made a point of visiting her mother every time medication was due to be administered to make sure it was. Once the medications were administered, she would then read to her Mum until the pain subsided.

Fall and winter passed quickly. Spring came and went in the blink of an eye. The girls turned eight in April, and Alex tried to do what she could to make the day special for them, despite her weakness. She told Jonathan what to cook for breakfast, then lunch, which Kathleen shared with her Batman, Erin with her dad, and finally, the girl's favorite dinner. She also sent him out to get Kathleen more journals to write in and Erin a new playhouse.

Although her daughter Kathleen had to make the cake, they gathered in Alex's room to blow out the candles and share in it. Alex did her best to pretend she was eating by putting the cake to her lips before lowering her fork to break it into smaller pieces. Her fork then spread the pieces out to look like left-over crumbs.

Kathleen never went to bed until 1:00 a.m., after everyone else was asleep. So, she would sneak into her parents' room and climb in to share her mother's hospital bed. Alexandra had lost a great amount of weight. She was tiny and thin, while Kathleen was so small they fit comfortably together.

At 4:00 a.m. on June 24th, Jon was shaken awake by a loud shriek of his young daughter's cries.

"Tell God to give her back! I need her; tell him to give her back!" Kathleen turned and ran back to her mother's bed. "Mummy! Don't go, Mummy!"

Jon jumped out of bed and ran to his wife's side, placed his hand on hers, and felt the coldness. Without letting go, he fell to his knees and sobbed.

Kathleen lay on her mother's right side, hugged her, and cried, continuing to beg for her not to go. She refused to leave, and the coroner later had to peel her off the body to take Alex away.

No laundry was done. No breakfast was made. That day was a blur for all of them. Jon made calls to arrange the funeral at the end of the week—on Friday, July 1st. He had to take the girls with him to choose a casket and speak to the priest.

When the arrangements were made, it was time to make the dreaded call to England. As usual, he couldn't get past Isabel's secretary. "Yes, I would like to leave a message. Please inform her that her daughter has passed away!" Jonathan's throat immediately closed up, so he slammed the phone down.

No more than five minutes later, his mother-in-law's secretary called back, requesting details of the funeral arrangements and informing him that Isabel Harrington would be in attendance.

Jonathan went to find Kathleen, who sat on the couch downstairs, just inside the glass doors overlooking the beach. She stared at the hill, knowing her friend would not come. He was away with his family to visit his grandmother in Rehoboth again. Batman wouldn't be coming home until Friday, the same day as the funeral.

Jonathan's tense shoulders dropped, and he put a hand to his stomach when he saw her. "Are you okay, Princess?"

Tears filled her eyes as she shook her head back and forth. "I miss Mummy and Batman."

Just then, he saw a tear fall to her lap. He sat beside her, laid an arm around her small body, and said, "He'll be back. You'll see. And you can always talk to Mummy—she can hear you." When she didn't answer, he asked, "Guess what?" Jonathan tried to sound cheerful.

Kathleen finally looked at him expectantly with her swollen, tear-filled eyes.

"Your Grandmother is coming to stay with us."

"Mummy's mum?"

"Yes, Princess, and I'm sure she's very excited to meet you finally."

He was wrong.

A few days later, her grandmother arrived, and Kathleen immediately disliked her. "She never looks at us, Da. When you insisted that we hug her, did you see how she lifted her arms? I think she was afraid to touch me."

Jonathan tried to be sympathetic, "She's only here for a few days. Remember, she just lost her little girl. She's in mourning, love."

Kathleen was kept busy that week helping her father. She had become his shadow the way she had once followed and helped her mum.

Jonathan didn't seem to have the same appreciation for it. "It's okay, honey; I can make lunch."

"Then I'll set the table, Da," Kathleen replied, walking towards the table.

The funeral was a shortened mass at their church, with only a few of Jonathan's friends from work in attendance. Standing at the gravesite afterward was too much for Kathleen and Erin. They clutched their father's waist and hid their faces in his side while they cried. Jonathan reached down to pick Erin up, and she wrapped her arms tightly around his neck. His other arm reached down to rub Kathleen's back and head as his own eyes filled with tears.

When they returned home, Jonathan made them all a light dinner, during which Grandmother spoke only to Jonathan. "Well, it looks as if you haven't done much with the place. Have you even attempted to keep up my property?" Even during such times, Jonathan sensed the hatred she had toward the decision her daughter made.

Jonathan and the girls ate quickly and were glad when the old woman insisted on retiring early.

"Da?" Erin said.

"Yes, Princess?" The three of them were making their way up the stairs.

"Can I sleep in your bed tonight?"

"Yes, of course you can," Jonathan replied while Kathleen went to her room without stopping.

July 2nd

In the morning, Kathleen awoke early as usual and finished her studies. She left Erin to sleep, remembering Batman talking about how he liked to sleep in on weekends. After gathering everyone's laundry, she took it down to get it started and closed the door behind her.

After starting the load and ascending the stairs to return to the main floor, she heard her grandmother and father's voices in the sitting room, which sounded like an argument. She chose not to open the wall and sat on the top step to listen.

"It's only for a holiday, Jonathan. They must know from whence they came. They'll get to meet their cousins and Uncle Robert."

The frustration was evident in Jonathan's voice, "But the timing...They've just lost their mother, for heaven's sake."

"Yes, and what better way to recuperate from it than to be surrounded by a loving family?"

Jonathan knew she had no intention of giving up the idea, and he hadn't the energy or a viable argument to win. Then, a thought came to him, but he only mentioned one. "Erin has motion sickness, so a car and plane ride is out of the question.

Motion sickness? Since when? Kathleen thought.

Jon continued, "However, Kathleen has always been curious about her mother's birth home."

"NO! I won't go!" cried Kathleen, exploding from the hidden staircase. She ran to her father with pleading eyes and tightly wrapped her arms around him. "I don't want to leave."

Jonathan put his arm down around his daughter to comfort her, but it was her grandmother who spoke. "Your mother would have wanted you to know her family. Would you deny your dead mother such a wish?"

"That's enough!" Jonathan looked at the old woman with disgust. He then knelt and tried to reason with Kathleen. "Honey, it might be fun-"

"No, Da, please! I don't want to go; I don't want to go!" Kathleen pulled away from him and ran. Through the window, she could see a figure coming down the tree-covered hill, and she headed back down the stairs to the glass doors. As she passed through and stepped out to the beach, she saw her Batman.

He was coming down the hill more slowly than usual and dressed differently. His typical dirty t-shirt, ripped pants, and worn sneakers were absent, replaced by a smart, dark suit coupled with shiny shoes and a bow tie. As she drew closer, she could see that his curly hair was combed back, and his skin was at least three shades cleaner than she had ever seen.

Kathleen was still in her nightdress. Her feet were bare, and her hair was askew. Her face was wet with tears as she screamed, "Batman, save me!"

She needed Batman to really save her today and hide her until the old woman gave up and returned home. But when she got within a few feet of him, she was met with a face full of sand. She began spitting and desperately wiping her eyes to see again. When she succeeded, he was gone. He had run back up the hill out of sight.

What did I do? What...why is he mad at me? Kathleen had a million questions.

"Kathleen!" She heard her father call again and felt his hands on her shoulders as her eyes still searched the hill for some sign of her friend.

She let out a long breath, her shoulders curled forward, and she let her father take her inside, clean her up, and pack her bag. Then they waited for the car that would take them to the airport. Kathleen had soaked up the situation and knew she couldn't do anything now, but all she thought of was why her Batman did not save her today.

When no one was looking, Kathleen snuck into her parents' room, took her mother's diaries and the only photo album, and slipped them into her bag. She didn't know it, but she was being watched from the hill.

Batman sat, hidden by the thick brush, his head still reeling from what had happened. He had worked so hard last night and this morning, helping his mother clean the house and insisting that she cook something fancier than hotdogs and hamburgers. His birthday invitations went out with the same inscription: "Sunday school attire required."

He had told all his friends about the Princess he knew who lived in the house on the hill. No one believed him, but they would see! "She's beautiful and doesn't sound like us either."

Jeff, his best friend, was always the antagonist, "Why would she leave her house on the hill for your birthday party?"

"She will. She said she loves me," Mike barked back at him.

Jeff kept at him. "What if her father, the king, says no?"

"Then I'll ask her to run away with me for the day. I'll show her how to sneak up the hill."

"And if she won't?"

"Shut up, Jeff! I'll ask her dad myself, and I won't take no for an answer!" He claimed.

All his friends arrived at his house early, dressed as he had asked and anxious to see the princess he had promised. He left them all there and went to retrieve her.

He made his way through the neighborhood, crossed Buckley Road, and started up the hill, following the tree line. Over the two years he'd been coming to visit, he had worn a path in the grass. Once at the top, he slowly and carefully worked his way down through the trees to the beach. He was so proud of how clean he had managed to stay, not sliding in the dirt even once.

When he reached the beach, he looked at the glass doors expectantly and saw them open. His heart leaped until his eyes focused on her.

She isn't ready, he thought. *She's not dressed.* And he knew instantly from her demeanor and the wetness that showed on her face that she wasn't going to be able to come.

Panic struck him. He looked down at the ground and thought about how he had told all his friends. *They'll be waiting when I get home—I'd said I wouldn't take no for an answer…Jeff will never let me live this down.* All his fear, frustration, and disappointment seemed to explode within him; it radiated through his body, legs, and feet. Sand went flying up into the air, and when his eyes followed it, he saw that it all landed and stuck to the wet face of his friend. "Aww, no," came out through his exhale.

She was choking, spitting, and wiping her eyes. He stepped toward her to help but heard her father calling from the glass doors, and shame overtook him. Batman ran back up the hill without caring for his clothing, which the branches and bushes scratched and tore. He hid in the brush at the top of the hill and cried, looking at his princess.

From where he was sitting, he had a perfect view of the beach, the side of the house, and most of the front. Batman's tears turned into a fit of anger directed at himself. *Why did I run?*

Sometime later, Batman watched a black car pull up the long driveway and stop at the house. The driver got out and opened the trunk. Then he watched as her father handed him two suitcases. After closing the trunk, the driver opened the door to the back seat. An old woman he had never seen before got inside—and then his princess, Kathleen. He knew it wasn't Erin because of the pants she wore, while Erin stood in a dress watching.

Batman watched her father waving at the car as it drove back down the long driveway.

Why the suitcase? Where's she going? He had to know, so Batman mustered up the courage to walk around the upper rim of the cliff to the front door and knocked. When Jonathan answered it, he recognized the boy immediately.

"Batman, correct?"

"Hello, sir. I was wondering where Princess Kathleen was going. I, uh, well, I owe her an apology, sir."

Jonathan saw the sincere guilt on Batman's face. "She's gone on holiday with her grandmother. We have family back in England that she's never met. Why don't you come in, son, and have a drink of milk with Erin and me."

Batman followed him in and was about to sit in the sitting room when he stopped and noticed a photo on the floor. He smiled when he looked closer because it was a picture of him with Princess Kathleen on the beach that her mother had taken of them.

He handed it to Mr. Yule, who seemed to stare at it long before giving it back to him. "My wife keeps—kept—an album that has many more of these. You go ahead and hold on to this one."

"Thank you, sir, I will." Batman tucked the picture into the side pocket of his jacket, grabbed the glass of milk being offered, and sat down. He noticed Erin was nowhere to be seen.

Jonathan and Batman sat and talked about Kathleen for a while. They even spoke of the sand and why he had kicked it.

Her father assured him, "Have no fear; she has probably already forgiven you. Your visits mean everything to her." Jonathan even kidded around about the mood she would be in if her beloved Batman didn't come. "Unbearable, I tell you. Neither her mother nor I could speak to her without her overreacting or starting a fuss." Batman giggled in embarrassment.

Batman finally realized the time and remembered his party at home. He stood up to leave. "When will she be back, sir?"

"I told her grandmother she could stay with her for a few weeks. I'm not sure exactly what day she'll return." Jonathan's voice trailed off slowly in hearing himself.

As Batman reached the door, he turned back. "Is it okay if I come back and check in?"

"Of course, you are always welcome here, my friend." With that, Batman was gone.

When he returned, his mother and all the kids waiting at his house that day couldn't believe their eyes. Batman's perfectly pressed pants were ripped and torn and covered in dirt, along with blood from the branches that had scratched his legs. His shiny shoes were mud-colored, and his curls had fallen back over his eyes like they had always been.

Of course, that didn't stop Jeff from giving him a hard time. He started with, "So? Where is she?"

"She left with her grandmother today to go to England, but she'll return soon. Wanna see what she looks like?" With that, Batman proudly held out the picture Mr. Yule had given him.

While all the kids looked at the picture, his mother was not amused. Although she still allowed him to have his birthday party, she made him pay for the damage to his suit with extra chores the following week.

The following week, Batman returned to visit Jonathan, and he noticed he looked tired and beaten down. He couldn't have known that Jonathan had not heard a word from Kathleen or her grandmother, and they didn't seem to be taking his calls again.

Batman came back every day. Three weeks after she left, he'd stopped at the mailbox to get Mr. Yule's letters on his way to the door. One of them had England in the return address. *It must be from Princess Kathleen*, he thought. He ran to the front door and, without thinking, didn't knock. He rushed in, screaming for Mr. Yule, and shoved the letter in his hand. He barely stood still while Mr. Yule ripped it open and pulled out the inside pages.

Mr. Yule's hands began to shake. "No, no, not Kathleen!" Batman watched in horror as Mr. Yule fell to his knees. "Oh God, what have I done? I didn't mean for this. Oh God, please forgive me. I didn't mean for this!" He dropped the pages, covered his face with his hands, and sobbed uncontrollably. Batman watched as the man, twice his size, curled into a ball and rocked back and forth, sobbing, praying aloud.

Batman knelt and picked up the pages, spying the scripted words at the top of the second: "Certificate of Death." He wondered where Erin was and looked around the room and up the stairs, but he was surprised she hadn't come to the screams of her father. He looked again at the pages. The first page was a letter from Kathleen's grandmother, explaining that although she "hadn't the heart to tell him personally," Kathleen had contracted pneumonia shortly after her arrival and "probably due to the stress of losing her mother," her small body had not the strength to fight it. Mrs. Harrington had seen fit to have her granddaughter's body cremated and buried in the private family cemetery near her father right away. She attached the death certificate for his records.

Batman put the letter and certificate on the end table while his thoughts raced. Unsure what to do next, he stepped back over to Mr. Yule. He took one more look with expectancy to see Erin but finally knelt on the floor and put a hand on Mr. Yule's back, patting him lightly. *Pneumonia? Cremated? Family cemetery?* Batman stayed with him until he stopped rocking, and the sobs softened.

Finally, Jonathan let out one last prayer. "Take me, God, I can't bear the pain. Please, God, you should have taken me, not Alex. She would never have made Kathleen go."

Made her go? Hearing this, Batman's throat started closing, his face began to contort, and his eyes began leaking. *Kathleen had pneumonia. She died and was cremated.* His thoughts were now more focused; he thought about what death was, but he had never experienced losing anyone close to him. His heart began to pound at the memory of her face and the words she had screamed on the way to him, "Batman, save me!", then seeing her choke on the sand and wipe her eyes. *I can't say sorry. I'll never get to say sorry.* He jumped to his feet and ran from the house, wiping away the tears as he cried his eyes out remembering his princess.

Memorial

Jon scheduled a memorial service for Kathleen at Holy Angels church.

Losing Alex was devastating, but the loss of Kathleen seemed to stir anger inside him. His most common thought was, *why is God punishing me?* To make it worse, Erin's belief that she is alive somewhere only inflames it. *I need her to accept her sister's death for both our sakes.* It was torture hearing her beg for him to find her.

When he entered, Erin sat quietly in her room, staring into space. "It's just the two of us now, Princess. The two who cannot cook. Should we order a pizza tonight?"

She snapped back to reality and looked intently at her father, "You need to find her, Da."

"She's not lost, Erin. You know where she is. Mommy's family has a private cemetery in..."

"She's not dead!" Erin exclaimed.

"Erin, please. Someday, I hope to take you to Europe and visit Kathleen's grave."

"Stop it, Da!" She's not dead, and we need to find her. Why won't you believe me?" Erin raised her voice with frustration in it.

Jon stood up, "You stop! I know death is difficult, but you need to accept that they're gone. Mummy and Kathleen are GONE."

Erin watched as he stomped out, but she called out at him, "She's scared, and you don't care!"

Jon slammed the door behind him.

In the neighborhood across the highway, Batman's mother hung up the suit she had purchased earlier that day to replace the one her son had destroyed. She knew he would need it when she heard

Jonathan Yule had planned a memorial. It looked a little big on him, but he didn't seem to notice when he put it on the next morning.

Batman had not spoken much to his parents since seeing Mr. Yule collapse, and he had not left the house or spoken to his friends either. He was quiet and lost in his own thoughts, not interested in talking, eating, playing, or much else all week.

When Batman's parents pulled into a spot at the church, his door opened immediately. It was Jeff. Batman climbed out and found he was not alone; behind Jeff was Jessica, Joe, and Alan. Ray was walking up to them from his parent's car. They were all dressed in the same clothes they had worn on his birthday.

Seeing all of them caused his emotions to explode, and the tears flowed. He kept his head down, but none of them teased him for crying. Jessica put her arm around him, and they escorted him into church. As was their custom, the five sat together in the second pew back, which was across the aisle from the Yules. Erin was sitting in the front pew alone with her head down, but Batman noticed no tears. Her Dad stood nearby, being consoled by other adults, including Batman's parents.

Looking over at Erin, Batman felt the heat in his face rise. *She's hard to look at,* he thought. *Why did Kathleen have to go alone? Why did she have to die?* The anger stopped his flow of tears – at least for a short while.

Jonathan turned back to his seat and saw the kids. Batman bowed his head again and didn't notice, but Jonathan gave the others an appreciative nod.

The service was beautiful. There was a lot of music and a few readings. When it was time for the priest to read from the Gospel, he announced, "I have decided not to read from the usual passages but have chosen to read Kathleen's favorite passage because I feel it best reflects the little girl I knew.

II Corinthians, 13:1-7

[1] If I speak human or angelic tongues but do not have love, I am a noisy gong or a clanging cymbal. [2] If I have the gift of prophecy and understand all mysteries and all knowledge, and if I have all faith so that I can move mountains, but do not have love, I am nothing. [3] And if I give away all my possessions, and if I give over my body in order to boast, but do not have love, I gain nothing.

[4] Love is patient, love is kind. Love does not envy, is not boastful, is not arrogant, [5] is not rude, is not self-seeking, is not irritable, and does not keep a record of wrongs. [6] Love finds no joy in unrighteousness, but rejoices in the truth. [7] It bears all things, believes all things, hopes all things, endures all things.

Father Jackson then spoke about the little girl who would be so awake and eager to celebrate mass early on Sunday mornings. "She was a bright young girl who knew her faults. Since she had not yet made her sacrament to give confession, she did it openly. She was never afraid to tell me aloud what she had done wrong that week and how she was trying hard to treat her sister better. She once said that the two could be like water and vinegar, but she loved Erin and was always trying." At hearing that, Erin raised her head for the first time and showed some emotion in her eyes when they met the Priests.

Father gave her a quick smile and then continued, "Speaking of her loves, Kathleen also loved to argue – well, let's say debate – the bible." Many of Johnathan's friends made sounds of amusement, including him. "I had to do more than study and prepare for the week's readings because she knew the bible by heart, and I never knew what she planned to hit me with on any given Sunday." He gave a few examples and then mentioned the most recent conversation. "Kathleen told me all about her best friend, Batman." The congregation giggled, but Batman looked up at the priest, now looking toward him and his friends. "Her father assures me the young man exists, and his friendship was surely of 'superhero' status."

The priest closed the mass, and most got up to leave after he processed out. Jonathan and Erin didn't move, and when someone approached to offer condolences, Erin hid her face in her Da's arm. He tried to get her to acknowledge those who offered her their sympathies, but she didn't budge. She resisted the idea of accepting that her sister was gone.

Batman didn't budge either until the last had walked away from them. He slowly stood up and went to the front to stand before Mr. Yule. He wasn't sure what to say, but once he saw him face to face, his throat closed up again, and his tears turned into full-throated sobs.

Jonathan grabbed the boy without getting up and pulled him in for a hug.

Erin lifted her head and saw Batman's eyes squeezed closed with his head on her father's shoulder. She waited, and when he opened his eyes, Erin whispered, "She's not gone. I know it. If she were, I would feel it."

He lifted his head, never taking his eyes off Erin. *What? What did that mean?* Batman's head was reeling when Mr. Yule's voice broke through, "You were her best friend, and she appreciated and loved you."

Batman nodded, pulled away, and ran out of the church.

Jon knew what Erin had said to Batman, which made his blood boil. He stood to leave and started down the aisle.

"Da, wait. You're walking too fast." Erin ran to catch up, and when she did, she tried to take his hand in hers, but he pulled away.

They got in the car, and he just sat there.

"Da?" Erin spoke to break the silence.

He turned around to look at her. "Never again! Never again do I want to hear you say your sister is still alive. Kathleen is dead. Her grandmother buried her in England. She's gone." Now shaking his finger at her, "Not another word about it." Jon turned back around and started the car. His wheels squealed a bit when he pulled out, but he slowed down after leaving the parking lot. Realizing he was in no rush to return to their cold and empty house.

Erin Starts School

It would be Erin's first day in a real school. Jon had sent them everything his wife had in her education thus far, and they determined that she was past the third grade. They wanted to start her in the fifth grade, but Erin refused. "I don't want to be with older kids, Da. I'll never make friends."

"Your education will suffer if you spend years reviewing what you already know," he replied.

"Please, Da, this is scary enough." Erin's eyes filled with tears.

The school and her father relented, and Erin started that Monday in the third grade.

The teacher introduced Erin to the class by explaining that she'd been homeschooled. While most kids ignored the introduction, one girl, Maggie Kelleher, listened with great interest. Maggie was tall for her age, plainly dressed, and looked disheveled. Her shirt was half tucked in and half out. Her hair was clean but just hung limp to her shoulders. She looked at the new girl, Erin, and thought she was beautiful. *She looks like a doll.* Smart looking dress, shiny shoes, and her hair neatly put in ponytails.

Erin had gone from one morning class to another, never speaking or being spoken to by the other children. She was painfully aware that she was overdressed compared to the others. Very few wore dresses, and the ones that did wore tights under very short skirts. Now came the worst she suspected: recess.

The children filed out to the playground and ran into their comfortable cliques. Erin sat alone on the curb surrounding the parking lot and watched until someone poked her shoulder. "Hi, Erin, right?"

"Yes," Erin remembered Maggie in class. She was always the first to raise her hand when the teacher gave them the opportunity with a question.

"You're eight years old? You look younger." Maggie sat next to her as she asked. Before Erin could answer, she continued. "So why were you homeschooled?"

"My Mum was homeschooled, so she wanted to do the same for us."

"Us?"

"I have a twin sister."

"I haven't seen her; did she go to a different school?"

"My grandmother took her to England after my Mum's funeral, and she's still there."

Maggie asked her next question more slowly, forming it as she did. "Why would only your sister go and, well, not you?"

"My Da lied to her and said I get motion sickness sometimes, and he didn't think I could do the trip. My sister didn't want to go either, but she didn't have a choice. Now they say she's dead." Erin put her head down and concentrated on a small stone she pushed around with her shoe, but the word dead hung in the air.

"Wait, what? You lost your mom, and now your sister, too?"

"No. Well, oh, never mind." Erin looked away. She knew her father didn't believe her, why would Maggie?

"Please don't say never mind, you can trust me." Maggie put her hand on Erin's arm.

Erin sighed, "She's my sister, my twin sister. If she were dead, I would know it. I would feel it, and I don't. Instead, I feel anxious and dread, but they aren't my feelings."

"That's because it's scary starting at a new school with kids you don't know," Maggie said.

"No, they aren't MY feelings, they're Kathleen's!" Just then, a yard mother looked over at her, and Erin realized what she'd done.

She turned and pleaded with Maggie, "Please don't repeat any of this. I know you don't believe me, nobody does. I'll get in trouble with my Da if he finds out."

"I said you could trust me, and you can trust me." Maggie put one hand on her heart and the other in the air, "I won't say anything, I swear."

"You really think she's still alive?" Came a voice with a large shadow behind them.

Erin snapped around and saw a familiar face. "Batman? You go here?"

Maggie giggled, "Batman?"

"My real name is Mike, and yes, I go here. Do you really think Kathleen is alive?"

Erin took a deep breath, "Are you going to make fun of me now?"

He repeated his question, only louder this time, "Do you really think she's alive?"

"Yes." She answered.

"It doesn't make sense. I saw the death certificate; how do you explain that away?" He asked.

"I can't explain anything; I just feel it," Erin replied.

"I feel something, too," Mike said as Erin looked hopeful. "I feel like the wrong sister was sent to England." He turned and walked off.

"You are such a jerk!" Maggie yelled after him, but Erin patted her leg.

"Stop, it's okay," Erin said quietly.

"That's not okay. That was so mean." Maggie replied.

Erin wiped a small tear from her cheek and took a deep breath. "Batman and I were never friends. I was never nice to him either."

"I don't care; that's still not right, Erin."

Erin seemed to shake it off. "He doesn't bother me. It's my Da that does. I think he also wished he had sent me and not Kathleen."

"Why would you say that?" Maggie asked as she sat back next to Erin.

"He used to say she was eight years old going on 40. My sister could do everything adults could do." Erin replied.

"So what?"

"I think my dad wished she were here doing his laundry, helping with the cooking, cleaning the house, and all the other things Kathleen did when my Mum got sick."

"I think he would be mad that he let her go, but not that you were there. What I mean is he probably didn't want you or her to go. He probably wishes he still had both of you."

Erin never looked up, still playing with the stone, but replied, "I wish she didn't go either."

A bell went off, and all the kids filed back into school. The first class in the afternoon was English, and the teacher handed out a test. When she arrived at Erin's desk, she said, "You don't need to take this today; I know you haven't had time to study."

"I would still like to try," Erin replied.

The teacher smiled, dropped one off to her, and moved on. Erin smiled for the first time all day when she read the questions. *This is kiddie stuff.* When they were done, they had to pass the papers up to the front desk, and then the teacher told them to take out their red pens and put their pencils back in their bags. Erin had to raise her hand.

"I don't have a red pen."

After the teacher lent Erin hers, she mixed up the rows and handed papers back out for students to correct other student's tests. The teacher then gave the correct answer for each question. When they were finished, the teacher asked each student whose test they had and what score they received.

The boy next to Erin grunted and put his face in his hands. "She just wants to embarrass me for not studying," he whispered to himself.

Finally, she heard a student say, "Erin Yule."

"And what score did she get?" asked the teacher.

"A 100," said the student.

Erin smiled and looked over at Maggie, who was smiling back. However, the students between them were not, which made Erin snap her head back toward the teacher. When the teacher finished marking her book with all the scores, she asked for the tests to be passed to the front and collected. Erin noticed that only Maggie and herself had received 100s.

The day ended at 2:20 p.m., and the final bell couldn't have rung soon enough for Erin. She gathered her new books, homework notebook, and sweater and lined up when the teacher called for 'car riders.' Erin got in line to end her school day and was grateful to have someone to follow out to the proper area to meet their parents.

Jon Buys A New Home

Erin saw her father's car and made her way toward it. "Da?"

"Yes, princess?" Jon replied as he drove.

"I looked stupid today in this dress. None of the other kids wear this sort of thing. They wear pants, mostly, that Maggie called jeans. Can we…"

"Already on it." Jon cut her off. He had also noticed how she stood out from the others. Shortly after, Jon went to a clothing store and allowed Erin to pick out a new wardrobe. The jeans she chose usually had beaded pockets or stitching down the leg, and the shirts she found matched their design in some way. She still bought some skirts but paid close attention to the mannequins and got leggings to go under them.

"Ready?" Jon asked once she had a pile in the cart.

"Yes, thank you, Da."

"Good, because I have something to show you."

Her Da drove them to the neighborhood just down the street, past the one directly across from their house. He stopped in front of a lovely, two-story home with two garage doors.

"Why are we here?" she asked in confusion.

"The cliff house belongs to your grandmother, and she sent a notice to vacate."

"She's kicking us out of our home?!" Erin cried.

"I know you love that house; I do, too, but it isn't ours. This one is. I saved a lot of money over the past eight - nine years since we never paid rent."

Erin didn't move from the car lost in her anxious thoughts. *What if Kathleen finds her way home or tries to call, and we're not there?* She thought. Her father had come around, opened her door, and pulled at her arm to get out. "But what about our mail? What if a letter comes to our house and…"

"It'll be forwarded to our new address." Her father answered quickly.

After the quick tour, Erin went back out and sat on the small front porch.

"Erin? Erin, what are you doing here?" Maggie was crossing the street towards her.

"We're moving in here. Where did you come from?"

"I live across the street, just up a house. The one with the green shutters." Maggie pointed, and Erin followed with her eyes. It was the same style house, just different colors.

Maggie couldn't hide her excitement, "This is so cool! I finally have a friend in the neighborhood."

Erin had noticed that Maggie wasn't very popular at school. "Don't any other kids live in this neighborhood?"

"Yeah, half our school lives here or in nearby neighborhoods. The kids who don't live here in Springfield are from Clarkston County." She explained and after a moment of awkward silence, Maggie continued, "I'm glad we're friends, but don't worry, I know we won't be forever."

"What do you mean by that?" Erin asked.

"Well, you're pretty and smart, and the other kids will like you. You can't be my friend and be popular, and I think you'll be popular soon."

Erin wasn't sure how to answer her at first, but she spoke anyway. "I've never had a best friend. I've never had a friend at all. So, if other kids decide to like me, then fine, but they must like both of us because you are officially my first and oldest friend."

"Almost a whole day old! Hahahaha," Maggie replied with glee.

After Erin laughed at Maggie's joke, she asked, "Do you know where Bat- I mean Mike lives?"

"In Scottfield, I think, behind the cemetery right across from the house on the hill." Maggie flinched when a large hand appeared in front of her.

"Hello, I'm Erin's Da, and you are?" Jon waited to shake Maggie's hand.

"Hi, I'm Maggie. Erin and I are in the same class."

"That's wonderful!" Jon looked down at Erin, "That'll be great for Erin. We've always lived so far away from anyone her age."

"Where is that?" Maggie asked.

"Most call it the cliff house, but it's…" he started to answer her.

"The cliff house?! I've always wanted to see inside the house on the hill. You are so lucky."

"Well," Johnathan answered, "The cliff house isn't ours, but we should be get'n back to it."

"Ooo, can I come?"

"You'd have to ask your parents," Jon replied with a smile.

"I live right there; I'll go ask."

"Wait, maybe we should all go over. I would love to meet a neighbor." Jon started and then waited for Erin to stand up and follow before the three went to ask Maggie's mother.

Nora, Maggie's mother, was very kind and gave her permission. *Maggie has a friend. God, please let this one stick,* she had thought.

They arrived at the cliff house, and Erin took Maggie for a tour. She loved the hidden staircase that led to the beach and the beautiful piano up by the back doors to the patio. "It's going to be tough living in my neighborhood after living here. This is beautiful." She claimed. They made their way to the kitchen, and Maggie noticed a door. "Where does this go?"

"To nothing. It's just a big empty space," Erin replied as she opened it.

"Oh, my goodness, you could fit 20 cars in here."

"Seems weird, right? My Mum used to wonder why the builder never made anything of it."

Erin pulled Maggie back, and they went up into her bedroom. Erin whispered, "It'll be even tougher not living here, knowing Kathleen won't know where we are. If she calls, we won't be here to answer."

"Here are some boxes." Jon ignored their surprised looks and left them just inside the door. "You can start packing whatever you won't need for the next month."

"Thanks, Da." Erin looked at Maggie with big eyes, opened her dresser drawers, pulled out her summer clothing, and dropped it in the box.

Maggie wandered out of the room and walked to the only room Erin had not shown her yet. The room was perfectly neat and well organized – more Maggie's style. There were not many toys, but a lot of books and notebooks lined up on the shelves. The clothing in the closet was different, too. They looked the same size as Erin, but there were mostly pants and shirts instead of the dresses that filled Erin's closet.

"Kathleen hated dresses. Da made her take the few she had." Erin said as she came in and watched Maggie.

"So, this was her room – she keeps it like I keep my own. I like knowing where everything is." Maggie replied.

Erin ignored the comment, "Yeah, I wish I had worn something of hers today, but her clothes are so plain. She always wore just solid colors."

"What are all these notebooks?" Maggie asked, looking at them lined up on the bookshelves.

"My sister liked writing stories."

"Can I read a few? Can we take them?"

"I guess so." Erin turned back to keep working on her packing.

It was Sunday, and Jon sat in the pew closest to the choir. Maggie was a member and encouraged Erin to join.

Jon was startled when he felt a hand on his shoulder, "Hello. Jonathan, is it?" Without waiting for an answer, she continued, "I'm Martha Kilgore."

Jon stood up and shook her hand. "It's nice to meet you, Martha. Please, call me Jon."

Martha didn't let go of his hand and instead put her other on top as she asked, "I understand you play the organ, correct?"

"Yes, well, I play the piano, but I don't assume the organ is much different." Jon was getting a bit uneasy at her persistent handholding.

"We're losing an organ player to college. I was hoping you could fill in. Would you be interested?"

"I suppose I could." Jon was angry with God, but the church was still the only place to hear and sing music regularly. He missed hearing Alexandra and the girls singing while they did just about everything. Now and again, he would swear he could hear Alex singing from the laundry room or the large storage area off the kitchen. The wish and the memory haunted him.

"Wonderful! We can work out a practice schedule after mass. You live in the cliff house, correct? I could come there…"

"Not for long, we're moving…"

"Moving? Why?" Martha's smile faded, and she seemed to shrink about an inch.

"The house doesn't belong to us; it never did. Now that my wife is gone, her mother has requested that we vacate it."

"Well, can't you offer to buy it? Maybe you could rent it?"

"I tried both, but she wasn't interested. Erin and I will move to a house in Drummond Hill in a few weeks."

"Oh." Martha and Jon stood there a bit awkwardly in silence before she continued. "Well, we'll need to start practicing right away," she said less enthusiastically. "Should I come on Tuesday and Thursday of this week?"

"Seven o'clock too late for you? I must get Erin fed and…"

"I'll see you at seven on Tuesday." Martha finally let go of his hands and turned quickly to make her way to lead the choir.

Jon spent the rest of the mass daydreaming about his wife, Alexandra, only focusing on singing when the music started. He found peace in the music. When mass was over, he found himself looking forward to Tuesday and filling the house again with songs.

July 2nd - Rewind

Kathleen felt a hand on her back, guiding her to climb in beside her grandmother before hearing the door slammed shut behind her. She immediately jumped up and turned around to watch her home. She found her father standing on the porch waving as the car pulled away.

As it turned onto the main road and the house fell out of sight, she sank back into her seat facing the front. Sitting as close to the far door as possible, her grandmother began to speak. Although the old woman never turned her head in Kathleen's direction, it became painfully evident that the conversation was for her ears only.

"You should never have been born. I told your mother she would have been better off if she had just rid herself of the problem. It's too late now, though. Now she's gone, leaving her problems for the rest of us to tolerate. Jonathan was good enough to take my daughter on in her condition, but he needn't be bothered with you anymore. Now, he can move on and start a real life for himself without having the responsibilities of someone else's sniveling little brat hanging about. Well, at least the one he didn't want."

The comments brought Kathleen to tears and she tried not to be too obvious when she wiped them from her eyes. "My daddy loves me. He tells me so every day."

"Your real father was a gutter rat who had the good sense to go off and get himself killed. Your 'daddy,' as you call him, was just a lustful teenager hoping to get a payday for taking on my pregnant daughter."

"Take me back! I want to go home!" Kathleen's begging was met with silence. Not another word was spoken for the next seven hours. Upon reaching the airport, they boarded their flight, and the plane ride was torturous. Kathleen didn't like sitting still for so long, and although she spent most of it writing, she hadn't even noticed that she'd dozed off for her daily 20-minute nap.

When the plane landed, they were met by a man who immediately offered to take their bags out to the car for them. Once there, he opened the door to the back seat and stood while Grandmother got in. Kathleen started to follow, but the door was shut before her. The window rolled down, and they looked eye to eye for the first time since meeting in America. "Your ride is over there. Geoffrey will escort you." And with that, the window rolled up as her head turned forward again.

Although only eight years old, Kathleen had a good sense of what was happening. Her grandmother intended to do what she believed her mother should have done long ago, "rid herself of the problem."

The car Kathleen sat alone in stopped about an hour later at a large dwelling. The giant letters on the front of the building read Willington Boarding School.

The steps leading up to the entrance were vast and numerous. The large front doors opened to what Kathleen surmised was a castle. The foyer seemed never-ending, with staircases leading to heaven from every corner.

A tall, broad man approached, causing Kathleen to take a step back. He quickly extended his hand to hers and, with a friendly smile, said, "Welcome, Kathleen. We hope you're looking forward to your stay with us."

Before she could reply, he worked his way around to her side and gently guided her to walk with him. He escorted her to a dorm just off to the right of the entrance and introduced her to her new roommate, Sara. She was also eight years old and short in stature. Sara was very thin and frail-looking, with dark auburn hair and pale skin. Kathleen thought she looked as though she could be crushed with just a hug.

The windowless room had two beds, two closets, and two desks with accompanying chairs.

The first thing Kathleen did, even before unpacking her things, was to sit and write her father a letter on borrowed paper. As Sara looked at her in confusion, she explained to her, "I'm only here because of my grandmother's evilness. I know my father really does love me and will come for me straight away."

Having lived at the school for as long as she could recall, Sara had heard this before. There were many variations to the "someone is coming for me" story, but they all ended the same—she thought Kathleen's time would be better used getting unpacked and settled in. So, she played quietly while Kathleen concentrated on her letter.

After giving her letter to the headmaster to mail, Kathleen found Sara anxiously awaiting her. "Do you want to play?"

"Play what?"

"Chutes and Ladders. One of the L.O.s gave it to me. Well, not really. She was actually throwing it out, but I saved it."

Kathleen gave her a questioning look. "L.O.s?"

"Loved Ones. Ya know, the children who have families and get to go home for holidays."

Kathleen wondered; *does she even know how sad that sounds?* "What are you then?"

"They call us the T.A.s—throwaways."

"Well, not anymore!" Kathleen said, raising her voice with a sense of anger in it that surprised even her.

Sara sat back a bit from the game before she replied. "What do you mean, 'not anymore'?"

"I'm going to love you like a sister—I've always wanted another sister. And that means you are a loved one, too."

Sara smiled but returned to laying out the game without a response.

They barely started playing the game when Kathleen, who had played it with her mother many times, said, "That's not how you play."

"It's how I play it." Sara smiled.

"Read the directions; it says no such thing."

"I can't read very well. Here, you read them." Sara handed her the directions paper.

Kathleen shoved the paper back at her. "There's only one way to get better at it."

Sara ignored her and started to turn away. "Let's play dolls instead."

"No, Sara, read. I'll help you if you get stuck."

Sara didn't want to, but she tried anyway and proved herself correct.

Kathleen felt her stomach tighten at how slowly she read and how often she struggled with the most straightforward words, but her face never showed it. Instead, she remembered how her mother taught her and chose to encourage Sara. "You really aren't as bad as you say, and I love the sound of your reading voice."

"Really?" Sara couldn't help but smile.

When Kathleen answered her with a polite smile and agreeable nod, she continued to read on.

They enjoyed each other's company all day and giggled through dinner in the great hall that evening. When they returned, Sara immediately started on her homework, so Kathleen sat down to write a second letter to her father.

Dear Da,

I will have a surprise for you when you come- another daughter! My roommate is a throwaway, which means her family doesn't want her, but I want her, and so will you when you meet. Her name is Sara...

Kathleen was so excited she folded it up, asked Sara for another envelope, and took it straight to the headmaster.

When he opened the door, he seemed glad to see her. "I would be happy to send it off for you. So, love, do you have everything you need? Night dress? Toothbrush?"

"Oh, yes, sir."

"Wonderful. I'll be in to check on you both in a bit then."

Kathleen skipped back to her room, beaming. *I have a sister — that I like! If only mummy could have met her, she would have loved her too.* She stopped skipping just before reaching the door at the memory of her mother, but that was soon replaced by her thoughts drowning in math problems as she helped Sara with her homework.

"Sara?"

"Yeah."

"Why do you have opened suitcases over there?"

"We just moved into this dorm, and I haven't had time to unpack."

Kathleen didn't know that the headmaster was new to the school and had quickly come to understand the difference between the 'loved ones' and the 'throwaways.'

The night before Kathleen arrived, he had gathered the very young female throwaways—only five then—and moved them into a separate dorm. When you entered the school, all the other children would go to the stairs on the left, but this dorm was on the first floor to the right by itself. The dormitory was old and had not been used in years. It had a common area, with two doors on each side when you first walked in. The headmaster took the fifth suite at the opposite end of the entrance. The girls were doubled up in the other three bedrooms, leaving only the loo.

The headmaster knocked and then peaked his head in. "Are you girls okay? Ready for bed?"

Both girls were already in bed, Sara almost asleep.

Kathleen whispered, "Yes, we're fine. Thank you, sir."

She heard him sigh and reply, "Okay then, see you in the morning."

Kathleen used a small light and used the time to write stories until she was tired enough to sleep.

First Day Of School – Europe

Kathleen awoke early, as usual, dressed quietly, and spent the extra hours writing and looking at her mother's photograph book. When Sara finally woke up and readied for school, she insisted on doing Kathleen's hair.

"Did you even brush it this morning?" Sara asked while she pulled the brush through the knots. Kathleen wouldn't allow her to put it in ponytails, but she did allow Sara to pin the front up in frilly barrettes.

It was time, so Kathleen followed Sara to her first class. She was about to sit in the first seat, but Sara tugged at her sleeve. "No, no—back here."

"But I don't want to sit in the back." Nevertheless, Kathleen allowed herself to be led past all the nice school desks to the plain chairs against the back wall.

Sara dropped her books on the floor next to one and sat down. Then she focused on Kathleen and whispered, "Those chairs up front are for the L.O.s."

Kathleen didn't like sitting so far from the instructor, but she waited to see if there were enough L.O.s to fill the other seats.

The teacher was a young woman who looked more like a student than an adult. "Good morning, everyone."

The class responded in unison, "Good morning, Miss Beaks."

"Did you all practice your times tables over the weekend?"

There was only a soft murmuring, which grew louder as she started handing out a pop quiz.

When she handed one to Kathleen, she got a confused look from her. "Miss Beaks?"

"Yes?"

"I already know my multiplication facts."

Miss Beaks tilted her head and smiled. "Wonderful, then this should be easy for you."

The teacher finished handing out the papers and then sauntered across the back of the room and up the far aisle, returning to her desk at the front.

"Miss Beaks."

Startled, she turned around to find Kathleen holding out her paper. "Done already?"

"Yes, Miss."

Before Kathleen could turn back to her desk, Miss Beaks asked, "What school did you transfer from, dear?"

"I've never gone to one—this is my first. My mum taught me at home."

"And you've already learned your facts? Well, I see."

"Years ago, ma'am."

"Wait here." Miss Beaks walked back to her desk, wrote a note, folded it, and told Kathleen how to get it to the main office. The note explained to them that she should probably be placed in the third-grade math class. However, that teacher sent her back to the office with a note sending her to the fourth. Eventually, the office grew tired of seeing her, as this same pattern happened with every teacher in every subject.

"Kathleen? Where have you been?" Sara was running down the hall with a worried look. "Did you get in trouble?"

"No, they kept moving me about, but I'm good now. They say I'll be tested tomorrow by a specialist to see what grade I should be in."

Just then, Sara's head jerked forward, and the boy who had hit her started laughing. "Hey, throwaway—how's he like it?!"

Kathleen noticed that all the students had stopped to watch and listen. As he walked away, they all joined in his merriment before losing focus and returning to whatever they had been doing.

"What was that about?" Kathleen was angry at the act and could feel her insides catching fire.

"Forget it, let's go." Sara's head hung noticeably forward, and her eyes only looked at the ground before her.

Kathleen didn't have any homework since she hadn't been in any class long enough, but as they were walking back, she decided to help Sara, "Sara, do you need any help?"

Sara shrugged. "I have to memorize this by tomorrow."

"Let me see. Oh, good heavens, I made up a song for this once to help my sister. Want to hear it?"

That night, they realized Sara could memorize almost anything if put to music.

"Sara?"

"Yeah."

"Did you notice the other girls in this dorm—they aren't terribly friendly."

"They used to be but haven't been very happy since we moved down here. Maybe they had better roommates or something before."

"They looked so unhappy; it's sad. They don't like the headmaster either, do they?"

Sara looked up at her with a crooked brow, thinking. "No, they don't. They almost looked scared of him when he came around to announce dinner."

Kathleen smiled and shook her head. "Yeah, I think that's silly. He's so nice."

Later that night, while they were getting into bed, they heard the headmaster out in the hall. "Unlock this door! Now!"

Kathleen and Sara looked at their door to make sure he wasn't yelling at them. Soon after, they heard a door open and then close again—violently.

The next day, Sara went to class, and Kathleen went to the main office to meet the specialist.

The girls met up at lunch and then again immediately after classes ended to go back to their dorm. As they reached their bedroom, the headmaster was entering the common area.

Kathleen looked at him anxiously. "Sir?"

"Yes?"

"Have you heard from my father yet?"

"Yes. I'm sorry, sweetheart, but he thinks you should stay here at Willington."

"Did he send a letter?"

The headmaster stood over her and looked straight down. "Yes—to me."

Kathleen was devastated by the news and could not believe what she had heard. She lost her appetite and didn't go to dinner that evening, so Sara went with the other girls from the dorm. With another letter written to her father begging him to write back to her, she was just about to take it to the headmaster when he opened the door to her room.

"Oh sir, I was just bringing you a letter for my father."

"Okay," he replied. He took it from her and slid it into the inside pocket of his jacket, never taking his eyes off her. Then he pulled at his collar, slid his jacket off, and threw it on her bed. He walked over, pulled the chair out from Sara's desk, and sat down, facing the open room. "Come here, Kathleen."

When she approached, he picked her up and sat her on his lap. "I know you're upset."

She initiated her explanation with a break in her voice, "I've never been away from home before. I just don't understand—why so far away?"

"Because this is where you belong, sweetheart. With me." His hand then landed on her lap, his fingers between her legs.

Kathleen looked down, and every muscle in her body tensed. "Can I get down?"

"No." His hand slid up her leg a little more firmly. "I want to play a game. Do you like games?"

"Um, yes," Kathleen replied, trying to wiggle out of his grip.

The headmaster smiled. "So do I. I like touching games."

When Sara returned an hour later, Kathleen was already in bed with her back to the room.

Sara could hear her new friend sniffling and thought *she must still be upset about not getting a letter*. She finished her homework by herself, quietly murmuring made-up songs to memorize definitions before going to bed.

Sara noticed that Kathleen had become as quiet as the others the next day. She did all she could to cheer her new friend up, and by dinner, she'd succeeded. Kathleen's mood lightened slightly at Sara's relentless jokes, but she seemed to go quiet again upon returning to their room.

Kathleen heard the headmaster's door open just before it was time for bed, and she stopped breathing. She only let out a breath when she heard another door, one of the rooms across the common area, open and closed.

Kathleen watched Sara very closely over the next few days. "Sara? Do you still like the headmaster?"

"Yes. I told him of the collage you helped me do for class, and he said he would visit us tonight to see it."

Oh no, Kathleen thought. She looked at the closet and, for a brief moment, considered hiding in it. *I could pull dresses down to cover up in the corner.* She made sure to leave the closet door open.

Later that evening, the headmaster did come for his promised visit. Sara was so excited and immediately pointed at the collage she had displayed on her desk.

"That looks wonderful. You must have put a lot of hard work into it."

"Yes, and Kathleen helped me."

The headmaster then turned his attention to Kathleen. With a noticeable giggle in his voice, he said, "She is a good little girl." Then he looked back at Sara. "Your nightgown is very pretty."

"Thank you, sir." Sara grabbed both sides of her nightdress, fanning it out to model it while she twirled once playfully.

He watched and then took a step forward. "Now take it off," the headmaster said, standing over her expectantly.

Sara stopped cold and dropped the ends of her dress.

"Wh-what?" she asked.

With a strange calm, he repeated, "Take it off, I said."

Sara was scared but slowly started to lift her dress.

Kathleen lunged toward Sara, pushing her into the closet directly behind her, and locked the door.

Sara hit the back wall and hadn't gotten her wits about her yet when she heard the headmaster shout at Kathleen. "What do you think you're doing, young lady?"

Kathleen wasn't sure what she was doing. Her eyes teared up, and she let out a breath of defeat. She shook as she heard herself reply to his angry stare with, "Don't hurt her. I'll play. Please don't hurt her."

Sara couldn't see her hands before her face because of the darkness, but she did not make a sound, slumping to the floor and curling up. She could hear only muffled voices coming through the door and couldn't decide if she was more scared of the dark or the door opening.

Eventually, the closet lock turned, and as Sara escaped, Kathleen was climbing into bed with her back to the open, empty room.

Sara sat gently on the edge of Kathleen's bed. When she laid a hand on her back, Kathleen jerked away, closer to the wall. "Do you feel like talking?"

"No," Kathleen whispered between sniffles.

"Do you feel like listening? I can read to you."

There was a long pause, but just as Sara became convinced that Kathleen was asleep, she heard her whisper, "Okay."

Kathleen Starts University

The specialist, Ms. McCarter, Headmaster Stone, and the student administrator, Ms. Croll, sat to discuss Kathleen's testing.

The specialist, Ms. McCarter, started with her results: "She is well past the 12th grade. You will need to graduate her and figure out how to continue her education. She seems hungry for learning, and you wouldn't want to discourage that."

"No, I would not want to discourage that. We could use her to blow our trumpets someday, that Willington was chosen to care for such a brilliant intellectual," Headmaster Stone replied.

"I have a friend who is a professor at the nearby University. Should I call and see what she can do to help?" the administrator, Ms. Croll, asked.

"Yes! Let's see if we can get her enrolled. I'll ask Kathleen what courses she would be interested in," said Headmaster Stone. "My only worry is that classes have already begun. She'll be starting behind."

The specialist smiled wide. "I doubt catching up will be any struggle for her. I give her a week before she is leaps and bounds ahead of her class."

"How on earth…" Ms. Croll began before getting cut off.

"You don't understand; Kathleen remembers everything she sees and hears. Everything. She can read the textbooks immediately and be ahead of the class, which probably slowly works through them. How many other students do you know that read ahead like I know Kathleen does?"

Headmaster Stone and Ms. Croll responded in unison: "None."

"Then it's settled. We'll contact the University and get her enrolled as quickly as possible. I'll keep her busy with tutoring until then. She's also a great teacher, I must say. She said she had schooled her sister for the past few years, and I think I learned more than she did in our time together," said Ms. McCarter.

Headmaster Stone called the meeting to an end and anxiously waited for them to leave. He picked up the phone, dialed, and after a short delay asked, "Isabelle Harrington, please. This is Mr. Stone from Willington."

After a short pause, Isabelle answered, "Hello, Mr. Stone. We agreed we would never speak again," she said bluntly.

"You told me she had no family, but I've just learned Kathleen has a sister. Where is the sister?" he asked.

"Dead," Isabelle replied. "If that was all, I have a schedule to keep, Mr. Stone. I assume this will be the last call, correct?"

"Yes, Ma'am," he replied before hearing the click of her receiver.

The University agreed immediately, intrigued by such a child. Headmaster Stone took her to meet with the dean and discuss the options.

Kathleen took charge of the meeting as soon as the introductions were complete. "I want to take two majors, computer science and business."

"Two? I think we should start you off with one major and see how you settle in," the dean replied amusedly.

"I would prefer to start with two and drop one if it becomes too much. It makes more sense than playing the 'could-of, would-of, should-of game later," Kathleen replied. The Dean smiled and was about to answer when she spoke again, "I'm used to people like yourself underestimating me. The only question left to answer is whether you will be brave enough to chance my proving you wrong for having done so."

The Dean looked at her intently, waiting. Finally, he spoke slowly with less amusement. "I will allow you the two majors on a one-month trial. If you aren't flourishing in both, I will insist you drop one at that point to focus all your attention on the other. I will speak to your professors to determine the best course of action."

"Fair enough," Kathleen replied with a pursed smile. "Where do we pick up the books? I want to get started straight away."

"That will take a few days to see about scheduling two majors. If you would like, I could see today's schedule. Would you like to sit in on a class or two?" The Dean couldn't help but return her smile. He could see her excitement and found it contagious.

The Headmaster cut in, though, "Shouldn't we walk the campus so you can learn it first?"

Kathleen took a deep, slow breath in. "I've already studied the map of campus and feel comfortable I could lead that tour. I would prefer to sit in on classes," Kathleen replied without turning her head to look at him, but her eye contact with the Dean also fell off to gaze at the objects on his desk.

The Dean gave an awkward cough and pressed a button on his phone to call for his assistant. "Ms. Kline, can you tell me where any business or computer science classes are at the moment?"

Kathleen sat in on a few classes and got the proper books before they left. Only three days later, she had a schedule and had already read through all her books as usual. Her first class was almost occupied, but she found a single open seat about halfway down and three seats in.

"So, whose kid is this?" asked Scott Beavers. He sat in the next seat and was instantly irritated by her.

"Is there a problem?" she asked him.

"Whose yer daddy, kid?" he replied.

"I'm a student here, the same as you," Kathleen replied with an eye roll.

"What? You're like 10."

At this point, every student she could see looked back at them, watching. Kathleen put her chin on her shoulder and gave her best cutesy face. "Aww, that's sweet, calling me a 10. However, I must tell you I don't find you the least bit attractive." This garnered quite a laugh from the students and irritated Scott, but he didn't get a chance to respond. The teacher entered the room and asked everyone to take out a notepad.

Scott noticed Kathleen did not have a notepad or even the book assigned to the class. She held only an unsharpened pencil in hand. He leaned over and whispered, "Came unprepared, did ya?"

"No. I'm fully prepared. I don't need a notepad. I have an excellent memory." Kathleen shot back.

"But you don't have the book we'll be working from either."

"I've already read it," she replied.

The professor cut in the arising argument, "Is there something you two would like to share with the class?" asked the professor as he approached them. Looking at Scott, he asked, "Your little sister?"

"NO!" Scott and Kathleen said in unison to the resounding laughter of the class.

Kathleen followed it up, "I'm a student, sir. If you have any questions, please direct them to the Dean."

"You don't have a notepad out as I instructed, and I don't see your textbook," the professor replied.

"I don't need them, sir."

"We work heavily through the book, Miss?" he queried.

"It's Kathleen. I've already read the book. I assure you I can keep up, sir."

"You'll need the book, young lady…"

"Open yours and pick a page," Kathleen instructed confidently.

"Excuse me?" the professor asked.

Kathleen repeated more slowly, "Open your book, sir; pick a page and tell me what paragraph you choose."

The professor had a pursed smile, but he did as she asked. "Page 105, third paragraph."

Kathleen closed her eyes for a moment, diving into her brain, and then opened them, reading word for word from the page she had seen in her memory. She had the whole class's full attention, who were quickly flipping to the page. When she finished reciting the paragraph, she concluded with, "I'm actually glad you chose that page. I have a few questions regarding the current tax liabilities."

"Very impressive. Very, very impressive, but I'm afraid your questions will have to wait until the rest of the class gets caught up." He gave her a huge smile and a wink before returning to the front of the room.

Kathleen could feel Scott's eyes burning a hole in the side of her head. "Can I help you?" she asked without looking at him.

"Do you tutor?" he asked with a smile.

She turned her head toward him and returned the smile, saying, "I'm carrying two majors, but I'm sure I could fit you in."

Safe Space

It was Saturday, and Sara was sleeping in as usual. Kathleen grew tired of writing quietly and tried to sneak out without the headmaster knowing. She had only just closed the main door to the dorm when she realized he was already up and out in the large foyer area. She took a hard left and headed to the front doors. Once outside, she noticed some kids walking down the hill, some with bags and most without. Curious about where they might be heading, she followed.

When she had crossed almost half the yard, she looked back and noticed he was following her as usual.

The kids she followed arrived at the school's ice rink, and before Kathleen entered, she looked back again and saw the headmaster had stopped halfway and was turning back toward the school.

Inside, she didn't get in line for skates. Instead, she went to the short wall surrounding the ice and watched as the kids went around in circles. Suddenly, a whistle blew, and everyone started getting off.

A huge machine came out through open doors at the opposite end and started driving in large oval patterns on the ice. In its wake was clean, wet ice, melting away the scratches.

Kathleen was mesmerized. *It's like God's forgiveness. No matter what they do to the ice, it all gets wiped away for a fresh start,* she thought to herself. Her mother had said something similar when Kathleen confessed how she felt about teasing Erin. "Each day God gives you is a fresh start."

Kathleen kept glancing back at the doors, expecting him to enter. At her last glance, she saw Dannie and Rachel come in. "Are you going to skate?" she asked them.

"Yeah, I'm not very good at it, but it's something to do," said Rachel, followed by an embarrassed laugh.

Rachel was a tall, thin, black girl. She was beautiful and seemed to garner unwanted attention from the boys.

"Are you going to?" asked Dannie. Daniel was her real name, but Rachel had nicknamed her Dannie, and she didn't seem to mind. She was as tall as Rachel but had a larger build. Her skin wasn't white or black, but something in between, and her eyes were narrow. She and Rachel were never seen apart.

"I've never skated before." Until today, Kathleen had never even seen an ice rink.

Dannie pointed back toward the entrance, "Go get some skates. You can suck at it with us." They all giggled while Kathleen returned to get in line for skates.

She was nervous as she laced them up, paying attention to the older girls who seemed hell-bent on making them as tight as possible. When she stood up, she realized this would only get scarier when these thin blades were on slippery ice. Hesitant to find out, she tried walking a bit first from the far wall with the shoe lockers she had used toward the front door of the rink.

She watched as others entered the ice first. Some went straight out without issue, while others held onto the wall that enclosed the frozen circle. Holding onto the wall seemed to be the best course of action.

"Kathleen!" Just as Kathleen was about to step on the ice, she looked back to see that Sara had come.

Sara had her skates in hand as Kathleen made her way back to a bench. They sat down while Sara laced hers up. Her skates were white with black scuffs, and the toe area barely held together. "One of the L.O.s threw them out last year, but I rescued them. They're my size," she explained.

"Here is my locker key. Do you want to put your shoes in with mine? I can make my way back to the other end with you," Kathleen asked.

"We can skate them down to the other end," Sara replied, taking the key from her.

"Did you see the monster outside?" Kathleen asked. 'Monster' had become the agreed-upon name for the headmaster.

"He was talking to a teacher on the front steps," Sara replied.

Kathleen wondered; *he follows me everywhere else. So, why not here?*

Kathleen was uneasy on the ice, and her legs hurt when the whistle blew again. She waited to take her skates off until she watched as the scratches were melted away by the huge box-looking vehicle, leaving the ice renewed.

The next day, Sunday, Kathleen headed down to the school's ice rink again and found that the monster would not follow her past that same point. She spent all day Sunday free from the monster and wasn't alone. All her dorm mates, Dannie, Rachel, Sienna, Julie, and Sara, seemed to spend a lot of time there. Today, however, she did not turn her skates back in. Instead, she put them in the locker, where she got her shoes and retook the key. She had a plan.

Kathleen chose the lowest locker in the column closest to the back door. She had stuffed cardboard into the lock of the same door so it would open easily from the outside.

The last part of her plan was to find a way to escape the school late at night and early in the morning. This proved more difficult than she had thought, but at 4:00 am, she snuck out of her dorm to figure it out.

When she exited the dorm and turned to the left, toward the entrance, she noticed for the first time a small stairwell that only went down. It led to a landing with a door to the outside, but the stairs kept going to what she assumed was the basement. She would have to find more cardboard to fix it. It was vital that she be able to sneak back in before the others awoke.

It took another two days to find what she needed to fix that door's lock. Her first attempt failed immediately when she tested it. The lock was older and heavier built. The cardboard would not stop it from locking, but she figured the heavy clay she took from the art room would hold two nails in place. It worked brilliantly.

She gathered her courage the following day to see if the clay and nails held. They did, so she went to the rink's back door. The inside of the rink was pitch black. It didn't have any windows even to allow moonlight, so she had to move slowly and count her steps to the lockers. She ran her fingers down to the bottom locker and guided the key in to remove the skates. She sat on the floor to put her shoes halfway into the locker, stopping the door from closing completely.

Lacing up the skates was challenging but doable. Next, she had to figure out how to get around.

It was ten steps to the ice from the locker. She wouldn't turn on lights and take a chance they could be noticed from the front of the building, facing the school. Learning to skate would be challenging in the dark, but knowing where she was on the ice at all times was even more challenging.

Over time, visiting the rink once in the early morning and again late at night strengthened her other senses. Her listening skills helped her hear the echo off the walls to navigate around the rink. Her memory was solid in both mind and body. She knew how many seconds it would take her to go from one wall to the other at any speed she chose.

Scratching the ice for at least two hours every night and an hour in the mornings gave her the sense that she could feel the rink. She could see it clearly in her head as if her eyes were open and the lights were on.

Kathleen never thought of it as ice skating but as scratching the ice. That's what it was about – the scratches. The marks of anger, humiliation, resentment, and loathing scratched into the ice she knew would melt away and left pure for her to scratch again. *His games are getting worse, and they hurt; they really hurt now.*

Oddly, the young man who drove the giant machine that melted them away never seemed to notice when he cleaned the ice in the mornings.

Torture Of Sisters

Kathleen knew when the monster said he loved her, it wasn't real, it couldn't be. She was loved by her Da; he never loved her like that. She never felt uncomfortable or dirty after playing games with her father. The pain from what the monster was doing now was causing her to bleed.

An older student at the university, Tina, heard Kathleen's panic cries in the loo and asked if she could help.

After some prompting, Kathleen opened the stall door and let her in. "I'm bleeding, and I can't make it stop."

Tina gave her a sympathetic smile before reaching into her purse to pull out a maxi-pad. "Put this in your underwear to catch the blood. Don't worry, this is normal. You're a woman now."

Kathleen listened as Tina explained why girls bleed and then a quick lesson on how to deal with it. Unfortunately, she said it would last five to seven days, but that wasn't true. This bleeding wasn't the menstrual cycle she described, but she was too ashamed not to go along with it.

While Kathleen tolerated the majority of his abuse at night, it was the other five girls who endured abuse from the rest of the school throughout the day. The other children started teasing them horribly with comments like, "Hey, throwaways! Want a cigar to practice on?" The girls were pushed and shoved, and their books slapped out of their hands onto the floor while the others kicked them about. They had to start wearing shorts under their dresses because the boys would pull up their skirts to humiliate them in front of their classmates.

The other students were harassing the five of them every day— all day long. Kathleen was the only exception, as she spent most of her days at the university and wasn't fully aware of how bad it had gotten.

"Sara? Are you okay?" Kathleen had just returned to Willington and entered the room to find her crying with her head on her desk. *He better not have touched her!* She thought.

Sara looked up, and Kathleen could see that she had a bloody scrape on her arm. "What happened?"

"They were trying to put me in a trash can in the hall." Sara looked down, humiliated at hearing herself.

Kathleen cleaned her up while Sara told her what the L.O.s were saying and doing to her and the others. She also told Kathleen how their friends, the other throwaways, were dealing with it. "Daniel's a fighter and got detention for kicking one of the boys between the legs and punching another right between the eyes. Rachel has a mouth on her and has been spitting ugly words back at them. Julie and Sienna just hide away every chance they get. I'm not even sure where they go."

Sara always tried so hard to be liked, and Kathleen could not bear seeing her feel so tormented. She'd had enough.

The headmaster entered that night, cheerful. "Hello, love."

Kathleen didn't move and looked him straight in the eyes with a cold face. "You don't protect us."

His look of shock was momentary, but before he could morph into the monster he truly was, Kathleen continued. "The other children … they tease and taunt us, and you do nothing. You say you love us, but you don't protect us."

His face corrected itself, and he looked at her with honest sympathy. "I will, you'll see."

His sympathy was short-lived and did not save her from a night of pain and humiliation. His games were getting worse.

During assembly the following day, he excused all the teachers wanting to speak to the student body directly. Once the teachers filed out, he began. "You call them the throwaways," he began. He took a few steps toward the edge of the stage, looking down and shaking his head. Then, raising it with a smile and a slight chuckle in his tone, he continued. "Yet, compared to them, most of you will likely become thrown away." This captures the student's full attention.

"The children I have chosen to oversee are the ones I see the most potential in. Regardless of their school grades, they are the children I see as having a glimmer within them. A glimmer of brilliance that can't always be measured on a math or English test." Then, tilting his head with an inquiring expression, he asked them, "Don't you think it odd that all of them happen to be those without families? And odder still, all girls?" He stared directly at many of the boys when he said it, raising his eyebrows at them.

Those boys thought of it as a joke and giggled.

The Headmaster continued, "It is sad to see so few of our male students proving to be as great. So, few showing any reason for me to take pride in them."

The boys' faces went blank as he stared them down.

"My goal is to encourage these clever girls and brag heavily about having had them graduate from Willington someday. One has already advanced to the university at age eight." His voice became intense as he declared, "And for me to be successful, I will no longer be tolerant of any misconduct in their regard."

He dismissed the students, believing his point had been made, but not all the children initially took him seriously. They learned swiftly. Two boys earned detentions, having to clean out the bathrooms for a week after being seen nudging Sara in passing. Others had to clean the front steps with toothbrushes when he found out they had said nasty things to Sienna and Julie.

Kathleen followed up by talking with the other throwaways. She told them, "Keep your chins up and your heads high, no matter your feelings. Never show weakness. I assure you that weakness is like food for those dogs, and they'll eat it up." She drew from her memory of Batman; his confidence was her source for pretending she had the same.

Within six months, things turned around, and they found themselves the envy of the others. The girls couldn't help breaking a smile when they saw their fellow students trying desperately to get noticed by the headmaster.

They also noticed the headmaster and Kathleen had a rather strange relationship. The regular students and her fellow throwaways saw how he doted on her. He ensured she was always protected and knew where she was whenever not at the university.

The abuse at night was getting worse. It was no longer a touching game. He was hurting her, and she was dreaming of death more often now.

Engagement

"Da?" Erin called.

"Yes, love," Jon replied as he placed the last of the grocery bags on the counter.

After Jon gave her a look of expectancy, Erin started to unpack the bags and put them away.

"I noticed you and Martha have been spending a lot of time together on the weekends."

Jon didn't answer at first while assisting her.

"Da?"

"Does it bother you, love?" he asked, avoiding eye contact with her.

"No, and that's why I brought it up. It seems you've been sneaking around when I'm at Maggie's," Erin said with a sly smile and a bit of song to her voice.

Jon just looked down with a smirk and took a deep breath.

Erin struggled to push the sugar onto a higher shelf than she could reach. She spoke while her father's hand appeared to help push it up into place. "Da, you don't need to try and hide it from me. I hate us keeping secrets."

"I'm sorry, you're right; we shouldn't keep any secrets from one another." Jon turned back toward the bags still waiting to be emptied.

"All but one, of course," Erin replied sheepishly.

"And which one is that?" Jon asked, smiling, expecting a comic comment from her.

"My belief that Kathleen…"

Jon quickly lost the smile and sighed loudly, causing Erin to stand still. Her heart started racing, and her eyes watered. They continued in silence, and she never looked up at him again. The silence was soon converted into tension that filled the kitchen.

Once Erin put the emptied bags away in the cupboard below the sink, she attempted to escape.

"Erin," Jon called.

She stopped in the doorway but didn't look back at him. Jon thought quietly of what to say, but the words weren't coming. The seconds counted for a whole minute before Erin broke the silence.

"No secrets then–just us agreeing to disagree." She waited only one more second before leaving the kitchen.

Jon had been sure she would grow out of the thought that her sister was still alive. *If she were, she would have contacted us immediately*, he thought. He prayed she would. He prayed he had been wrong. He looked over the death certificate and re-read the letter Isabelle had sent more times than he could count. It was filed first and most prominent in the bottom drawer of his two-drawer filing cabinet— her name on the label, written in big, bold letters: Kathleen Erin Yule.

Jon missed Alexandra and Kathleen. His eyes glazed over as he felt the familiar ache for the happiness they knew as a family. He had turned the old house upside down, looking for his wife's photo album, and now constantly questioned himself. Did he remember to check all the dresser drawers? Did he check under the mattresses? Did he... *rinnnnggg*. It was Martha calling.

"Hello, Jon. We need to talk, might I..."

"We do! I just had the most interesting talk with Erin. She is very comfortable with us and said I should stop trying to hide it."

Martha cleared her throat before answering, "That is very good to hear since we won't be able to hide it much longer."

After a small silence, Jon asked, "Martha?"

"I wanted to tell you in person, but I'm, umm, I'm pregnant, Jon."

While she waited anxiously, she finally heard laughter come through the phone. Martha could now listen to him calling for Erin.

"Jon?" Martha asked, but the phone wasn't at his ear. She could now hear Erin answering him.

"Da? What?" Erin asked as she made her way back downstairs.

"Martha has some great news she needs to share with you." While handing the phone to Erin, he said, "I'm taking the two of you out to eat – er, three of you if you want to invite Maggie. Tell Martha I'll pick her up in two hours, okay?" He was gone before she could agree. She heard the front door open and close before turning her attention to the phone she was holding. Erin put it up to her ear.

"Martha? What is the news?"

"I can't believe…I umm…oh my goodness, Erin, I'm pregnant. I'm so sorry." Martha was at a loss for words. The awkward silence didn't last but a few seconds, though.

With all the excitement she could muster, Erin said, "Congratulations. I guess I'll see you in a few hours to celebrate." However, she sat down when they hung up and felt slightly confused. How could she be pregnant? She thought to herself.

Maggie's parents agreed, and she arrived at Erin's straight away. "Martha is pregnant? Is it your Dad's?"

"They both seem excited about it, so I guess so," Erin replied dryly.

"You'll have a baby brother or sister. That's kinda cool. I'm an only child and have always wanted a little sister."

Erin showed no emotion when she replied, "I already have a sister."

The girls hung out, listening to music until Jon came to pick them up. Martha was already in the car, and the restaurant was one the girls had only heard of. The prices on the menu and the food that arrived did not seem to match in their eyes. Erin couldn't help herself when they placed the small meal before her.

"Da, it looks like you are paying for the view of these pretty plates." After her father gave her an amused smile, she continued, "We'll have to hit a McDonald's on the way home. I don't sleep well on an empty stomach."

Maggie gave her an approving nod while Jon and Martha giggled.

Martha finally spoke up, looking at Erin, "Are you excited about having a little sister or brother?"

"I already have a sister, so I would prefer a brother. You know, to mix things up a bit." Erin smiled back.

"What should we name him?" Martha asked.

"Keith Erin."

"And if it's a girl, Kathleen…" Martha started before Erin cut her off.

"We already have a Kathleen Erin!"

"No, no, I wasn't saying another Kathleen Erin; I meant we could give a little girl a middle name of Kathleen. I would love to honor your sister's memory."

Erin could feel the heat rise in her cheeks. "My sister went to live in Europe before we met you. How can you honor the memory of someone you don't remember?"

"Erin, that's enough," Jon snapped before continuing, "It's a kind thought, and you should acknowledge the kindness." He reached over and took Martha's hand, "I think we should call a little girl Caitlyn, maybe Caitlyn Martha."

"Molly. I prefer my middle name." Martha forced a small smile but then looked down at her dinner.

Jon gave Erin a stern look and flicked his head for her to make things right.

Erin's face morphed into a smile, but not a kind one. Then she turned her attention to Martha. "I'm sorry, Martha. I didn't mean to be like that." Martha looked up with a small smile, but then Erin continued. "My father and I don't keep secrets from one another, but we agree to disagree about my sister Kathleen. He believes the word of a woman even my mother didn't trust that says my sister is dead."

Jon slammed his palms down on the table, dropping his fork. "Erin, you are pushing my patience this evening." Now Jon could feel the prickling heat in his skin. The waiter rushed to their table and immediately placed another fork on his plate before picking up the dropped one.

Martha placed her hand on his, "I want to hear her out. Erin, what do you believe?"

"I feel her. She's suffering, and I don't know why she hasn't contacted us, but I feel her. She's alive." Erin was surprised that Martha didn't dismiss her belief but looked at her with seriousness. "She'll come back. I don't know when, but she'll come back."

"As you know, I work with children and have had a few twins in my office. They say twins seem to have their own language. They can often speak without words." Martha explained.

Erin smiled and let out a sigh. "Thank you. I don't think you believe me any more than my Da does, but I appreciate being able to say it out loud."

"You are always welcome to talk to me. Although to be honest, it isn't as difficult for me to hear it. I didn't know her, lose her, or, worse still, didn't have another child I had to move on with and create a life for."

Erin put her fork down on her plate, never taking her eyes off Martha.

Martha continued, "As an adult, I'm sure it was very difficult to move on after so much loss, but your father had to for your sake. You'll learn as you grow up that acceptance of yesterday is often the only way to see tomorrow's path forward."

Erin gave a small nod, "I think I understand what you're saying, and I appreciate what my Da has done. But I used to think he wished I had gone to Europe and Kathleen had stayed behind because…"

"Oh, Erin. Why would you think that?" Jon asked.

"Because you wouldn't hear me out, and Kathleen was like Mum. She could cook, she could clean, do laundry…"

"But you've been a huge help to me," he retorted.

"You would have listened to her." Erin looked away from him and over to Martha. "Kathleen had a way of making my parents listen to her."

"A real force to be reckoned with, huh?" Martha asked.

"Yeah, she was a force, all right. When Mum got sick, it was Kathleen who home-schooled me for that last year. She made me get my baths, do my hair, and stood on a kitchen stool to cook the meals. You should have seen the nurses who came to care for Mum gush over her."

Martha smiled, "You were a help…"

"No." Erin shook her head and looked down. "I never helped."

"What I meant was you were a help to your sister," Martha said.

"How so?" Erin asked aghast.

"From what you describe of your sister, it sounds like she needed someone to care for. Jon once mentioned that Kathleen and your Mom had a very strong bond, the same way you and he did. When your Mom was sick, Kathleen undoubtedly felt lost."

"Da loved her too…"

"Oh honey, I'm not saying your Mom and Dad didn't love you both. Oh heavens, I didn't mean that at all." Martha shook her head and seemed stressed.

"Maybe we should change the subject," Jon interjected.

"No, wait." Martha looked at Erin with a kind smile. "Did your parents give you identical gifts at Christmas or for your birthday?"

"Oh no. I always wanted dolls or coloring books, while Kathleen always wanted pencils, notebooks, or more books to read," Erin replied.

"That was my point. They loved you both equally but differently."

"But how did I help my sister? She did everything and rarely asked me for help."

"You allowed her to act as the person she had the stronger bond with, your mother. You allowed her to fill her days with what she was comfortable doing and made her feel she had a purpose. That was surely better than her wasting away in constant worry and depression, watching your mother get sicker."

"I hope my sister agrees and believes that. I don't want her to hate me when she comes back." Erin's eyes teared up, and she focused on her plate, which was even emptier after a few bites.

Maggie added, "If you can feel her emotions, she can probably feel yours too."

Erin nodded in agreement before finally looking over at Maggie.

For the remainder of dinner, Maggie and Erin talked amongst themselves, as did Jon and Martha. When the waiter returned, Jon asked the table before he could, "So what will you all be having for dessert?"

"Are you trying to get out of taking us to McDonalds?" Erin spurts out.

"Aha, if you still need to go to McDonalds after dessert, so be it," Jon laughed.

"Maybe their deserts will be bigger and more filling," Martha retorted.

When the waiter took their orders, Jon popped up and excused himself from the table. He didn't return until the waiter led him with three deserts on his platter. He put one in front of each of the girls, and then he made his way around to place the last in Jon's empty seat. All three of them watched, surprised he skipped Martha. None of them noticed Jon kneeling next to Martha's seat with her dessert in his hand.

Martha gave the waiter a small smile and a nod before she turned back toward the girls, finally noticing Jon out of the corner of her eye. "Oh, Jon! What are you doing?" she asked.

"I wanted to deliver your desert personally." He held up the plate containing a brownie and whipped cream. Sparkling from the top of the cream was a beautiful diamond ring. "Will you marry me, Martha?"

Tears came to her eyes and a smile on her face. "Yes, yes, I'll marry you."

After the initial shock, Maggie looked to see Erin's reaction and found her smiling. *It seems Martha won her over.*

Hospital

Time passed slowly for Kathleen. It had been two long years since she'd arrived. She and Sara were almost 10 1/2 years old, and Kathleen was acknowledged as the girls' leader, although it was unspoken. The other throwaways were glad the headmaster no longer visited their rooms much, while Sara complained about how much more time she spent in the closet.

Kathleen hated his constant attention. When he would visit, she desperately attempted to delay the abuse with conversation, which proved good for everyone else. As he took her personal, private power from her, he seemed to give her more power in the school. He would listen to every suggestion she made and usually act on it immediately, earning her respect and credibility throughout the student body. Of course, it didn't make up for the pain and humiliation it cost her, but more visits came and went without abuse because she realized his love for debate. She exploited their political difference every chance she could. She looked for any topic that would spark his attention – away from why he had initially come to her room.

Her only solace was that Sara was protected and seemed happily unaware. She was also grateful that her secret safe place and sneaking out to it had gone undiscovered. It gave her something. Something to be hopeful about that was just hers. She controlled it. She owned it.

Tonight, when Sara went to turn on the light in the closet in preparation, Kathleen reminded her that he wouldn't be visiting. "He has a staff dinner tonight."

Sara turned the light back off. "Thank goodness! Can I sleep with you tonight?"

"Yes," Kathleen answered without showing her frustration, but having Sara in her bed made sneaking out more difficult.

Sara climbed into Kathleen's bed and talked until Sara fell asleep.

Kathleen carefully snuck out of the dorm and headed toward her safe space outside the school. She was getting good at removing her slippers, lacing up the skates, and walking confidently and blindly to the ice.

Kathleen was getting better every day. Staying up on the skates was no longer a problem. She could skate confidently frontwards and backward, doing twists and spins. She was now doing more difficult tricks she had practiced in the gym. If she could do them right once, her memory would allow her to do it correctly every time.

The gym mats were great for piling up and forcing her to land on them without losing her balance. She figured if she could train herself to land in the air before the blades hit the ice, she could do just about anything, let it be cartwheels, flips, and what she called 'air twists,' all were becoming old-school to her. She had become addicted to the feeling of flying.

Kathleen cut her time short this evening, unsure when the headmaster would return, so she replaced her shoes in the locker with the skates and made her way back up to the school.

She was only just getting settled in bed when she heard his footsteps. They stopped outside her room, but Kathleen closed her eyes and pretended to be asleep.

Suddenly, the headmaster flung open the door, turned on the light, and staggered in. The smell of alcohol filled the room immediately.

When he saw the two girls together in one bed, he demanded, "Dij you haf fun witout me then?" He stumbled over, picked up Sara, and threw her like a rag doll to the far wall, where she bounced off and fell to the floor lifeless.

He stepped toward her again, but Kathleen jumped onto his back, reaching around to his face, and started scratching at his eyes. "You promised you wouldn't hurt her! You promised!" The last thing she remembered was the floor—coming at her very quickly.

Caitlyn's Birth – Kathleen Is Slipping Away

Erin was awoken at 3:00 am and told to get dressed. She and Martha had prepared for this and had packed her a bag to go to Maggie's when the moment came. She could see lights on in the front room of the Kelleher's house as she ran over.

Jon had already called to wake them up and watched her make her way as he pulled the car out of the driveway. He stopped and watched until he was sure Erin was safely in their house before taking Martha to the hospital.

The following day, Maggie and Erin played close to the house, waiting for news from her father. Maggie was teaching her how to play 'hopscotch.' She had drawn out squares on the sidewalk while Erin sat quietly.

Maggie started to show and explain but realized Erin hadn't heard a word she'd said. As she turned her attention from explaining the game to watching Erin, she saw tears streaming down her cheeks. "Hey, are you alright?"

"I'm alone," Erin replied while sitting in a daze.

"Umm…I'm right here," Maggie replied.

"No," Erin said in a whisper and then let out a long sigh. "That's not what I mean." Erin just sat there in a daze thinking to herself, *Kathleen? Kathleen, where are you?*

Maggie sat down next to her. "Then what did you mean?"

"I don't feel her. I can't feel Kathleen." Erin started to shake, and the tears were flowing faster.

Maggie put her arm around Erin but wasn't sure what to say, so they sat quietly.

"Erin! Erin, your father is on the phone," Nora called from the front door.

Erin choked out an "okay." She raised and wiped her eyes and headed into the house.

Maggie had never seen such a look of defeat as she did in Erin's eyes. Even when her father's football team lost, he never looked that empty. Maggie followed her in and watched as she forced happiness to the news of her new sister, Caitlyn Molly.

It was agreed that Erin would stay the night. Martha was not due home until the next day or maybe another.

Maggie knew her mother would become concerned and start nagging Erin about her mood, wanting to fix it. Nora Kelleher couldn't stand a long face and would have exhausted herself trying to make Erin smile and even laugh.

"Let's go for a walk," Maggie proposed. Erin never responded, but Maggie took charge and guided her back outside. Once they were back out in the yard, she told Erin if she didn't want to walk, Maggie would keep playing hopscotch so Erin could relax and think. "I'll try to keep my Mom from nagging ya, but will you make me a promise, Erin?"

"What?" she replied.

"Trust me and tell me everything. You can trust me about Kathleen."

Erin stared at her momentarily before saying, "I can usually feel something from her. Anger, fear, frustration, even happiness, but nothing. I'm not feeling anything." Tears filled Erin's eyes again. "Do you think she's gone? Something happened, and she's…" She put her face in her palms, unable to say the word. She sniffled before saying, "I want to go home."

"We could tell my Mom we're just going over to get some clothes."

"No." Erin shook her head, "I want to go home. Do you think we could walk there from here?" Erin asked.

"The cliff house? It would take us all day, and Mom would kill me if she found out." Maggie said, watching Erin put her face in her palms again. She leaned down to her and whispered, "But it would be a short walk from Scottfield. If you called Renee and got us invited over, we could walk from there, easy."

They tried, but unfortunately, Maggie's mother, Nora, wouldn't allow it and said, "Your little sister is coming home. I think you should be here when she does. Your father said he may stop by tonight with pictures and would be hurt if you weren't here."

Jon did bring pictures that night and asked Erin to come home to help him prepare the house for Martha and Caitlyn's return. Maggie insisted on helping as well.

They cleaned the entire house early the next day, ran the laundry, remade the beds, cleaned the kitchen, and prepared lasagna for Martha and Caitlyn's expected arrival the following day.

They were having lunch when Jon noticed Erin and was worried. "Did I tucker you out today, love? You look tired."

"No, Da, I'm good," Erin replied quietly.

"You don't look okay. Something you want to talk about?" he pushed.

Erin took a deep breath, took another bite of her sandwich, and looked at him. "I want to go home," she said.

Jon immediately reached out with his hand to feel her forehead.

"Daaaa? What are you doing?"

"Checking for a fever. You are home, honey."

"No, I mean, I know, but I just really want to visit the old house."

"We no longer have a key…"

"I know we can't get inside, but I could look through the windows."

Jon wasn't upset; he understood because he, too, missed the old house. "What if someone else lives there?"

"Then I'll knock and ask if I could just look around or visit the beach. They may say no, but…"

"Okay. We'll go after we clean up lunch," Jon stated with a smile.

Erin took the last bite quickly and didn't have to be asked to clean up the lunchmeats and wipe down the counter where they made their sandwiches. Jon also showed a little excitement and finished quickly, throwing his paper plate away and grabbing his car keys. "Maggie, call your Mom and let her know while I start the car. Erin, lock up behind you."

Jon drove up the long driveway when they arrived and parked right in front. Erin got out of the car the second it stopped and ran to the door to knock. She then stepped to the right and took a peek in the window. "Da! It is exactly how we left it. Even the note you left on the side table is still there – the one asking the new tenants to contact us if they find Mom's photo album."

"And look at the dust," Maggie noted while standing next to Erin and looking in.

Jon said nothing while he made his way up and also looked in the windows. They stared inside each window, working their way down slowly to see inside the kitchen and even the empty storage area. *I wish I had made a copy of my key instead of handing them all in. I could have done one more search. Isabelle hasn't even rented it out again.*

After taking in all she could looking in the windows, Erin left the porch and walked along the top of the cliff that overlooked the beach. When she finally reached the hill at the far end, she slowly started to make her way down. Maggie, of course, followed.

"This is the coolest backyard ever. Did you ever own a boat to go out on the water?" Maggie asked.

"Hahaha, no, we never did," Erin replied. "Da did show us how to fish from the beach, though."

They both walked to the water's edge, kicked off their shoes, and got their feet wet.

Jon finally made his way down but headed straight to the glass door to the house. He could see how corroded they had become and took a chance at pulling to the right to see if it would open. It didn't budge.

"My Dad put a stick in our sliding glass door because he found that if you lift the handle while sliding it, you could jump the lock," Maggie said as she approached.

Jon knew he wasn't showing a good example even trying, but it didn't stop him. He grabbed the handle and lifted it while pulling, and 'click,' he jumped the lock. The door was still difficult to slide, but he managed it.

Erin didn't wait. As soon as it was opened enough for her to fit through, she was in and running up the stairs. By the time Maggie and Jon caught up, Erin was gone.

"Erin? Erin, where are you?" Maggie called.

"Upstairs!" she called back from Kathleen's room. Erin realized they had touched nothing in her room when they left. Even the pictures of Mum, Da, Kathleen, and herself on her dresser were still there. The room was dusty, but the bed was neatly made, and everything was in its place as Kathleen liked. She opened the closet and found a bookbag Kathleen would use to carry her notebooks, pencils, and library books to the beach. She grabbed it.

Erin could hear Maggie pulling a few notebooks off the shelves, "Can I take a few more of these to read?" Maggie asked.

"Yes, I want to grab as many of the later ones as we can carry," Erin replied as she also took the pictures from her dresser and put them in the bag. As she went through Kathleen's desk drawers, she also found sketchbooks. As she leafed through the pages, she found her sister's artistry impressive. None of the pictures of her Mum, Da, or herself were staged. She discovered that her sister had drawn a detailed picture of Erin playing with her dolls that she had never been aware of. One of her Mum cooking, and another of her Mum and

Da dancing on Christmas morning. And, of course, numerous pictures of her beloved Batman.

Erin filled the bookbag to the point she couldn't zip it closed, so she carried it by wrapping her arms around it like a hug. Maggie also carried a pile of notebooks. They were leaving her room when they heard noises from her parent's old room.

Jon was lifting the mattress and then the box spring, rechecking every drawer before pulling the dresser out to look behind it.

"What are you looking for, Da?" Erin asked.

"Your Mum's photo album. It has to be here…somewhere."

"Kathleen has it," Erin stated very matter-of-factly.

Jon stopped frantically looking and sat down on the dusty bed. "You think so?"

"Kathleen always insisted Mum let her put the new pictures in. She considered it as much hers as Mum's."

Jon closed his eyes and shook his head slowly, "Of course."

"Mum used to have a lot of pretty jewelry she would allow me to play dress-up with. Did you…"

"Yes. I have it safely put away for when you get older." Jon stood back up and was ready to leave the room. "I'm surprised she let you play with it. Your Mum's family was very well-to-do, so that wasn't costume jewelry; it was real. I suspect a few pieces were family heirlooms."

"Snotty grandmother…" Erin began.

"Oh no, not from your grandmother Isabelle's side of the family. She grew up very poor. They would have come from your grandfather's side. His family has a long history of wealth."

The three of them carried their treasures back out to the beach. Jon slid the door closed as best he could before he took the pile of books from Maggie to carry up. Maggie took the overflow from Erin's bookbag so they could zip it up. Erin then followed Maggie to help push her when she could have used her now-filled arm trying to climb back up.

"Why didn't we put all this on the front porch, lock it back up, and then climb this hill?" Erin pondered aloud. They didn't answer her other than private eye-rolls at realizing her brilliance that was too late to consider.

Jon drove back home and got cleaned up to visit Martha at the hospital. Erin kept the bookbag when she and Maggie returned to the Kelleher's.

For the first time, Erin was content to finally read Kathleen's stories. It helped to distract her for the next few weeks of summer.

Kathleen Awakes

Kathleen's next memory was a very white room with bells and whistles ringing in her ears. "Where am I?" she choked out in a froggy voice.

Sara screamed, "You're awake!"

"Where are we?" Kathleen asked again, clearing her throat.

"You almost bled to death. We weren't sure if you were going to make it, and they kept wanting to take me back without you. But I didn't let them! I've been fighting them for almost two weeks."

"I've been in here for two weeks?"

"Yeah, they were keeping you in a coma until you were healed enough to wake up." Sara smiled, "I knew you were going to wake up today. You were talking to Erin again in your sleep. You kept saying, "I'm okay, Erin, stop worrying.""

"To Erin?" Kathleen asked in confusion.

"You talk to her a lot while napping during the day. Oh, that reminds me, who is Caitlyn?"

"Not sure, why?" Kathleen spoke as she observed the room she was in.

"Just a name you mentioned while sleep-talking," Sara replied.

Kathleen had no recollection of her dream or the attack. She learned from the doctors that after hurting Sara, she became the focus of all his rage until he passed out next to her. Her face was swollen a bit, but her arms, stomach, and legs were horribly bruised. She also had two stitches that closed up just inside her left thigh.

Kathleen scooted over and invited Sara to lie with her. Moving was painful, like her insides had bruises too. The doctors protested and would insist she get out, but once they'd leave, she would climb back in with the blessing of the nurses.

"How do you feel today?" Sara propped herself up on her elbow next to Kathleen.

"Angry. I want to break every bone in his body and watch him bleed." Kathleen's voice was animated, and her hands were tightly clenched into fists.

"He's in jail now. Ms. Penney came to visit and told me he's in jail," Sara said. "She was the teacher Rachel went and alerted after finding us."

Before leaving the hospital days later—together—a nurse asked to talk to Kathleen privately. "Sweetheart, I'm afraid I have some tough news for you. The beating you took caused some internal bleeding that had to be stopped. Has the doctor explained what that means?"

Kathleen could see the seriousness in her eyes. "No, what does that mean?"

"Well, some of the damage affected your uterus."

Kathleen just stared at her with a crooked brow.

The nurse tried to be gentle, saying it in almost a whisper. "You will never be able to carry a baby."

Kathleen thought for a moment before answering with a question, "So, I should never marry?"

Now, the nurse looked back at her with a crooked brow. "You can marry; you just can't have your children. You would have to adopt or something."

"Thank you for telling me." Kathleen put out a hand to shake hers before walking back to Sara.

Kathleen and Sara climbed out of the car, now parked at the front steps of Willington. Ron Harkins, who was sitting out front, jumped up to greet them. He was the boy who once tormented Sara in the halls but had befriended them after the headmaster's tirade.

Ron stood up as they started to ascend the steps. "Hey! You're back. How was your holiday?"

The girls looked at each other with crinkled brows before Kathleen decided to go with it. "It was fine. So, did we miss anything?"

Sara just looked at Ron expectantly, following Kathleen's cue.

"Didn't you hear? We have a new headmistress, Ms. Brookes. Oh, and two of your friends went home."

"Who?" they asked in unison.

"Um, Sienna Brennan and Julie Carmichael. It was weird, but both of their families came about the same time and insisted on taking them home for good."

"Thanks, Ron." Kathleen pushed Sara's back to nudge her to walk.

That leaves only the four of us, Kathleen thought. *I hope Rachel and Dannie have been okay.*

Sara took a few steps when she saw the funny-looking magazine Ron was holding. It had a very artsy cover. "What are you reading?"

"It's an American comic book. *The Adventures of Batman and Robin.* They save Gotham from the evil Joker in this one." Ron said as if the two girls already knew the characters.

Kathleen couldn't believe her ears. "May I see it?" *Batman, Gotham City, he was playing a character. Oh my, he was pretending to be a character, a superhero, and I never asked his real name.*

After convincing him to loan it to her when he was done reading it, Kathleen and Sara headed inside. As they entered the doors of Willington, they turned toward their old dorm when a short, plump woman stepped in their way. "Hello. Allow me to introduce myself. I'm the new headmistress, Ms. Brookes."

Sara replied first. "I'm Sara -- nice to meet you." When Kathleen said nothing, Sara spoke for her as well. "And this is Kathleen."

Ms. Brookes smiled, "Where are you going?"

Finally, Kathleen spoke up, "Back to our dorm. We've been away for a bit and…"

Ms. Brookes cut her off, cheerfully saying, "I have reintroduced all the girls into the regular dorms. I have a new room for both of you as well."

Kathleen became instantly enraged. "Absolutely not! The throwaways are my family, and I want them returned immediately." Before the headmistress could argue, Kathleen held up her hand and announced, "This is not up for negotiation," and she marched off to her dorm.

Sara wasn't sure what to do, looking between Kathleen walking off and the new Headmistress with pleading eyes.

Ms. Crow, Ms. Brookes' assistant, was appalled. "Young lady, get back here!" She then looked at Ms. Brookes and said, "How dare she speak to you like that!"

Ms. Brookes caught Ms. Crow's arm and stopped her from going after Kathleen. She waved her other hand a bit at Sara and, with an approving nod, said, "It's all right."

Sara smiled with relief and ran to catch up with Kathleen.

Ms. Brookes turned her attention back to Ms. Crow, "Don't be bothered by it; I'll take care of it. What can you tell me about them?"

The headmistress watched the two girls enter their dorm. She had been unable to get much detail from the other girls but knew from the damage done to Kathleen the hell they must have had to endure. Only Ms. Brookes was privy to the doctor's reports. *It would be best to obey her wish rather than aggravate the situation,* she thought.

"Well, the blonde girl, Kathleen, doesn't attend school here," Ms. Crow started. "She was immediately graduated from the twelfth grade when she arrived, and…"

Intrigued, Ms. Brookes cut her off, "How old was she when she arrived?"

"She was eight – home-schooled by her late mother, as I understand it. She attends the University but lives here otherwise." Then, in a gossipier tone, she said, "She seemed to be his favorite pet. He followed her everywhere and even drove her to and from the university every day," Ms. Crow finished.

"And the other? Sara?" Ms. Brookes asked.

"Her roommate. Sara struggled in school before Kathleen arrived, but now she's at the top of her class."

The Board of Directors had only given her vague responses when asked where the last headmaster had gone, but she knew one teacher was there when the ambulance arrived.

"Ms. Crow, where could I find Ms. Penney?"

"She teaches in room 306 and oversees dorm 300A."

"Thank you, Ms. Crow. Please find and escort the other two girls, Daniel and Rachel, back to their old dorm to greet Kathleen and Sara. I'm sure they'll be pleased to find them well." Ms. Brookes headed off before hearing Ms. Crow's answer.

Return To The Dorm

Kathleen entered the dorm and planned to put her night bag in her room when she saw the blood-stained, wooded floor. She dropped her bag and charged to the open doorway of the headmaster's room before making an abrupt stop. Nothing had been touched or removed yet.

Sara had followed and stood beside her when Kathleen asked, "Are you sure he's gone?"

"Yes. I told you he's in jail," Sara answered.

Kathleen entered the room and immediately found one of his jackets, a shirt, and pants that she proceeded to stuff full of every other piece of clothing she could find.

"What are you doing?" Sara whispered so as not to wake the dead while she stood frozen in the doorway. There seemed to be an imaginary barrier stopping her from proceeding through.

"I'm creating a dummy. Help me find things to stuff into it." Kathleen opened the top drawer of his dresser, and she found three letters while pulling out all his socks to use for stuffing. All three were unopened, and she recognized the writing immediately. She pulled them out of the drawer and read the address on the front a few times to herself.

Sara stared at Kathleen. "Are they what I think they are?"

Kathleen folded them up and put them in her back pocket. "Yes, he must have known I was telling the truth, and my father would have come for me."

"Are you going to send them now?"

"No. Maybe someday, but not now. Da wouldn't understand." Then Kathleen stopped for a moment and looked at Sara. "Besides, I couldn't bear to leave my sisters here now. I need you."

That seemed to open the imaginary door, and Sara started to help her stuff the dummy. When it was done, they dragged their creation to the common area and put a hat on him.

Dannie and Rachel returned, rather shocked at the sight. Kathleen greeted them, saying, "Go to your rooms and choose your weapon of choice."

Daniel returned with a hanger, but she was still hesitant to go near the stuffed dummy.

"Hit him." Kathleen prodded.

Dannie just stood still and stared at it. Rachel also had a hanger and stood still looking at the dummy.

Kathleen slipped off her shoe, got on her knees, and hit it. "You bloody bastard!" She slammed it a few more times before standing back up. She then kicked it a few times, separating the stuffed pants from the upper half.

That was all Dannie and Rachel needed to see. The two started beating the dummy, screaming until stuffing littered the room. All three of them exhausted themselves, kicking and stomping on every last piece of the dummy until they collapsed on the floor surrounded by it all.

Kathleen finally blurted out. "I hated most having to touch him. He was so gross!" Her eyes filled with tears, and she became choked up. Kathleen, Dannie, and Rachel spent the rest of the day crying out the pain he had caused.

Sara just cried, listening, realizing what she'd been spared. *She saved me. Kathleen saved me.* It was like a broken record in her head as she heard of the horrific things he did and made them do. *He's been torturing them, and I never knew it. She saved me. She saved me.*

Sitting with her knees tucked close to her chest, Sara shook and cried quietly until Kathleen noticed her. They stared into each other's eyes, and without a word, Kathleen raised her arm, and Sara crawled over until it fell around her shoulders.

Ms. Brookes had stood outside the door, listening from the start. When her assistant tried to approach, she stepped away from the door and asked quietly that Dannie and Rachel's things be repacked and brought down immediately. She also wanted her to ask the maintenance man for boxes to pack up the old headmaster's room.

When they returned with the girl's belongings and the boxes, they left them outside the door per Ms. Brooke's request. Only after the room had quieted down, hours later, did she finally knock lightly. After a minute, Sara opened it slowly.

Ms. Brookes looked down at her and said, "I have the girl's things out here; should I bring them in?"

The door suddenly swung open out of Sara's control, revealing Kathleen. "We'll get them, thank you." Her face was swollen from crying.

"I also brought some boxes to start packing up the…the um…" Ms. Brookes stuttered.

"I'll pack his things and leave the boxes in the hall when I'm done. I think you should plan a bonfire." Kathleen said. "I have plans for the room, so I hope you have no intention of moving anyone else in here."

Ms. Brookes took a deep breath, "I hadn't planned for any of you to be in here, so I had not planned for a new supervisor, however–"

"We won't require a new supervisor, thank you." Kathleen started to close the door, but Ms. Brookes raised her hand and stopped it.

"Kathleen, I'm doing my best to work with you, but you must do the same. My job requires that I know you are safe at all times."

"We'll be safer now than ever," Kathleen shot back.

Ms. Brookes tried again, "Kathleen, I'm responsible…"

Kathleen cut her off, "Spare me the blustering about how we'll be safer with an adult. We've been on our own for most of the past two years, and we can get through the next eight the same way."

"You will have to negotiate on this with me, Kathleen." Ms. Brookes replied with a higher voice. She could feel the frustration building and took a deep breath before starting again. "I can't be locked out. I must be afforded the ability to check in with you on occasion."

Kathleen looked about to respond when Ms. Brookes continued quickly and louder, "If not, I will lose my job, and you will be forced out of this dorm and worse." She knew now she had Kathleen's attention and lowered her voice again. "Again, I'm here to work WITH you, but this only works if you're willing."

Kathleen finally agreed to allow the new young headmistress to stop in and check on them regularly. Kathleen also asked if the school had funds for paint. She wanted to paint the rooms and insisted they would do it themselves. Ms. Brookes agreed she could provide the paint, drop cloths, rollers, and brushes.

"Are you sure you don't want any help? How will you get the ceiling done?"

"A ladder," Kathleen responded bluntly.

After that day, Ms. Brookes often sat quietly in the common area to listen to them talk. She quickly learned that just before bed was the best time. Kathleen had started a tradition where they would all sit on one bed and discuss their day and anything else before turning in for the night.

Ms. Brookes gained credibility with them by turning some of their thoughts into reality before they even made a formal request. For example, one spoke of wanting to learn how to fight so no one could hurt her again. Ms. Brookes immediately hired a trainer and held open classes for students interested in martial arts. Kathleen, Rachel, and Dannie flourished. Kathleen kept earning belts faster than all of them. Sara seemed to have the least momentum but still did well.

One evening, while Ms. Brookes sat in the common area, she overheard the girls talking about God. Sara was sarcastic when she said, "A God? I think not. If there were a God, he would never have allowed the headmaster to hurt you."

The room fell silent momentarily, but then Ms. Brookes could hear Kathleen slowly respond. "God gave us free will. We can't have that and then hold him responsible for how we choose to use it. No, what happened to us isn't his fault."

Sara, who had no religious background, asked, "Then what good is he? Is he just a gatekeeper for when we die?"

Kathleen's voice was very soft, "No, love. He's the one who listens to you even when you aren't speaking aloud. He's the one who is always rooting for your success when others are not. He's the one hoping you'll make the right choices in life. But more importantly, he's the one who stands by you even when you fail and is always willing to help carry the burden. I've prayed that he helps carry the pain so the weight doesn't break me. And yes, he's also the one who cradles your soul in his arms like a newborn and takes you to heaven to live with him when your body dies."

"How do you know he does all that if you can't see or hear him?" Sara asked, now curious about God's existence.

"You could hear him if you chose to listen," Kathleen answered.

That weekend, Ms. Brookes invited them to the local Catholic Church. She had not gone in years but soon found herself committed to singing with the girls in the choir every Sunday.

Despite everything Ms. Brookes did, Kathleen was very untrusting of adults, and the new headmistress was no different. *They should have stopped him. They knew and did nothing,* she often thought to herself. Kathleen did her best to be respectful but never let down her guard.

Kathleen behaved like a mother to the girls. She liked feeling she had a purpose. She pushed them to finish their homework every night and go to bed on time. She would wake them in the morning and help them make their beds or do it for them when they overslept.

The girls' grades and attitudes improved, and Rachel got fewer detentions for acting out. She was currently on a three-month streak of not getting even one reprimand.

America: Self-Empowerment

"So, you feel her again?" Maggie asked.

"YES! She's alive," Erin replied as they walked into school.

"But what happened? You hadn't felt her for weeks."

Erin smiled ear to ear. "I have no idea, but I can feel a renewed energy in her." She whispered the rest as they made their way to homeroom. "She's still suffering something. It's hard to explain…"

"She's still suffering?" Maggie asked with a crooked brow.

"How can I explain this," Erin thought aloud. "Okay, imagine a home. The basement is dark with cobwebs and scary shadows, right?"

Maggie nodded in agreement as she hated the basement in her own home.

"Now imagine two kinds of homes above that dark basement. The first house was horrible with broken windows, a leaky roof, and, um, rats running around."

"Ewwww." Maggie physically cringed.

"That describes what I felt for her until I lost her weeks ago. But now, the house above that basement has gotten new windows, the rats have been run out, and she's, well, fixing the place up. She's finding power in the cleaning and decorating. Oh my God, does that make any sense at all?" Erin asked as she struggled with words to explain her feelings.

"I think so. Something bad happened, but it's in the basement. And she's building something better on top of it," Maggie replied, "You are so good at visuals."

"It's how my mother taught us. She was very good at visualizing something that made whatever the lesson was make sense. My sister was just as good at it when my Mum got sick, and she took over my lessons." Erin's eyes looked dazed in memory when she continued, "It's nice to know I picked up something from both of them."

Samantha and Molly then approached Erin to say hi and ask about her summer. Erin immediately noticed how uncomfortable Maggie became.

"You two remember Maggie, right?" Erin asked.

They both shifted slightly to stop blocking Maggie from the conversation when Samantha said, "Yeah." With a little giggle in her voice, she continued, "We remember Mag-pie."

"My best friend," Erin stated matter-of-factly. "And the reason I had such a fantastic summer. She even made church more fun, insisting I join the choir."

Molly smiled at Maggie and Erin both, but Samantha gave a weird smirk.

Erin continued, "It's never a dull moment with Mags. So, how were your summers?"

Maggie smiled back at Molly but then moved away to find her seat and secure another for Erin to be beside her.

Samantha then lowered her voice, "But Maggie is weird."

With a giggle, Erin smiled and said, "I know. I guess that's why she doesn't bore me like so many others do," Erin winked back at Molly before going over to the seat Maggie had secured for her.

Most of the boys learned just as quickly not to give Maggie a hard time if they wanted to win Erin's favor – and most did. Samantha was the only hold-out until her birthday party in October. Erin decided that since Maggie wasn't invited, they would have an early Halloween party for the class on the same date.

Although a few girls did go to Samantha's party early, none agreed to spend the night so they could attend the Halloween party after dark. Even the boys were invited to the haunted house, so the entire class, minus Samantha, planned to go.

About two hours before their party began, Erin made a call. "Hello, this is Erin. May I please speak to Samantha?" Whoever answered put her on hold until she heard the receiver pick up again.

"Hello," Samantha said.

"You're coming tonight, aren't you? I was too busy setting up the haunted house, but we planned something special for you." Samantha didn't answer other than with a sigh. Erin continued, "It's a haunted birthday house. It has lots of scary things in it, but I'll need to show you what ropes to pull to scare everyone."

"A haunted birthday house?" Samantha asked.

"Yeah! We did up the entire basement. Maggie and I used your birthday as the theme. You'll greet everyone standing high on a table, but it'll look like you were hung. My Da built it, so it's totally safe, I swear. We'll attach fishing line to your wrists so when you move, you'll make things pop out."

"What do I wear?" Samantha asked with a bit of excitement in her voice.

"Maggie and I went to the Goodwill and found clothing we could rip up, and my Step-Mum took me to get a lot of makeup stuff. Can you get here soon so we can make you look scary in time? We only have a few hours before…"

"MOM?! Can you get me to Erin's Halloween party right away? They need to get me into costume."

Erin could hear Samantha's mother agree, so she said, "Okay, we'll see you soon!"

"Okay, bye," Samantha replied before hanging up.

Martha listened and gave Erin a curious look.

"I know what you're thinking, Martha." She looked to ensure Maggie wasn't nearby and whispered, "Samantha didn't invite Maggie to her birthday, and I wasn't going without her. She is all about being the center of attention, so Maggie thought this would win her over."

"Very clever of you two," Martha said.

Erin and Maggie set up tables with cups and a punch bowl in the garage. They hung ghosts, bats, and black streamers too. They thought a dirty, ugly garage was the perfect place to begin before sending them to the haunted basement. Martha had bought some snacks and made others that looked or felt gross. She had peeled grapes to feel like eyeballs.

Their fathers had done all the work setting up the haunted house, but it was their mothers who dressed up and scared the kids. Even old Mrs. Nantais from next door dressed up to help.

When Samantha arrived, she allowed Maggie to do her scary makeup and dress her in a white dress with fake blood dripping down it. When she was ready, Jon showed her how to put her hands in the loops of fishing line and her head through a rope that she had to be careful not to pull too hard on. It was only attached high up with a very thin fishing line that would break easily but was hidden from view.

"Oh my God, you really look like you've been hung," Erin said with wide eyes and excitement. "You are going to scare them to death."

Samantha smiled and laughed as Martha took pictures.

"Maggie, you should add some blood to look like the rope is cutting her neck," Erin said.

Maggie grabbed the fake blood goop they had made and climbed up on the table next to Samantha. As she started to apply it, Martha snapped a few more pictures, making sure to get Maggie and Samantha laughing together.

Erin and Maggie's idea had worked even better than they had planned. After everyone had gone through the haunted house, they kept asking Samantha, "Who did your makeup?"

Maggie and Erin both took a little joy in hearing everyone praise Maggie's work with each inquiry. Molly got first in line, asking Maggie to make her look scary, too, but others followed.

Martha also helped solidify it when she took her pictures to the one-hour developer and the copier place on Sunday afternoon. She made a collage that would fit on one sheet of photo paper. She copied enough of them for the girls to hand out in school on Monday. Martha showcased the one of Samantha and Maggie laughing together in the middle of all the snapshots she used.

Britain: A New Me

It had been almost a year, and Sara, Dannie, and Rachel had turned 11. Kathleen tried to make their birthdays special. They would treat the birthday girl like a queen for a day. They couldn't afford gifts, but sometimes they would make them. When she could find good material in the lost and found, Sara could sew clever items like purses or belts.

Today was Kathleen's birthday.

"Key!" Dannie yelled.

Kathleen turned around, giving Sara, Dannie, and Rachel a strange look. "What key?"

"You're Key." Sara pointed at Kathleen and said, "You're Key!"

Still confused, Kathleen asked, "Why do you want my key? Did you lose yours again?"

At that, all three girls started giggling. "No, silly, you ARE Key. We've decided your new nickname is *Key*."

"A nickname?" Kathleen still looked at them with crooked brows.

Sara stepped closer. "Yes, if you had to speak your initials—K. E. Y…"

"Yes, I'm well aware my initials spell key." Kathleen smiled and rolled her eyes while Rachel stepped up to chime in.

"We think it's appropriate since you have been the 'key' to our survival."

"And to keeping our sanity," Dannie added.

"You are always telling us we can start fresh, that learning from today's experiences can make for a better tomorrow. So, we're giving your fresh start a new name for your birthday."

"I love it. A new name to reflect the newest me is a great gift. Thank you," Key said as she hugged them all.

The new name felt powerful somehow. She could now file all the bad memories under the old name and all the new memories they were making under her new self, Key.

Key was determined not to answer to Kathleen anymore. She would ignore those who chose not to recognize the new her.

"What were you doing before we interrupted? Oh… that folder. What are you always writing in that folder?" Dannie looked over the top of it, then at Key.

As Dannie called it, the folder was a leather-bound binder that allowed Key to add pages as necessary. Her mother had given it to her when she turned six.

Once a story was complete, she would remove the pages, tie a string through the holes, and add it to a shelf in the bedroom. She now had more of her own stories than books.

"Just stories. They fill my head, and it helps to put them on paper so I can… well… stop obsessing over them."

Dannie understood, or so her facial expression led Key to believe. "What are those envelopes?"

"Old letters I wrote."

"To Sienna and Julie?" Dannie asked.

"No, Dannie, I'm still waiting on Ms. Brookes to give me their home addresses," Key replied.

"Well, let's go to the ice rink. You don't skate with us anymore," Dannie complained.

"Okay, let's go," Key said, laughing and joking as the girls walked to the rink.

Later that evening, while the girls sat on Rachel's bed for their 'good night' talk, there was a light knock on her door.

Sara answered it and found Ms. Brookes' face flushed and her hands shaky.

"I have some devastating news, girls."

"What is it?" Sara asked immediately.

"I contacted both Julie and Sienna's families…" her voice trailed off.

"Won't they allow me to write to them?" Key asked. "I just want to keep in contact–"

"I'm sorry, but they are no longer there." Ms. Brookes started again.

"Oh my God, did they throw them away to a different school?" Racheal barked.

"We'll call every school and find them–" Key began.

Ms. Brookes took a deep breath, finally exhaling, "No, they are angels with God."

"Angels? They both happened to die? Bullshit!" Rachel screamed.

"Rachel, watch your mouth!" Key barked. She always had to correct Rachael's language and was determined, even tonight, to do so. After Rachel gave her an acknowledging look, Key continued, "I don't believe they died mysteriously. I think they did what we've all considered doing but have fought against."

The room fell silent.

Dannie finally asked quietly, "They…they did it themselves?"

All the girls watched and followed Key's eyes, staring directly at Ms. Brookes. "I'm correct, aren't I?"

She didn't need to answer; her tears spoke for her, but she still gave a slight nod in the affirmative.

While tears took over every eye, Key continued, "I want to know where they are buried."

Again, Ms. Brookes could only nod before choking out, "I'm so sorry. They might have survived, if—"

"If what?" Rachel asked angrily.

Ms. Brookes swallowed hard and took a few deep breaths to get her voice back, "If I hadn't contacted their families when I arrived. The board of trustees thought it would be best, but if I hadn't contacted them—"

"I don't understand why the board thought contacting their families, that threw them away in the first place, would be a good idea," Key said with disgust for the board in her voice.

"Ms. Brookes, did you know what had happened here? Did the board know when—" Sara started.

"I did not know, but I think the board did. I had been given very little information when I arrived but knew something devastating had caused the injuries the hospital reports described." Ms. Brookes wiped her eyes. "It wasn't until I searched out Ms. Penney, who had found you, that I learned enough to deduce what must have been going on," Ms. Brookes replied.

They all stayed silent, but Key reached out for Sara and Dannie's hands, and they reached out for Rachel's. The visual only made Ms. Brookes break down into harder sobs.

Sara pulled away, slid off the bed, and hugged Ms. Brookes. Dannie and Rachel followed suit, but not Key.

Ms. Brookes looked at Key and choked out, "I'm so sorry, I know it's my fault—"

"That's not true. I didn't know what was happening, and I shared a room with Key," Sara said, pulling away to look Ms. Brookes in the eyes. She then looked back at Key.

Key looked at the girls but couldn't follow them into hugging Ms. Brookes and even she wasn't sure why. She decided to do the next best thing. She slid further on the bed, up against the wall, and patted her hand on the empty space. "Come on, there's enough room for a fifth tonight."

Revenge Of A Throwaway

The girls were a few months shy of turning 12 years old, and the media continued to scratch at the walls of the school in hopes of getting the inside scoop on why the old headmaster had been arrested. The trial that followed was kept confidential to "protect the children."

Key did not feel protected, though. The lawyer wanted the girls to testify, but Dannie and Rachel refused. Making sure he was put away fell on her shoulders alone.

Seeing him again and feeling the humiliation of having to describe those two years changed her. Key was well past denial and had moved past depression straight to anger that overwhelmed her. A rage she knew she needed to find a release for.

"You know what, Sara?"

"What, love?"

"I was thrown away to this school because my grandmother thought of me as her family's dirty little secret. And now we're being sheltered here as the school's dirty little secret."

Sara stopped fiddling with the hand-me-down camera Ms. Brookes gave her, sat back, and watched Key. "And your point is?"

"So, I intend to stop being a secret. I've written my life story, and I'm going to submit it to some publishing companies."

"Wow, are you sure you want to do that?"

"Absolutely. Do you want me to use a different name for you in it?

"Are you using your own Key?"

"Yes. My real name will be on the cover."

"Then, no, don't change mine either. Heck, I'm not even sure it's my real name anyway! What have Rachel and Dannie said?"

"They agreed, although they didn't want their real names used," Key replied.

Key sat quietly in her room, reading over her draft. *I'll title it the Forgotten, no the…Unloved.* And then it dawned on her: *The Throwaways.* The title stirred something inside her. *This is stupid. Who would want to read about my life? The scribblings of a forgotten child.* She opened her bottom dresser drawer and pulled out her old folder. Inside the front cover pocket were the three letters, still unopened. She ran her thumb across the letters written by her naïve, eight-year-old self. Her finger slid into the corner of the envelope, and the dried glue lost hold with a quick slide across. Although she remembered every word she had written to him, rereading the words bit at her memory, and the hope they represented stung her heart.

My book wouldn't need to be so depressing, so 'woe is me.' I could make it about hope, like the hope my real father, Erin, had when he joined the armed forces so he could marry Mum. Like the hope my mother had when she agreed to marry a man she hardly knew. And the hope my Da had when he asked her to marry him, willing to take on a family that wasn't his and leaving all he knew to make a fresh start in a strange country.

Key held herself and got to work, pulling out her mother's diaries, which she had stolen the day she left America. She decided her story would begin with the reckless, yet pure, young love of two teenagers.

Although she once blamed her Da for letting her go and not coming to find her, no matter how angry she was, she couldn't hate him. She chose to believe better of him. *Father is probably working hard back in America, believing I'm being raised and spoiled rotten by my wealthy grandmother. He never would have guessed her level of hatred and evil and would no doubt have sold his soul to get here if he knew where I was…and what she'd done.*

When she completed her rewrite, she composed a letter. She mailed out nine copies to the various publishing companies with a short introduction to the book. Unfortunately, after she received nine replies, Ms. Brookes had to be made aware. All nine letters insisted that Key be 18 years old or have the approval of an adult guardian.

Ms. Brookes and Key had a long discussion about the idea of the book.

"Key, please understand. It would put my livelihood at risk. My job is to protect the school and its children."

Key nodded and looked down for a moment, leaving Ms. Brookes to believe she'd won. *She should have known better…*

After gathering her thoughts, Key looked up at her again. "If you do not allow me to publish it now, then you should warn those you answer to that I will publish it the day I turn 18. And I assure you, they will dislike that version even more."

"Key, please." Ms. Brookes pleaded.

Key sat back, confident. "You could choose to see this as an opportunity, you know. This is the only chance the school will have to negotiate with me on what is said. I can either describe them as supportive and understanding or later describe them as harsh and uncaring."

It only took two days for Ms. Brookes to return with a "yes." However, Key had to agree not to use any of the other girls' real names. They were minors, and the school would not permit her to do so. Therefore, in the book, Sara became Susan, Dannie became Donna, Rachel became Rebecca, and Siena and Julie's names didn't change, but she promised never to include their last names. She decided she would do the same for herself in a sense. She chose to use her mother's maiden name, Harrington, rather than Yule.

Key sent out a letter from the school with permission. They were all surprised that the publishing companies were tripping over themselves to get the rights to the story. They were hoping for the inside scoop on the scandal but got much more than they had bargained for.

Before she chose the publisher who would receive the honor, she replied to them with yet another letter. This time, she said that the publisher she chose would also have to agree to publish two more books that she had written – a drama and a mystery – both fictional novels.

That letter only received one return, but it came in the form of a personal carrier who waited not only for her decision but also for their signatures on the attached contract. It was a small, family-owned publishing company.

The terms she proposed mattered more to Key than the size of the publishing company. She didn't care how small it was; she insisted Ms. Brookes sign.

The Show

Key's stories were fun, and the girls loved reading them but felt they were going to waste.

"These would be great plays for the drama department," Dannie had once suggested during their Good Night talks.

Key accepted the challenge and took one of her favorites to dissect it into scenes for a play.

Figuring out how the show would work was a fun summer project for them. Sara and Key did most of the songwriting, while Dannie and Rachel worked on set designs. Musicals were their favorite.

"Now that the other students are returning from holiday, I think we need to start having auditions so we can start fleshing out these scenes," Key said.

"When are we planning to put on the show?" Sara asked.

"Soon, I hope. I'm excited." Rachel replied quickly.

"No, not until the end of the school year." Said Key.

"Next June?" Dannie said at a higher pitch.

"Yes. You know me, I want it to look professional, not amateur."

"Seriously, Key? But we are amateurs." Dannie replied with pouty lips.

Key just looked at her for a bit. "If you want to do this half-ass, I'm out. We haven't even finished all the music."

"Oh, relax, all of you. We'll plan to put it on when we ALL think it's ready to be put on. Fair?" Sara looked each of them in the eye until each nodded in agreement. Then she thought to herself, *which means whenever Key says it is.*

They did as Key had asked and started auditioning the interested students. If they weren't comfortable singing, the girls began working with them. They created a Vocal Club after school, and even the students not selected for the main parts were invited to attend the club if they wanted to be background singers and extras on stage. Key insisted anyone interested in being a part of the show could and she would ensure it.

Dannie and Rachel found their expertise was stage direction. They were brilliant in using all of it strategically.

The year was eventful, primarily because of the release of Key's book. Although their fellow students struggled with what they had learned, working on the show with the Throwaways seemed to have a calming effect. It allowed the students to accept the Throwaways, and soon, the school's rhythm slowly returned to normal.

The following May, they were ready. Parents and teachers got involved in making costumes, although they were not allowed to watch rehearsals. None of the kids were allowed to tell the story to anyone before show night, which came quicker than even Dannie realized.

"Why are you wearing a wig for this, Key?" Dannie asked.

"I don't want any chance of my face showing up on someone's social media," Key replied.

"The stage makeup should remedy that, but yeah, I get it."

Senior graduation was only a few weeks away, but the students were a buzz about the show.

The first night, the crowd was familiar and expected—mostly teachers and parents. However, one of those mothers worked for the newspaper and was so impressed that she took pictures and wrote an article that came out the next morning. She added to the end of her article that she would be attending it again on Saturday night because she enjoyed it so much. She also hoped the school would sell recordings of the songs.

Ms. Brookes acted quickly and got a video company to record the next night's performance so they could sell them. She also spoke to the music teacher about getting the songs recorded.

The next day, the theater was sold out by showtime. Because of so many calls for tickets, they added another matinee for Sunday and then one more that night.

The story Key wrote had everything in it. The audience laughed most of the time, but they got angry and booed at some characters until they found their eyes leaking with sympathetic tears. It had a 'happily ever after' ending, though. Fortunately, the kids who got the boos were older kids, so they took it well. Key thought she would have to keep that in mind if they ever did another.

The Monday after their last show, Dannie waved a paper in the air as she and Sara ran into Key's dorm room. "Momma-Key! Key! Have you seen the newspapers? "

"More about the play?" Key asked.

"No, there's a write-up about your book!"

"Seriously? Let me see." Key grabbed the paper from Dannie while Sara crunched up beside her on the bed. "Ouch." Key's expression became strained as she readjusted.

"What's wrong?" Sara asked.

"I have a bruise on my hip, and you plunged yourself right into it."

"How did you get another bruise?"

"Oh, I'm such a klutz, I fell, no big deal," Key replied quickly before turning her attention back to the paper.

The local newspaper made it front-page news. The headline read, "Revenge of a Throwaway." It described how the book "outed" her grandmother, a very prominent figure in society at the time. Her grandmother wasn't alone, though, as the entire upper crust of English society was outed for their process of throwing away their children. And, finally, the headmaster for the crimes he committed.

Key read aloud, "Although he spent the last six years comfortably in prison without anyone knowing what he'd done, he was later found dead in his cell after the publication of Ms. Harrington's book, which was made available in the prison library. Evidently, mass murderers and the like have a strong distaste for child molesters."

"He's dead!" Dannie cheered.

Key couldn't stop or hide the smile that came over her.

"Oh my God, I have to go tell Rachel." Dannie jumped off the bed and ran out.

The book shocked the other students when they learned the truth. Many became more awkward around them – at least at first.

Many of the students gathered in Cynthia Cromwell's room one night. She was a junior, about to be a senior, and one of the most popular students. Everyone was abuzz about the article, but they stopped to listen when Cynthia spoke up. "I know all the names in the book were changed, but I think we all know who they are."

All the kids nodded in agreement.

Cynthia continued, "Can you imagine while being tortured by that old monster, Key still thought of all of us?" After hearing a few gasps, she went on, "For instance, I once complained to her that I was a vegetarian, and she said she would see what she could do. That. Same. WEEK, I suddenly had more options in the cafeteria. And Joan, remember how cold your dorm was for so long? All you did was mention it to Key once, and the windows were resealed, and the heater was fixed immediately."

Another student chimed in, "Yeah, and when I told her that George and them were bullying me, she said not to worry anymore about it. Next thing I knew, they wouldn't come near me, like they were afraid to."

George was in the back of the room and replied, "The headmaster came down pretty hard on us. He practically threatened our lives." The comment garnered a few giggles from the room.

Little did they understand that Key used their issues as a means of delaying the torture. Hoping that speaking about heaters or menus would ruin the 'mood'.

The Throwaways was only the first of many books she would have published, but it was the only one that bore anything close to her real name. As per the agreement, Key mixed Julia and Sienna's names up. The dramas used the name Julie Brennan, and the mysteries were written under the alias Sienna Carmichael. She did it to honor the two friends they'd lost, Sienna Brennan and Julie Carmichael.

Using an alias also helped to protect Key's privacy, so she never held book signings or other public events. Nevertheless, even without the usual personal appearances, her books always did very well. The once small, family-owned publisher was most grateful for their newfound success.

Those who had turned their backs on the girls became less popular for doing so. The vast majority of students felt a need to be known as a friend to the throwaways, making them the most popular, powerful group in school.

"Key?" It was Markus Quinn, a handsome young man who was only a year older.

"Yes? Oh, Markus, how are you?" Key noticed how all the girls in the hallway were watching them. Markus was considered the most sought-after boy for his good looks and family name.

"How about dinner tonight? We can sit in the date-area of the cafeteria." Markus proposed.

"Sorry, but I already have plans. Thanks for the offer, though." Key replied, starting to turn away when he took hold of her arm.

"Okay, no problem, we'll do it tomorrow night."

Key put on a big smile, stepped closer to him, and said lightly, "You're charming, Mark, but no, sorry." She pulled away as gently as she could without making a scene and left Mark standing there, unsure what to think. He had never been turned down before.

Sara was the only one who thought she knew the real reason Key wouldn't accept. When they returned to the privacy of their dorm, Sara let her have it. "I know you are too young to marry anyone right now, but you turned down MARKUS! Good grief, just because you can't have babies? That's stupid. If it actually led to marriage, you could always adopt."

Key stared at her momentarily, wondering where the thought of babies or marriage even came from. Finally, calmly, she replied. "Sara, I believe adoption is a good way to build a large family, but I don't wish to condemn a man to never having a child of his own. I figure I can wait until I'm in my 30s or 40s and find a nice widower or divorced man who has already had all the children he wants."

"And I REPEAT—that's stupid! Millions of men and women can't have children who adopt."

Key took a deep breath and replied in a very calm manner. "Yes, I know. But they often don't know they can't have kids until after they're already married. I'm different. I already know and would feel like a con artist if I waited until a man fell in love with me before I told him the truth. Although, it's not exactly a first date conversation, is it?"

Sara knew in her heart that Key was lying. *That's not it at all*, she thought.

"For heaven's sake, Sara, we're too young to worry about that stuff. I wouldn't be the first to wait until I'm 18 or so to start dating, and that's five years away. Besides, that wasn't the reason I turned him down."

"Then why?" Sara asked.

"He doesn't measure up. I can't see dating anyone that doesn't measure up," Key replied.

"Measure up to what? He's gorgeous!"

"Not what, to whom. Markus couldn't hold a candle to my Batman."

Suing Grandmother

Having published three books quickly and a fourth in the works, Key could now afford things she never imagined. The most important of them were for her sisters. She could afford them an allowance, allowing them to buy proper clothing. They could finally afford birthday gifts, Christmas gifts, and so much more. Key had the girls pick out bedroom sets, curtains, a dining table, and sitting area furniture. Their dorm finally looked like a livable place they could call home which previously appeared like a human storage area.

Sara's first purchase was a replacement for her old camera. She planned to decorate the place with fun pictures of all of them.

Of course, Key had to receive approval for every expense since she was a minor, but Ms. Brookes didn't argue, especially since one of her requests included a summer holiday.

Ms. Brookes had hired an independent finance company to oversee Key's new financial windfall. Any purchases or investments needed the approval of their agent, Ms. Brookes and Key.

This change in the life of the girls had brought positive mindsets and Key felt strong enough to make bigger decisions now. Key had been writing while Sara worked on homework when Key broke the silence. "I called a lawyer this morning. He thinks it will be an easy case against my grandmother," Key started.

"How much are you going to sue her for?" Sara had turned away from the science project she was working on to face Key expectantly.

"My birth home."

"That's it?!"

"I want nothing else from that old hag. The house was nothing more than a property to her, but it was my home. I want to visit it soon. I'm planning a trip for us to America."

Sara had never gone far from the school, let alone another country, "So, when do we leave? We'll have to fly – oh my God, in an airplane. How long will we be there? Where will we stay?"

Key giggled, watching Sara's excited and panicking at the same time. "I arranged it so we would arrive there on July 2nd." *It's only fitting since it's the day I left.* "It's a long flight; are you nervous about flying?"

"The whole trip scares me a little, but I still want to go. Are we going to go to your birth home and see your father?"

"I may go to the old house to see if I can look around, but the lawyer said the property is vacant. It's been empty for years now." Key replied in a lower voice.

Sara was afraid to touch on what that might mean, so she tried to change the subject. "I can't believe just the four of us are…"

"We're not going alone."

"Who else is going?" Sara asked.

"Ms. Brookes has to escort us since we're still underage, but don't worry, I insisted on separate hotel rooms."

Sara wasn't worried. She liked Ms. Brookes. She saw that the headmistress had been trying hard to earn Key's trust over the years. Just then, she saw the headmistress approaching them.

"Key?"

"Yes, Ms. Brookes?"

"Sorry to interrupt, but you had a call." She handed Key a small piece of paper. "He said he was your Uncle Robert. I'm sorry, dear, but I have little information about your past. Most of what I know, I learned from your book."

"My mother had a brother, Bobby."

Ms. Brookes looked concerned. "He could be a scam artist just after your book earnings or out to exploit you. I don't want you meeting him anywhere but here, where I can keep an eye out— okay?"

"Actually, I think I'll call my lawyer first to see if I should talk to him at all. I am suing his mother." *And he's just another family member who abandoned my mother,* she thought.

Key went right to her room to make the call. *What would he want with me? He probably wants to talk me out of the lawsuit. Well—the hell with him!*

"Mr. Sunstrum, please, it's Key Yule from Willington." Key realized she had worked herself into a tizz and took a few deep breaths to regain her composure.

"One moment, please," came a woman's voice.

"Ms. Yule?"

"Yes, Mr. Sunstrum, I received a call from a man saying he's my Uncle Robert. I was hoping for some advice."

"Call him."

The reply left Key confused, "Are you sure?"

"Yes, call him. I'll let him give you the good news."

"Good news?"

"I've already said too much, so I'll let you go. I'll be seeing you soon enough. Good day, Ms. Yule."

"Good day."

Key had barely hung up when she started dialing the number on the piece of paper Ms. Brookes had given her.

A very dry, male voice answered. "Hello, this is the Harrington residence."

"Unc…um, Robert Harrington, please." Key was shaking inside and had to sit down to compose herself.

"May I ask whose calling?"

"This is Key Yule, his niece."

The dry voice perked up a bit and started stumbling around upon hearing the name. "Oh yes, one moment, please."

Just a few seconds later, a different voice hit the receiver, "Hello? Kathleen?"

"Yes, this is Key."

"Good heavens—finally!"

There was an awkward silence before he continued. "Ya know, I was only 12 when my sister and Jonathan married. It did my heart good to hear that she was happy, having gotten to know you."

"I'm glad. I'm not sure I expressed it enough in the book, but she really was the best mother in the world."

"I'll bet she was. She was the best sister, too. Have you spoken to your stepfather yet? I'd love to thank him."

Key's heart skipped a beat. *Stepfather?*

"Hello? Kathleen?"

"Yes, sorry, umm, no, I haven't."

"Do you need help finding him? I could hire a…"

"No! What I mean is, I found him—I just haven't spoken to him." Key hated to lie but was still flustered. After another awkward silence, Key asked, "Would you make me a promise, Uncle Robert?"

"Anything, love. What is it?"

"Promise me you won't contact my father—stepfather. Ever."

The line went silent again, and she heard Robert clear his throat. "You're my niece. You have my loyalty, but why?"

Key let out a small sigh and explained, "He's moved on. The attention my book has gotten could only cause him harm."

"But…your sister…"

Key didn't want to argue, so she quickly changed the subject. "My lawyer said you had good news for me?"

"Yes, yes, the house—the American house you wanted. It's yours."

"Oh, good heavens! She's settling?"

"Well, not exactly. She signed it over to me."

Key thought to herself for a moment about what that might mean before responding. "Oh, she's evil. She wants you to hate me too."

"No, I disagree, love. I know you think she did it, so you'd have to take it from me, but that's not true. She knew I would give it to you. Actually, love, she ensured I would before signing it over." He let out a frustrated sigh before continuing, "Your grandmother is a complicated woman."

Key's mind was racing, and she didn't know what to think.

"Kathleen, your grandmother would like to see you."

Graduation – 'V' House Assistant

"Two down, two more to go," Key said with a smile, hugging Sara and her girls.

"Congratulations, Key. Your speech was wonderful, very uplifting," Ms. Brookes said.

Sara looked at Key with a crooked brow. "Wait, you said two more to go? You don't have to do another day of school if you don't want to."

Key giggled at the comment while she handed her cap to Sara to hold. She was taking the gown and the sashes off. "I still have another five years before I'm of legal age, so I may as well use it wisely."

Sara just rolled her eyes and shook her head, "Whatever. So, what do you plan to study this time?"

They all started to walk out of the auditorium. "The Dean said I could continue to work on my computer science project even though I've graduated. I'm thinking of law and physics this time. The business degree was helpful in creating a few ideas and using them in my books. Having more knowledge of law and science would round them out, especially my mystery novels."

"What's the computer project you are working on?" Ms. Brookes inquired.

"Want to see it?" Key asked.

They all agreed, so Key led them to the computer science building. She pulled a key out of her purse to unlock the door.

"They gave you a key?" Sara asked before the others could.

"Yes. I have made quite an investment into both my project and the building, so-" She opened the door and walked them down a long hallway of doors until they reached room 110. "This one is mine."

She opened the door, turned on the lights, and shouted, "Wake up, V-Key, it's time to introduce yourself."

A large monitor that occupied almost the entire six-foot table lit up.

"Oh my God, that's you!" Dannie exclaimed.

"Hello, my name is V-Key." It looked as if it was a live feed of Key herself. It was so real.

"I would swear she's making eye contact with me," Rachel said.

"She is. The monitor I created has a billion little eyes. She can follow all of your movements, including your eyes." Key replied.

"That's crazy, she looks just like you. Now you have a triplet!" Dannie laughed.

"Not exactly like her. V-Key has green eyes, and Key's are blue," Sara commented, to their shock. None of them had noticed. "So, what does she do?"

"She's a personal assistant I plan to install in the American house. I have also designed a phone with her loaded so you can always have your assistant with you."

"Why not just an app that can be loaded on your phone?" Rachel asked.

"I want my assistant to have access to everything, and your current phone isn't capable of doing that," Key replied instantly.

"So, you can talk to her – have a conversation with her?" Dannie asked.

"Yes. I've uploaded as much of my brain to her as possible, but that'll be a never-ending process, of course."

"V-Key, tell me something I don't already know," Sara said to the screen to the giggles of the girls.

V-Key asked Sara in perfect Key style, "Do you know what political party Abraham Lincoln was in?"

"Ummm…no. Wasn't he an American President?" Sara replied.

"Yes, he was. He was the first Republican President in America. He was a member of the anti-slavery party created in 1860 and wanted to free those enslaved in the southern states. It cost America many lives in a civil war, but they won for the good of the country."

"Wow, she really does have your brain." Everyone giggled again when Sara followed it by saying, "But it wasn't fair to ask me about America."

"You need to learn it if you want to return with me. We'll need to get you nationalized so you can stay." Key replied. "You are going with me, aren't you?" This time, Key looked at all her girls.

"But then we can't come back here," said Rachel.

"Of course we could. I'm talking about dual citizenship. I've already been granted as much here, so you would need to get…"

"You have?" asked Ms. Brookes.

"Yes, the university sponsored it, and I have an excellent lawyer. My mother was also born here," Key replied. "I intend to get the girls the same when we get to America. I've already started the process."

"Sometimes I forget that you're only 13 years old," Ms. Brookes said with a smile.

Dannie had a look that bothered Key. "Are you okay? What's bothering you, Dannie?

"I'm not sure I want to move to America and leave all my friends here."

"I have to go home to my family there. I've waited patiently, but when I'm 18…" Key began.

"I know, I know you do. And I want to go back with you when you reveal yourself to them. I just, well, I'm not sure I want to move there with you, leaving everything behind" Dannie put her head down and fidgeted.

"We don't have a choice, though," Rachel added. "We get kicked out of Willington when we graduate, and we can't afford to live on our own."

"Girls, you are only 13 years old and worrying too much – too soon," Ms. Brookes tried calming the girls.

Key was quiet, and Sara could see how tense her jaw had become.

"Key has already said she's sending all of us to university–any university we choose," Sara said while taking Key by the hand. "If you decide to attend a university here in England, then we'll have somewhere to visit!"

In a quiet voice, Key added, "But America has a lot of universities, too."

"Five years. A lot can happen in five years. Can we all chill out right now?" Rachel insisted, which calmed the situation down.

First Trip To America

The day arrived, and they were packed and ready to go. Sara was giddy all morning—in the car to the airport, in line through the metal detectors, in the terminal while they waited—but it was a different story once they got on the plane.

"Sara! You're going to break my hand," Key complained.

"Sorry," Sara replied with a shaky voice. Her grip loosened enough to let Key's blood flow again, but she couldn't let go completely.

Key did all she could to distract Sara from her fears with jokes, games, and stories. Eventually, about an hour later, they were well into a card game, almost forgetting they were on a plane.

They got off the plane, made their way out of the airport and got a car. Key insisted the driver stop first at the graveyard across from the house. She had purchased a small bouquet and placed it at her mother's grave. She knelt on the grass and spoke. "I've missed you, Mum. It has been a long journey back, but I'm here. I'm finally here."

The next stop was the old house. Key couldn't hide her emotions as she usually did. As she made her way to the front door, she let out a breath that sounded to Sara like she'd been holding it in for years. Tears followed as she soaked in every piece of wood, paint, stone, and blade of grass. Her hands shook, but she finally inserted the key into the tiny hole and turned the lock.

She stood just inside and took in the familiar smell. It was from the sand, stone, and water that always seemed to overtake the place. As they walked further in, Sara saw something.

"There's a note here, Key," Sara said before opening it.

"What's it say?" Key asked.

"Aha, they didn't know you took your mother's photo album. It looks to be from your Da, and he gave their new address in case whoever takes over the house finds it."

Key took the note from Sara and read the address before placing it back on the table.

Just inside the door was a large living area, now covered in inches of dust. To the right was a door that led to the kitchen, with another door to a large section her family never used. To the left, under the balcony, was another door that went out to the garage. Further inside, also to the left, was a curving staircase that ended just outside the first three bedrooms.

Sara put her hand on the small of Key's back. "Where's your room? I want to see your room."

"It's upstairs." Key started for the steps that led to the balcony above but stopped. "My room was the one in the middle." She walked past the stairs to the window just before the hidden doorway and looked out.

Tears filled her eyes again as she remembered that last day and what she felt was her only hope—Batman. Just past the window was what looked like a wall that protruded into the room. She gave the trim a light tug, and the wall opened to another set of stairs. Key went down to the small room with the glass doors and the old couch where she would sit and wait for him. She put her hand on the door latch but paused when Sara screamed, "Key! Your room!"

Key turned back and headed up to see what Sara was talking about.

"The room in the middle looks like it's for a little girl, and everything was left behind. There's a closet full of small clothes, a bed, a desk, a bunch of notebooks…"

"My stories!" Key ran up to the balcony and into her old room. "Oh my God, it barely changed since the day I left. Although they took my pictures." When Key turned to look at her bookshelves, "Aww, and they took most of my stories."

Walking back out of her old room, leafing through a notebook, she noticed Ms. Brookes wiping the tables downstairs. She realized a lot of work needed to be done to make the place livable again. "I'll need to make some calls, I think. Starting with a maid service to help us play 'catch up' and some contractors to look at everything else."

Ms. Brookes looked up at her. "I agree, and I'm glad we got rooms at a hotel. None of the electricity seems to be working, and the water in the kitchen doesn't run."

"All right, just give me a few minutes, and we'll go." Key turned back toward her room but stopped and looked at her parents' room. She pulled out the drawers and looked in the closet. *Everything of my mother and I's is still here — left behind, forgotten.*

After looking through everything, Key finally went down to the beach. "Look, the door was unlocked."

Sara helped her slide the door open, and they made their way out. Both kicked off their shoes to walk through the sand to the water's edge.

"Your beach seems to be a collection of trash that probably washes in," Sara commented, looking around.

"This could be helpful, though." Key picked up a wooden board that she wedged in the sliding door. "No one will be able to slide this open again while we aren't here."

It was time to leave, so they locked it back up and headed to the hotel not far from the house, down on Paper Mill Road. It was also very close to a restaurant and grocery store—close enough to walk to them both.

Ms. Brookes made the necessary calls on Key's behalf, pretending to be Uncle Bobby's assistant. The house had to be in his name until Key turned 18. She only agreed because it helped to hide her identity in America until then.

Key thought their next order of business was to search out her father. She asked Ms. Brookes to call again for the car service. Ms. Brookes wished she had the freedom of her own car but couldn't comprehend how they drove on the wrong side of the road as they did here.

Now that they had her father's address from the note, Ms. Brookes, Sara, and Key headed out. Dannie and Rachael chose to stay behind. They were both suffering from jetlag.

The driver found the address, but Key instructed him to drive past it, turn around, and park a few houses away, across the street. At first, the driver hesitated to take orders from the little girl, but Ms. Brookes nodded at him, and he followed what Key said. Once parked, they sat and waited.

Twenty minutes later, Sara lost her patience and started to whine. "Are we really just going to sit here all day? What if he's away on vacation or something?"

Key started to feel silly and was about to give in when a car pulled into the house's driveway. "It's him! That's my father!"

"Who's that with him?" Sara leaned against Key's back, pressing them both against the door to look out the rear side window.

"Key? Would you like me to have the driver pull up and get their attention?" Ms. Brookes asked.

"NO!" I don't want him to know I'm here. I don't intend to make a fuss for him."

Key said it so loudly that Sara jumped back on the seat. "Why not?!" Sara barked at Key.

Key spoke, never taking her eyes off her father. "If we get his attention, he may want me back. Is that what you want? Do you…"

"Oh my God!" Ms. Brookes exclaimed.

But Key kept speaking, "Do you want me to leave Willington and come live in America? He'd have the legal right to make it happen."

After her father, a woman, and a small child entered the house, a girl who looked like Key emerged from the place they were parked in front of. The girl kept stealing glances at the car, and Key ducked behind the driver.

Ms. Brookes and Sara were sitting there with their mouths gaped open. Key snarked, "I told you I had an identical twin." Neither replied as all three watched Erin walk home and enter the house before they had the driver pull off.

The subject came up again just an hour later when they prepared to leave for dinner.

"What is that?" Sara asked.

"A wig. You saw her yourself. I can't go out looking like my sister Erin," Key replied. "Imagine the mess I could cause."

Dannie laughed, "Red looks good on you, but you'll need some help. I can see your blonde locks peeking out."

"Take it off, I'll do it." Sara managed to twist, pin, and flatten Key's long hair to hide it under the wig. "Where did you get this thing anyway?"

Key looked at Ms. Brookes and carefully answered, "I borrowed it from the theater supplies."

The restaurant wasn't far, but it was crowded. They were lucky to get what looked like the second-to-last table. The only other table was a long set of square ones right next to where they were seated. It had reserved signs on each table, which they had pushed together to prepare for a larger party.

After giving their drink orders, that long table started filling in. Right next to Key was the head of that table, and there sat a very tall, handsome young man. He couldn't have been much older than Key and the girls. To his left was a younger girl, maybe 6 or 7 years old, who looked a lot like him. Next to her were his parents. To his right was a tall, red-headed boy, two brown-haired boys, and a sandy-brown-haired girl at the opposite end. Key found it easy to figure out the family members but assumed the others were just friends.

While the girls and Ms. Brookes waited for their meals, they realized it was the handsome boy's birthday dinner. Every guest stopped to say as much before taking a seat. Finally, the young girl to his left handed him a wrapped gift.

"For me?" he said as he accepted it. The young girl looked very anxious, so he unwrapped it as slowly as he could, obviously torturing her. The young girl had had enough, grabbed the paper, and pulled it away. Everyone laughed, but he held up the book and said, "My favorite author. Thanks, Dee."

"Put your bookmark in it," the young girl prompted.

"But I haven't started it yet."

"Awww, come on, Mike, put your bookmark in it."

The young man put the book down, reached back with his left hand, and pulled out his wallet. He flipped it open with the same hand and pulled something out. He held it sideways, away from his little sister, to torture her more, which allowed Key a long, easy view of it. He held it there while he flipped his wallet closed again and slowly stuffed it back in his back pocket.

Key took a deep breath, followed by another, and then another. She was doing all she could to prevent her emotions from overtaking her.

Sara was to her right and leaned over to quietly ask, "Key, what's wrong?"

"Nothing, nothing; I'm okay." Key looked back at the table and tried not to reveal her secret.

However, Sara noticed Key sneak peeks at the table next to her and was anxious to get her alone. Once she made eye contact with Key again, Sara said, "I need to visit the loo."

Key knew what she was doing and immediately offered to go with her to find it.

Once alone in the restroom, Sara asked her, "What is happening? What upset you?"

"Sara, I need you to do me a favor. Did you bring your camera?"

"I always have it with me; why?"

"I want you to take a picture of me, but make sure you get Batman in it," Key said with a huge smile.

"Batman? Oh my God, are you serious? Did you recognize him?"

"No. The boy I knew had longer, lighter hair, but it's him," Key replied.

"Wait, then, how can you be sure?"

"He took a picture from his wallet, and I saw it. Remember I said there were six pictures of him and me in my mother's photo album, but one was missing?"

Sara nodded, she remembered.

"Well, it's not missing anymore. The young girl next to him asked him to take it out and then asked to see his "princess Kathleen" again."

"Princess?" Sara asked.

"He started calling me that after he heard my Da use it once."

They returned to the table, and Sara did as she had promised. But just before snapping it, Sara slammed the table as hard as she could. Every table around them stopped to look, including Batman's. Once the young man looked over in curiosity, she snapped it. She got the red-headed Key and him in the same shot.

Key didn't share the news with the others until they were safely back at the hotel. Rachel was impressed with how good-looking he was, but Dannie was mad because she ignored who was at that table and didn't remember him. Sara promised to show her the picture of him before she gave it to Key.

The following day, Key woke up earlier than the others, so she decided to walk back to the cliff house. She put her wig back on to be sure and left them a note before heading out.

The property that belonged to her now was vast. It stretched a few miles in either direction from the main house. She knew she would pass a few large openings from the East, where she came from. The first was just into the woods, but a secondary opening was a driveway leading to an old barn and a small cottage.

When she passed the first opening, she saw an old car she assumed someone had just dumped on her property. Curious, she approached it and was startled to find two people sleeping inside. She stepped back as the man opened his eyes.

"Scram, little girl." He said while rolling down his window.

"Oh Frank, be nice," said the woman beside him, rubbing her eyes, waking up.

"I don't have to 'scram.' This is my property." Key shot back at him.

"Shit." He said.

"Frank! Don't curse in front of her." The woman had gotten out of the car and was walking around the front of it. She wore a T-shirt with cut-off sleeves and a tattoo on one arm. Her hair was thick, frizzy, and uncombed. "I'm sorry, he's awfully cranky in the mornings."

Key took a few more steps back. "Why are you parked here?"

"We ran out of gas." The woman said, "My name is Dee; what's yours?"

"Key."

The bald, tall, largely built man with a goatee mustache started to fold out of his car, and Key took five more steps, scooting more quickly backward.

"Don't worry yourself, I ain't gonna hurt ya," he said. He walked around the car, out of sight, until Key could hear the sound of water running.

"Shouldn't you be at work?" Key asked.

"I wish we were, but I lost my job, and he can't get one," Dee said.

"Why not?"

"He just got out of prison, and no one hires ex-cons." Dee leaned back against the car. "I'm still looking, though."

Key's voice cracked a bit when she asked, "Did he kill someone?"

"Oh no, noth'n like that," Dee replied, waving her hand up and down.

"Then I'll hire you."

"Is that right?" Frank said with a smirk as he made his way back around, standing next to Dee.

"I live in England, but this is my property, and my house is just up there. There is also a small cottage just before reaching the main house. You can use that." Key saw they weren't sure of her, so she continued, "I'm not sure how much I can pay you yet, but it should be enough to live on. You won't have the rental expense of a flat, so…"

"A what?" he interrupted.

"A flat," Key answered.

"She means an apartment or house…a place to stay." Dee chimed in.

"Yes, of course," Key said. "Without that expense, whatever I can afford should be enough, considering your current predicament."

"It sure would. So, what would we be doing?" Dee asked.

"Helping to organize the contractors. The main house needs a lot of work, and I haven't seen inside the cottage yet. I would assume it will be just as bad. Ultimately, you will be my eyes here after we return to England in a few weeks."

"Frank loves working outside, so he can maintain the land, and I can make the calls and meet with the contractors. I would love the job, but I still need to know how much you can afford to pay us." Dee looked at Key with amusement. She was so tiny but obviously older than her short stature made her seem. *Maybe she's one of those little people,* she thought.

"I'll have to look closely at my finances and budget for the work I want done. I think I can afford about 40..."

"40 dollars? Hahahaha," Frank laughed.

"No, 40 thousand." Key shot back at him. With a harsh sigh, she continued, "I can find someone else if you aren't interested."

"We're interested!" Dee exclaimed, punching Frank in the arm.

"Alright then. I'll have to talk to my lawyer, who will want to talk to you and get your information, I'm sure of it. I'll have him forward you a starting payment so you can get a working car. We'll need to be driven when we visit."

"We can do that," said Dee.

"Would you like to take a look at the cottage? As I said, I'm not sure what condition it's in." Key started walking up the path to it. "Your first chore will be to get the water and electricity turned on."

Dee and Frank followed. When they arrived at the small cottage just down from the main house, Key handed them the key to the door.

"Don't you want to see it too?" asked Dee.

"I'm not comfortable being in there with two strangers. You can report your needs later when I see you again." With that, she continued walking up to the main house.

"Can you believe that little girl? She's probably 40 years old, and we don't know it." Dee giggled.

"Seems too good to be true to me," said Frank. He was impressed with the workmanship of the shelving, floors, and doors, even though they were covered in dirt. "This place is going to need a lot of work."

"Perfect. We can probably do most of it ourselves, babe." Dee said before walking into the next room. *Tomorrow has hope.* Dee took a long, deep breath in. *Tomorrow, for the first time in so long, has hope.*

Key's thoughts were of her safe space at school. *I'll need a rink. I'll have to start looking into getting one built on the property.*

Key entered the old house and, with a smile, took in the scent of it before going to the window again to look at the beach. *What is that?* She could see something in the middle of the beach, stuck in a mound of sand. She quickly opened the hidden doorway to the stairwell and down to the glass doors. She removed the wedged board, but the doors were eroded and difficult to open. She wouldn't give up until they finally moved enough for her to squeeze out.

A rose. A single rose was sticking out of a small mound of sand in the middle of the beach. *Who would do this? Why?* Upon further inspection, the rose was horribly wilted, as if it had been out there for some time. *It wasn't here yesterday morning – I would have seen it.*

Key left the flower and returned to the house to clean. A few hours later, Ms. Brookes and the girls showed up. Key thought it best not to mention Frank and Dee right away. But of course, she told Sara, she kept nothing from her. Sara was always the exception.

However, she was especially glad she didn't mention it to the others when she asked to stay back while they went sightseeing. Ms. Brookes never would have allowed her to stay if she had seen them. She was sure of it.

Not long after they left, there was a knock at the front door. It was Dee.

"Hello. So how bad of shape is the cottage?" Key asked her while inviting her in.

"I was able to call and get the electricity turned on, but I'm not sure how I'll pay the bill when it comes," Dee replied.

"No worries; I'll make sure you can. I'll need your information, though. Let me see if I can find some paper and a pencil." Key opened a drawer in the table by the front window and found her mother's old notepad, which she would use to leave phone messages for her father. She instructed Dee on what information to jot down.

"Does the water work in the cottage?" Key asked.

"Yes. Frank had to turn it on, but it works," Dee replied.

"Do you think he could do the same for this house?"

"Yeah, of course!" Dee replied, looking at him and wondering, *why didn't I think of that?*

"Do you have a bank account? You'll need one."

"I do, but it is down to the lowest limit, so I can't take another penny out," Dee said.

"Well, I can write you a check to carry you over until your position is solidified," Key replied, swinging the pencil while looking at her.

Key spent the rest of their holiday cleaning and planning how she wanted to restore the old house. Frank was able to turn on the water but quickly realized the loo in the kitchen had a leak and couldn't be used.

They never did run into Mike or Erin again, but it was not for a lack of trying. Per Key's insistence, they ate at that same restaurant every night. Sara kept an eye out everywhere they went, every shop, every museum, but nothing.

Return To Britain

On the first full day back at Willington, Key called her agent to discuss the house in America. "I've hired a husband-and-wife team to organize the contractors and maintain the property."

"Do you have their information?" The agent asked.

"Yes, I'll fax it over. I had mentioned paying them a salary of $40,000 in American dollars. I have looked at the numbers, and that works well for now. I could afford a little more in my budget, but it may be best to hold it back for a Christmas bonus if they do well." Key explained.

After hearing some computer keys ticking away, he said, "I agree. 40 is good if they agreed, and yes, you could easily afford more, but it's always good to be conservative until you're sure about them."

"I'll need to purchase a proper vehicle for them right away. They will also be our drivers when we visit. I'm sure there will be much more equipment, like a work vehicle, to use around the property. I'll price check, crunch the numbers, and get back to you."

"Great. Talk to you soon, Ms. Yule."

Key hung up and called back to America to give Dee the good news. After working out some details, she thought they best have a heart-to-heart. "Dee, can I trust you?"

"Of course, girl. What's up?" Dee replied.

"I need to keep my identity private. No one, and I mean no one in America, can know of my existence."

Dee could hear the slight trembling in Key's voice. "Your secrets are safe with us, but I'm not sure I understand who ya are, so it makes it kinda tough to know if I'm protecting or hurt'n ya honey."

Key was slow to explain but managed to make it clear that if her family in America were to find out about her existence, they could "rip her from her life again."

Dee had many questions, and Key did her best to answer them. "I'm a writer, Dee, and I'll send you my first novel. It should explain a great deal more than I care to go into. However, until I'm of legal age, the house will still show to be in my Uncle Robert's name."

"Are ya never gonna let them know you exist?" Dee asked.

"When I'm 18, they'll know. I plan to move back to America with my new family of sisters and hopefully join them with the old." Key replied. "Oh, I have one more crucial detail…"

"What?" Dee asked.

"Did you notice I was wearing a wig when we met?"

"Yeah, honey, it was a very good one. Are ya sick?"

"No, I have an identical twin sister," Key replied.

"Really?"

"Yes, she's a natural blonde, so use that to differentiate her. I'll show you the next time I'm there, but please be careful not to assume someone who looks like me."

They did not speak much longer, but Dee did promise to make Frank aware of the situation and promised she could trust him. Just before they hung up though, Key had one question that had been on her mind.

"Dee, what did Frank go to prison for?" Key asked.

"I'm embarrassed to say, but he was sell'n drugs for a friend to make some extra cash," Dee replied instantly and continued. "He'll never do it again, I promise ya."

"I appreciate your honesty, and I pray you're right. Thanks, Dee," Key concluded and hung up.

Sara was surprised to learn of his crime, and she didn't help Key's fears on the matter. "What if they decide to use your secrets against you and extort more money?"

"I can only pray they won't, I suppose," Key replied hesitantly.

"You took an awfully big gamble, Key. What do you know about these people?"

"Only that they needed a job and a place to live. I didn't even know their full names until I met with them before leaving America."

"Oh my God! That is so unlike you. You research everything and trust no one. Why…"

"Sara, you aren't helping!" Key put her hands in the air. "I acted irrationally. I know. I needed them, and they needed what I could provide. It seems a little too neat now, but I thought it a good solution at the time."

Sara sat beside Key on the bed and put her arm around her. "I'm sorry."

Key looked at Sara. "I admit I acted hastily, but it isn't like I've been terribly careful until now. I wrote a book with my name on it. My grandmother, who hates me, could use it to contact my Da."

"No." Sara shifted and sat sideways to look straight at Key. "I would think she would be more afraid of what he could do to her after what she's done. Every day she holds the secret is a day she continues to walk free." Sara then put her hand up to Key's cheek. "You are white as a ghost."

"Even if Izzy doesn't contact him, I'm surprised the media has yet to. It could just be a matter of time before one of them looks up my Mum's wedding record and finds his real name. They made the connection to Izzy so quickly." Key replied in a softer tone.

"That book only became a limited best seller in our area. Maybe they assume he has also passed away," Sara replied.

"And my twin sister?" Key shot back.

The Letter

Ms. Brookes walked quickly toward Key and stopped her before entering her dorm. "We received a letter I think you'll find interesting."

Key looked at her inquisitively and took the letter. They both entered the dorm and sat on the couch to read the letter.

To whom it may concern,

My name is Erin Yule, and I am a freshman at Saint Mark's High School in Springfield, Main, America. In my English class, a fellow student read an article about a play one of your students wrote. It described its tremendous success in raising money for your school in detail. It also mentions that the author did not want to share it or to be known, but I'm hoping their love of the arts will entice them to save a drama club.

Our club was told this year that the school could not afford to pay for the rights to a famous play. Only the parents of the kids performing attend, and it is rarely enough to cover the initial cost.

This is my first year at Saint Mark's, and I, like my best friend Maggie, have been looking forward to the opportunity to be on stage. However, with the news of financial restraints, we are experiencing a lack of interest in participating, even among the students.

If you would allow us to put your play on here, we could use that article in our advertising. It could generate interest among all the school's parents and even our local paper.

Lastly, the article mentions that the author wanted to be referred to as the 'Drama Queen' when pressed for a name. From one Drama Queen to another, thank you in advance for considering my request.

Sincerely,

Erin Yule

"Thank you, Ms. Brookes. I'll reply right away." Key got up from the couch and disappeared into her bedroom.

Ms. Brookes was curious and had to know, "Are you going to send your sister the play?"

Key turned back with a huge smile, "Of course I will! She's a drama queen herself." Ms. Brookes smiled back and left the room, allowing Key to do her job in peace. Key immediately sat down at her desk, pulled out a piece of paper, grabbed a pen, and took a deep breath before letting out slowly.

Dear Erin,

I was glad to receive your letter and am happy to help save your drama club in any way I can.

All I ask is that you don't rush the production. Please take your time to find the right people to represent each character and then practice, practice, practice. We built the story the summer before and put it on the following May.

Enclosed are the script, stage directions, music sheets, and set building instructions. I recommend you get as many students involved in more ways than just performing. Ask the teachers to make the costumes an assignment if you have a sewing class. Do the same with music teachers to get the musicians involved. Maths teachers can also be approached for set construction projects. The more student groups you get involved in, the more parents you attract. We were fortunate that one of the parents we drew happened to be a journalist.

I can also send other items and props specific to that play. I hope the address you provided will accept them.

Sincerely,

Drama Queen

Key immediately gathered the paperwork she had promised and found a large enough envelope to fit them all. Now, she needed to gather the props she mentioned to get them boxed up.

"What are you so excited about?" Sara asked, entering the room.

"Look! My sister wrote to me." Key handed her the letter before she started to mumble to herself the list of things she would need to find. "A large box…I can get that from the loading dock…I stored the props-"

"She wrote to the Drama Queen," Sara said after reading the letter and immediately putting her hand up in the stop position. "And yes, before you state the obvious, I know that's you."

"Well, of course, she doesn't know she wrote to me specifically, but how fantastic is it that I can help her save her drama club?" Key replied. "I think I'll also anonymously send a note to Mrs. Markum, letting her know that I've consented to allow an American high school to use my story."

"Why?" Sara asked.

"Alerting the original journalist could help gin up interest if it crosses the pond to America. It reached them once in a theater magazine; maybe I can help it reach them again in the newspapers."

After boxing things up, she sat in her room, allowing the realization to sink in. *I'm helping Erin.* Just then, the phone rang.

It was her Uncle Bobby. In her joyous mood, she allowed him to persuade her to go to the main house and meet his mother—her grandmother. Unknowingly, he had called at the most opportune moment. Key would've accepted anything if asked politely enough at the moment as her brain was occupied with only one thought: *My sister sent me a letter…*

Early the next day, Key had a car service take her the hour to the Harrington mansion. The driver took Hobb Street to get there, and for the first time, she saw what her mother had described in her diary. The tall building of flats her fathers lived in and the café across the street was still open and looked busy.

They drove up the large driveway to the impressive house. Key was suddenly regretting her decision to come.

She made her way up to the front door and knocked. She was greeted by an average man with thinning, light blonde hair and a belly that hung well over his belt.

"Kathleen? My heavens, you're beautiful!"

Key couldn't help but smile. "Thank you—Uncle Robert?"

"Yes, yes, come in, love. Please call me Bobby." Before the door closed behind her, he gave her a hearty hug.

Uncle Bobby was as blonde as she and her mother were. He was a bit overweight, she noted, but a jolly fellow. "I meant to ask you, Uncle Bobby, are you married? Do I have any cousins?"

"No, dear, not anymore. I was married to a widow for a short time who had a few kids. After a few years, she took me for everything I had."

"Oh, I'm so sorry."

"Well, never mind that. Your grandmother is anxious to see you." With one hand on her back, he gently pushed her along.

Living in a school the size of Willington, Key was rather unimpressed by the large foyer and lavish rooms as they entered the great room.

"Mom? Kathleen's arrived."

An old woman stood up from a chair in the far corner and slowly approached them.

Key felt her heartbeat quicken, and the hairs on her arms stood at attention.

"Oh my, how you've grown," said the old woman.

Isabel was wearing an expression Key had never seen on the familiar face and didn't quite expect—a smile.

Her grandmother stopped just short of her and paused. She then took one step closer and started to raise her arms.

Key turned abruptly to her right and, pointing at a chair, "Is it alright if I sit here?"

The look of annoyance on her grandmother brought Key some comfort. So, when she sat, she leaned back and put her feet on the coffee table. She was instantly uncomfortable. *This may have been overkill–this furniture is so stiff,* she thought. But Key wouldn't show her discomfort or regret; she wouldn't give the old woman the satisfaction.

"So, Izzy, why did you wish to see me?" Key asked.

The name seemed to physically sting her. Determined, however, Isabel took a deep breath and went to the couch to face her granddaughter. "I understand you went to America this past summer. Did you visit the house?"

"Yes, I did." Key purposely didn't offer any more.

"Was it still in good condition?"

"It's going to take some work, but I'll enjoy restoring it." Key couldn't take it anymore and lowered her feet to sit up properly.

Isabel felt confident about how their meeting was going as she sat down. "I could help if you'd like. What all needs to be done?"

Key made eye contact with the old woman now sitting opposite of her. She smiled and then broke out in laughter.

Isabel was taken aback, unsure how to respond.

The laughter slowed as Key began to rise from her seat. "Is this why I'm here? To give a report on MY house?" She followed it with one last giggle and a roll of her eyes.

"No, I've…" Isabel realized her granddaughter would be a formidable opponent. She fidgeted in her seat, took two deep breaths, and let each out slowly before speaking again. "My only…my only concern is that you're happy."

"Oh yes, I'm very happy. And you? I understand the papers have not been very kind." Key gently sat down again.

"No, they haven't." Isabel looked down. "Quite deservingly so, I suppose."

Key looked over to her uncle. "Uncle Bobby, do you think we could get some tea? I'm parched."

Isabel became immediately flushed. *How dare she order tea without being invited! Calm down—good heavens, calm down—*two more deep breaths.

Isabel began again. "Kathleen, I don't expect forgiveness for my actions." Now, returning her gaze at her granddaughter, "My intentions are simply to do what I can to right the wrong. I have the means to make your life quite comfortable."

Key crossed her legs and folded her arms before her. "How?"

"I could buy you the finest clothes, ensure you have the best of things, and take care of your every expense. If you were to live here…"

"With you? Here, with you?" Key giggled, tilted her head, and looked at her grandmother with a large grin.

"Yes, well, it would make it easier to provide for you."

"Interesting. I wouldn't be a 'problem' anymore?"

Remembering their only conversation in the car so many years ago, Isabel mentally gave Key a point on her imaginary scoreboard. In hopes of winning one for the home team, she tried again. "You are my granddaughter, Alexandra's child." Looking away as her servant brought in the tea and handed each one, she continued, "So, of course, I love you and feel horrible about what I've done."

"You love me?" Key asked.

Isabel answered as she stirred her tea, "Yes."

"Then look at me when you say it." Key uncrossed her legs and leaned forward, looking right into her grandmother's eyes.

With a clatter, Isabel put her tea on the table and returned her glare. "You didn't come here today with any intention of giving me a chance, did you?"

Key let out a long sigh. "You're wrong. You had a chance—but you threw it away." She stood up, shaking her head while she made her way out of the room.

Isabel jumped up and followed. "No, Kathleen, you should take the side door if you insist on leaving. It will get you to the car much quicker. Robert can drive you back."

Key looked back at her, feeling a sense of power at her grandmother's obvious stress while looking at the front door. "No, I'll be leaving the way I came in. My taxi is out front."

As she opened it, she saw the mob of reporters out front, waiting and yelling questions.

"Ms. Harrington! What did you talk about?" Asked one.

"Have you two made amends?" Asked another.

"Will you be moving home now with your grandmother?" Asked a third.

Finally realizing her grandmother's plan, Key turned back to look at her. "This wasn't quite the outcome you were hoping for, was it?" And with a final smirk, she stepped out, telling the reporters, "One question at a time, please," as she closed the door behind her.

Key didn't stay or answer many questions but enjoyed knowing her grandmother would think she had.

"Have you and your grandmother reconciled?" One reporter asked.

"No," Key answered as she walked off the porch.

"So, you won't be moving in with her?" Another asked.

"No," Key said again while she pushed her way through to get to the car.

When Key returned to Willington, she went on with her regular schedule. No one knew, except Sara, that she had gone. If Ms. Brookes saw anything in the papers, she didn't mention it.

As was tradition, they gathered together on one bed to rehash their day that night.

Sara was shocked when Key told them what had happened. "Oh my God, are you kidding me? It was just a set-up?"

Key just nodded in the affirmative.

"That woman is pure fucking evil." Exclaimed Rachel.

"Rachel!" Key gave her the 'look.'

"Sorry, but it's hard not to curse when I know someone is mistreating any one of you."

Key shook her head. "That's no excuse, and you know it."

"Yeah, I know. Sorry, Momma-Key." Rachel always got the 'look' because she was the only one still finding it difficult to control her words.

They all giggled, including Key, because of the title Rachel and Danny had given her lately. Key wasn't sure she liked it, but she understood it. She had filled the role of parent to both of them. The only way she could keep her deal with Ms. Brookes was to ensure they all stayed out of trouble and never gave her a reason to move an adult into their dorm.

Only a week went by when Uncle Bobby called again: *Riiiinggg.*

"Hello?" Key answered.

"Kathleen?" She heard a familiar male voice ask.

"Yes. Uncle Bobby?" She asked.

"Kathleen, I have a huge favor to ask."

"What can I do for you?"

"Give her a chance?"

"Uncle Bobby…"

"I know she doesn't deserve it. I'm not saying she does, and I'm surely not defending anything she's done." He hesitated, and after not hearing a reply, he asked, "Kathleen?"

"I'm still listening." Key sighed heavily.

"She's all I have." Bobby finally said.

"I understand. However, I don't know what I can do. She doesn't love me, and I honestly don't believe she's capable of it."

"She's capable. My mother has had a difficult life."

Key rolled her eyes, "Uh huh. I'm sure which gold or pearl necklace to buy must have been horrible."

"She didn't start out like that. She was lucky to get a meal a day until she married my father."

"Is that so…" Key said, suspicion dripping from her voice. "I'm curious: Do you know that as a fact, or is that just what she's told you to gain sympathy?"

"My father told me. She took all her frustrations out on him shortly after Alexandria left for America. My father told me what he knew about her life to make me understand."

Key said nothing for a moment. Then, after a long sigh asked, "What do you expect from me? She tried to set me up the last time I was there."

Bobby didn't answer right away.

"Bobby? What are you asking of me?" She asked again.

"I'm not sure, actually. I know she won't try again. She knows you don't trust her," he replied, sounding defeated.

Key took a deep breath and exhaled loudly. "So, you expect ME to make the next move. You want ME to try again with HER? Are you kidding me?"

Bobby replied in a low voice, "I'm sorry I asked. It was too much to ask. I'm sorry."

They remained on the line in silence. Finally, Key needed to know, "Why? Why is this so important to you?"

"I miss my sister. It's hard to explain, Kath…" He cleared his throat, "Key. We both loved Mom, but it was always us against her. I had a partner. I had someone to suffer through with, I guess. When she left, I had my father for a short while…" Bobby's voice trailed off.

"You'll have a partner in me, Bobby. You can always talk to me." Key tried comforting him.

"No, it's not the same, although I appreciate that. I'm not asking for someone I can call to complain to. Never mind, I can't explain it."

"You want someone there at Thanksgiving dinner to make faces to, is that it?"

"Yes! Sounds silly, doesn't it? But you can't be at the dinner table the way things are. You know what I mean? You can't be here for me if you can't be here."

Key couldn't help a small giggle. She felt she understood enough and was rethinking it. "Would I be allowed to come visit you, or do I have to have her permission?"

Bobby sounded a bit chipper. "You could always come to see me."

Key promised to "see him soon" but didn't go right away. The thought of her grandmother made her blood boil. Her memory would torment her, and she'd think back to the car ride and the horrible things her grandmother had said. Then the memories would either go backward, and she'd see and feel the pain of her father waving goodbye and the loss of her Mum, or it would go forward, and she'd remember the agony of her arrival here at Willington. If the memories went forward, the pain was almost unbearable. That's the curse of having a genius memory; you can't forget even when you want to, and time never heals or lessens them. The emotion was as strong remembering it now as the day she experienced it. She felt abused again and again each time.

Just before they all met up on Rachel's bed tonight, Key went to take a shower. She sank down and just let the water rain down on her while she wrapped her arms around her stomach and cried in silent, hard sobs.

Drama Queen Replies

A huge manilla envelope with Erin's name on it was on the kitchen table. The return address read, 'Drama Queen, Willington Boarding School.' "She replied!" Erin picked up the phone immediately to call Maggie, "Drama Queen replied!"

"Seriously? Already? So, what did she say?" Maggie asked.

"I haven't opened it yet. Don't you want to be here when I do?"

"Yes! I'm going to get out of my uniform and be right over."

They hung up, and Erin ran upstairs to get changed as well.

Erin and Maggie couldn't believe the Drama Queen agreed and sent so much to get them started.

"I'll need to ask Ms. Baxter for that article Dana handed in as her assignment. I'll need to make copies of it and send it to the papers with a copy of the letter from the Drama Queen." Erin was looking through all the papers carefully. "I'll also need to contact all the teachers to see how they can get involved."

"We should write a letter and put one in each teacher's mailbox right away," Maggie suggested. "We should also plan this for Spring. There is so much to do to get it right, and I don't want to let the Drama Queen down."

"Let's get the message written and see if we can email it to them tonight. Then we need to read the play and take notes on the characters we'll need." Erin put the papers down and smiled at Maggie. "I can't believe this!"

Dear Saint Marks Teachers,

We need your help. The Drama Club has received an amazing gift from a writer in Britain, but it is a large project. We suspect it could garner attention from the press, so it needs the entire school to get involved. With everyone's help, we are sure to make the gift-giver proud.

I have attached an article describing the play written by a student at Willington Boarding School in Britain. It received so much praise from their local newspapers that their original shows sold out, causing them to add more. It further tickled the interest of many theater companies who requested the same as we did but were not granted the same gift.

Until now, the author has rejected all offers. However, my letter to the author and her response are attached to the article.

Please consider adjusting your lessons to help get your classes involved in making this a great event. We're sure we don't need to express the importance of saving the arts at Saint Mark's.

Thank you in advance for your consideration,

Erin Yule and Maggie Kelleher

"How are we going to attach them?" Maggie asked.

"I found the article online, so that'll be easy. I guess I could ask my dad to take a picture of the letters with his phone and email them to me to attach."

"Do you think Mr. Patch will be angry we did this?"

"I didn't even think of that, but he only oversees the club. We, the students, should be able to fight for its survival," Erin replied.

The girls worked all weekend on a plan. They read the play, listed the characters, and made plans to call Holy Angels school for younger characters. Willington has students of all ages, but Erin and

Maggie decided that older students could do many of those characters. A few would need to be younger, though.

Erin opened her laptop to type another letter to Drama Queen when she noticed she had new emails. At first glance, they looked like spam, but they all had "Drama Queen 2 Drama Queen" in the subject line.

Dear Erin,

I noticed you included your email address on the back of your letter. I hope it allows the pictures I have attached to come through. I thought they might be helpful when considering costume design.

I also made notes of what the seamstresses had to do for some to make them work.

My original letter did not clarify, but I have entrusted you with the packet I sent and wish it not to be sold or passed on to others. If my trust proves righteous, we can speak again for future shows.

Sincerely,

Drama Queen

"Look at these, Maggie. She sent us pictures from their production."

Maggie and Erin celebrated as they felt their show succeeding with the help of their beloved drama queen.

On Monday, Mr. Patch was not upset, but he wanted the packet that had been sent to Erin.

"I'm sorry, sir. I can't." Erin replied when he insisted, saying he would need it to put the show on. Erin opened her laptop and showed him the email. "If I give you the packet, then I will lose her trust, and I'm not willing to do that. I can share what needs to be with those who help, but I must keep the packet in my possession at all times. I promised."

"Then how am I supposed to direct this?" Mr. Patch asked.

"I guess Maggie and I will be. Isn't teaching us what you know about directing just as important?"

"I thought you wanted to be in it?" Mr. Patch asked.

"We do! And I feel we should be permitted to choose our parts at least for this first one." Erin said with a sly smile. "And we wouldn't be the first actors to direct as well."

"Okay, I'll help in any way I can," Mr. Patch responded, returning the smile.

"Great! You can start by talking it up in the teacher's lounge. We haven't heard back from any of them yet."

Mr. Patch did as she asked, but the New York Times did the rest. It would seem the Drama Queen's note to the journalist in Britain did as she had hoped. It reached across the pond to America. The story was such a hit that even nightly news programs were reporting on the mystery writer and the story they wouldn't share – until now.

The attention fired up the school's administration to get involved and make formal requests to the teachers to help out. They explained that calls were already coming in requesting tickets. That forced them to set a formal date of Friday, May 14th, for the first show, with another on Saturday and a matinee on Sunday.

The computer teacher immediately had her class design tickets to be mailed out, as well as posters and flyers. The teacher agreed that once the show was cast, they would start designing the program.

The Home Economics teacher worked with Erin on getting the costume designs. The Art teacher, with a few of the advanced Math teachers, worked with Maggie on set design. The Music teacher changed his lessons to accommodate, and even the English teachers got involved volunteering their time to help students learn their lines.

Erin allowed Mr. Patch to read the play while they set up times for casting calls. Erin and Maggie approached a few people they were afraid would not audition but knew they fit specific parts. A few linebackers on the football team would be perfect for the tough guys needed. "Denise Richards would be perfect for the frail character, but she's very quiet and has only a few friends. It would take some convincing her."

"Everything is really coming together quickly," Erin told Maggie. "We'll be able to start rehearsals next week."

"Even Denise is onboard and willing to do it," Maggie replied. "Honestly, I think she liked the attention we gave her."

"I agree. Maybe this experience will help build some confidence in her. Okay, now we need to schedule rehearsals for the various groups. We need to work around the athletic schedule, or we'll lose a few of our main characters."

"Maybe we could get Denise involved in helping us, like an assistant. I'm just saying—"

"I agree. The more we get her involved, the more confidence we'll help her build," Erin replied.

"Erin!" Jon called from downstairs.

"Yeah, Da?" Erin called back. She and Maggie appeared at the top of the stairs, looking down at him.

"Care to go for a walk? It's so nice out, but Martha's not interested."

"Actually, could we drive first and then walk the beach?" She asked with an awry smile.

"I guess we could do that." Jon smiled as he grabbed his keys.

After getting there, Erin noticed the note was missing, and the place looked cleaner. They immediately made their way down the steep hill to the beach.

"Someone's been here! There's a stick in the door." Erin was devastated she couldn't get back in.

"Then we should get back to the car and off the property before we get caught." Jon turned toward the hill and the girls followed, but Erin kept looking back at the window up above.

Alexandra's Room

Key got a taxi to visit Uncle Bobby. When she knocked on the front door, her eyes widened when her grandmother, Izzy, opened it.

"Kathleen?"

"It's Key. Can I come in?" Key asked.

The old woman stepped backward to let her pass.

They stood still in the foyer, not saying anything. Finally, Key broke the silence. "Do you still have any of my mother's things?"

"Her room hasn't changed."

"May I see it?"

Izzy led the way up the stairs and down the hall to Alexandra's old room. It was beautiful. It had a canopy bed, soft, blue-painted furniture with white knobs, and beautiful blue and white flowery curtains.

Key started to open drawers to find most of them empty. *It truly looks like it hasn't changed in years waiting for its owner to return. The tapestries may be yellowing, but the room is dust-free and obviously cleaned regularly.*

"You should look in her closet," Izzy said, pointing to the shutter doors.

Key opened the doors and saw boxes that were left behind on the floor.

"Let me help you." Izzy grabbed a box and put it out on the bed. She took off the lid, reached inside, and pulled out a notebook, handing it over to Key.

Key recognized her mother's handwriting immediately.

"I've read every one of my daughter's stories. It seems you aren't the first writer in the family." Izzy pulled out another and started turning the pages. "She made up stories about everything."

Key sat on the bed and looked at Izzy. "Why did you hate her so much?"

"Hate her? She was my daughter!"

"She believed that you hated her," Key repeated.

"No, she did not! That's a horrible thing to say."

"I have her diaries," Key said softly.

"No. No, she didn't really believe that. She couldn't have really believed that." Izzy started breathing heavily.

Key tried to keep her voice steady and soft, but she could feel her pulse quickening. "You punished her by locking her away in her room a lot. You hated the man she loved and…" Key had to take a deep breath. "You were going to force her to have an abortion."

Izzy met her eye-to-eye.

But it was Key who continued, "You tried to kill Erin and me." Key would swear she saw Izzy's eyes water before her grandmother looked down again at the notebook she was holding.

"Not because I hated her, because I loved her." Izzy shook her head and sniffled.

"Her diary said before my Da asked to marry her, that even if she had the baby, you would have 'sent it off.' Would Erin and I have both ended up at Willington?"

Izzy wiped her eyes, stood up, and turned to leave saying, "You can take what you want," before she disappeared out the door.

Key was left shaking a little. *I'm going to break her,* she thought. *She can't pretend she didn't know the pain she caused.*

Half a minute passed, and Uncle Bobby came in asking, "What did you say to her?"

"The truth," Key replied as she put the notebooks back in the box and returned its lid.

"Can't you two just be civil? She's trying."

"I remember everything-" Key started to say.

"I know, but…"

"No, Uncle Bobby, you don't. I remember everything I see and hear. Everything. Time does nothing, the memories don't fade, and my pain never gets better. The hurt never lessens." Key took a long, deep breath. "Knowing why I was hurt helps. It can help me make peace with it."

"Why did that ability skip my generation?" he said, scratching his head. "My mother has the same memory."

"Then she should understand my need for an honest conversation." Key picked up the box to leave. "It doesn't end here."

Bobby laid a hand on her arm. "Key, if you push too hard, she'll lash out. She may even call your father in America."

"Then you should warn her what prison will be like. She took me under false pretenses and had me held against my will. She's looking at a lot of years in a very cramped cell."

His hand slid down off her arm, but Key didn't move. "Grab a box out of the closet and follow me down. Then you can take me for a tour of the house."

He hurried his way to grab a box and they left it down by the front door. Then, he walked her through the various rooms. Bobby showed her where her mother was married, her grandfather's office, and his personal favorite, the basement. He explained that he and Alexandra used to love playing down there amongst all the storage items and boxes. They would make forts and get horribly dirty, frustrating their mother.

As they made their way back to the main floor, they heard clinking sounds in the kitchen. They made their way in and surprised the occupant.

"You're still here?" Isabelle asked.

"Yes. Uncle Bobby gave me a tour. You have a beautiful home," Key answered.

Isabelle nodded before replying, "Thank you."

"Could we join you for tea?" Key asked.

Isabelle let out an uneasy sigh and then proceeded to take out two more teacups and saucers and put them on the table with her own.

Uncle Bobby pulled a chair out for Key, mostly directed at her while she sat, saying, "I do hope we can have a civil, relaxing teatime."

Key smiled in return, but did not make him happy replying, "We're a family who haven't seen each other in many years. We also live over an hour away from one another. So, it's important we use our time wisely and be as productive as we can, every chance we get."

"What are you trying to accomplish exactly? Revenge?" Isabelle shot back.

"No. Understanding. My mother taught me that family is forever. The only love a family should have and know is unconditional love."

Isabelle finally brought over the teapot and filled each cup before placing it back on the stove.

Key continued, "Despite everything, I know my mother loved you both. So, despite everything, I would like to try. But I can't without making peace with what's happened. I need to understand."

"Why can't we just start with a clean slate and let bygones be bygones?" asked Uncle Bobby.

Isabelle perked up and looked at Key expectantly.

Key stopped stirring her tea, placed the spoon on the saucer and replied, "So asks the man who wasn't exiled to a different country, with a man she hardly knew, to save a pregnancy."

Uncle Bobby kept his head up, but his eyes got lazy while Isabelle's demeanor deflated completely into her chair.

"Also says the man who wasn't stripped from his family, thrown away to a boarding school in a strange country and handed over to a pedophile for his personal pleasure. So, no offense, but-"

"I didn't know he was a monster. I swear, I didn't know." Isabelle's head was swaying furiously back and forth.

"I'm glad to know that," Key answered with a song in her voice. "See? We've already made progress! I had assumed the worst, but now understand my mistake."

Isabelle started to nod again, now understanding what Key wanted, as did her son whose head was still down, but nodding in understanding as well.

"I can't stay much longer today, but I plan to keep visiting…unannounced."

America: May 31st

The play was a huge success. Everyone had worked so hard for almost four months that the Principal added a weekend before the original date, just for Saint Marks students and parents at a discounted price. Due to the demand for tickets, they also added two more weekends in May before finally ending it so the senior class could study for their finals.

The photography department took pictures and filmed the event every night, including the additional weekends. They promised to piece together the best performances and create one video masterpiece.

Erin was unaware that her sister, the Drama Queen, had been keeping track through the media.

Dear Drama Queen,

You did it! You saved our Drama Club.

Thanks to your enormous generosity, we can now afford to do Fall, Winter, and Spring shows next year. Of course, we hope our Spring show will be another of your amazing plays. We understand your show this year was just as popular as this last one.

Please find enclosed your original packet as well as pictures of our production of it. I also added copies of our flyers, tickets, and newspaper clippings of the coverage we received. Our Photography classes are putting together a video. I will surely send you a copy as soon as they say it's complete.

We are forever in your debt,

Erin and Maggie –

They didn't have to wait long. Only a week later, she received a reply through email.

Dear Erin and Maggie,

Thank you for the pictures and clippings. My sisters and I are so happy to see that the play was used for a good cause.

I may have written the initial play, but I couldn't have done all the songwriting, music, stage directions and costumes without their aid.

Maybe one of these years, we'll take a holiday and catch your show.

Your friend from across the pond,

Drama Queen

"Wouldn't that be wonderful!" Erin practically screamed after reading it. "And it sounds like she's agreed to send us more of them."

Maggie laughed with excitement too, but then asked, "Have you ever considered asking her about Kathleen? If she's ever heard of her?"

Erin's face immediately became pensive. "Do you think I should?"

"Yes. Why wouldn't you?" Maggie asked.

"I feel there's a reason she hasn't contacted me, but I'm going to ask anyway." Erin sat down at her laptop but was slow to type. "How in the heck do I explain this?"

"Start with the importance of your name. Ya know, how your names are inverted," Maggie said.

Dear Drama Queen,

As I've mentioned before, my name is Erin Kathleen Yule. I only mention it because I have a twin sister whose name is Kathleen Erin Yule. It's a long story, but I believe she is there, in Britain.

I haven't heard from her since I was eight years old and was curious if you have ever heard of her?

Your friend,

Erin

Bad Dream

Sara started to stir. When she rolled over to look at the clock, Key was rushing by her toward the closet, crying and talking in a muffled voice. "Key? Are you okay?"

"Hurry, he's coming," is all Key said before getting into the closet and closing the door.

Jumping up, Sara turned on her small desk lamp and scanned the room. She made her way to the closet and slowly opened the door. "Key? Key, are you okay?" She could see that Key was wrapped up in a tight little ball in the back corner and not budging.

Sara knelt down and touched Key on the shoulder, but she whimpered louder and curled up even tighter.

After sitting back against the wall, confused and unsure, it dawned on her. "Kathleen, the monster is gone." She immediately saw her loosen up a little. "Batman came and saved us and locked the monster out."

Key stopped making any sound, and Sara could see her body become very relaxed. "We need to get back to bed." Sara started to pull on her arm saying, "Kathleen, get up, we're safe. Let's get back to bed."

Key wasn't moving; she was fast asleep, and Sara knew there was no waking her up when she was. Sara hated leaving Key alone, even when she took her 20-minute nap in the middle of the day. Once, when the school did a fire alarm test, Key never came out. Even that didn't wake her – nothing did.

Sara got Key's pillow, slid it under her head, and threw a cover over her, leaving the closet door open before getting back into bed. She was restless though, afraid waking up in the closet – and wondering why – might bother Key and bring back painful memories.

About an hour later, Sara stirred awake again, but this time, she saw Key carefully closing the bedroom door behind her. *Where in the heck is she going this early? Oh my God, is she still sleepwalking?*

Again, she jumped up, pulled her jeans on under her nightdress, stepped into her slippers, and opened the door to see Key closing the door to the entrance of their dorm. She ran to the door, made her way out, and saw Key dressed in all black and taking the stairs to the basement. *Is she sleepwalking again, or am I?*

Sara could hear a door open and close as she made her way to the top of those stairs and realized Key had left the building. She skipped steps to get down to the door and quietly opened it. Key was walking fast down the hill toward the ice rink, so Sara started to run to catch up.

Just as Key opened the back door of the rink, she jerked in surprise at Sara's voice. "Ahhh! Sara?!"

"What are you doing?" Sara asked.

"Nothing. Go back to bed. It's too early for you to be up."

"Not until I know what you're doing."

Key ignored her and went in, hoping the darkness would spook Sara and the door would close behind her, but it didn't. Sara had followed.

Forty-two steps to the locker – Key was counting them out when, to her horror, the lights went on. She spun around to Sara, "Turn them off! Someone may see the light from the school."

This time, it was Sara's turn to ignore Key as she walked by saying, "You can't see the lights within this building from outside.

"Are you sure?"

Sara took a deep breath that made her attitude clear. "Yes, I'm sure. They had a birthday party in here the other night, and only those invited knew about it because the lights don't show outside.

Key sat down in front of her locker and was pulling the skates out when she asked, "They invited you and not me?"

"No. I only knew of it because I overheard them talking on their way to the rink. It was underclassman." Sara watched as Key laced up her skates, which didn't look anything like the rink skates given to the students. "New?"

"Yes, I splurged on some new skates for myself. The used ones I had been using were starting to tear apart."

"How often do you come here to skate?" Sara asked.

"Every morning for almost two hours and every night for at least two hours." Key stood up and made her way to the ice and seemed uneasy stepping on. "I really would prefer the lights be turned off."

"Are you insane? It would be so much harder in the dark."

"But it's how I learned. I'm not used to being able to see the ice." After a short staring contest between the two, "Oh never mind, I'll just close my eyes."

Once her eyes closed, she immediately flowed on the ice like a bird. It's what she did next that caused an audible sound from Sara.

Key had been on one leg, with the other stretched out behind her. She also had one arm stretched out in front when suddenly both arms swung up while her back leg bent up and she managed to catch her skate above her head. She looked like a tulip with a thin stem.

Sara was impressed by it, but that isn't what caused her to gasp. She gasped when Key let go of her skate, allowing her leg to come swinging down and continue until she managed to flip completely over. Key didn't seem to pay any mind to Sara when she started the process over again, but with the opposite leg.

Sara tried to ask her a question, but Key was oblivious with her eyes closed cascading on the ice. So, she sat down and watched her sister flip, twist and do cartwheels between dance moves. *The bruises!* She thought.

Finally, Key stopped to take a drink from the water bottle Sara doesn't remember seeing out there on the wall.

"You shouldn't be doing this alone! You could fall and break your neck, and we wouldn't know for hours."

After taking a few short sips from the bottle, Key just pursed her lips and rolled her eyes.

"I'm serious, Key. This is dangerous stuff you're doing."

"Sara, please let me have this." Key's eyes looked like they were pleading desperately. "This is my time, my safe space. I'm not giving it up, not even for you. And so help me, God if you tattle and have it taken away from me. I...I..."

"I wouldn't," Sara said. "You don't even need to try and think of something horrible that I know you could never do anyway. I'm just saying it's dangerous."

Key took a deep breath, and her entire demeaner relaxed. "Thank you. I understand your concerns, but I need this. It's worth the risks."

"Well, I'm coming in the mornings, and you need to let Rachel or Dannie come at night – at least on the weekends. Otherwise, I may do something rash that you'll need to forgive me for."

"If we tell two friends, they may tell two friends and so on. You know the commercial," Key replied with a hint of anger in her voice.

"But they aren't just friends. They're our sisters. You can trust them, Key."

"I don't want to trust them. I don't want to have to worry about trusting anyone. This is mine, Sara. I just want this to be mine and in the dark."

"I'll make you a blindfold to wear, and you have to – as you say to us all the time – get over the rest."

"Only on the weekends, not the school nights," Key replied sternly. "And before you argue..."

"I won't argue with that. It's settled. One more question though: Why no music? Are you afraid they'll hear it outside? They won't-"

"I was just so afraid of losing this I wasn't willing to take any additional chances. Besides, I would have had to count a lot of steps and directions to make my way up to the booth."

Sara giggled and stood up, "I gotcha." Within a few minutes, Sara had the music playing, so Key closed her eyes again and lost herself in it.

Two hours later, Key finally got off the ice and said they should sneak back into school.

"You should compete. If you tried, you would win the gold in the Olympics."

"Thanks, but I don't scratch the ice for anyone but me," Key replied, walking back to Sara.

"Why do you call it that? 'Scratch the ice' I mean."

Key stopped and looked up at Sara. "My first time at the rink was like a religious experience. The monster had been following me until I came here. This was the first place I found peace, true peace. Then I watched all these skates scratch, dig at, and chip away the ice, which is how I was feeling at the time, like I wanted to tear at something, anything. But then this huge machine…"

"A Zamboni," Sara interrupted.

"Is that what it's called? Ok, anyway…"

"Oh. My. Goodness. I actually know something you don't!" Sara said excitedly.

Key laughed.

Sara continued excitedly to teach Key something, "Some guy named Frank Zamboni invented the first machine that cleaned the ice. That's why they refer to them as a Zamboni."

"Okay, a 'Zamboni' came out," Key said with a nod of appreciation, "and melted it all away like none of it ever happened. It reminded me of what my Mum used to think of God. The way he forgives and lets us start fresh."

Key returned her skates, dawned her shoes once more and showed Sara how she had rigged the doors not to lock her out.

"Did the fact that our dorm is so close to the exit you sneak out of play a part in you not wanting to lose our dorm? You know, bring Dannie and Rachel back and all?"

"It may have played a very small part, but I just really wanted the four of us to stay together. I knew they had suffered as I did and needed a private place to vent, scream, or cry," Key replied.

When they returned to the dorm, Sara laid down for another hour while Key went about her normal morning routine. She ran some laundry, ate a muffin, and then sat down to do some writing. Her email showed new messages, so she decided to get those out of the way first.

"Oh no," Key sat back and stared at her laptop.

"What's wrong," Dannie asked as she came out, rubbing her eyes.

"Erin asked me if I have ever heard of her sister, Kathleen Erin Yule."

Dannie moved more quickly to read the email over Key's shoulder. "What are you going to do?"

"I won't outright lie to my sister. I can't." Key just sat there and couldn't move.

"Then don't. You are brilliant at non-answer answers." Sara said, groggily exiting her room as well.

"I thought you were going to try and get a little more sleep?" Key asked.

"I couldn't, especially after you two started talking." Sara pointed to Key's laptop, saying, "Just give her one of your non-answer answers."

Key sat back up, placed her fingers on the keyboard, and typed,

Dear Erin,

Willington is a prestigious boarding school, and not all who apply are accepted. I have found that those who are not often opt for private tutoring at home. The ability to afford a private education has become just as prestigious as attending a highly regarded school.

I'm sorry I don't have better news for you, but I hope you will hear from your sister in the future.

Your friend,

Drama Queen

"Well done," Sara said after reading it. "Send it."

"I should probably warn Izzy. What if Erin writes to her directly?" Key picked up the phone and dialed.

"Harrington residence."

"Uncle Bobby?"

"Key, I'm so glad you called." His voice lowered a bit, "I hate how we left things the other day."

"My visits will continue to be difficult for both her and me, so please don't let our relationship be affected. It's going to take time," Key replied with a genuine tone.

"I understand, I guess. So how can I help you?" He asked.

"Remember when I asked you to make me a promise not to contact my stepfather?"

"Yes, and I haven't. I understand why now."

"Thank you, but I have an issue that has come up, and I need you and Iz…your mother to understand what to do."

"What issue?"

"My sister, Erin. She may write to you or your mother asking about me. I need you to promise you won't answer it before letting me know."

"Wait, why would she be asking? Doesn't she think you're deceased?"

"Good question. I've been emailing with her…"

"So, she does know."

"No, sorry, she doesn't know it's me she is communicating with. It's a long story, but I promise I'll explain it on my next visit. However, her email did make it sound like she believed I was alive. She asked if I had ever heard of, well, myself. Will you promise Uncle Bobby not to let her know of me?"

"Of course, I would be too afraid to reply something stupid."

"And you will tell your mother? Remind her that it would be in her best interest not to reply. She could face jail time for what she has done." Key said this to drive home the point.

"I will indeed."

"Thank you. I have to go, but I'm sure I'll see you soon. Love," Key said.

"Goodbye, love you too," he answered.

Key looked back at the email on her laptop and hit send.

Returning To America

Key and Sara wanted to continue their visits to America every July, but neither Rachel nor Dannie were interested in going back. Although Key referred to them as her sisters, they considered Key their mom and, like most kids, looked forward to some 'free' time.

When Key, Sara, and Ms. Brookes arrived, Key did the same as the last visit. She went to her mother's grave first and left flowers. Then to the house, which they found livable now, not terribly pretty, but still somewhat easy to rest eyes on. So, they were able to cancel the hotel and move in after shopping for bed linens.

Next, she stalked her father and Erin until she felt certain they were doing well. Unbeknownst to Ms. Brookes, Key had hired a private investigator to keep tabs on them while she was in Europe. He wasn't able to find her Batman, 'Mike.' He needed more information, so he agreed to be at McGlynn's restaurant on July 2nd upon Key's request.

Ms. Brookes finally met Frank and Dee, who had been in constant contact with Key all year about the house. She was a bit 'put off' by the tattoos they had but liked them both once she gave them a chance. Even Frank had lightened up a bit. Having Ms. Brookes there also made it possible for Key to enter the small cottage Frank and Dee were living in. They had cleaned it up very nicely.

"It looks so fresh and clean," Key said.

"Yeah, but I liked the natural wood trim throughout. I couldn't bring myself to put paint over those," Frank replied.

"I'm so glad. They add character to the rooms. Does the plumbing and electric work throughout as well?"

"Yeah. When they were coming to do the main house, Dee scheduled them to start here since we were trying to live here." Frank said it strangely, as if he was admitting to a crime.

"Dee is very smart and has been a great asset to me. You're a lucky man, Frank." Key gave a smile and a wink, letting him know they hadn't done anything wrong. Key thought, *Dee didn't do anything without letting me know first, but obviously isn't sharing that with him.*

The main house now had a badge system to get in. The badges were only one inch high and two inches wide. They showed the owner's image and then a bar code. There was a real key as a backup, but the lock was well hidden. The system to make the badges was inside, which Sara wanted to learn immediately. The main system was down in a room under the barn, which was just past Dee and Frank's cottage. Key had actually created the system herself and Dee helped to find contractors that would install it. The larger computer system that was wired throughout the house that Key wanted was very complex, so she was eager to get it configured while they were there.

The building of the ice rink had only just begun, so she would have to wait at least another year before she could use it. Although now that Key had a much larger house to work with, she hoped not to miss the ice as much. She had grand plans for that large empty space past the kitchen. She was going to recreate Hobb Street. It would have a hotel down most of the back side, so its windows would look out to the water. Across from the hotel will be a music store, candy shop and part country store as well as a café. The cobble 'road' will end at the Blacksmith shop. She could see the whole recreated street clearly in her head.

"I swear your house looks taller," Sara mentioned.

"Only the long room attached to the kitchen. I wanted it to be two floors like the rest of the house." Key replied as she led Sara through the kitchen to go look at it.

What Key called a long room; Sara had described as an empty warehouse after their first visit. However, it wasn't empty anymore. There were open walls dividing the space into numerous sections on both the left and the right. And each of those rooms had a room above it. There were wires and pipes, and Sara couldn't make sense of any of it.

"On the left will be a hotel with six guest rooms. On the right, we'll have some stores, but above them, you will also have a sewing room and photography lab. The last one will be my computer lab." Key watched as Sara stared at its current progress with a crooked brow.

"And it is going to look like we walked outside?" Sara asked.

"Yes, it'll have a cobblestone street running down the middle with what will look like old gas street lamps. The ceiling will also have a lighting system with three settings: night, dawn, and day."

"What will be in the stores?"

"The candy and clothing store will be where we can hang and store our off-season clothes. I plan to design it like an old country store with candy in glass jars on the counter. We can also buy some sweats, shorts, and T-shirts for guests who come unprepared but want to stay over. The music store is where we'll store all of our instruments, and I figured we'd build a small recording booth. The last is the café and it'll be only half a building with an outside sitting area with trees and an umbrellaed table."

"Is that what Hobb Street looked like? I've been on Hobb Street–"

"No. That was my original plan, but the next store was a furniture store, so I added the clothing store instead and I'm doing a café that isn't completely enclosed."

"Well, I'm excited to see it done, but we need to get you ready if we're going out today." Sara turned back into the kitchen and disappeared.

Key hated wearing costumes to hide her identity. She had bought a better wig and colored contacts for her eyes. They looked so much more realistic. She hated wearing makeup too and usually didn't, but Sara loved doing it, so she convinced Key it was necessary.

"A little extra shading here and there can change the entire look of your face," Sara had told her.

The disguise worked well. A few days after Batman's birthday, they were outside of a café and found themselves at a table next to Mike and his friends, Jeff, Jessica, and Ray.

Jessica was teasing Jeff after the fifth girl stopped to flirt with him. "So, Jeffrey, is there any girl here besides me that you haven't claimed to sleep with?" Jessica looked at him expectantly with pursed lips, waiting for an honest tally.

Mike rolled his eyes. "Yeah, let's hear it, Romeo."

"It's not just sex. I made love to all of them," he answered with theatrical flair.

"You try to have babies with all of them?" Key blurted out in surprise, causing their entire table to look at her oddly.

"No!" Jeff said, "Where'd you come up with that?"

Sara shook her head and put her hand up to Jeff, while addressing Key. "I think he's just using the fancy name, but he means he shares himself with them all."

"Fancy name?" Jeff asked, intrigued.

Sara looked at him with amusement. "Key believes 'making love' is just a fancy name for sex. That it should only refer to making babies—you know, what's making love if not something to actually love."

Jeff refocused his attention on Key. "Sex is sex. Making love is romantic. I believe—at least when I'm with them—that I truly love them."

"I believe you do, but like you said, 'sex is sex.'" Key responded, shaking her head. "Sex is a dirty but necessary animal instinct that society has tried to dignify. It's like going to the loo."

Now Jeff became more than a little intrigued, and he leaned toward Key, placing one elbow on their table and putting his chin in his hand to give her his full attention.

"You wish me to elaborate?" she asked, turning her head toward him.

"Please!" Jeff said with wide eyes.

"Once upon a time, the cavemen used to squat to do their business anywhere they pleased, and it stank where they left it. Eventually, as society grew, they tried to dignify the act by digging holes and building privacy around it. They invented indoor plumbing, then toilets and even flowery sprays to hide the odor. But I don't care if your lavatory is lined with diamonds and your toilet made of gold, you are still squatting to do your business, and it still stinks."

"Sex is no different. Again, society tried to dignify it with privacy and rules, like only after marriage, only between a man and a woman, and so on. But there again, in the end, sex is still a dirty little animal instinct. That's why brothels never go out of business and children get molested."

Michael was stunned at the last remark. "You can't be serious."

"Don't get me wrong. I like what society tried to do. I believe it should be between adults who love one another and all that. God intended it for reproduction, which is why it's necessary. I simply recognize it in its purest form."

"And you don't like the fancy names?" Michael asked before he thought to himself, *why would seeing it in its 'purest form' be so important?*

"No, I don't. I prefer the truth. I call it *sex, playing,* or—if you need to be more romantic about it—then you could call it *sharing yourself.*"

"But not *making love?*" Michael knew there was more behind it but wasn't sure how to ask.

"Correct, unless you are trying for a baby. Just a personal choice." Key said in a concluding tone.

Jeff was curious now too, but not as discreet as Michael. "When was the last time you *shared yourself?*"

Key's mouth gaped open a bit, and her face turned red.

Sara, seeing the panic in her eyes, spoke up. "That's a very rude question to ask of a lady. New subject!"

Jeff felt bad at seeing how uncomfortable Key became and moved back, sitting up. "I'm sorry, you're right."

Jessica had to interject though, "It doesn't matter what you call it, he's all talk. None of them have slept with this fool."

Mike led the laughter while punching Jeff in the arm, but they all joined in.

When the laughter died down, Mike took over the conversation. "So, your name is Key, but what's yours?" pointing at Sara.

"I'm Sara."

"Where are you from?" he asked.

"Well, I'm from England, but…"

Key cut her off saying, "We both are." Key gave Sara a cold stare.

"So, what brings you to Springfield, Main?" Jeff interjected.

"Looking in on some distant relatives," Key answered.

"How long are you staying?" Mike asked, looking only at Key.

"A few weeks." She replied.

"Where are you staying?" Mike placed another question.

"We're renting a house close by." Key started to get nervous and wanted to change the subject. Sara picked up on it and introduced a different topic.

"Where do you all go to school?" Sara asked.

"St. Marks High School. We're seniors. How old are you?" Mike asked.

"We're 15," both Key and Sara answered in unison.

"Soooo, going into the 10th grade then?" Jeff asked.

Key gave Sara another cold stare before Sara responded simply, "Yes."

Mike looked at Ms. Brookes, "And you are? Their Mom?"

"Oh no, I'm their headmistress. They can't travel alone." As she finished, she felt Key's cold stare on her now.

"Wait…" Mike started.

"We're throwaways," Key said bluntly. "Our families in England left us at the boarding school until graduation. That's what wealthy families do there when they don't want to raise their own. But we were looking into our family connections and found that we had some distant relatives here that we came to find."

"Did you find them? Maybe we could help." Jessica offered.

"Oh no, thanks anyway," Key said quickly.

Ms. Brookes spoke up. "We actually found their family members, but they weren't interested in reconnecting, so we're just enjoying a wonderful holiday here in Maine." Ms. Brookes looked at Key and received a smile of appreciation.

"Well, we're going over to the arcade if you wanna join us," Mike said.

Sara responded, "We'd love to!" After a quick glance at Key she asked, "But what's an arcade?"

They all giggled while getting up and throwing their trash out.

Mike took a special interest in Key and hurried to walk next to her. "So, what does Key stand for?"

"My name."

"But is it a nickname? Like your initials or something?"

Key didn't want to lie to him. She was never very good at lying, so she twisted it back at him. "What would make you think that?"

"I knew a girl with those initials once. She was short and petite like you but had blonde hair and blue eyes."

Key never looked up at him while she walked, "You no longer know her? You said, 'used to'."

"She died of pneumonia when she was eight years old."

Key played along, "Died?"

"Yeah, but she has a twin sister, Erin, who thinks she's still alive."

"Why? I mean, what makes her think that?"

Mike sort of shook his head and shrugged his shoulders. "She says she can feel her."

"Feel her?" Key said with an odd look on her face.

"I know, sounds crazy, right? If I could get to Europe, I would probably be the first to visit her grave. She didn't really know anyone else in England."

Key thought to herself while Mike and the others spread out to play the various arcade games. *Can I take the chance to tell him? I still have three years left before I turn 18, and if Da finds out, I could be in for a horrible legal battle. Would he try to force me to come back? Maybe he wouldn't. Maybe he'd understand.*

"Key? Are you okay?" Ms. Brookes' voice broke in.

"Yes." She replied.

"Are you thinking it over? Reconsidering your decision not to say anything?"

Key looked at her in awe. "Wow, it's like you were reading my thoughts."

"I just appreciate the situation, I guess. It's what I was thinking because I'm also in a difficult situation."

"How so?" Key asked.

Ms. Brookes twisted and coaxed Key outside, "If the school's board knew what I knew, they would have wanted me to contact your father. It won't bode well for me if they find out I didn't."

"I never thought of that. I'm sorry. That's why I was so careful not to give anything away about him in the book. I was afraid they would try to find and contact him."

Ms. Brookes just smiled.

"They could still figure it out. I've gone over numerous ways they could track him down and am incredibly surprised none of the media have bothered yet," Key said, reasoning her own thoughts.

"Agreed. I'm wondering if they think it's in their best interest to keep you in England. Maybe they believe the longer it goes on, the bigger the story for them later. Is that crazy?"

Key smiled with a wondering look. Finally, she asked Ms. Brookes, "Do you think he would force me to come back and live here before I was 18?"

After a brief sigh, Ms. Brookes answered, "I keep wondering the same thing, but I'm not sure. I don't know him."

"I know. I'm his daughter, but I'm afraid I don't know him well enough either. He was much closer to Erin when we were young." Just then, Key saw Erin. She was heading to the arcade. "Oh no."

"What's wrong?" Ms. Brookes turned to see what Key was looking at. "Oh."

"She's my sister, she might recognize my voice, and I can't change it now. Mike and the others have already heard me."

"I'll go in and get Sara, make up some excuse, and we'll get out of here. Walk over there to the bench, and we'll come get you." Ms. Brookes immediately took off to find Sara while Key turned her back to Erin's direction and started slowly walking toward the bench.

Finding Peace

On this visit, Uncle Bobby answered the door. "Hello sweetheart. Sorry, but I was just heading out."

That's okay, is Izzy home? Key asked.

"Izzy? Key, you really shouldn't disrespect your grand–"

"She has to earn it. She's not 'grandma' until she does."

"Fair enough," came a familiar voice behind him. "Although I can't imagine I could possibly do enough to please you." Izzy walked up and gave Robert a peck on his cheek. "Have a good day, dear."

When Izzy shut the door behind him, Key commented, "I think you'll be surprised to learn just how little it would take." They were caught in a cold stare. "Sooo, am I invited to stay?

Izzy turned toward the kitchen. "I'm going to make some tea."

She found Izzy laying out two cups with matching saucers on the table. She turned to look at Key. "Well, go ahead and sit down. Let the hate-fest begin."

"I don't hate. I get angry, disappointed, and from you, hurt, but I try not to hate anyone." Key said while she took a seat.

"You also feel a need for vengeance, though, correct?"

"You mean my book, The Throwaways? Yes, I guess I did. I was angry at the lack of control I seemed to have over my own life."

"But you don't have to apologize when you lash out, I suppose." Izzy's voice with indignation.

Key's eyes were a blur. *I'm no better than her. I purposely hurt her, and I've gotten joy out of–*

Izzy's voice cut off the thought by asking, "Even if I said sorry, would you believe me? Would it just make everything better?" Izzy continued.

"

Key focused again, "No. Just hearing sorry wouldn't be enough. Understanding why you did it, though, would help. Knowing "why" is the only way I've ever been able to make peace with things."

"You said you made peace with what that monster did to you. Did he explain why?"

"No, he didn't. I had to do a lot of research on pedophiles to understand the sickness. Only through that did I find peace with it.

"You have forgiven him?" Izzy asked.

"I'm not quite there yet. I can't forget, and time doesn't fade the memories because I can't forget. So, forgiveness comes slowly for me. But I can't even pray to get that far until I make some level of peace with what happened. Don't you find the same?"

Izzy poured the hot tea into their cups and sat down at the table. "I never thought of it like that. I guess I never concentrated on trying to make peace with it first."

"You drowned in the anger instead, didn't you." Key said it more as a statement than a question.

Izzy sat back, slowly sipping her tea. Now, her eyes had gone into a blur, although she still said what she was thinking aloud: "I wouldn't even know how to make peace with my life."

Key prompted her, "I suggest start with the earliest one that you can't let go of."

"Oh my, we'd have to go back to when I was just a wee girl. Cindy Morgan. She was so mean to me. There was no reason for it, but I was smaller, so I was an easy target."

"How old were you?"

"Seven."

Key smiled a little but wiped the smirk off her face when she thought, *I shouldn't mock her.* "Okay, well, it's too late to confront her about it. Unless you know where she is now."

"I do. She died a few years after high school."

"Okay, then you must do all the work yourself like I did for the monster. You have to think of all the reasons she may have treated you badly. Keep in mind that kids are impressionable and can be influenced by everything in their environment, including the people in it. Maybe her parents…"

"Her parents? They weren't around enough to influence her." Izzy snarked.

Key put her hands up and sat back in a dramatic fashion. "Oh my God, do I have to spell it out for you? She was lashing out because…"

"She wanted attention from her parents." Izzy finished the sentence.

"Probably. Of course, forgiveness comes later, but can you even see peace in the future about it?"

"I think I already feel the peace in it. I get it now. I should forgive her too. We were so young, and all kids do stupid things."

Key smiled at her. "Then let me begin by saying I'm sorry for letting my anger control me. Nothing you did is an excuse for my own bad behavior."

Izzy scoffed, "You know you don't have to make any apologies…"

"Owning my behavior is a huge part of making peace with the actions of others. So yes actually, I do."

"You make it sound like it's so easy." Izzy put her cup down on the table.

"It's not. I'm angry, Izzy. Just because I apologized for my behavior doesn't mean I forgive you for yours. So far, I have nothing to go on to help me make peace with any of the hurtful things you've done."

"Why do you need to make peace with my actions?"

"BECAUSE LIKE YOU, I CAN'T FORGET!" Key's rage surprised them both, causing Izzy to jump in her seat a bit. Key's eyes filled with tears. "You hurt my MOTHER! You hurt ME. You hurt my SISTER!" She had tears running down her face, her cheeks were red hot, and she was shaking all over as she continued, "I can't understand how you can hurt so many and care nothing about it!"

Izzy stood up in a shot and, in a flash, was outside the back door, walking across the yard toward the trees with her back to the house.

You aren't getting off that easy, Key thought as she jumped up and followed her out. "Why won't you help me find peace? Do you really hate me that much? Do I not deserve…" Key couldn't go on, she was sobbing. She just stood there and watched as Isabelle kept walking farther out in the yard, never looking back.

Key sat back, getting a hold of herself and waited for 20 minutes before Izzy finally came in the back door. *I probably should have taken a nap before I came. Not sure I have the strength for this.*

"You're still here?" Izzy asked when she entered the kitchen,

"I can't leave without feeling like I understand something about you." So, Key asked her earlier question in another way. "You have a reputation for being angry. Why? What are you so angry about?"

Izzy sat again and stared at her teacup for so long that Key wasn't sure she was going to answer. *Is this her version of the silent treatment?*

Finally, Izzy spoke without looking up. "I used to live in an almost constant state of anger. My past would haunt me."

"Why did you take it out on those who loved you?" Key asked.

"Every torturing day I lived under my father's rule would haunt my memory. My anger would be so overwhelming I had to release it somehow. Lashing out at those in my presence was the only way to deflect from the memory."

"How's that worked for you?" Key asked with a hint of sarcasm.

"Allowing my past to destroy…" Izzy stopped, and Key could see a teardrop on the table.

They sat there in silence for a while before Izzy spoke again. "Bobby has given me another way to let it out."

"How's that?" Key asked.

"He gave me an oversized pillow with a circle on it. When the memories overtake me, he said to imagine the face of my father, or whoever I'm angry at, and punch it as hard and as much as I can."

Key smiled. "How many times have you seen my face in that circle?"

Izzy finally raised her head and looked at her granddaughter. "Only once."

After Key gave a surprised expression, Izzy added, "So far."

Later, Key walked into the dorm while Sara was working on her photos. She stopped and asked, 'How did your visit go today?"

"Remember the day we returned from the hospital?" Key asked.

"Yes."

"I created that dummy of the monster because I felt the need to beat the hell out of something." Key dropped her bag and sat, slumped in a chair. "I should have stolen some of her clothes to build another one."

"I'm A Ted"

Saint Marks was buzzing with news that a horrible incident happened off school property over the weekend. Two students had attacked a third. The boy who was attacked was someone Erin and Maggie knew well. His name was Ted, and he was a competitor with them for the top grades. Ted was quiet and was often seen talking to himself, but both Erin and Maggie were always kind, and the three of them would often compare test scores in class.

Saint Mark's had five levels of competency for each subject. They grouped kids with similar competencies and called them 'Phases.' Out of the 5 phases, the 5th represented the most accomplished students, while the lowest phase represented a student's struggle with that particular subject. Most kids had a combination of phases in their schedule. They could be a phase 5 English student and a phase 3 in Math. However, Erin, Maggie, and Ted were in phase 5 in all subjects.

The student body was in shock to hear of the attack. They beat him unconscious at a park in their neighborhood and then left him for dead. Ted didn't remember what happened when he could finally speak to the police at the hospital. Fortunately, a few of the neighbors reported seeing a car and two teens they recognized leaving the otherwise empty park at the time.

Erin and the other cheerleaders were sitting around talking about it after practice on Monday. Maggie approached them and sat down next to Erin. "We're a perfect example of why this doesn't need to happen."

"What do you mean?" Erin asked, surprised.

Maggie seemed to have everyone's attention. "Back when we met, I was the 'Ted' of our class. I was the one everyone called different and weird. Other students never had anything nice to say to or about me, but you refused to be one of them."

Erin got a smirk on her face that only Maggie understood when she said, "You were my first and oldest friend."

"Wait, you were a 'Ted'? I find that hard to believe. You're beautiful and stylish and not weird at all, but Ted…" Dana spoke up.

"But I was before I befriended Erin. She's the reason I wear my hair this way and she does most of my shopping as well." Maggie laughed as she continued, and it seemed contagious to everyone. "She's the fashionista, not me." When the giggles died down, Maggie continued, "Ted obviously never had a friend that was willing to believe in him like that." She took on a more serious tone, "All I'm saying is we have a story to tell that may help students look at others differently. Maybe we could save the next 'Ted'."

"I'm in. I'm not sure what I'm agreeing to, but I know you have a plan, and I'm in," Erin said instantly. Then, with a big, expectant smile, she asked, "So, what exactly did I just agree to?"

"Well, Principal Thompson said he is planning to have the entire school attend an assembly tomorrow about bullying. I thought we could put a presentation together showing me as my former 'Ted' and what you've done for me."

Dana spoke up again, "Wow, are you sure? I mean, I've got your back either way, but are you sure you want anyone to know you used to be a 'Ted'?"

Another cheerleader, Renee, spoke up this time to answer her before Maggie could. "I hope you do because I think it would be a powerful message. I have to admit, when I first met Erin in elementary school, I thought you were, well, a bit weird. When I said something to Erin, she dismissed my comments and told me it was what she loved the most about you."

"Same here," said Molly. "It made me want to be different."

"Maybe all of you should help with the presentation then. I know I'm new to Saint Marks, but as I said, I never would have guessed it about Maggie," Dana said.

Erin gave Maggie a more serious look, "You remind me of my Mum. While I would have been satisfied with us just talking about it, she would have wanted to do more." Erin smiled to all the girls in the circle, "I remember when we were just wee bits, my Mum would take us to the library for storytime. One day, we showed up to find out they had canceled it. While other mothers were complaining, my Mum picked out a book, sat in the open space, and read it aloud. All the kids that had come for story time surrounded her and listened. The librarians immediately asked if my mother could do it every week, and they would give her the same reading room they had been using. It turned out that their volunteer couldn't come anymore."

With an approving smile, Erin continued, "So, I'm glad we're doing more than just talking or complaining about it, too. That's exactly what Mum would have done."

The next day, the students were called to the theater, and after they took their seats, the lights dimmed, causing them to quiet down. Suddenly, a huge picture of Maggie as a 7-year-old appeared on the screen, up on stage. After quite a bit of laughter, they heard her voice.

"I was a 'Ted'." Maggie suddenly appeared from stage left and walked out with a microphone. The laughter stopped abruptly. "I used to be the weird kid, the one everyone saw as 'different.' So why haven't I suffered the same fate?" She took a dramatic pause. "Because I made a friend that made all the difference."

A new picture appeared of Maggie and Erin at age eight. Maggie was still a bit disheveled looking, while Erin looked pristine. Erin emerged from the opposite side of the stage. "I had been homeschooled up until I started at Holy Angels School at the age of eight. All the kids there had known each other for years, and none of them knew me, but one reached out. Maggie was the only one to welcome me to the school and befriended me the first day." The pictures on the screen slowly scrolled through Maggie's transformation over the years as they continued to talk.

Maggie continued, "I never expected the friendship to last, though. I had friends before, but never for long. The other students would make fun of them for being my friend, causing them to join the majority in hating me. Peer pressure can be tough." Maggie took a few more steps toward the middle of the stage.

Erin mirrored her steps toward the middle as well. "They tried that with me, telling me she was weird, but I had already realized that her differences made me better. While I was consumed with superficial things like hairstyles and clothing design, Maggie challenged me to work harder in school. Because of her, I haven't taken my education for granted. And yes, I still love doing my hair and love fashion, but she introduced me to helping out at the food bank and singing for the elderly."

Maggie and Erin both took a few more steps toward the middle, "Erin became well-liked and very popular because she was so pretty and considered 'normal,' but rather than throw me aside like the others, she brought me along. She defended me and dismissed the comments the others would make."

A new voice came from the same side as Maggie walked out. It was Renee. "The first time I saw Maggie, I was judgmental and not realizing she and Erin were close. I said as much to Erin."

Now, a voice came from Erin's side of the stage. It was Molly who continued Renee's thought. "I did the same, but Erin just dismissed my comments. She said 'normal' people bored her."

Renee continued the thought again, "Because they offer her nothing. People who are different, though, can challenge us, challenge our thinking."

Erin and Maggie took a few more steps until they met in the middle, while the others took the same amount to get closer as well.

"On my first day of third grade, I wore a frilly dress, with frilly socks and shiny shoes that my late mother had made me. I had no idea of current styles and realized I stuck out like a sore thumb. Today, I'm still proud of that frilly dress because of the love my mum put into making it. It still hangs in my closet." Erin also allowed a dramatic pause before finishing with, "I'm a Ted."

"I had no fashion sense and usually looked disheveled and plain. Worse yet, I still would be if Erin didn't constantly nag me. I'm a Ted," Maggie said.

"I have OCD and need things in order and often touch things a particular number of times. It can look weird to others. I'm a Ted," Renee followed.

"I have two Dads and no mother. Father-daughter dances were always an adventure." The student body giggled before Molly ended with a smile and "I'm a Ted."

"I'm a Ted," said the quarterback of their football team, who stepped out from the curtain next to Molly.

"I'm a Ted," said the class president, stepping out from Renee's side.

Students from various athletic teams, the drama club, the chess club, and the list went on, came out calling themselves a 'Ted.'

When the stage was full, Maggie spoke up again. "If you judge and hate someone because you think they're different or weird, then you are a coward. Don't fear us, Teds of the world. Challenge yourself to find out what we may have to offer to your life and what you might have to give back."

Erin took Maggie's hand and reached out to Renee. Everyone on stage followed suit.

The entire student body gave them a standing ovation. Random students also called out, "I'm a Ted!" while others cheered.

After a few minutes, the quarterback stepped up again and waved his hands, motioning to calm them down. "The bookstore has donated notecards for each of us to write a note to Ted Wheeler while he recuperates at home. We're going to pass them down the aisles. Please write something kind and then drop it in the baskets we have at the exits. Principal Thompson will make sure he gets them."

While the students were pulling out their pens and passing the cards, Maggie walked over to the principal. She tried to hand him the microphone, knowing he had planned on giving a speech, but he put his hand up and waved it away. "Nothing I was going to say could top that. Very powerful. Thank you all."

Writing Mike – Visiting Again

"I'm going to let Michael know we're going back," Key said as she sat at her desk typing.

Sara heard a note of excitement in Key's tone and, as usual, grew hopeful. "That sounds like fun. Michael seems nice enough in his emails."

Key stopped and looked at Sara. "You've been reading my emails again?"

"Are you seriously going to lecture me for the hundredth time? I mean, it hasn't worked yet…" Sara said with a wry smile.

Key giggled back at her, "You don't read my books, but you'll go through my personal emails? I seriously don't get it."

"Who says I don't read your books?"

"You've never opened one of them."

"Because I've already snooped and read the first drafts. Although I could barely keep up with this last one. You wrote it so quickly."

"That is because I wanted to hand it in before we returned to America." Key explained.

They arrived in America on July 1, early in the morning, allowing Key to leave flowers on her mother's grave and check to see that her father and his family were doing well.

The next day, she decided to wait and finally catch the rose bearer. Every year, someone at some point had been leaving a red rose stuck in a mound of sand in the middle of the beach. She sat on the couch just inside the glass doors and used the time to work on her next story.

Her laptop slowly powered up, but before she could get started, she sensed some movement on the hill. She immediately jumped up and stood by the glass doors, only peaking a little so as not to be noticed.

She couldn't believe her eyes. It was Mike and he was carefully making his way down, holding onto branches, stepping carefully, trying not to slide down the steeper sections. Once at the bottom, he looked intently at the house, specifically the glass doors.

Key panicked and ran up the stairs to the window where she could use the curtains to better hide herself while she watched. He never looked up, still intently watching the glass doors until he finally stopped, knelt down, stuck the rose in his teeth and built the sand mound. Once it was high enough to hold it, he stuck the rose stem down the middle.

Key watched as he stood up and stared out to the water. *Batman, oh Batman.*

"Watcha looking at?" Sara asked, making her way to the window.

Key caught her arm before she could move the curtains to see. "My Batman," she said in a whisper. "He's the one leaving the rose every year."

Sara was very careful to get behind Key and look over her shoulder through the sliver of the curtain until Mike turned to leave and climb the hill again. "Well, you will see your handsome Batman in a few hours. Did we get him a birthday present?"

Key giggled before saying, "I got him one."

"Aww…only from you?" Sara complained.

"Actually, I was thinking you could give him the Julie Brennan drama that was meant to go with my latest Sienna Carmichael mystery."

"But he likes mysteries."

"Imagine you being the one to make the connection between the two. No one seems to be figuring out that the characters I build in the drama are the same ones I transfer over to the next mystery," Key explained.

"Ooo…okay! That sounds cool." Sara replied with a new excitement. "So, we should get our story straight about how I was reading the drama and you the mystery and, through conversation, realized we were talking about the same people."

"Sounds good to me. The drama is on the shelf, and the gift bags are in the drawer below."

That evening at dinner, Mike had saved the seat next to him for Key.

Key always received the first printed copy of her novels, and knowing Mike had written to her that he was a fan of Sienna Carmichael mysteries, she wrapped it immediately. Upon receiving the gift he was very surprised. "Thank you, Key!

His mother gasped saying, "But how did you get it? It's not due to be released for another week or so."

Key, knowing they might ask, had prepared a cover story. "The only thing I can figure out is that the publisher is based in England. Maybe that's why it's released there first."

"Open mine!" Sara pushed.

"Okay, okay." Mike laughed and pulled it out of the bag and just stared at it looking for the right words. "Wow… a drama…" He said dryly.

"Yes, it is. I know you like mysteries, but I think you'll find a new appreciation for the mystery if you read my book first. Trust me."

Mike gave her a smile, "Well, thank you. It was nice of you to think of me."

Key leaned over as he was putting it under the mystery novel on the table, "You really should trust her." Key then slyly pulled the drama out from under the mystery and put it on top. "Promise me you'll read the drama first, then the mystery."

"Absolutely, I promise," Mike replied, nodding with a smile.

Key seemed to have that effect on him. He could feel the chemistry between them and looked forward to seeing her all year. The one girl he sort of dated since last summer broke up with him because of his incessant talking about Key. The girl also did not appreciate knowing he was constantly writing or calling his "friend" in England.

That same night, as they sat with Mike's friends, eating dinner and taking turns getting up to dance, Key noticed something sticking out of the book she'd just given him.

When she pulled it out to look at it, Mike watched her.

"Oh, that's just my bookmark. It's a picture of an old friend and me on the beach as kids. I keep it in my wallet when it's not keeping my page in a book."

"It's very cute, but that's you?" Key said, pointing at the boy.

Key was desperately trying to pretend she had never seen it before.

"Yeah, I used to let my hair grow long even though my mom hated it. Oh, I think I told you about her once. Her name was Kathleen Erin Yule, so she had the same initials as your name."

"Oh, yes, I remember you mentioning her. Remember, though, you need to put this in the drama, not the mystery first. You promised." Key handed it back to him before hearing Sara stir things up.

"So, who is everyone's favorite superhero?" Then she turned and continued, "Keeee?" Sara smiled.

Key answered with a sarcastic tone and tilted her head to send Sara an evil glare. "Well, I guess it would have to be Wonder Woman as there weren't many other choices for us, were there?"

Jeff started to chuckle as he nudged Mike on the shoulder. "Out of all the superheroes to choose from and all the magnificent things they could do, I forget, Mike, which one did you choose to be OBSESSED with for most of your adolescence?"

Mike just nodded his head a few times in acknowledgment of his teasing while everyone else at the table had a good laugh. Sara cleverly realized they weren't supposed to know the answer, so she piped up to ask, "Anyone care to fill us in on the joke?"

Jeff answered her with a laughing sound of disgust in his voice. "Batman. His favorite was Batman. Who would choose Batman over, say, Superman with the ability to see through women's clothes?" This comment prompted a punch in the arm from their friend Jessica, who was sitting next to him, but the guys at the table grunted in agreement.

"An above-average, intelligent child, maybe?" Key blurted out.

Everyone stared at Key with amused curiosity. "You can't strive to be Superman and suddenly gain impossible powers. But you can strive to be a regular man who overcomes impossible handicaps and still manages to save the day." Key turned slightly toward Michael, and with her best Vanna White impression continued. "All you need to be Batman is grow tall, dark and delicious looking, and own a chick-magnet car—"

Everyone looked at Mike and smiled, knowing he had a black '69 Camaro outside.

After that dramatic pause, Key continued, "And, well, at least one great toy." While she let her eyes wander downward for a second, she finished with, "Although I'm afraid I don't know him well enough to answer that."

While everyone chuckled, understanding her inference perfectly, she sat back, confident that she had defended her hero—the man she now called Michael, not the boy Batman—the best she could.

Mike stared at Key in awe. They had been teasing him about his obsession with Batman since childhood. Yet, it took her only one short argument to render them speechless.

He also enjoyed the slight flirtation. Mike believed any guy who earned her attention should feel lucky. She was intellectually stimulating and yet never spoke over anyone's head. She was beautiful but didn't seem to know it. And she had a fabulous sense of humor when she chose to share it. Although, he noticed, she usually sat back, giving Sara center stage.

Letter From Izzy

Sara brought up the mail so they wouldn't be seen walking down the long drive to the box. She handed it to Key who became excited to see a letter that had been forwarded from Willington.

"It's from my grandmother, Izzy." Key ripped it open immediately.

Dear Kathleen,

I'm not the writer you and my daughter were, so forgive me, but I have been thinking a lot about our conversations and felt compelled to send this letter.

Allow me to begin with the most important. I did not hate my daughter, and I do not hate you.

The weight of my actions is heavy, but I realize now they weighed heavier on you.

I am sorry for sending my daughter off so I could not see her every day. She was the light that filled every room she entered. I saw my actions more as punishing myself — not her. I was the one going without and never thought my absence in her life mattered. She always seemed to be trying to get away from me long before she left.

I resented your father for getting my daughter's last years. He brought her the happiness I could not. However, like you with your book, I still had no excuse for taking my anger and resentment out on any of you. My behavior is mine, as you say, and mine alone.

As for trying to get her to an abortion clinic, I can only say that I am glad she fought me and prevailed. She had two beautiful daughters that she can be proud of, and I know she is watching you from heaven.

I know it is difficult to believe when I say I wanted it out of love for her, but I honestly believed it was for the best, at the time. When you focus, as I did, on how people would look at her, whisper about her and demean her socially, you can understand my motherly instinct to protect her from all of it. I was wrong. I see that now, but I promise you it was only from my cowardice and short-sightedness, not from a lack of love for my daughter.

Admitting to the horrible things I have done does not soften the memories of doing them or bring me any peace. Nevertheless, you seem to think it will help you, so I pray it does.

Sincerely,

Your Grandmother, Isabelle

"I hate that I understand her thinking," Sara said, looking at Key with a blank face.

Key turned her head to see that Sara had been reading along with her. "We shouldn't, but I understand how you feel."

"Are you surprised?"

"I am. Her letter shows that she was actually listening even though she storms off from the conversations," Key replied.

"I assume you'll keep at her then?" Sara asked.

"Of course," Key replied.

"Good, because I think you're helping her as much as the answers are helping you. It's never too late to stop her from hurting someone else."

"I think she's done hurting others. She and Bobby seem to have a special bond," Key replied. "I honestly believe his insistence was more for her than himself. Don't you think? I mean, he always finds a reason to leave her and me alone when I visit."

"I could answer you if I knew them better. Are you ever going to invite me to go with you on the next visit?" Sara asked.

"You're welcome to join me any time, but it's a long drive for a short visit. It takes an hour, and I probably wasn't there much more than five minutes the first time."

"Do you care if I'm there? Please be honest. Will my presence hamper the conversation?

"If you think it is, you could disappear with Uncle Bobby." Key giggled.

"Then it's settled. I want to go at least once. If your visit ends quickly, we can go shopping in the area, and you can show me where your two fathers lived and the café where they met."

Ice Rink – AMERICA

Early that Saturday morning, Key had Frank take her to get groceries. However, before getting out of the car, she noticed her father and two young girls exiting. "Follow them, please." Frank did as she'd asked and parked a few spots away when they arrived at an ice rink.

Key watched as Jon's daughter and her friend jumped out of the car and ran inside. He tried to catch up before remembering to go back and lock the car.

When Key made it inside and paid her admittance, she saw the girls sitting on a bench getting their skates on. The one with dark hair was yelling at her Da saying, "We can do it ourselves!" Eventually, she saw him make his way up the bleachers to the top, just under the heater vents. She noticed that he had brought a book to keep himself busy.

Key had brought in her own skates that she kept in the trunk and quickly put them on. Before making her way to the ice, she realized the girls were still struggling with theirs.

"You should tighten your laces a bit."

The dark-haired girl looked up at Key, "Oh, no, they're good."

"You would be able to skate straighter; your ankles wouldn't bend this way," Key said as she demonstrated on her skate.

After standing up, the young girl immediately understood as her ankles bent inward.

"Can I help you tighten them up?" Key asked.

She sat back down with a defeated look and allowed Key to undo, tighten and re-tie her laces.

When Key was done, the young girl stood up, "Wow – that's a big difference. Thanks!" She stomped in place a few times.

"It was my pleasure. Do you need help?" Key asked, looking at the other little girl. "By the way, I'm Key."

"I'm Caitlin, and that's Amanda," she said as she pointed to her friend, who had paid attention and was finishing up her own laces just as tightly.

Key looked over and smiled at Amanda, then focused her attention back on Caitlin. "That's a pretty name. Do you know what they would call you in Ireland if they saw your name?"

"No, what?"

"Kathleen. Caitlin is the Americanized Irish name Kathleen."

"My Dad's from Ireland, but he never told me that." Caitlin looked at the bleachers where her Dad always sat and found him looking back at her.

Key also turned to look and immediately spotted her father, who had now stood up. *No doubt he's intrigued to know why we're both looking at him,* she thought.

Key turned back to Caitlin. "Well, I hope you have the luck of the Irish with you today. It looks like a wild crowd out there this morning."

Caitlin and Amanda both giggled as they watched Key make her way to the ice.

Amanda, who was always intrigued by Mr. Yule's Irish accent said, "That lady was really pretty, and she looked like your sister, Erin."

"My sister doesn't have red hair or green eyes."

"No, I was just talking about her face. Where do you think she's from – did you hear her accent?

"I bet my dad would know." Caitlin looked up and noted that her father was sitting again but still keeping an eye on them. She motioned for him to come down.

When he approached, he could see that his daughter was excited about something.

"Dad, a lady just told me that my name, Caitlin, is the same as Kathleen in Ireland – is that true?"

With a surprised look, Jonathan answered, "Yes – sort of."

"Why did you name me Kathleen?" Caitlin stole a quick glance at the rink and then back at her father. Before he could answer, she went on…"She has an accent. If you heard her, would you know what kind it is? It sounds like a royal."

"Well, if I heard her, I could probably confirm that much."

Just then, he saw the same red-haired girl skate by the open doors to the ice. *She looks familiar,* he thought. Without taking his eyes off her skating, he asked his daughter, "What was her name—did she say?"

"Key. Daddy, I'll try to get her attention so you can talk to her."

He looked back down at Caitlin and Amanda. "Why? Why not just ask her yourself?"

Both girls gave him a dead stare, then shrugged their shoulders and said, "Okay."

The girls ventured onto the ice and clumsily made it around the rink, working their way toward the middle.

"Do you see her?" asked Amanda.

"Oooh—there she is!" Without looking, Caitlin started cutting across to catch her.

"Ahh!" Caitlin was bulldozed by a much larger boy.

The boy immediately circled back and knelt down, horrified when she started to cry. "I'm so sorry. Are you okay?"

"She'll be fine; it was just an accident", came the familiar accented voice.

Caitlin felt herself being lifted up and saw it was Key supporting her as she skated her back to the open doors.

After returning her to the bench where they'd met, Key knelt down in front of her, holding her feet. "Can you move it?"

"Are you alright, sweetheart?"

Key's heart began to pound at the sound of his voice. Her father had knelt down just beside her.

"I'm okay." Caitlin rubbed the front of her leg with one hand and her tears with the other.

Key gave her a smile and a wink as she stood up, turning away from where her father was. As she started to walk off, she heard his voice call after her.

"Thank you!"

She only turned halfway, gave a wave, and said, "You're welcome; I was happy to help." Key was breathless. She had gotten to meet her father's daughter, Caitlin, and was no more than inches from him. The fact that they exchanged words was exhilarating, no matter how meaningless the conversation. She couldn't wipe the smile from her reddened face as she made her way to the loo to catch her breath.

Key was staring at herself in the mirror, thinking *I should probably get out of here and not push my luck,* when suddenly she realized she was being watched.

"Hi," Caitlin said.

"Hello again—looks like the leg is working well." Key grabbed a paper towel from the dispenser and pretended to dry her hands. She noticed how much this little girl looked like her father—same skin tone, hair color and even the same facial expressions.

Caitlin finally mustered up the nerve to ask, "Are you from England? Your accent sounds like it's from England."

"Not originally, but I did most of my growing up there."

"Where are you from then?" Cathlin asked curiously.

At the excitement of talking to her sister, she said much more than she'd planned to. "Here, actually. I was born in America but thrown away in England at age… at um… an early age."

"Thrown away?" Caitlin asked, leaving her mouth open.

Key's smile faded. "That's what the wealthy families do with the children they didn't want. They dropped them off at boarding schools to be raised by teachers."

"That's sad. Why wouldn't they want you? You're pretty. You do look a lot like my sister, Erin."

Key was so taken by the comment she had to swallow the emotion that seemed to rise within her. *I should have had Sara do my makeup.* "I'm not sure, but thank you, love."

Caitlin entered a stall, and Key left the restroom a little nervous that her father might be waiting outside. She hadn't realized she'd been holding her breath until she relaxed at the sight of her father seated once again at the top of the bleachers.

Key sat on the bottom bleacher on the opposite side, facing her father, glancing up to find Jonathan staring directly at her. She reached down with a small smile on her face to remove her skates and put her shoes back on.

Jon sat in a daze. It had been years since he'd let his mind wander back to his days in England and his wife, Alex. He felt a wave of shame and a pang in his heart for the little girl he had sent off. That's when it flooded his memory, "My name spells key – Kathleen Erin Yule. Your name spells Eky – hahahaha," she would tease Erin. The book in his hand slipped, and Jonathan was jolted back to reality when he tried to catch it before it could fall beneath the bleachers. Grabbing it on the edge, he could see the wet grime that now colored the back cover. He rubbed it along his pant leg before returning it to his lap. As he looked across the rink to where the pretty young lady had been seated, he saw that her spot was now empty – she was gone.

Key took the opportunity when he dropped his book to make her way out to Frank. "We need to get that grocery shopping done. I have deliveries coming today."

"What deliveries?" Frank asked.

"Since my ice rink is done, I bought workout equipment for Sara and the girls and some mats to practice my stunts before trying them on the ice. And since Sara insists on watching me skate, I bought some lounge chairs too."

"No stadium seats?" Frank asked.

"No. No need for them. I just wanted the ice."

"I noticed there are no walls around the ice either…seems unsafe to me."

"It's safer, actually. Trust me, when I fall and slide, it hurts like hell to slam into a wall at high speed." Key said with a giggle.

Frank smiled in acknowledgement. "Makes sense, I guess. Ya know, you probably wouldn't fall if you opened your eyes. Dee told me that you skate with your eyes closed. Is that true?"

"I learned in the dark, so it's comfortable. I can feel the ice and space when my eyes are closed."

"Then I guess walls don't matter; you'll be seeing none anyway." Frank laughed, and Key giggled back at the comment.

Frank drove to get her groceries, which she did quickly before they headed home. After dropping her off and heading down to the cottage, Key noticed another car pulling in. One she had never seen before.

"Sara, are you expecting anyone?"

"No, why?"

"Someone's here."

Sara looked and saw the car come up and park. She was shocked to see who got out. "Oh my God."

Key immediately called Dee, "Erin is here. She's out front, and it looks like she and a friend are coming up to the front door."

Ding

"Correct that. They ARE at the front door."

"Calm down, I've got this. I'm on my way." Dee hung up and bolted out the cottage's front door to make her way up to the main house, racing past Frank.

She saw they were about to ring the bell again when she called up to them, "Can I help you?"

Erin and Maggie looked to see where the voice was coming from and started to walk down the long porch. "Yes, hello. I umm…I used to live here."

"Really? That's wonderful." Dee replied simply.

Erin continued, "I was wondering who lived here now and if I could see the house."

"Oh, I'm sorry, that won't be possible. The owner is a very private man, and he would never approve." Dee said with the sincerest tone she could muster up.

"Hey!"

Dee turned around in a flash to see her husband coming up and knew he would say something wrong. While she replied to him, she held her finger to her lips, hoping he would get the hint. "Hey, honey. This young girl says she used to live here. Dee then turned back and said, I'm sorry I never got your name. I'm Dee, and this is my husband, Frank."

"I'm Erin Yule, and this is my friend Maggie." Erin couldn't take her eyes off Frank's face. He looked surprised and frozen in place when he caught up to Dee. He and Erin seemed to be locked in a staring contest.

"Well, it sure is nice to meet you two, but I'm afraid I can't let you in. As I said," which she was repeating for Frank's ears more than theirs, "the owner is a very private man."

"Do you work here?" Erin asked.

"Yeah, he aint here very often, so he needed help looking after things year-round," Dee replied.

"Is he home? Can I at least ask?"

"Oh no, his friends are using the place while they're in town. I would feel even more uncomfortable asking them. And even if they said yes, he wouldn't be happy about it. Sorry."

"Well…" Erin was running out of ideas. "Can I leave you my name and number and could you ask him? I was born here, and we left a lot of stuff behind. I would love to know what he may have done with it." Erin shrugged her shoulders, "but mostly, I just want to see the old place."

"Sure, I would be happy to take your number."

Maggie pulled a small pad and pen out of her purse for Erin to write down her name but gave them Maggie's home number. As Erin handed it to Dee, she said, "Thank you. I would really appreciate it if you tried to convince him. It would mean a lot to me."

"My friend, Erin, is a twin, and this is the last place she saw her sister before she was told her sister died in England. So, it really would mean a lot to her." Maggie added.

"Died?" asked Frank.

Dee gave his arm a bit of a squeeze.

"Yes, my grandmother had come after my Mum died and then took my sister back with her to England. We got notice of her dying from pneumonia sometime later." Erin answered him.

Dee spoke up before Frank could, "We're so sorry to hear that, sweety. I'll do what I can for ya." Dee still had a strong grip on Frank and stood there until the girls returned to their car, backed up and left the way they came.

"Care to explain?" Frank looked down at Dee while they turned back to the cottage.

"I told you no one can know that Key is here, and you just met the number one reason. If you insist on not reading Key's book, then I'll read it to you."

Izzy Owning Her Actions

"Good morning. Grandma Izzy home?" Key asked.

"Did you just call her grandma?" Uncle Bobby asked.

Key smiled and giggled while asking, "Is she home?"

"She is. I think she's reading." Uncle Bobby turned toward the great room and announced to her. "Mum, Key is here."

The old woman closed her book and put it on the end table before she started to get up.

"Don't get up. I'll join you there," Key said as she walked toward her.

"Oh, thank you. So, how was your trip to America? How is the house coming?" Isabelle asked as she sat back comfortably again in the large leather chair.

Key handed her a package of pictures. "The house is coming along great. Those are pictures of the before and the now, not quite the after yet. I hope you'll come to see it when I'm finished."

"What is this?" Isabelle asked, holding up a picture of a stairwell.

"That is the hidden stairwell that leads to the beach. Down the right side, you can see how they built it down the side of the cliff and how the wall to the left is brick. I added more lighting. The plumbing to the laundry room was interesting, but I was able to get what I wanted in there. Instead of one huge washer and one dryer, I put in several smaller ones. I do laundry every day, so it allows me to keep everyone's loads separate while running simultaneously."

"Oh, my goodness, where is this?" Isabelle asked again.

"That is the large open space next to the kitchen. I had the roof raised, and I'm building a two-story hotel, some stores, and my wood shop. It's going to look like you walked outside!" Key said with great excitement and a huge smile.

"Oh, sweetheart, that sounds amazing. I would love to see it when it's done, but you know I would be arrested the moment I landed in America," Isabelle said as she handed the pictures back to Key.

"I didn't come here to show you pictures. I came to thank you for your letter. It meant a lot," Key smiled, taking the pictures back from Isabella.

Isabelle's eyes got lazy while she took a few breaths. When she opened them again, she said, "But not enough."

"Don't look at it from the negative. It was a great start. You owned your failure to control your anger and need for revenge. You explained your thinking about abortion, and I understood it. I really tried to put myself in your shoes and I understood it. Although I'm glad you still recognized it was ultimately the wrong decision," Key explained.

"I could never apologize enough, though. I could never–" Isabelle started.

"It's not about apologizing enough; it's about letting your defenses down and owning it every time. For example, if we talk tomorrow and the memory hits me and I make a comment, you humbly owning it again will help me through it. Or, like Mum always said, love me through it. Even if the memory stings again at a later date, I may not feel the need to mention it a third time if I know your answer already and know you'll own it. Does that make any sense?" Key asked.

"I think so," replied Isabelle. She took a long, deep breath before continuing, "Okay. I'm ready for your worst."

Key smiled. "Let's talk about when things started to get complicated between you and my Mum."

Isabelle's head started to bob a little, "I think it was when she got old enough to date. She thought she was ready at a much younger age than I thought she was. I guess I also had my ideas on the kind of boys she should be choosing, but her ideas were very different in that as well."

"I looked at superficial things only. Your father, your real one, I did not know him at all. What I knew was that he did not have a proper job and that he was born and raised Irish. I know I was wrong to judge him like that, but can you understand at all how I felt? She was my only daughter—"

"I can. My sister dates and I wouldn't want her dating some shlub. My expectations are high for her as well, so I guess I can make peace with that," Key replied calmly.

"I know judging him for being Irish was very wrong. You are half-Irish, and I don't think less of you for it. I also appreciate everything Jonathan did. It sounds like he was a wonderful husband to my daughter."

"I like this new you, Grandma," Key commented.

Isabelle gave her a small smile, "I do too. Taking responsibility for my bad behavior feels better than feeding the anger with excuses. I wish I had known you earlier. You could have saved me a lot of horrible years. Not just me, obviously, Alexandra, Robert, William, you, and your sister–"

"Better late than never, they say. Can you tell me about my grandfather? Why were you angry with him?" Key asked.

"I wasn't really. I just took it out on him like a coward. His father bought me from my father, and I couldn't take it out on them, so my husband suffered my anger," Isabelle replied.

"Wait, what? His father bought you?" Key asked.

"I was only 17, just like Alexandra was. My husband had told his father my name when he was asked who he was interested in. To hear my husband tell it, he was as surprised as I was to be told about our wedding date. It seems his father immediately found out who I was, approached my father and offered him money for his gambling and drinking habits to deliver me to the church."

"Oh my God, that's crazy," Key was shaken.

"I felt like a bought whore," Isabelle replied.

"Did Grandpa William treat you like one?" Key asked.

Isabelle took a long, uncomfortable breath before she admitted, "No. He was a very sweet man. He treated me like a queen and was very generous. I was new to having money, but he was very patient in teaching me everything he knew. He also turned a blind eye to my overspending in the early years."

A small smile escaped her lips as she continued. "We did have some good times, especially after the kids were born." Then Isabelle's mouth showed every bit of her regret. "But when left to drown in my memories, the anger would build, and I would lash out," This time, a tear escaped her eyes and fell to her lap as she looked down.

"I can understand that 100%," Key replied. "I, myself, try not to leave myself too much time to think. I stay very busy with my computer program, businesses and restoring furniture. It helps to keep my mind occupied, usually on accomplishing something. So, let's not drown in those memories. I would love to hear about those good years with Grandpa," Key encouraged her.

Isabelle gave her a nod of determination and started it with a forced smile. "He was such a doting father. Of course, he worked long hours, but when he came home, he would be so excited to see them. Alexandra would run to the door to greet him. Robert was six years younger but would desperately try to crawl to keep up with her. I would be there beside them on my good days but loved watching it even on my worst."

"Once the kids had grown too old, I was the one greeting him at the door. As you can imagine, his work hours started getting longer and longer as the years went on." Isabelle started to shake her head again and sniffled.

"Then let's say a prayer for him," Key said as she reached for Isabelle's hands.

Isabelle offered her hands over while Key spoke, "Hello God, it's me again. We're thinking of my grandfather today. I am confident you have him with you, so please conference him in if you could."

Isabelle looked up at Key who gave her a smile and a wink.

"Grandpa, although I never had the pleasure of knowing you, Grandma Izzy has been telling me what a wonderful man you were here on earth. My Mum, who I am just as positive is there with you now, told me the same."

Isabelle put her head down again but thought, *she speaks to God like no one I have ever heard before.*

Key continued, "We're thinking of your life, but your wife worries about what you suffered. I know you're at peace where you are, but please watch over her with a forgiving heart. She wants to see you again and is working hard to earn her ticket to heaven. Okay, I love you Grandpa and you too, Mum. Love!"

Isabelle looked up with tears in her eyes but a smile on her lips. "You never say goodbye. Robert and I have both noticed you always just say 'love.'"

"I hate goodbyes, and I don't think people hear the word love often enough," Key replied.

Isabelle squeezed Key's hand again before letting go, "I love you, and I should say it more often."

Key & Mike Get 'Close'

This year was special. It was December 8th, and the girls were packing their bags for a special trip to America. Mike's little sister, DeAnne, was going to dance in a Christmas pageant and they had promised to attend.

Michael's mother, Madison, had insisted they save the money on a rental or hotel and stay with them. Sara, not thinking, had accepted the invitation with great excitement.

"I'll have to wear a wig the entire time I'm there, Sara!" Key had reminded her, but it was too late.

This trip was also special because Ms. Brookes allowed them to go without her supervision. The headmistress had spoken to Madison herself to work out the details, and they were sure to call the school when they arrived safely.

Their flight ran late, but Mike found them quickly in the baggage area. They arrived at Mike's house only two hours before the event. The girls quickly settled in, grabbed a quick bite, and freshened up in time to take the seats that Madison had saved them.

Mike was embarrassed to have them sit through a long production of young kids dancing and singing. Although not when his sister's group came out. His pride in his little sister was obvious. DeAnne could dance like an angel as far as he was concerned, and he was her biggest fan.

At the end of the event, they waited in the theater until DeAnne came out.

"Ooo, here she comes!" exclaimed Sara.

"The pageant was wonderful," Key told her. She and Sara handed her small candy bouquets they had made themselves from an array of options only found in Europe.

"What is a Crunchie?" DeAnne asked.

"Just my favorite! It's a crunchy honeycomb toffee with a sugar center. Oh my goodness, it's to die for," Sara said, making all their mouths water.

"The Cadbury Twirls are my favorite. Their crunchy milk chocolate flakes are coated in smooth milk chocolate. I may be a bit biased though, because they originated in Ireland, and you don't just get one, you get two!" Key added.

"I'm hungry now after hearing all of that. Let's get dinner," Mike said, laughing.

Madison suggested a local restaurant, so they headed out. The eatery was busy, and they had to wait almost an hour before they were seated, but the food was worth it.

After a long night, Madison turned to her son, "Mike, I think DeAnne is wiped out." His mother gave him a look that said, *It's time to go.*

However, Mike, Jeff, Sara, and Key weren't quite ready to leave. Key leaned over and whispered, "Michael, offer to let them go on. I'll call the car service to pick us up later."

Mike proposed the idea to his parents. Madison and his father agreed and got up to go. On the way out, DeAnne stopped to give Key a kiss on the cheek before doing the same for her brother, Mike.

While Key watched them walk away through the tables full of patrons, Mike whispered in her ear, "So, are you ready yet?"

She turned about with a lost look. "Ready for what?"

"To move here to America, full time."

"Good heavens, that was random." They both giggled.

Michael put his arm around Key and beckoned to the waitress to order another round of sodas. "Okay, let's celebrate."

"What are we celebrating?" Jeff asked.

"Key and Sara deciding to move to America when they turn 18, of course."

For a moment, Sara wondered, *wait, did she tell him? Does he know?*

Key answered her question with a surprised smile. "I don't know what he's talking about, I swear."

"Well, gosh, maybe it's something we should consider?" Sara said, causing Key to giggle.

"Yes, I think we should think long and hard about it. Springfield has a feeling of home. I could see myself living here," Key chuckled back.

Mike was excited to hear it, without understanding that it was Key's plan all along. Only Jeff felt there was an inside joke of some kind but said nothing.

An hour later, Key called Frank to come get them. As they walked out, Sara insisted on going back to the loo once more. Jeff offered to wait on her while Mike and Key headed outside.

Due to the crowds, probably the throngs of Christmas shoppers, Frank was doing his best to manipulate his way to the front. As they stood waiting, Mike noticed Key shivering and opened his long, black wool coat, inviting Key in one swift move to share in the warmth. Her body pressed into his, her arms wrapping around until her hands caught and grasped the large muscles on his back as she hid her face in the warmth of his chest.

The car pulled up, but Michael didn't tell her. Instead, he lowered his head, put his cheek to hers, and whispered, "I could get used to this." Her eyes opened, her face lifted as their lips met, and he kissed her.

She lost herself in the warmth of his lips until suddenly she pulled away and, with a look of panic, breathed, "No."

Just as Sara exited the restaurant and approached them, she heard Key say, "You deserve better, better than damaged goods." Sara watched as Key yanked herself from his grasp, quickly turning and climbing into the waiting car.

Mike and Sara were both in shock and slowly climbed in after her.

Key stared out the window and Mike gazed at the floor while Sara stared out the other window. Jeff seemed oblivious, talking up Frank from the passenger seat in front.

Sara spent the ride back trying to sort her thoughts. *Damaged goods?* She had never heard Key call herself such a horrible name. Nor did she recognize the tone in her voice when she said it, leaving Sara to wonder, *have the smiles she has been wearing since she was 10 years old been more bravery than reality?*

Sara poured over the years of memories and shockingly started to see things she hadn't noticed or comprehended before. The way Key has taken care of her and the other throwaways, protecting them and pushing them to believe in themselves and walk proudly. It was like Key had once said to them in school, "Keep your chin up and never show weakness." *That is what she has been doing all along.*

Have all the others been playing me for a fool as well? Do they all believe, as Key does, that they're damaged goods and not worthy of love? No, no, the others are in relationships, she thought. Then Sara realized, *of course, they believed in themselves, Key would not have settled for any less.*

It suddenly dawned on her, *oh my God,* Sara thought to herself. *How could I not have realized it all these years? No one ever protected Key. No one ever worried if she believed in herself."* Sara was painfully aware now that the "damage" was not solely the inability to bear children. *She's still a broken little girl. She can't forget. She's probably constantly being abused by her memory. Oh my God. How do I...what do I do to help her?* Sara's mind raced.

Back at the house, Key refused to discuss the evening with Mike or Sara and went straight to the bedroom. She changed into her sleepwear and curled up in bed.

Sara came into the dark room and sat on the bedside. "I know you don't want to talk, so just listen." She put a hand on Key, who was turned away from her. "I love you. I love you for the sister you promised to be to me long ago. You've protected, defended, and helped me through school in countless ways—more than homework. But I haven't returned it—have I?"

Key stirred a bit, wanting to protest, but she was too choked up to respond.

Sara continued, "I didn't protect or defend you. I just sat in that damn closet, worrying more about the dark and my own fears. You really were Wonder Woman in my eyes." Sara stopped to wipe the tears now running down her own cheeks. "And even after I found out what you had protected me from, I let you continue on as my caretaker when it should have been me taking care of you. What you did for the girls, I should have been doing to build you up."

This was too much for Key, who finally turned on her back to face Sara. "That's not true," she choked out. After clearing her throat a few times, she continued, "Letting me mother you, be so overbearing—it was that control that I needed, and you gave yourself to it." Key stopped and wiped her own eyes clear. "I'm not entirely sure why I'm so scared, but I assure you, it's not your fault."

Sara didn't bother to undress but instead laid down next to Key, putting her arm around her friend until she fell asleep. Key, however, couldn't rest. She stared at the ceiling, her mind racing until finally, she slipped Sara's arm from around her, slithered off the bed and put her wig back on the best she could.

As she descended the stairs, she could see a light was still on in the living room. Mike was sitting in the middle of the long couch, his head angled back and eyes closed.

Oh, good heavens, he's going to hurt his neck sleeping like that, she worried. "Michael?" she whispered. "Michael, wake up, love."

He didn't jerk awake as she'd expected but instead slowly lifted his head with opened eyes.

Key sat next to him. "You were awake?"

He looked down toward his feet. "Just trying to accept my reality."

She took a deep breath. "What reality is that?" Key knew she was opening the conversation to the earlier events, so she braced herself by taking another deep breath.

"I'm in love with a woman who isn't in love with me." Mike bent forward, put his elbows on his knees and rubbed his face in his hands.

Key watched him and then shook her head, "I don't think that's your reality at all. I think you just love a woman who is too scared."

Turning his head to look at her, "Scared of what?"

"Of revealing myself, I suppose. I've been through some things that are hard to talk about."

"You were abused, weren't you?"

Key looked up in surprise. "H–how?"

"I thought a lot about that conversation we had the first time we met. The one where you said, 'sex is sex', and you called it a 'dirty little animal instinct.'" Mike turned his body sideways and swung his left arm up and around behind her. "I knew there had to be something heavy behind not being able to call it *making love*."

The tears streamed down her cheeks now. "That's what 'he' called it." She started to shake. "It's an ugly name to me now unless you can imagine something beautiful coming from it. Something like a beautiful baby—a new life."

Mike understood but wasn't sure what to say. He sat for a moment, not wanting to press for more detail while letting her know he was open to listening. "I'm sorry, and someday I hope you feel you can talk to me about it. But please don't let it stop you from letting me love you."

Her eyes looked up and focused on his. "I've never let it stop me from loving you. But, oh God, what if I can't bring myself to share my body with you? Men need that sort of thing."

Mike couldn't help but see the humor in that old belief, and a smile overtook him. "We like it—LOVE it actually—but we don't *need* it. I wouldn't shrivel up and die without it."

"But to condemn you for…" she stopped herself. *I shouldn't assume we're talking about forever,* she thought.

With a slight sarcasm in his voice, he answered, "Yeah, geez, that'd be terrible to condemn me to love a woman who makes me happy, is a great cook, great conversationalist, smart, funny, and beautiful." He exaggerated his sarcasm even more and finished with, "The HORROR of it!"

A smile finally broke across her lips, and she curled up her legs, leaning them on his and putting her head on his arm. They didn't talk much longer.

The next morning, when Sara awoke, she was surprised to find them both lying together, fast asleep on the couch. She whispered, more to herself than for other ears, "I guess I'm making the coffee this morning."

When a voice from the couch said, "Oh no, you don't, I can't drink the sludge you make." Key had awoken hours before but didn't want to let go of Mike.

Key sat up, and when she saw Sara's big smile, she couldn't help but return it with one just as large.

The big smiles turned into a quick look of horror on Sara's face as her arms reached out and straightened Key's wig before Mike opened his eyes.

Mike tried to get up unsuccessfully, falling back to the couch pillow. "What time is it?"

The girls looked at him and giggled until Sara turned toward the kitchen. Key jumped up to race her to the coffee maker.

About an hour later, Jeff stopped in to pick up Sara. He'd promised to take her to a shooting range. "Jeff won't let me go hunting with him until he's confident I can handle a gun."

Key was surprised. "Why on earth would you want to go hunting?"

"Because I've never done it before."

The two of them just stood there in a locked stare until they started to giggle at one another. Key was speechless.

Mike's mom followed them out, taking DeAnne with her to church and then off to visit some friends. This left Mike and Key alone in the house.

Mike put his arms around her. "So, what do you want to do today? Your choice."

"Nothing special. I just want to enjoy having you all to myself for a change," Key replied.

The two of them played cards for a while, ate lunch, and then took a walk until finally, it was time for Key to take her afternoon nap.

"That sounds like a great idea." Mike took her by the hand and led her to his room.

"Are you suggesting I sleep with you?" she said with faux surprise.

"You didn't seem to mind it last night." Mike chuckled as he climbed into the bed and laid out his arm, waiting for her to join him.

She didn't hesitate to curl up against him in the same position she found herself that morning.

"Hey, beautiful? Is kissing a…ummm…can we…"

A huge grin came across her face. "I liked kissing, although I'm not sure I was any good at it. It was my first." Key waited with anticipation after leaving him that open invitation.

He rolled over so that his left arm was still under her head and the other now on the front of her waist. "Well, there's only one way to get good at something. Practice."

The kiss became very passionate quickly, and Key started feeling a strange euphoria. His leg slipped down between hers, and her leg instinctively bent up to almost curl around it.

Michael got caught up in the moment, and his hand slid underneath her shirt before he caught himself. "Sorry," he said in a deeper voice than normal.

Key was aroused, and in the moment, she found the bravery to say, "I want to try. Share myself – I want to try."

Michael went slowly and made it all about pleasing her, although she was very aware that doing so seemed to make him very happy. Her body felt like it had already exploded inside. She was ready, her body prepared, and Michael was eager—when it dawned on him, "I don't have any condoms."

"It's okay, I'm clean-blooded," she said with a hint of desperation, squeezing her legs around him.

"I wasn't worried about that."

She was breathing hard with frustration now, "You mean you don't want to get me pregnant?"

"Yes."

"I can't." Key closed her eyes, expecting questions to follow, but she got a warm sensation inside of her instead. She squealed with delight and finally understood what Sara had described to her in so many of their late-night talks.

Barely an hour later, Sara and Jeff walked into the house, and Sara knew Key would probably be taking a nap, so she started up the stairs. Jeff went immediately to Mike's room. "Oops—sorry!" He closed the door quickly.

"What oops? What's wrong? Is Key in there?"

"Ummm… they're taking a nap. I think we should leave them be." But Jeff's face gave away more, so Sara pushed past him before he could protest.

Although no vital parts were showing, Sara could tell they were naked. "Oh heavens!"

Both Key and Michael turned toward the door. Sara quickly turned her back to them. "Keep the jewels covered, my boy – we needn't share too much today."

"Sara, what in heaven? You scared me to death!" Key bounced her head on the pillow, letting out an "Ugh!"

Sara turned back and jumped on Key, straddling her. "Was it consensual?"

Mike, obviously offended, answered in unison with Key, "Of course!"

Key just lay there with a huge grin on her face.

"Ahhh!" Sara started jumping on her knees while Key laughed. She stopped abruptly and looked down at Key. "Was he any good?"

Key whispered it with a giggle, "It was wonderful."

Mike held tightly to the covers and looked directly at Sara. "Ahem! I'm still here."

"I know!" Sara bent down, grabbed his face, and gave him a long kiss on his forehead.

"Are y'all alright in there?" Came a voice from outside the door.

Sara answered him while still jumping about. "Oh Jeffrey, come in, come in!"

Mike put his hand up. "Woe-woe-woe!"

Although Jeff never entered the room completely, he did poke his head in and said, "Here's a crazy idea. How about Sara and I leave you lovebirds long enough to get some clothes on?"

"Brilliant!" Mike replied instantly.

Jeff gave a wry smile, reached for Sara's arm, and pulled her off the bed and out of the room. "Yeah, I'd hate for your mom to come running in next."

"Fine—whatever," Sara said as she jumped off the bed. But she pulled away from Jeff long enough to turn back and give Key one last kiss on the cheek. She exchanged excited smiles with her before closing the door on her way out.

343

Key Turns 17

"Are you sure you won't be coming back?" asked Dean Roberts.

"No sir, not to attend classes anyway. Thank you for everything, sir." Key said while shaking his hand goodbye.

"Well, don't forget us. I look forward to seeing what you'll do with all your new knowledge."

Key, Sara, Rachel and Dannie all walked away with a wave back to him.

"I wish we were graduating this year," said Rachel.

"I know. One more year, but it feels like it's forever away," replied Dannie.

"Thank you all for coming today," Key said, appreciating their presence.

Sara started to giggle causing all of them to look at her. She then whispered, "How angry do you think the other students were to have a 17-year-old graduate at the top of their classes?"

"Oh Sara, all the ones I knew were very supportive," Key said, shaking her head at her while the other two had huge smiles on their faces. "Don't encourage her, girls." But although they tried to wipe the smiles off, they never fully succeeded.

"Probably not nearly as angry as the ones who watched a 13-year-old do it four years ago," Dannie finally blurted out.

"They were actually more supportive four years ago," Key said simply.

"So, what now? You have to wait another year before we're done." Sara asked.

"Start preparing for home, and I can put a lot more energy into our finale show," Key said bluntly.

The girls went out for a celebratory lunch after Key's graduation and then headed back to Willington. The phone was ringing as they walked into the dorm and Key answered it. "Hello?"

"Key? It's Gus, and I have some news for you on your friend, Mike." He is the investigator that Key had hired to keep tabs on Mike as well as her family.

"Is he okay?" Key asked.

"He's in the hospital. He hadn't been out of the house for some time and then suddenly, an ambulance came and got him. I spoke to a nurse, and all I could get was that he has pneumonia before she realized I wasn't family."

"Oh my, how bad is it? I'm surprised he would need an ambulance…"

"It must be pretty severe. He's in the intensive care unit."

Gus gave her all the details he had before they hung up.

"Sara! I need to get home immediately."

"You mean America?"

"Yes!"

"Why?"

"Michael is in the hospital, in the intensive care unit. I want to go see him."

"Don't they usually only allow family in?" Sara asked while watching Key throw a few outfits in a bag.

"Money talks, that's family enough for most," Key replied. "Can you do your magic and look for the quickest flight back? I'll go inform Ms. Brookes I'm going."

"You mean that 'we're' going."

Ms. Brookes wasn't happy about it because she couldn't chaperone with school in session, but she trusted Frank and Dee to watch over them, so she relented.

"I actually got us a flight for tomorrow, but we'll be landing pretty late, Sara explained.

"Thank you," Key responded.

When Frank picked them up, she insisted they go straight to the hospital. Key was correct about a few bribes being 'family enough' for the overworked nurses.

The room was darkened overall but had a small light on the wall that looked like it was meant to highlight a painting that wasn't there. The lighting didn't help shelter her from the shock of seeing him lay there with tubes coming out of his mouth and taped to his chin. More disturbing was seeing his wrists tethered to the sides of the bed, although she knew it was to stop him from reaching up to pull at the tubes.

She stood beside the bed just watching him and started to say a silent prayer when his eyes opened. Key smiled, "Hello, handsome."

Mike's eyes closed again for a few seconds before opening again. His lids looked too heavy to lift, so they only opened to small slits.

"You need to get strong; I can't lose you." Key noticed his eyes rolled back a little before his lids closed again for a few more seconds. She wasn't sure he could even hear her over the beeps and buzzing of monitors.

His eyes had closed again, but she continued, "I once asked you if you loved me, and you wouldn't answer." His eyes opened into thin slits again. "But I said I loved you and promised I always would, and I have. I've had to do it from afar but have never stopped loving you." His eyes closed for the last time; he was asleep. She stayed and held his hand until a nurse came in and insisted they needed privacy. Key understood and left the room.

"He was sleeping, I hope," Sara said.

"Why?"

"Because we didn't even think of putting your wig on. Did you bring it?"

"Yes, I brought it, but I don't think he'll even remember my visit. He seemed to be in and out of consciousness – mostly out while I was there."

Sara couldn't miss too much school, so they had to fly back after being unable to get in the next night. They only had to wait one more day before Gus called to say Mike's condition had improved, and they were planning to remove him from the respirator. "Thank you, Gus. Thank you so much for keeping me informed."

Key decided to make another visit, but this time to Izzy's.

"Hello? Hellooooo?" Key called as she made her way into Izzy's house.

"I'm surprised to see you," Izzy replied from the kitchen door.

"Making tea? I could use a cup." Key made her way back to the kitchen and sat at the table by the bay window that looked out to the backyard.

"Please don't start up on me straight away. I already have a headache I haven't been able to shake."

"I only have one question today, but it's one that I've been meaning to ask you." Key was very calm and sounded almost friendly. "I think I understand why you did it. I guess I just need to hear it from you."

"Okay." Izzy put both hands on the counter, bracing for it.

"How did you convince my Da that I was actually dead?"

Izzy put her head down and closed her eyes. She stayed quiet until the water was ready. She turned the oven off, grabbed the teapot and brought it to the table.

Key pushed her cup forward and watched as she poured. "I already know you said I died of pneumonia, if that helps. I was just curious how you convinced them of it."

Izzy took a deep breath and sat down. "A forged death certificate," she finally answered.

"Is that it? You sent a death certificate, and he didn't ask anything?"

"I sent it with a letter about how sorry I was and how sudden and unexpected it was. He thinks you're buried in the Harrington family cemetery." Izzy said, staring at her cup of tea and never looking at her granddaughter.

Key gently took another sip of her tea and placed it back in the saucer. "Has he ever called?"

"A few times wanting to buy the house. I never took the call."

The two sat quietly for a while until Izzy refilled their cups. The gong of the hall clock could be heard reverberating into the kitchen. Finally, Key broke the silence. "Are you worried about when I go back?"

Their eyes met this time. "Yes. I'm sure to go to prison. The only question is, where?" After another deep breath and long exhale, "I assume they'll want to extradite me to America to try me there."

Key couldn't reply at first, just fiddling with her cup.

"You'll be asked to testify against me, so I hope you get all your answers to make peace with it before then." Izzy pulled her hands to her lap to hide their shake.

"I won't testify," Key said bluntly.

"Well, they probably won't need it. The letter and death certificate will be enough evidence."

Still Believes

"Hey old man, I'm here to break you out of this joint," Jeff said as he watched Mike trying to get his shoes tied.

"I thought my dad was coming?" Mike answered.

"I volunteered."

"Thanks man. Can we stop at Chic Filet? I'm hungry for something with taste to it."

"Sure. You ready?"

"I'm supposed to wait to be wheeled out," Mike replied as he sat and looked at Jeff.

"Gimme a break, man, let's go." Jeff started walking out and didn't turn back, so Mike followed and caught up.

Mike's friends were back at the house waiting to surprise him. He realized it when Jeff passed the Chic Filet without stopping.

Nevertheless, Mike acted surprised to see his usual gang waiting for him when he arrived. Jessica gave him a bouquet, but not of flowers, of candy bars on sticks. Of course, the guys didn't bring him anything. Jess is the only one who thinks of that stuff. Oddly, the guys only think of it when it's time to do it for Jess in return.

"So, how ya feeling man?" Ray asked.

"I'm good, just tired. I had a visitor you wouldn't expect though."

"Who?" Jeff asked, listening in.

"Erin Yule," Mike replied.

"No way. That's just weird, you haven't spoken to her in years," Jessica added.

"Well, it gets weirder. I was in and out a bit when she came, but I swear she told me she loved me and always had." Mike said it with a smile and laughter in his tone.

"She's cute," Joe said. "I'd take that."

"Out to dinner is what you mean, correct?" Madison, Mike's mother asked sarcastically.

"Of course, Mrs. Young. What did you think I meant?" Joe became very animated and exaggerated his expressions. "Oooooh, you and your dirty little mind, woman." It caused the entire room to break out in laughter.

"So, you gonna be good by Friday night?" Jeff asked.

"Yeah, why?" Mike asked.

"The carnival starts."

"Are we still going to the school carnival tonight?" Maggie asked.

"Yeah, you want to go early? I told Molly and them we might, and she said they may go early as well," Erin said.

"Yeah, we can eat there."

The rides were running when they got there, although it was mostly the kiddie rides with mothers standing all around them. Jon had made sure both girls had enough money for tickets and food before they left. They decided to eat first and then walk around afterwards before doing rides.

"Crud," Erin said as she started to rise back up from her seat.

"What's wrong?" Maggie asked.

"I forgot ketchup for my fries." As Erin turned to fetch it, she started waving frantically. "Hey! Over here!" It was Samantha, Molly, and Bethany from school. The three of them filled in around Maggie and Erin's seat at the table. "I need ketchup. I'll be right back."

Erin grabbed a few ketchup packets from the vendor's tub and turned back quickly. She immediately ran into a wall, or so she thought. When she looked up, it was Mike, which made her smile fade quickly. She made her way around him saying "sorry" as she did.

"Hey," he called after her.

Erin stopped and slowly turned around to look at him.

Mike made a few steps to catch up to her. "It's been, what, nine years? I'd like to think I've grown up a little."

Erin found his smile contagious. "You must be referring to your maturity because height-wise, you've grown more than a 'little'." His smile became a chuckle, so she continued the jest, "there probably isn't a big foot costume in the state of Maine that would be tall enough to fit you."

"Funny you should say that because you're right. I've looked," he retorted.

After a quick chuckle from them both, came an awkward silence. Erin wasn't sure if she should say more or goodbye or just turn to go.

Mike broke it with a sudden seriousness, "By the way, I have a friend who lives in England, and she could visit that family cemetery."

Erin's face contorted into instant rage. "So, what color is my sister's gravestone?"

"I'm not…"

"How tall is it?

"She didn't…"

"Does it have an inscription, and if so, what did it say?"

Mike stopped trying to answer her until he was sure her list of questions had come to an end. Then, in disbelief, he asked, "Oh my God, you still believe she's alive?"

Erin stared at him with pursed lips for a moment before answering, "Nine years may seem like a long time, but right now, it feels like no more than 10 seconds." She turned quickly to head back to her table.

"I'm sorry, Erin." Mike took a deep breath. "I'm, I'm…ugh."

Erin stopped and also took a deep breath before looking back at him again. "I know you think I'm crazy, and that's fine." After a sigh, giving her frustration away, she continued, "But I can't ignore what I feel. I can't ignore it." Her eyes were watering now, and she shook her head.

"But how can you still think…"

Erin shrugged her shoulders, "It's not that I think she's alive – that's just it – I KNOW she is. I have more overwhelming confidence in her being alive than I have in…in…in whether I'll take my next breath." She took a step closer to him, "I feel her. I…I…oh my God, I just can't with you, I'm sorry."

Mike was speechless as he watched her walk away. *It's been almost 10 years; how could she still think Kathleen wouldn't have contacted her by now?*

Last Visit

The house was finally getting close to being completed, as Key imagined. She had been refurbishing old, but solid, furniture with soft leather for the great room. The coffee table was actually a huge old trunk that she protected with finish, and all the tables were made from reclaimed wood.

The laundry baskets had also finally been cut and completed. They were next to each bedroom door, in the shape of a swivel box. When it was swiveled inside the room, they could throw their laundry in it. When Key would gather laundry in the morning, she need only pull the small knob and swivel it to open to the hallway. She liked not having to enter anyone's room and interrupt their sleep.

Sara had also been adding her own touches. She had installed a flat-screen TV and over it a mechanical scrolling picture to reveal it. Key hated TVs and could never sit still long enough to watch anything, but Sara had insisted on one. Key simply wanted it hidden when not in use. The scroll was a painted copy of her favorite picture of the four sisters, Key, Sara, Dannie and Rachel.

"You seem tense or something this visit," Sara mentioned as they brought their bags in. "I would think you would be more relaxed since Ms. Brooke didn't accompany us."

"I think I'm going to try something really stupid."

"You? Do something stupid?" Sara's laugh was exaggerated before continuing, "I doubt it."

"Well, doubt no more. I know what I'm planning is stupid and dangerous, but I'm going to try it anyway."

"Try what?"

"I'm going to play 'Erin' and see if I can get inside my Da's house."

"What the hell? Why would you do that? While your Da is home? Are you cra–"

"No, not while he's home," she said with the same attitude another may have just said, 'Duh'. "My sister usually goes to her friend's house, and I know my Da takes his daughter skating on Saturdays."

"But why would you need to get into their house?"

"To find the letter and death certificate that Grandma Izzy sent them."

"Ummm…so again, why? Who cares about the letter and certificate? Why would you want them? I'm sure your Da will show them to you next year when you return home."

"So, do I, that's the problem. If he still has them, he can use them against Grandma Izzy. Kidnapping is a federal crime, and she could go to prison for the rest of her life."

"And you don't want her to?"

"I know you think I'm crazy, but no, I don't. I don't want a big, public family feud when I finally return home."

"You've forgiven her. Don't bother denying it, I can tell."

"How?"

"You always said she would have to earn the title of grandmother, and it sounds like she has. At least halfway since you still call her Izzy."

Key responded with just a shrug of her shoulders.

"Let's get unpacked. It sounds like we have a wild weekend ahead of us," Sara said while shaking her head in awe. As they headed up the stairs with their bags, Sara made a confession. "Key, I have to admit I don't hate your grandmother."

Both girls stopped at the top of the steps. Sara's face started to contort and her eyes filled up with tears. "If she hadn't thrown you away–" Her throat closed up, and she couldn't choke out the words.

Dropping her bag, Key embraced her. "I know exactly what you're thinking. I have the same internal fight going on in my head." She pulled away to look at her eye-to-eye again. "How can I hate the woman who gave me such wonderful sisters?"

"But-" Sara couldn't speak and just put her head down, shaking it from side to side.

"But you know what it cost me. Sara, seriously, I understand. Dannie and Rachel have both said as much in private."

"It's a horrible, selfish way to think, though." Sara finally said.

"The way I see it, God put me where I could be the most use to him. Both Dannie and Rachel believe they would have gone the route Sienna and Julie took if all they'd had was a school counselor to talk to once a week. It had to be God working through me to insist on staying in that old dorm. As determined as I may have appeared, I dreaded the thought of going back to it. But, together, we became a family and lived our healing process every day, all day long."

The next day, Key woke up at 4:30 am as usual, but instead of starting the laundry, she ran over to her mother's grave for a visit. She could find it in the dark, but the moon was extraordinarily bright this morning. Sara never gets up on time on their first day back. It takes her a day or so to acclimate to the time change. So, after visiting her mother, she went and scratched the ice in the dark like she prefers. She was there for two hours before returning to a quiet house. Sara still wasn't up, so Key made herself a simple breakfast with the few groceries Dee was kind enough to get them before their arrival. Then she sat near the window in hopes of seeing her Batman leave another rose.

"What are you doing?" Sara asked, rubbing her eyes.

"Waiting to see if he brings another rose this year." Key never looked away from the beach but asked, "Are you hungry?"

"Did you eat already?" Sara asked.

"I had a bagel and cream cheese. I could whip you up some eggs though, she got us a dozen."

"No, I'll just toast a bagel. So, what's the plan for today?"

"I need to plan my mission. I plan to ask Dee to drive me over, but I'll tell her the truth before allowing her to agree. Then, I need to take just about every color T-shirt, shorts and long pants. I want to be able to match Erin as closely as I can in case I'm caught."

"That isn't today, though, correct?"

"No, Saturday," Key answered.

"Tonight, we see your 'Michael'. Are you excited? Hahahaha…stupid question I guess, look at you."

"Ooo, here he comes!" Key watched Mike's ritual of carefully making his way down the steep hill at the far end of the beach. He walks to the middle, always watching the glass doors before stopping to stand the rose up in the sand mound. He skipped a few stones across the water before finally climbing back up the hill and out of site.

"I have a company coming in later this week to carve and install cement steps down the hill. It's terrible, but I wanted to watch him climb down one more time before they were installed," Key said.

Later that night, they arrived at the restaurant early and found Mike was already waiting out front. He 'cheeked' Sara as she had taught him years prior before hugging Key and then giving her no option other than his lips for a quick kiss. Key became flushed after doing so, and Sara noticed.

Sara smiled and thought *she's no longer a romantic virgin.* She had a quick memory of a conversation on Rachel's bed years ago. Key insisted she was no longer a virgin and had nothing to give away. Sara had countered, *but you are a virgin in a sense. You have never given anyone a real kiss, you said so. You have also never shared yourself by choice. So, the way I see it, you are a virgin, a romantic one.* Sara came out of her daze when she heard a familiar voice.

"I see you wore the tight jeans you know I like. I appreciate the gesture." Jeff said with a huge smile before leaning down, cheeking Sara, who was also laughing.

"The table is probably ready by now if we want to go in." Mike then looked down at Key and then back at Sara, "and I hope those gift bags have what I hope they have in them."

"I probably should have gotten you something you wouldn't expect. Very lazy minded of me." Key replied.

"Oh no, I would have been heartbroken if you did that. By the way, I guess you knew that the author must write under two alias'?"

"Yes, we knew, which is why Sara gave you the other. So, you read them in order as she told you?" Key asked.

"Yes, which wasn't easy. I was so excited about the mystery but was glad I followed directions," he said as he turned back to Sara.

"Good boy," Sara replied. "You could learn a thing or two from him," she said, turning to Jeff.

"Oh, I never learn. Where's the fun in that." He jested.

After sitting and opening his gifts, he thanked them both again. "So, tomorrow, I was wondering…"

"I have plans in the morning," Key said quickly.

"What?" Mike asked.

"I have errands to run. We just need to get settled, but what did you have planned?"

"Nothing really. I was just fishing to see how early I could see you. So where are you staying, and how early can I come and get you?"

"Oh, no need. Our driver…"

"Why won't you ever let me pick you up?" Mike asked. His smile had faded.

"The house we decided to stay at is a little embarrassing. It's a bit extravagant for just the two of us."

"I don't care where you're staying or how nice it is. I'm glad you aren't staying in some seedy hotel."

Key looked to her right and realized Sara was listening intently. She could read Sara's tells and knew she wanted Key to take a chance. She turned back to Mike and said, "We're staying at the house on the cliff on McCoy Road."

"The cliff house? You're staying at the cliff house?"

The entire table is now paying attention.

"Yes, it's owned by a man in England who has connections to our school," Key responded as confidently as she could. *I'm not really lying. Uncle Robert is connected to me."* She thought.

"Can we go there tonight? Can I take you home?" Mike asked.

"No, but after I'm done my errands tomorrow, I'll call you."

"But..." Mike started.

Sara cut him off, knowing they would need time to prepare, so she shot back at him, "We just got here, and I'm tired. Do you understand the difference in time zones?"

Key smiled, "Michael, you're lucky we made it here tonight, but I promise, I'll call you tomorrow, and you can come pick us up."

After dinner, Key called Frank to let him know they were ready. Mike walked them out to meet him. Again, he cheeked Sara and gave a peck of a kiss to Key before they got in and drove off.

"I have so much work to do before tomorrow. All my novels are on the bookshelves, and we have pictures throughout the rooms..." Key was lamenting.

"We'll get it done tonight, but I may not get up with you again tomorrow," Sara joked.

Mike's Visit

Key and Sara tried to remove their identity from the house, including Key's books and the sweatpants and T-shirts that Key had purchased to fill the shelves in the new country store she created. She had purchased them in almost every size for future guests who decided to stay over. They had Sara's new website logo with 'Key2Sara.com' on the front, and Key thought it best not to advertise it to them.

Sara has been very careful to hide Key's identity on the site, only showing her in costume and makeup for school plays or just her voice with scenery video to accompany it. She also had a site called 'IceScratcher' where she posted Key's ice scratching, but only the one's where she wore a long nylon hood that came down over her eyes and nose, revealing only her mouth.

Key was not yet aware of that site. Sara knew Key would allow it but thought it might affect her scratching if she knew it was for an audience. Key made it very clear it was something she did only for herself.

When morning came, Key only scratched the ice alone, for about an hour. She couldn't stop thinking about her mission. After getting a shower, she made a breakfast casserole. Once Sara woke up and ate, Key had her pin her hair up to hide how much longer it was than her sister's. They picked out multi-colored t-shirts, shorts and long pants. Until they knew what Erin was wearing, Key wore her usual white t-shirt and jeans. They still had a while to wait for Dee to come pick them up.

Sara opened her laptop. "Hey Key!" Sara called from the sitting room.

"What?" Key yelled back from the kitchen.

"My website has 2,142,000 viewers!"

"Really? 2,142,000? I haven't seen it in a while. What else have you added?"

"Oh, good heavens, I've been adding content almost every day. When we write, and I record another of our songs, I post it. I've also…"

"Sara!" Key came running out of the kitchen.

"Relax! I don't post videos, just audio. The only videos have me, Rachel and Dannie—never you."

Key's entire body visibly relaxed while she let out a long sigh before ending with a smile.

"I do post videos of you, though, but before you freak out," Sara quickly added, "it's only when your hood is on." Sara was referring to the black nylon hood attached to her skating suit that Sara had specially made. Although, it also had another purpose. The hood was thicker over the eyes to make it easier for Key to skate with the lights on at the rink.

"You mean of me scratching the ice?"

"Yes. I do it only on the IceScratcher.com site," Sara replied. "My numbers have shot up by thousands from just yesterday, but oddly, for both my sites."

Just then, they heard a knock on the door as it was opening. "You two ready for this?" Dee asked. "I am so nervous, but I'm here for ya girl," Dee said as they headed back out to the car. "You look so different with blonde hair. I like it better than the red."

"I just hope I don't get caught," Key replied.

Sara explained, "If you do, run through the houses; don't come straight back to the car. We'll pick you up at the Stop N Shop."

"Then what?" Key asked.

"Then Dee drives us to the airport. I got two tickets back, just in case. We each have a bag to throw in the trunk," Sara replied, pointing to the two bags by the door.

"You're brilliant. Thank you, Sara."

"But why shouldn't she just get to the car? Wouldn't it be quicker?" Dee asked.

"If they're running after her, they would make a note of the car and maybe even the license plate. That could be the beginning of a nightmare for you, even if we can get on the plane," Sara replied.

"Wow, you are brilliant," Dee said. "Almost scary, brilliant."

Finally, Key relaxed a little at the implication that they were brilliant criminals while they all giggled at the notion.

They parked toward the entrance where they would be able to see Jon's car come out and Erin if she crossed the road to Maggie's. "If he is going to take her skating today, they should be leaving any minute now."

"But what if they need to go pick up her friend, and they've already left?" Sara asked.

"Get down!" Dee yelled. Both of the girls ducked low while Jon's car passed by.

"Was Caitlyn with him?" Key asked.

"Yes, there were two little girls in the back seat," Dee replied.

Again, they waited. And they waited. And they waited until it was a good half-hour since Jon had driven past them. "Why won't she leave the house?" Key lamented.

"Maybe she stayed at her friend's house last night," Sara said.

Another fifteen minutes had passed, and Key was about to give up when, finally, they saw Erin and Maggie both walking from the Yule residence over to the Kelleher's.

"What luck," Sara said. "She's in a white t-shirt and jeans. What were the odds?"

"With sparkly pockets," Dee added. "Nuthin you can do 'bout that."

Key didn't move right away. She was shaking while she waited until Erin and Maggie were in the house across the street.

"You don't have to do this, Key," Sara reminded her.

After a deep breath, Key slowly exhaled and exited the car. She got to the house quickly but opened the front door very slowly. She knew Erin's stepmother would still be in the house, but as she entered, she didn't see or hear her. Until that is, when she closed the door and it made an unexpected, very loud 'click' sound.

"Erin? Erin, I need your help."

Key panicked and froze in place for a moment. The voice sounded like it was in a hole. She looked to the right, and before the stairwell, there was an open door, so she stepped inside it. Realizing it was an office, she ran in and hid behind the large, dark wood desk.

"Erin?" Martha called again. She was climbing the stairs from the basement when the front door opened, and four footsteps made their way in.

When Martha made it to the first floor and saw Erin and Maggie about to ascend the stairwell, she was angry. "Why didn't you answer me? I've been calling you!"

"We just walked in," Erin replied.

"I called when I heard the door shut." They started to protest again knowing they didn't fully shut it this time, but she cut them off.

"You said you washed my red blouse, and I can't find it. I've torn my closet apart looking for it, but you have a bunch of stuff downstairs."

"I think it's hanging…" Erin started, but Martha had already turned to make her way back, so she followed her downstairs.

Key started opening and looking through the desk drawers as quickly as she could. Then she noticed a short filing cabinet near the door and opened the top drawer but it was packed with what looked like tax documents. She closed it gently and opened the bottom drawer. *Kathleen Erin Yule* said the folder label of the first, most prominent file. She grabbed it and was about to make for the door when she heard them climbing the steps again. She slipped behind the open door and stood against the wall, trying to breathe as calmly and quietly as she could. She turned her feet out like she imagined a ballerina would do, so she could hold the door as close to her as possible.

All three hit the landing of the first floor, and Key could hear Martha again. "Take this up and lay it out on my bed, please."

"Sure," came Erin's response.

Key heard the two of them go up the stairwell and worried, not knowing where Martha was. She quietly made her way from behind the door and peeked out. She tip-toed toward the door, watching the kitchen, stopped, and held her breath. Martha was at the sink with her back to the door. *It's now or never,* she thought. Grateful the front door had not been closed completely, she quietly opened it wider and ran out. The screen door slammed closed behind her, and again, she knew she had made a huge mistake.

"Erin!" she heard Martha call after her. She was too scared to run across the lawn to get to the car. She stayed close to the front of the house until she had gotten around the corner to the side yard. She stood frozen with her back against the house, feeling her heart pumping, her breathing labored, and sweat forming on her brow.

Key heard the screen door swing open and then, "Ah! Erin, I thought you ran out," Martha said.

"No, but I heard the door too. Who was it?" Erin said while they all stepped out onto the porch.

Key slowly made her way along the side of the house and then darted across to get behind the neighbor's house. She hid behind a huge bush and watched as they looked curiously around before going back inside. *I'm not made for a life of crime. Oh my God, I'm going to be sick.*

Key made her way back to the car, got in and ducked low, putting her head on Sara's lap. Dee took off quickly.

"We didn't know what to do when we saw Erin and Maggie heading back to the house. Are you okay? I assume they didn't catch you, but did you find what you were after?" Sara asked.

Key was still trying to catch her breath. "I'm not sure. All I found was this folder."

Sara put an arm around her while Key tried to catch her breath.

Dee pulled up to the house and all three went in. Key sat down on the couch, still shaking with the folder on her lap.

"You want something to drink?" Dee asked.

"I think I would choke on it. A life of crime is not in my DNA. I feel like my heart is going to pump right out of my chest."

Just then, they heard a knock at the door.

Sara, without thinking, was headed toward answering it when Dee came running out of the kitchen. "Don't answer it!" she said in an alerted whisper. "It's Mike."

Sara stopped cold and locked eyes with Key. "Let's get upstairs and get your wig on," Sara said as she grabbed Key's hand, pulled her up from the couch, and led the way.

"Once you're out of sight, I'll get the door," Dee whispered again while another knock on the door could be heard.

By the time Key's wig was properly set, and she had calmed down enough, they descended the stairs, but Mike was nowhere in sight. Once on the first floor, it was obvious where he'd gone – the hidden door was left open. Key stopped at the window first and could see her old friend out on the beach, skipping stones on the water.

Mike's head snapped to the glass doors when he heard them opening, and Key found herself wanting to scream *Batman! Save me!* Her heart was pounding again, so she tried not to look straight at him while she made her way to the rose still stuck in the sand. She knelt to it but didn't touch it until a large shadow was cast over her.

"That rose is for the friend I told you about a long time ago, Princess Kathleen." He held out his hand, and Key took it to stand up. Michael pulled her in for a hug, and she turned her head toward the water and pressed it up against his chest, wrapping her arms around him and holding on to the muscles in his back. She remembered something her mother had written in her diary about her Da, "…his arms were now like a warm blanket."

Michael kissed the top of her head and then whispered, "I haven't felt this strongly or sure about someone since her." He then tried to pull away a bit, hoping she would look up for a kiss, but she didn't. Her hug became even stronger.

Key's mind was racing, *can I tell him? Should I? I can trust him, but can I trust who he might confide in?* Finally, she said slowly, "My 18th birthday is next May, only 10 months away. I'll be of legal age to do as I please, come and go as I please," as she pulled away enough to look at him, "To live where I please." The last comment brought a smile to his face and a kiss to her lips.

Sara and Dee had been watching from the window and rushed to look busy in the kitchen when Mike and Key were making their way back into the house. They had poured four glasses of iced tea and carried them out to meet them in the main room.

"This room looks so different from what I remember," he said as he accepted the drink. "The furniture wasn't nearly as comfortable looking as these cushy, leather couches do. Oh, and I think this room had an ugly yellowish rug." Mike was turning around slowly, taking in every detail.

Key just smiled fearing if she said anything, she would give away her role in the changes.

However, her heart skipped a beat when she heard Sara say, "Have you seen the courtyard past the kitchen? That's our favorite area."

"The courtyard? No, I've never been farther in than the kitchen. I had lunch here once, but that's as far as I've ever seen." Mike followed Sara, but he stopped to look at the large kitchen first. "This is completely different. It's like, what would they call it, something like country chic?"

"Well, get ready to walk into the old world," Sara said as she slid the farm door along its track to reveal the courtyard.

Mike stopped at the doorway and just stood, staring. "We're still inside? Are we still inside the house?"

"Yes. It's just made to look like we've walked outside and are looking down the street. Do you like it?" Key asked.

Mike finally started to walk along the cobble stones soaking in every detail of the brick building fronts, café with umbrellaed tables, stores with glass windows to show the goods and the streetlamps that gave a glow. He looked up to the brick hotel on his left and noticed that the upper rooms had their own balcony, looking down over the street. "So, what's in these? Storage space?"

"No, they're actually hotel rooms. Go ahead, open the door," Sara prompted him.

Mike walked through each room, upstairs and down and was more and more amazed with each one. "They're all different, and the sinks, that's clever as hell."

The faucet for one sink was actually an old-looking pitcher, spilling over. The dials for hot and cold were medicine bottles, one with a red label saying, 'Snake oil' and the other had a blue label saying 'Elixir.' In one room, the toilet was separated from the shower and sinks by a door that looked like an outhouse, with a half-moon cut out at the top and knotted rope to open and close it. All the rooms were country-chic with pipes for towel hangers, iron work, wood floors and beautiful wooden beds, but all with their own unique style.

"I never would have imagined the inside of these rooms from the outside of the building façade. They seem to go from rough, old country to elegant country chic. But the outside looks like, I don't know, old, with fire-lit streetlamps and all. I want to go over and look in the stores."

Mike was in awe at the incomplete collection of instruments in the 'Making Music' store and asked, "Do you think the guy that owns this knows how to play all of these?"

"I don't know if he does, but we do, and we're allowed to use them," Sara replied.

"Even the ones in locked cases?" he asked.

"Key was given the keys to those, so I guess so," she replied again.

"There are more cases than there are instruments. Maybe he's just a collector," Mike said.

"So, what's upstairs?" he asked as he headed for the stairs in the back of the store.

"We don't know. I guess it's his personal storage space because we don't have keys to those doors," Sara answered quickly.

While Sara and Mike were in the store, Key stayed out on the cobble road and spoke softly to her house assistant, V-Key. "I can't say V-Key before my commands, so I'll refer to you as 'V' for now."

"Yes, Miss," The system responded at normal volume.

"What was that?" Mike asked, heading back to the front of the store.

Key met him at the front and said, "V, please make it daylight."

"Yes, Miss." Suddenly, the ceiling lit up with a glow that made it look like the middle of a sunny day.

"Oh my God, that is so cool, but who are you talking to?" he asked.

"The house assistant, V. If you have a question or need help, just say V first and then ask."

"Okay. V, will you please make it night again?" Mike's smile was open-mouthed, watching the lighting change back, and the streetlamps come back on. "This is the coolest house I've ever been in. I can see why it's your favorite area – I'd be in here all the time."

He loved the candy store's front counter with glass jars currently holding unopened bags of candy sticks and gumballs, but the rest of them were empty. There were clothing racks with nothing hung on them and empty shelves along the walls.

Key and Sara had to throw all those things upstairs in the 'storage' areas to hide them.

"You gotta let me invite Jess, Jeff and them to see this. I would kinda love to invite Erin to see it, but that could be awkward," Mike said.

"Erin?" Sara asked while feeling the daggers coming from Key's stare.

"She was Kathleen's twin sister."

"Why would it be awkward?" Sara asked, hearing Key's frustrated sigh.

Mike didn't seem to notice as he kept inspecting everything. "I was in the hospital recently, and she came to see me. The drugs had me in and out, but she was talking about loving me since childhood, and I wouldn't want to encourage that. It was weird, but you know how they say two people have 'chemistry'? Well, Kathleen and I had it in spades, but I never felt any for Erin." Mike paused for a second and then continued, "I guess one's looks really have nothing to do with it."

Key couldn't stop the smile that came across her face, so she turned away as if looking over the area. *He remembers my visit.*

Sara agreed with him, "Yeah, that would be encouraging it. It isn't nice to lead someone on, and she would see hope in the invitation."

They could hear the phone ringing in the kitchen, so Key went to answer it and left them in the courtyard. "Hello?"

"Key, get home," Rachel said bluntly.

"Are you okay?" Key asked anxiously.

"Yes, but you won't be soon. Get home."

"What's wrong, what's happened?" Key asked.

"Sara posted videos on one of her sites, and one video ends with you taking off your hood. Evidently, those who were interested in how you skate, and there were hundreds of thousands of them on that site, are now very excited they know who you are. Everyone at school is talking about it. Get home!"

"Thanks Rach."

Key took a deep breath and then made her way back to the courtyard. "Sara, Rachel just called and said Dannie was in a car accident. We need to get back as soon as possible."

"Oh my God, is she okay?" Sara asked with a horrified look.

"She's alive, but I'm sorry Michael, we need to get-"

"You're leaving? Back to Europe already?" Mike looked down and shook his head. "I'm sorry, I'm being awful..."

"If we can get back, I promise we will." Key walked to him and gave him a quick kiss. "I hate to rush you, but…"

"No, I understand. Please keep in touch and let me know how she is, okay?"

"Of course," Key replied as she prompted him toward the kitchen to walk him out.

Once they saw him off, Key turned to Sara, "There was no accident, and Dannie is fine, but do you still have those plane tickets?"

Erin's Trust Fund

Jon wanted to get Erin's college funds straightened out, so he called the lawyer who oversaw the trust his late wife had set up for them. It was her father's money, they used, so Jon insisted it be from her.

The lawyer informed him he would need to provide Kathleen's death certificate. It was the only way to give the entirety of the trust to Erin. Jon had assured the lawyer he had it and would forward it immediately.

He opened the drawer and just stared for a moment. *Where is it?* he thought to himself, but wasn't truly processing reality. He finally went from staring to fingering the few folders in the drawer. "It's gone!" He stepped back, leaving the drawer open. *I must have misfiled it in the top drawer.* He kicked the bottom one closed and opened the top drawer, but nothing. He fingered it again, but her folder wasn't there.

His cell phone was on the desk, and he turned to grab it and sent a group text to Martha and Erin saying, "Does one of you know where Kathleen's folder went? It's no longer in my filing cabinet."

"I didn't know you had a 'Kathleen folder,'" Erin replied. Martha had also replied, saying as much.

Martha had been down in the laundry when she received the text before hearing a lot of banging and slamming noises upstairs. She ascended the stairs to see if she could help. When she reached his office, she saw he had pulled out every piece of paper and folder he had. They covered his desk and the surrounding floor. "What's in it that you need, honey?"

"Erin is 17 and applying to colleges, so I wanted to get the Trust her mother left her straightened out. It was split evenly between her and Kathleen. Naturally, I need to produce the death certificate to get Erin the full amount." Jon explained.

"Okay. We can methodically look for it first. If we don't find it…"

"But it has always been in the same place!" Jon yelled.

Martha stood still, put her hands on her hips and let out a long sigh.

Jon realized his mistake. "I'm sorry. I don't mean to take my frustration out on you. But I swear the folder has been in the same place all these years. I have never taken it outside this office. I swear."

"Then it has to be here. What did it look like?" she asked.

"Just a yellow folder with her name in block letters on the label."

They spent the rest of the afternoon going through everything. Every drawer, every folder and even through his bookshelves. It wasn't there and they were too exhausted to get too animated about it now.

"I'll have to request a copy from Europe," Jon said as they sat down in the kitchen.

"Maybe call your Mother-in-law and see if she can get you another," Martha thought aloud.

Jon rubbed his eyes. "That's a good idea, but I may have better luck looking up Alex's brother Bobby. I can't imagine Isabelle lifting a finger to help me."

Jon did some research online and found a number to the Registry office that should be able to help him get a copy of the certificate. He decided to try that first, but they couldn't find a record. Although he tried, he couldn't register the death without a medical certificate of cause of death given by the hospital.

Next, he tracked down the number and tried calling the cemetery's office to confirm when she had been buried, but they also had no record. Assuming the young woman he dealt with was simply incompetent, he now knew who he needed to call.

"Hello, this is the Harrington residence," came the dry voice.

Jon recognized him, although it sounded older now. "Yes, this is Jon Yule. I need to speak to either Robert Harrington or, if he is not available, his mother, Isabelle."

"And what is this in reference to?" the old house manager asked.

"My daughter Kathleen's death certificate. I seem to have lost the only copy Isabelle sent me when she perished nine years ago while in her care."

"One moment, please." After a few moments, he returned. "I'm sorry sir, the maid has informed me that they are both out for the afternoon. May I take your number?"

Jon gave him his number, but thought after having done so, *I should have just said I would call again. Now she'll know to avoid me.*

Erin came home just as he was hanging up. "So, what is a 'Kathleen folder'?"

"Where I kept her birth and death certificates. Are you sure you didn't touch it, honey?" Jon asked.

"Da, I swear, I've never seen her death certificate and didn't even know a folder existed until today. But why would you need either of those now?"

"The trust your mother set up for your education was evenly split between you. The lawyer says I need to prove…"

"That she's dead?" Erin asked with a wry smile. "Good luck."

Jon's mood changed quickly, "This is not the time for your sarcasm, young lady. That folder had never left my office, and now suddenly it's gone."

Erin stopped smiling. "And you think I took it?"

"It seems awfully strange that…"

"What seems awfully strange is that you would accuse me of stealing it, hurting myself, so that what – so I can say 'told you so'?" They stood staring at one another with cursed brows until Erin spoke again. "I'm not so stupid as to believe you couldn't get another one.

So, what point would there be in my taking it?" With that, she turned and ran to her room so he wouldn't see the tears now filling her eyes.

Moments later, he heard the front door slam and knew his apology would have to wait.

The next day, he called again and was told she had gone on holiday. "Both of them?" he had asked.

"Yes."

"Well, that's convenient. For how long?"

"I can't say, but they have your number, sir." Before Jon could protest, the house manager said, "Good day, sir." *Click*

Jon was determined, so he got the numbers for the hospitals close to their address and started to inquire with them to no avail. He also tried the police stations, but they were even less helpful.

The Ice Scratcher - Revealed

A still shot of what looked like Erin was all over Facebook. The girl was wearing all black and seemed to be pulling off a hood. The headline read, "Ice Scratcher Revealed."

"Erin! Oh my God, the Ice Scratcher, is you?" Alicia screamed as she approached Erin and Maggie, who had just gotten into school.

"What? Me? I wish," Erin replied with a half-laugh.

"That's you girl." Alicia held out her phone and showed them the picture.

"Wow, that does look like me."

"What does the article say?" Maggie asked.

"Not sure, I haven't read it." Alicia then pushed on the link to the article.

The article explained that a student from Willington Boarding School in Britain, known to students as 'Key' is the Ice Scratcher. The journalist confirmed that the videos online are the same as the rink on the school property. When he inquired as to her real name, the school refused to give one and no students seemed to know her as anything else.

Erin started crying and shaking. "She's alive. She's really alive."

"Who?" Alicia asked, scared and confused seeing Erin like this.

"My sister, Kathleen!" Erin answered.

Maggie also had tears in her eyes, "Oh my God, what do we do? Should you call your dad? Should we call Willington? Oh wait!" Just then, Maggie and Erin looked at one another, coming to the same realization.

Erin dropped in the middle of the hallway, pulled out her laptop, opened her email and started typing a message to Drama Queen.

Dear Drama Queen,

The Ice Scratcher is my sister! Could you please give her my email address and ask her to contact me as soon as possible? PLEASE!

Your friend,

Erin

All three girls stared at her Inbox for a few moments. "This is silly. She's probably not even awake. What time would it be there?" Erin choked out.

"They're actually ahead of us, but I'm not sure by how much. I just know they show their New Year's celebrations before we celebrate ours," Maggie said.

The hallways were starting to thin out.

"We need to get to homeroom. Please tell me as soon as she replies or if your sister emails, okay?" Alicia begged.

"We will," Maggie replied. She pulled Erin's arm and got her to stand up, but she had both hands holding her laptop. Maggie picked up her bookbag and nudged Erin toward their lockers. "We have English first, and she'll allow you to keep it out if you explain." Maggie couldn't be sure Erin was listening, so she made sure they both had the books they would need for morning classes. She then nudged Erin again to homeroom and then again to their first class.

Every student that passed asked Maggie if Erin was okay. "Yeah, she's good. They're happy tears." She replied over and over and over again.

Finally, they reached their first class and sat down. Erin placed the laptop on the desk and couldn't take her eyes off it.

Maggie knew she was breaking the rules, but she pulled her phone out and searched for the article to help explain it to Ms. Baxter, who had just come in.

"Ladies?" Ms. Baxter said as she stood over them.

"Erin is going to be useless today, Ms. Baxter. Can I show you why?" Maggie asked.

She allowed Maggie to follow her to her desk and then show her the article. "I'm not sure I understand. Why would her twin sister be in Britain?"

By now, the entire class had arrived and filled in around Erin. They listened in as Maggie explained the funeral, her grandmother and how her father had lied to stop her from having to go.

A fellow student, Steve, asked, "But why wouldn't her sister have told her or contacted her? It doesn't make sense."

"She had her reasons," Erin blurted out.

"So, what were they?" he challenged.

Now, in a whisper, Erin replied, "I don't know."

"Erin, would you like to go to the office and..." Ms. Baxter started.

Maggie cut her off. "If you leave and I don't get to see when she replies, I may never forgive you, Erin."

Erin looked up for the first time at Maggie and choked out, "I won't leave. You were the only one that believed me."

"Okay. It looks like teaching will be impossible, so I guess this is a free period today." Ms. Baxter was startled by the cheers of the class.

Maggie found herself telling Erin's story to every teacher that morning, and they all understood why Erin wouldn't close her laptop. Most taught around it, but others made it a study period.

In the last class before lunch, Mrs. Shopa asked, "Why wouldn't you want to go home and alert your father?"

Maggie didn't have to answer that one; Erin did. "He never believed me. All these years, he wouldn't even allow me to speak of it. Even with this evidence, I may need a blood sample to convince him."

By the time they made their way to the cafeteria, the news had spread throughout the school. Maggie made their way to the table they sat at every day and told Erin she would get their lunches. She took Erin's badge with her lunch card attached and walked away.

Suddenly, they heard the loudspeaker squeal before hearing, "Would Miss Erin Yule please report to the office? Thank you." There was an audible "aww" that rang out through the cafeteria. Erin got up, taking only her laptop with her, but gave Maggie an assuring look. "I won't leave without you, I promise."

When Erin reached the office, she was told her father was on the phone. Erin was put in a small, empty cubby the size of an old phone booth to take the call. "Hello?"

"Erin?"

"Who is this?" she asked.

"It's Mike. Sorry, pretending to be your dad was the only way I could get you. Have you seen the article about the Ice Scratcher?"

"Yes, it's Kathleen." The history between her and Mike evaporated. "I have a friend at Willington, and I've already emailed her. I'm hoping to hear back soon."

"The Drama Queen?" he asked.

"Yeah," she replied.

"Can I give you my cell number and ask that you let me know when you hear back?"

"Yeah, what is it?"

After reciting his number, "I owe you a huge apology. I should have…"

"She's alive. That's all that matters, *Batman*." The giggle it caused was the first smile she'd had in hours.

He chuckled too, and retorted, "Thanks, *princess*."

Erin was making her way back to the cafeteria when the email she had been waiting on came through. She stopped, about to drop, but thought of Maggie. She ran as fast as she could with both hands carefully holding the laptop. She didn't slow down when she entered the cafeteria and got back to the table quickly, plopped the laptop down next to Maggie and opened the email.

Dear Erin,

Key would prefer not to talk until you know everything. She wrote a novel called <u>The Throwaways</u>. *Do you have a Kindle or something so you can get it quickly? She wrote the novel so she would never have to tell the story again. You will understand after reading it.*

Once you have, email me back.

Your friend,

Drama Queen

"Crud! I do have one, but not with me," Erin lamented aloud.

"You can download the Kindle Books app to your laptop for free," Alicia said.

Erin immediately searched for the app, downloaded it, and found the book. Before she could even begin, one of the many students now surrounding the table said, "Read it aloud!"

"My battery is getting low. Is there a plug somewhere?" Erin asked.

Maggie was already pulling the power cord out of Erin's backpack, and after plugging into the laptop, they uncoiled it down the table to the nearest plug.

Erin started to read and had barely started when the bell rang. Again, there was an audible grudge sound from all.

One of the lunch monitors came over to break up the group when Steve, the student who challenged Erin earlier, said, "I officially call today, Senior cut day!"

The entire senior class cheered, and the echo in the cafeteria was deafening.

When the monitor protested, the students made it clear they weren't moving. Another brought over the microphone from the front and laid it on the table in front of Erin, encouraging her to continue. Holding the microphone in her hand and the book in front of her eyes, she did.

Eventually, the principal was called in, but Ms. Baxter, who had come out of the teacher's lounge and understood, stopped him. She pulled him aside and explained.

When she realized her mother had been in love with a man with her name, Erin slowed down immediately. Maggie understood and pulled the laptop over in front of her to keep reading aloud.

Learning what her father, Jon, had done to save their lives caused her to forgive him instantly for not telling her.

Maggie's throat was groggy, so Alicia took over. Kathleen had described her and Erin as "oil and water" but made it very clear that she loved her sister.

The next part brought tears to Erin's eyes. It described her mother finding out about the cancer and having to tell them.

When Alicia started reading about the funeral, she had to pause. Erin was in full sobs now and was being comforted. They gave her some tissues and a few minutes to compose herself before continuing on.

Now she was reading about the lie her father told and the grandmother taking Kathleen. There was a sense of anger that took over the group. Then, gasps as they learned she was refused entry into her grandmother's car.

Alicia couldn't continue when she reached the worst of it. They met the monster, and there wasn't a dry eye to be found. Finally, Steve prompted the student next to Alicia to get up, and he took over. However, even he had trouble getting through it. He was relieved when he reached the chapter on her release from the hospital and their newfound strength to overcome.

The last bell of the day had rung and some of the students started asking for rides home so they could miss their bus. Another student, who drove himself, announced, "We'll figure out how to get everyone home, so quiet down. Keep going, Steve."

He did, and only thirty-five minutes later, he closed the book.

"That was an emotional roller-coaster," Alicia said.

"Are you going to email her back?" Another student called from the group.

Erin wasn't sure who asked, but she replied simply, "Yes, at home." There was another audible disgruntlement from the class. "I promise to keep you all posted, though. Keep an eye on my FB page."

Cheers and agreement rang out.

She's Alive!

Maggie drove them home, and they had to explain everything to her mom, Nora, because of how late they were. While Maggie tried to answer her mother's questions, Erin sat in their front TV room and opened her laptop.

Dear Drama Queen,

You may find this hard to believe, but I've read it. The entire senior class now knows everything. I'll explain another time.

Please tell my sister and have her contact me as soon as she can.

Your friend,

Erin

A reply came back immediately.

Dear Erin,

Are you angry?

Drama Queen

Erin replied even more quickly.

NO!

It was probably only seconds before she heard back this time, but it seemed an eternity.

Dear Erin,

I'm so glad you understand why I couldn't contact you before now. As much as I wanted to see and talk to you, I needed my sisters, who suffered the same, in order to heal.

I also couldn't take a chance that Da would force me back to America. I had been ripped from one life, but being ripped from this one became a matter of life or death.

I love you,

Key

Erin and Maggie both stared and re-read the reply before reacting. "Drama Queen is Kathleen?" She wrote back foregoing the formalities.

Kathleen? Are you the Drama Queen, or are you just using her email? Are you coming home – ever?

E-

Key also stopped with the formalities.

I'm one in the same. I meant it when I said I was happy to hear from you and able to help your club.

Would you like to Skype? Our sisters are aching to meet you and I have waited so long to talk.

K-

Maggie immediately started to set up her laptop for Skype and connected it to the TV so they could watch a larger picture.

Of course! I haven't told Da yet, but everyone at school is aware, so it's just a matter of time. He would have found out anyway because he was trying to get a copy of your death certificate. He lost the one grandmother sent him.

E-

Did you see the certificate yourself?
K-

No, only heard about it.
E-

Good. It's okay that Da finds out. We're about to be 18 in just a few months, so there's nothing he can do about it now.
Let's Skype. Here's my address…
K-

Maggie is setting it up, but I hope it's okay that I texted Mike, your Batman. He called me first about the article that outed you as the scratcher. He was going to get the book.
E-

Maggie was finished and initiated the call. It rang more times than they expected, but then, four faces with huge smiles were looking back at them.

Key immediately asked her girls, "Do you need me to point out which one is my sister?" Everyone laughed as Dannie tapped her on the arm in gest. "Well, Miss Maggie, we all know who you are already, so allow me to introduce you two to my sisters. This redhead on my right is Sara, and…"

"You know me as Susan from the book," Sara added.

"Oh, that's right. They were minors and considering the contents of the book, the school wouldn't allow me to use their real names. Okay, so allow me to start over. This is Susan, real name is Sara. This is Donna, real name is Dannie and next to her is Rebecca, real name is Rachel. Sara, Dannie, and Rachael, got it?"

As Key was doing her introductions, Nora Kelleher had come into the room and sat on the couch behind Erin and Maggie. She was drying a bowl and had lost track as it dripped down her pant legs, while she stared with a gaping mouth and wide eyes.

Erin gestured back at her and said, "This is Maggie's Mom, Nora Kelleher."

Key and all three girls chanted back, "Hello, Mrs. Kelleher."

"And what a proper Irish name you have, Mrs. Kelleher," Key said in her best Irish brogue. Then she returned to her normal accent, "Maggie is truly your daughter. I can see where her beauty comes from."

Nora smiled and replied, "Hello, oh my goodness, hello. May I say you sound so much like Erin did when we first met her with that thick English accent."

"My sister does sound more Americanized, but don't be surprised if her old voice comes back once we're there," Key replied with a huge smile.

"You sound like Mum," Erin added.

Key put a hand to her heart and took a deep breath, "To compare me to Mum on any level was the kindest thing you could say." Key then continued, "I'm sure you have a ton of questions for me, but I have one I would really like to ask first, if I could."

Erin shot back, "Okay, shoot."

"I was under the impression you thought me dead, and yet your email to the Drama Queen years ago asked about me."

"I never believed it. The moment Da told me, I tried to tell him you weren't, but he didn't want to hear it. Even Mike mocked me, but I knew..."

"How?" Key interrupted and asked.

"I could feel you." Erin paused and watched as Key's brows became crooked. "It's hard to explain, but I could tell Maggie when you were scared, angry, anxious, I just knew. But I didn't feel them as you were. Your feelings were separated in a way that I knew what they were, but I didn't suffer them directly. I suffered them in a more sympathetic way." Erin stopped and shook her head a bit, "oh, I don't know how to explain it, and I'm sure I sound like a mad woman."

"I believe it," Sara replied with agreeing gestures from Dannie and Rachel. "We always knew you two had been communicating all these years."

"Why would you have thought that?" Key shot at her.

Then Key's head snapped over to look at Rachel, who added, "Because you talked to her almost every time you napped."

"What are you talking about?" Key asked in confusion.

"I know you don't remember your dreams, and I hate to bring this up, but do you remember waking up in the hospital and I told you that you woke up saying, "Erin, I'm okay, don't worry"? And then…"

"I do, but it could just have been a dream." Key replied.

"Yes, that part could have, but then I asked you who Caitlyn was." A gasp could be heard coming from Erin. Key also had figured it out, but Sara still made it clear to the others. "You said you didn't know a Caitlyn, but we now know that she is Erin's new little sister who had to have been born around the same time."

Everyone had become speechless for a moment until the sound of a cell phone went off. It was Erin's. She fumbled it for a moment before answering, "Martha?" A few seconds later, "No, I'm not coming for dinner right now, and you should turn it off and get over here." Erin looked in thought while she listened again to the caller. "Because I would like to introduce you to my sister, Kathleen." She choked up for a second before continuing. "We're Skyping with her now, and wild bulls couldn't pull me away." Staring into her sister's eyes, she finished. "Sorry, but I need to hang up. You and Da really should come over to the Kelleher's. Love you." Erin hung up and said, "sorry, that was Martha. I'm sure she's in shock right now. They had no idea."

"Da is home? He's coming?" Key asked with a shaky yet higher voice.

"Let's hope. I told her they should," Erin replied with a huge smile. "So, how did you know I had a little sister, Caitlyn?"

"I met her at the ice rink last year. Of course, I was in costume…" Key started.

"Wait, what? You MET her?" Erin shot back.

Key, Sara, Dannie and Rachel seemed to get fidgety, giving one another side glances before Key tried to explain. "I have been sneaking back since we turned 14 years old. The money from my books allowed us…"

"You came home? You were here?! Why didn't you tell me, contact me or something?" Erin now had tears in her eyes.

"Oh Erin, I thought you understood why I couldn't take the chance," Key replied. "I knew you and Da were so close, and I didn't think you would be able to resist telling him."

There was silence for a moment. Erin's face crinkled up, and tears flowed. Everyone just sat quietly with teary eyes. Finally, Erin took a deep breath and let it out slowly. "I know, I just," Erin said quietly before her thought trailed off.

"I'm so sorry I didn't confide in you. I should have, but I was just so scared." Key said. "I just felt in my heart that he would want me to return home, and I can't explain enough how important it has been to be here to heal."

"When are you coming home?" Erin asked in a whinier tone.

"The girls don't graduate until about the same time you do. I'm working hard, Erin, to wrap things up here so I can get home immediately after. I promise."

"Until we can, you should visit the house," Sara added. "We've alerted Dee and Frank to give you your badge key. You can go anytime."

"The house?" Erin asked.

"Yes, I got a lawyer, and Grandmother relented. I've been making improvements." Key replied.

"The house is yours?" Erin questioned.

"Well, technically," Key replied.

"Who are Dee and Frank?" Erin asked.

"I hired them to maintain the property, oversee the contractors and all that. They live in the little cottage just down from the main house. I believe you met them last time you visited." Key replied.

Just then, there was a knock at the door and Nora got up to answer it. It was Martha – alone. Nora directed her to the couch behind the girls, and she sat down with the same expression Nora had when she first saw Key.

"Hello, I understand you're Martha, Erin's step-mum?" Key acknowledges.

"Oh my…yes, I am. I…" Martha struggled to form a complete sentence.

All the girls giggled before Key started the introductions, although Martha had no idea what book she was referring to and real names vs. fake ones.

"Is Da coming?" Erin turned back to ask her.

"Um, no, sorry." Martha's face was turning red as a beet.

"Don't stress it, Erin," Key said. "So, where is Caitlyn? We were hoping to meet our littlest sister."

"She's eating dinner," Martha replied, suddenly getting very fidgety.

Key gave her a big smile, "Martha, please relax. My father and I will work it out over time, and I don't hold you responsible in any way for his decision not to come."

Martha took an audible deep breath and after letting it out, said, "Thank you for that. I'm sure you will. He loves you and misses you very much. So, where are you exactly?"

"We live at Willington Boarding School in England. And, Martha, before you start asking a lot of questions, I would ask that you read the book. You will understand why it's difficult to talk about."

"I'll let you read mine on the laptop or you could use my Kindle." Erin said.

This is only going to get awkward until they've all read the book, Key thought. "This has been quite a shock for all of us, I think. Maybe we should end this here and give it a night's rest. You could make a visit to the house if it's still early enough there, and we could talk again tomorrow. Okay?" Key asked.

They all agreed, but before they hung up the call, Key told Erin she had made something for both her and Caitlyn. "They are at the house, and Dee will retrieve them for you. Love!"

Old House – Photo Albums

Erin went to the beach house where she was welcomed by Dee. Key had already informed Dee of Erin's visit, so she had already prepared for it.

"You must be Dee. We've met before," Erin said as she walked to the front door.

"Hello, Erin. Yes, we have." Dee replied with a big smile on her face.

Dee showed Erin how to hold her badge up to the scanner and then watched as the front door opened automatically.

Everyone found it a bit frustrating, but Erin walked in very slowly, taking in every new detail. The bench in the small entrance with baskets underneath for shoes and hooks for coats. Maggie was right behind her and kept her mom and Martha from rushing her.

Erin gasped as she entered the main room. The old, tattered couches had been replaced by large, comfortable looking leather ones. The floor, which used to be an old, ugly yellow carpet, was now a beautiful wood, and the narrow wall between the open room and kitchen no longer had paneling, but a multicolored brick face.

As they all made their way in, the large picture on that brick wall started scrolling up, revealing a large TV screen. It was Sara looking in at them. "Hi again!"

"Where's Kathleen?" Erin asked.

"Everyone went back to their normal routines but working on my computer is my normal. By the way, since I have you alone, do you think you could get used to calling your sister Key? I think it would mean a lot to her."

"I could try, but why?" Erin replied.

"Princess Kathleen was the little girl you knew who had a wonderful childhood. Kathleen was the little girl who was helpless and abused. As you know, she can't forget anything she sees or hears, but Key represents the part of her that survived. She liked the new nickname when we gave it to her because it allowed her to really start anew and be who she wanted, no longer under anyone's thumb. She once told us she could compartmentalize the memories. Good, young memories under Princess, the really tough years under Kathleen and the new, good memories under Key. Does that make sense?"

"It does. I'll try to remember. So, how did you know we were here?"

"The house is wired with video and audio, so be careful. There's a house assistant, which you may have heard at the front door. She alerted me. If you have any questions, just start it with V." Just then, a voice that sounded like Key asked, "Yes, Miss Sara? How can I help you?" Sara dismissed her, but Maggie couldn't help giving it a try.

"V, can you tell me if there is any ice cream?"

"No, I'm afraid not. I believe the freezer and refrigerator are empty at the moment." V responded.

They all laughed in surprise.

"Are there cameras in every room?" Martha asked.

Sara giggled, "No. The bedrooms and each loo are camera and audio-free. Sorry, I mean the water closets or bathrooms, ladies' room, men's room, little girl's room, oh heavens, whatever of the 600 names you have for it. It seems every restaurant there has a different title for it." They all giggled before Sara continued.

"I'm going to let you go, but I wanted to make sure Dee found the gifts?" Dee gave her a nod and headed toward the bookcase. "And I wanted to mention that the items in the shops are free, but make sure V can see what you take so she can keep the inventory correctly. Oh wait, we emptied them before we left…"

"Shops?" both Maggie and Erin asked in unison.

"You'll figure it out, so I'm signing off. Love!" Sara ended the connection, and the picture started to scroll back down and covered the TV.

"Have you noticed they never say 'Bye,' they say 'Love' instead? I like it," Martha noted.

"V, what are the shops?" Maggie asked.

"The shops are in the courtyard, past the kitchen. There are three in total across from the hotel, not including the blacksmith shop at the end of the street."

Dee was trying to hand Erin the gifts her sister made for her, but Erin and Maggie both ran through the kitchen to see a new sliding barn door leading to what had been just an empty warehouse space. They slid the door aside and ran in.

"It looks like we've gone back outside!" Maggie squealed.

They spent an hour and a half in just the courtyard looking through the Café, Old Country Store, Making Music shop, Blacksmith shop which looked more like a carpentry shop inside and then each of the hotel rooms. Erin went live on FB for a bit, talking about how she was able to see her sister on Skype and the real names of her sisters in the book. She also explained how she got a key to her sister's house. She showed them the courtyard, panning from one end to the other before signing off.

"This is fantastic! I'm staying in room number three when we stay over," Maggie said. "That one's my favorite."

"I'll take the one next to it upstairs, so we can sit on our balconies." Erin replied.

They made their way back to look at the kitchen and then each bedroom and back deck. Even Martha, who had once practiced for choir with Jon and them years ago, was unaware of the hidden door.

Finally, Dee was able to get Erin to accept the gifts her sister had made for her and Caitlyn.

"I knew she took Mum's photo album!" She looked at Martha while she sat down, "And it looks like she made me a copy of it."

Maggie sat down on Erin's left and Martha on her right. Nora stood behind them to look at the book.

"What's in Caitlyn's?" Martha asked.

Erin closed her own and flipped Caitlyn's on top. "It's pictures of Da as a little boy. The labels say those are his parents." She slid Caitlyn's book over to Martha's lap and then reopened her own. The first few pages were the same as her mother's old one, starting with various ages of her mother growing up, but this one had new pages of both Jon and her biological father, Erin, growing up. "How did she get these? My Mum's book only had a few pictures of Da and, well, my other Da I guess, as teenagers."

"Your other Da?" Martha asked.

"You need to read her book. It says the beginning of Key's book was taken from my Mum's diaries." Erin stopped looking at the album and turned to Martha, "Da isn't my biological father, but he married my Mum to save our lives."

"I had no idea, Erin," Martha replied.

"Neither did I until today."

As Erin turned back to continue through the album, she said quietly, "he should have told me though."

"It's getting late, and you have school tomorrow. We really should head home." Nora said. "But thank you, Erin, for allowing us to come and see this. It is truly amazing, and I'm still in shock, so tomorrow should be interesting."

"I have been on such an adrenaline rush since this morning. I'll probably sleep like a baby tonight." Erin replied as she stood up.

Martha had finished looking through Caitlyn's album and handed it back to Erin. "I think you should be the one to give it to her."

"You need to give us some pictures of you growing up, and then Cate and I will have fun filling in the blank pages," Erin replied.

When they got home, Caitlyn was in bed, but Jon was not. He was in his office watching TV. Erin ran up and got into her night clothes, finally getting out of her school uniform.

Martha stopped to talk to him, though. "You need to speak to Erin." When he didn't budge, she said forcefully, "Tonight." Martha then made her way into the kitchen.

Erin was hungry when she came back down with albums in hand. This time, she stopped at the office door and when she had his attention, said, "Kathleen made a gift for Caitlyn, I think you'll enjoy. Come out while I get a snack." Erin didn't wait for an answer and turned back toward the kitchen.

Martha had already pulled out the leftover lasagna and had put a big slice of it on a plate for Erin and then one for herself. The microwave was whirling when Jon finally entered.

"Look Da! Kathleen did have Mum's photo album, but she added to it. She also used those additions to make a special one for Caitlyn." Erin opened the one that Kathleen made for her to the page of Jon as a little boy.

Jon sat on the counter stool and stared at the old photographs. "How did she…"

"I haven't asked her yet, but I'll talk to her again tomorrow. Of course, you could ask her yourself. I have her email address." Erin prompted him.

Jon didn't answer, and after he looked through the new pages, he flipped back to the beginning to see Alexandra as a little girl. When he got back to the pages of him and his old friend Erin, his daughter Erin pointed to the picture of the blonde-haired boy. "I look a lot like my father, don't I?" she asked.

Jon's head whipped up to look at her, and his eyes started tearing up. "You do." He wiped away the tears and looked at her again. "I would love to tell you all about my brother."

"Your brother?" Erin asked.

"Not by blood, but in every other way. Our mothers were best friends, and about the same time mine got pregnant, her best friend did too. Erin's Mum was unmarried though, so my parents took her in. We were born only a month apart and raised like brothers with two Mums and a Da."

"That's why you saved us and married Mum, because we were his only children," Erin said.

"How do you know that?" Jon asked.

"Kathleen, or actually, I should start calling her by her preferred name of Key, wrote a book. I learned about Mum's romance with my biological father and how he died. She said you didn't hesitate to propose to her in hopes of saving the pregnancy."

"But…but how would Kathleen know?"

"Mum's diaries. She took those too."

Martha put Erin's dinner in front of her and started the microwave again. "I have to say, Jon, looking at the screen and seeing Erin both in front of me and on the TV was very strange. And, oh, how she sounded like Erin used to. That really thick British accent."

"Have I lost that completely?" Erin asked.

"No, not completely, but it isn't nearly as thick as it once was. I suspect it may return once your sister comes home though."

Jon again shot up to look at them, "She's coming home?"

Erin now looked at him with a crooked brow, "Of course, she's going to come home. Don't you want her to?"

"I just didn't know. She hasn't contacted us in all this time, so…" Jon started.

"She didn't contact us because…she was afraid of you," Erin said.

"Afraid of me?" he shot back.

"She was afraid you would insist she come back to America. She wasn't going to be ripped out of her new life this time, so she waited until she was ready." Erin said.

"I didn't rip her out of this life!"

Erin looked down and said lightly, "You lied for me, Da. You protected me, but…"

Jon got up from the stool and stomped through the kitchen and out of sight.

Key Calls Batman

"Michael? It's Key. Please don't be angry with me. I can explain." Key wasn't sure what else to say to the answering machine, so she hung up.

"Did he hang up on you?" Sara asked angrily.

"No, it was a machine."

"Key? Are you in here?" It was Ms. Brookes.

"We're in here! Sara yelled.

"Hi girls. I, well, I wanted to see you before I go." Ms. Brookes said.

"Go where?" Key asked.

"I've been called to speak to the Board of Trustees. No doubt they want to know how much I knew about your situation."

"Nothing. You knew nothing." Key replied bluntly.

"Oh Key, they'll never believe that. They know about our holidays to America."

"Okay, then I'm going with you. I'll talk to the Board."

"That's not necessary. I knew this day would come, and I'm ready for what comes of it." Ms. Brookes tried to give her a reassuring smile.

"What time is the meeting?"

"I leave in an hour."

"Okay. I am going with you, but I need to do something first." Key said as she got up and made her way out of the room.

Key headed straight for Mrs. Burkhard's office, who has been the school counselor since before Key arrived at Willington. She knocked on her door and listened. "Come in," said a woman's voice from within, and when Key entered, she found Mrs. Burkhard sitting at a small writing table.

"Hello, Mrs. Burkhard. Do you have a moment to talk?"

The older woman's eyes became wide, and her eyebrows raised. "Are you finally agreeing to come talk with me?"

Key smiled. Mrs. Burkhard had been trying to get her into counseling since the monster was arrested. "Well, I need to today. I'm not sure you're aware but the Board of Trustees has asked Ms. Brookes to come in, and she believes it's to dismiss her"

"What is it you think I could do to help?" Mrs. Burkhard asked.

"I need you to tell them she did what was best for us and that you supported her" Key sat down on the stiff, wooden chair close to the writing table.

"I can't lie to them, sweetheart."

The two just stared at one another for a few moments.

"Mrs. Burkhard? Did you suspect what was going on back then? Did you know what we were suffering?"

Eye contact broke as Mrs. Burkhard's face became flush, and she looked down at her desk.

Key continued. "I didn't trust Ms. Brookes when I first met her because I didn't trust any adult at this school. But she's earned my change of heart" Key took a deep breath and let it out slowly. "We were powerless, so she gave us control. We were weak, and she gave us the strength to defend ourselves. We felt useless and abandoned, but she gave us cause and had our backs."

They locked eyes again, but Mrs. Burkhard was blinking away her watering eyes and said nothing.

"When the other students and teachers complained about how we were being treated differently, did you report her to the board?" Key asked.

The counselor shook her head sideways, motioning no. "Then you really wouldn't be lying. By staying quiet, you supported her," Key paused for a moment before continuing, "you were quiet when it was happening, and we suffered unimaginable atrocities. You were quiet while Ms. Brookes was making the decisions that ultimately helped us start the healing process. I'm simply asking you to speak up now on her behalf. Please, Mrs. Burkhard."

The room went quiet again until the noise of a drawer opening and a folder being slapped down on the desk broke the silence. "This is your file. You wouldn't talk to me, so I had to get clever about it," Mrs. Burkhard looked at Key again, "I'll be honest, I almost reported her only a few weeks into her tenure, because I thought you should have been forced to come see me as the other girls did. However, I decided to give her more time."

She started leafing through all the pages, and Key could see written notes, forms and even pictures. The file was more than an inch thick and the folder holding it together was starting to tear at the seam. "When you girls were all in class, Ms. Brookes would take me into your dorm. I documented everything, from how clean and organized it was, to how cleverly it was decorated over time. Even the precautions you took when you had the kitchen installed in the old headmaster's room." Mrs. Burkhard left the file open and put her elbows on it, bringing her hands together. "I also spoke to the teachers here about the girl's grades and found they went from being the worst students to competing for who would graduate at the top of the class."

Mrs. Burkhad sat back with her hands on her lap. "None of this is typical, considering what you all suffered. However, I'm still not sure what I have will be enough. Ms. Brookes knew more than she shared, and it was her job to share it."

"Do you understand why she kept my secret?" Key asked.

"Yes. You had lost two friends because they had returned home to families that didn't understand, and you were afraid to be the third."

"No, I was afraid to be the fifth. Suicide haunted all of us." A tear ran down Key's cheek, but she quickly wiped it away. "Would you have had me sent home?"

Now it was Mrs. Burkhard's turn to take a deep breath before saying, "God I hope not. I hope I would have done as she did."

Key slowly stood up to leave. "Mrs. Brookes will be leaving in less than an hour. I'm going to wait by her car and insist on going. We need her. We can't afford a new head that has no understanding" She slowly walked out of the office and toward the exit to the parking lot. *I can't believe she wouldn't help me now any more than she did then.* The thought brought another tear she had to wipe away.

The front door was only about ten feet away when Key heard her name. "Ms. Yule," it was Mrs. Burkhard with the large file in her arms and walking as swiftly as she could to catch up. As she approached Key she said, "I put you on my calendar for every Wednesday at 7:00 am" Before Key could protest, she put her hand up and said, "That's the deal, understand?"

30 minutes later, Key and Mrs. Burkhard were waiting at Ms. Brookes' car. "Mrs. Burkhard?" Ms. Brookes asked.

"I'm Key's counselor, and I think it's important I attend as well." Ms. Burkhard replied.

Ms. Brookes looked at Key and then back at Mrs. Burkhard. "Key has never agreed to meet with you."

"Well, she did today. I've been made fully abreast of the details, and Key has agreed to see me weekly until she turns 18." Mrs. Burkhard followed it with a wink.

Ms. Brookes shook her head and unlocked the car. "I'm not sure what you could do to help at this point though."

Shortly after they pulled out of the school parking lot, Mrs. Burkhard made it clear how she planned to help. "I'm sure it was difficult for you not to share Key's secret with the Board, but I hope to make them understand why it was important that you didn't."

Ms. Brookes took a deep breath but said nothing, so Mrs. Burkhard continued. "We lost two of the girls to suicide after they returned home, and none of us wanted to lose another. The decision I made-"

An audible gasp came from the back seat as Ms. Brookes looked at her quickly with a crooked brow before turning her eyes back to the road.

"Yes, the decision I made was in her best interest. If she was going to heal, she needed her sisters to do so with my counseling, of course."

"Are you sure you want…"

"I'm sure that I made the best decision for her wellbeing, yes." Mrs. Burkhard said with great confidence.

Ms. Brookes took a few deep breaths. "So, I…"

"You did what her counselor recommended, trusting that it would not go any further than your confidence." Mrs. Burkhard replied. "Patient-client privilege."

A few hours later, they returned and found Sara on the front steps waiting.

"Hey! Ummm…so, well, tell me how the meeting went," Sara said, stopping Key on the steps.

"She still has a job." Key smiled at Mrs. Burkhard as she and Ms. Brookes walked past them into the school.

"I'll see you next Wednesday at 7:00 am," Mrs. Burkhard replied before disappearing inside.

"She gotcha, huh?" Sara asked.

"Yes, that was the deal. Honestly, I know more about counseling now. It's not what I used to think it was, so I believe it could be helpful."

"You do?"

"I know Rachel and Dannie both appreciate her help. And Mrs. Burkhard knows about my memory, so I don't think it would just be her having me relive it. She may have ideas on coping, even for me."

Key watched Sara carefully while she was talking. "So, what's up? You seem antsy,

"You have a surprise inside, and I wanted to walk you in when you found it." Sara then turned to walk back to the dorm.

Key was getting more anxious every time Sara looked back with a huge smile on their way to the dorm but found her excitement contagious. Sara reached the door, knocked twice and then opened it.

Key had a huge smile when she entered, but it quickly turned to tears and froze her in place. She was so instantly choked up that she couldn't speak. Her hands came up and covered her face while she sobbed. They only dropped away once she felt his arms around her and she turned her head, pressed it against his chest and wrapped her arms around him to hold the muscles in his back.

"Shhh, I'm not angry," Mike said quietly.

Sara, Dannie, Rachel and even Jeff were getting misty-eyed watching. Finally, Sara cleared her throat and spoke up. "Ladies, let's take this dog for a walk." Sara took Jeff's hand and started pulling him out past Mike and Key, and the girls followed.

Key tried to wipe her eyes with one hand without losing her grip on Michael. She had found enough control to choke out, "It was me."

"What was you?" Michael asked.

"It wasn't Erin…in the hospital…it was me."

Michael's response was an even harder hug and kiss her on the top of her head.

They stood there for another few minutes before she tried to look up at him and speak. "I wanted…" but she broke down again.

"To tell me?"

Key nodded yes.

Michael bent down and put an arm under her legs to pick her up. He carried her to the couch and sat down. "I showed up just after you left, evidently, so I've had some time with your sisters. Sara, especially, had a lot to tell me, like what it took to invite me to the cliff house. But I think the most important was why you couldn't take a chance at telling me, even though Sara swears you trusted me."

Key shook her head in the affirmative again without a word. Then she laid her head on his shoulder and closed her eyes. Immediately, she was making a strange purring sound.

"Kathleen?" Mike prompted. "Key?" *She's asleep?* Mike chuckled and got comfortable, sinking down into the couch and locking his hands so she wouldn't fall back off of his lap. He was jetlagged, so he put his head back and closed his own eyes. He was sure he woke up from his own snore but then realized the door was opening.

"Hello?" Ms. Brookes said as she made her way in.

Michael whispered, "Hi. Sorry, the girls took my friend for a tour of the school and Key is asleep."

Ms. Brookes sat down on the chair across from him and spoke in a normal tone of voice. "I'm glad she gave in and allowed herself a nap. She does not always give into it. And you can speak in a scream, and it wouldn't wake her up. Once she's out, she's out." She paused for a moment and then questioned, "So, you must be her Batman?"

Mike laughed, "Yeah, that's me."

"I just heard you were here. It's good to see you again. I'll never forget how excited she was to find you our first year back."

"You mean when we met at the café, before going over to the arcade?" he asked.

"Oh no, the year before that. We were seated right next to your birthday dinner party. I understand you have a younger sister, correct?"

Mike nodded yes.

"Well, Key told us later that evening that your little sister gave you a book as a gift and then asked that you take your bookmark out."

"The picture. I have a picture of Kathle…Key and I as kids that I had covered in plastic."

"Yes, she saw it and then heard you talk about her. She was also glad to know she hadn't lost that picture forever. You know she has another five of them, correct? She has a photo album that belonged to her mother." Ms. Brookes said.

"I found the picture on the floor the day she left. Her father must have thought he still had that album when he said I could keep it." Michael readjusted a little, trying not to jostle Key too much.

"You could lay her down if you'd like. I promise you, it won't wake her up."

"No, I'm good. I'd prefer to hold on to her as long as I can stand it," he replied.

"The good news is, she never naps for longer than 20 or 25 minutes." There was a moment of silence before the headmaster in Ms. Brookes came out, "So, are you attending a university back home?" Ms. Brookes asked.

"Yeah, I'm going for a business degree."

"You'll get more business knowledge from Key in a day than anything you will learn at school. She'll be a huge help in your graduating with honors. Starting businesses seems to be one of her – well many – specialties. She likes to stay busy."

"She's obviously very intelligent, but doesn't make me feel stupid," Michael mused.

"You can thank her girls for that. When Key first started at the university at eight years old, I understood she got a big head about it at first. The girls didn't take that very well and taught her to be humbler about her God-given gifts."

"Wait, what? Started at a university at eight years old?" Michael asked. "She didn't mention that in her book."

"Yes, I wasn't here at the time, but I understand they had her tested and immediately realized her home-schooling had gone well past the 12th grade."

"Wow," is all Michael could say.

"Wait until you see what she's done with her birth home. It is the most…"

"I've seen it! She did that too?"

Just then the door opened again, and Sara led the pack into the room. "Oh good, she's napping. She needs that sleep you know, but sorry it happened now. How long has she been out?"

Mike and Ms. Brookes looked at one another, hoping the other would know.

"No bother, I'm just glad she wasn't alone. You know, in case the fire alarms went off, I trust you would have gotten her out." Sara sat next to Mike on his left so she could see Key's face. "So, how much did you get to talk before she conked out?"

"Not much, although I now know Erin is not in love with me," Mike replied.

All the girls and Ms. Brookes laughed.

Sara laid her head on Michael's other shoulder and was face to face with Key. "Feeling better, love?"

Key smiled and lifted her head to look at Michael. "I wasn't dreaming, you really are here." She lifted her hand to his cheek and gave him a kiss on his lips and then a few on his cheek. "How long are you here?"

"Until you come home," he replied with an ornery smile.

"That's months away."

"Then we should start looking for an apartment or a room for rent because I'm not leaving you."

"You're what every throwaway prays for," Rachel interjected. All eyes turned to her, so she continued. "Every throwaway prays that there is someone out there that remembers them, loves them and will come for them."

"We're here for all of you," Jeff said. "Well, he may be here for Key, but I'm here for all of you beautiful ladies. It's heaven."

The girls all giggled knowing what a 'player' he was.

"Not quite the same thing, ya bugger," Dannie quipped.

"No, but we'll take it," Sara quipped back, giving Jeff a giggle and wink. She turned her attention back to Key, "so, are you going to give Mike your collection?"

"Wha…" he started.

"Oh yes!" Key jumped off him and ran into her room, bringing out a box.

He took the lid off to find a pile of plastic-covered Batman comic books.

"Some are first additions, but others are later ones. The one on top isn't special to you, but it is to me. I got it from a friend who enlightened me that Batman may not have been your real name." Key gave Michael a pursed-lip smile.

He gave a guilty smile back but said, "I love the collection, but I think I appreciate the box more."

"It was custom-made," she responded. The box was a light tan color, faux marble looking, with the five pictures she had of them randomly covering the entire outside of the box, lid included.

Dannie got up and started toward the kitchen, which was the old monster's room. "I'm going to start dinner."

"Wonderful, but would you mind if I didn't help tonight?" Key asked.

All the girls giggled and stood up while Sara replied, "We got this. Come on dog, we'll throw you some scraps." She looked at Jeff and laughed.

"I'm not sure I like my new nickname here," Jeff replied as he followed her.

Ms. Brookes took the hint and also excused herself. "It was nice seeing you again and I'm sure your accommodations will be figured out for your stay." She winked at Key knowing full well that the boys would be offered the guest room that still had Sienna and Julie's old single beds.

Once they were alone, Key asked Michael to join her. She needed to have a more private conversation, so she took him into her room and closed the door.

"You look concerned. Are you okay?" Mike asked.

"Yes, but I have a huge favor to ask, and I'm not sure what you'll think of me after I do."

"Ask," he said simply.

"You mentioned once that you were there when my Da received a death certificate and letter."

"Yeah, I read them both. Is your grandmother still alive because she's going…"

"Yes, she is, and I don't want her going to prison."

"But…she…"

"I know you think I'm crazy, but I've been talking to her for years. I yelled mostly at first, but we finally had a breakthrough, and we've been making peace with the past."

Michael just stared at her quietly, his head shaking side to side slowly.

Key sat next to him on the bed. "I've forgiven her. She has the same issues I have with not being able to forget anything she sees or hears. That's not always the gift you think it would be. I relive every horrible experience over and over, as does she."

"That's no excuse…" he started.

"No, it's not an excuse for what she did. She's handled her gift-curse very badly and allowed her bad memories to rule her. I've been teaching her how not to…"

"You're a better person than I am. I would never have given her the time of day." Michael couldn't hide his anger. "She took you away from me, and she's the reason you were put in the position to be abused!"

"I know." Key wasn't sure if she should ask the favor now and just looked down at her hands.

After a few minutes of silence, Mike asked, "Are you asking me to forgive her?"

"No."

"Then what are you asking from me?"

Key didn't answer straight away. She started to get up, saying, "Never mind."

Michael grabbed her hand and pulled her around to stand in front of him. "Ask."

"I can't."

"Ask," he insisted.

Key took a deep breath and let it out slowly. "I ask for nothing. I only want to confide in you that I do not wish my grandmother to go to prison. Let's go join the others and help…"

"You want me to lie if I'm asked…"

"I ask for nothing," she snapped before continuing. "If Jon decides to go after her, then there's nothing I can do and what happens, happens. Whatever happens, it won't be with my help." Key then pulled away and started for the door.

"I want to meet her," Mike said without moving.

Key turned back to look at him. "We can go tomorrow," she replied. She stood there for a moment. "I'm sorry for hitting you with this. It's been weighing on my mind the more I think about moving back home."

"Are you nervous about confronting your Dad?" he asked.

Key started to walk back to him slowly. "I relive that moment every day—I can't help it. I hear him lie to protect my sister with such desperation. Then he offers me up without hesitation. I screamed and he didn't hear me. He didn't even wait to hear my grandmother agree before he was insisting, I go pack a bag." Key's eyes started to look teary. "We'll never know if she would have said 'all or nothing', because he was so intent to send me off."

Key was now in front of him again, and he took her hands in his. "I'm so sorry."

"Don't do that!" Key snapped.

"Do what?"

"Apologize for another man's sins. Tell me it sucks or that he was a jerk, but don't you say sorry for the pain he caused me. It's his to carry and no one else's."

Key was starting to breathe hard and fast. Mike put his arms around her and just held her until she calmed down. While still pressed up against his chest, she said, "My friendship isn't worth all this. I'm more trouble than I'm worth."

Mike pulled away enough to make her look at him. "I don't ever, and I mean EVER, want to hear you say that again. Do you understand me?"

Her lips curled down, and her head started to drop, but he cupped her head in his hands and forced her to look at him eye-to-eye. "Promise me."

She closed her eyes but nodded in agreement.

"I don't want to listen to my wife whine for the next 50 years with that self-pity nonsense."

Key's head snapped up with a crooked brow. "Your wife? That can't be me, Michael, that could never be me."

"The hell it can't." A huge smile took over his face. "I've watched how Sara nags you to get her way, so expect it, beautiful. You WILL be my wife. It's not a question in my mind."

She pulled away but with a smile now on her face. "I don't *always* give in to her," she said as she walked backwards toward the door.

Mike started after her, "You'll give in. I'm going to be relentless."

Key just giggled as they made their way out.

Key And Mike Go To Izzy's

"Nice house. She's still living large," Mike said with a hint of sarcasm as they pulled up to Grandma Izzy's.

Key knocked and Uncle Bobby answered. "She's in the kitchen making tea," he said as he bent down to cheek his niece. "And you must be Batman. Put'er there fella." Uncle Bobby put his hand out and Mike shook it.

"Sorry. Michael, this is my Uncle Bobby, my mother's younger brother. Uncle Bobby, this is Michael."

"You can call me Mike."

"Alright, Mike, welcome to our humble abode." Uncle Bobby stood aside to let them pass. "Now that there's some testosterone in the group, might I join you today?"

"You are always welcome, but you usually just get upset and leave," Key replied.

"Only when you two argue, which is most of the time."

Mike walked slowly behind them and took in the largeness of the entrance with the paintings he swore were watching him. *Feels like a museum in here,* he thought as he peeked into each room they passed.

"Hello, love." Grandma Izzy cheeked Key and then waited patiently.

"Grandma Izzy, this is Michael—Michael, Grandma Izzy."

Mike's face immediately became a scoffing look, and he didn't speak or gesture toward her. Although, he couldn't help but notice how attractive she was, considering her age. *She looks like an older version of Key, which is actually a plus,* he thought.

Izzy took a deep breath. "Well, should we sit down?"

There was already a tray with a teapot, four cups with matching saucers, milk and sugar on the table. Izzy started to pour the tea into each cup.

Mike started immediately. "So, I know Key has already forgiven you, but…"

Izzy stopped pouring and looked straight at him. "She has?"

"That's not the point. Continue Michael," Key said.

"But…I'm not sure I ever could. Why would you think anyone should?" Mike asked.

"I can't answer that," she replied.

"You mean you won't." he snapped.

"Because I don't know why anyone should. There is no excuse for my actions."

"Sounded like Key had excuses for you last night. She used your memory as an…"

"No, I didn't," Key said. "I specifically said it was not an excuse."

Before Mike could retort, Izzy did. "She's correct. It is not an excuse." Izzy placed the now-filled cups in front of each of them. "My granddaughter simply understood what drove my bad actions and explained it to me. Since she has the same gifts, she understood that I was not handling mine well. But no, it is still not an excuse for what I did to her. My actions were inexcusable."

They all took sips randomly and sat quietly. Mike wondered, *should I put my pinky out drinking from this dainty little thing?*

Finally, Izzy spoke without looking up from her cup. "Key wasn't the first person I lashed out at. Although I loved my husband, he took the brunt of it for years. It wasn't until Alexandra and Robert grew older that they started to suffer the same fate." Izzy took a quick sip of her tea and placed it back on its saucer. "And it cost me."

"Did it cost you 10 years of your life without family?" Michael snapped.

"More," she replied quietly. "It cost me the last eight years of my daughter's life. It probably drove my husband to an early grave and years of getting to know my granddaughters. Even if Key has forgiven me, as you say, Erin probably won't. Not ever. Nor will their stepfather, Jonathan. Oh God, how I've tortured that poor man."

After another minute of silence, it was Mike's turn to break it. "Last night, Key talked about the moment her dad lied to protect Erin. If he hadn't pushed Key to go with you, would you have agreed to take only her?"

"Hmmm…I honestly can't say for sure. I intended to take both. Actually, I did keep arguing for both while he was cleaning her up to go. He seemed to take control of the situation, which only made me angrier." Izzy looked at Mike. "I liked being in control of every situation. I feel lost when I'm not. Today is a good example…"

Again, silence. Mike was tapping his spoon against the cup, lost in thought.

After a minute, it was finally Key's turn. "You said you had some things for me?"

"Yes, I've been cleaning out and found some of your mother's things. They're from her childhood, but you may want to pass them on to your future children."

"You know I can't have any," Key said with a hint of anger.

"But you will. You said yourself that your sister Sara was willing…"

"I am not going to allow Sara to ruin her body to produce my children, and you know her future husband won't want her to either."

"Then you'll adopt…ah ah ah" Izzy wagged her finger at Key, who was about to protest, "you'll figure it out, I'm sure of it."

"Yes, we will," Mike said.

"Please don't start with that, Michael," Key said, sounding frustrated.

"But you love him," Izzy pushed. "You told me…"

Key stood up, pushing her chair back in one move. "Show me the stuff."

"So, how did it go?" Jeff asked Mike when they returned.

Mike rolled his eyes as he put a box down in Key's room. "It's hard to stay angry with someone who admits they did wrong, is remorseful and answers every question with complete honesty. Worse yet, I actually found myself on her side of an argument."

"Wow, really. So, you forgive her?"

"No. I'm not there yet, but I understand why Key could, I guess. They've been hashing it out for years."

Mike made his way out to the open sitting room and fell into a chair, allowing every muscle to relax. "What did you do while we were gone?"

"I finally read Key's book, but I have questions," Jeff said.

Key had overheard while coming out of the kitchen area. "What questions?" she asked while taking a seat next to Michael on the couch.

Jeff also sat down across from them but sat forward with his elbows on his knees. "Well," he hesitated. "I understand the things you did to help build the girl's confidence with the dummy you created when you returned and forcing them to sing and dance in front of audiences in the plays you wrote…"

"I resent that. I didn't force them – I encouraged them," Key answered with a smile.

"Okay, okay, you 'encouraged them' into doing what you wanted them to do. Got it." Jeff sat back now with a smile.

Key returned the smile for having been caught. She couldn't really argue with the accusation.

Jeff continued, "I understand how you helped them heal, but I don't understand how they really helped you."

Key's expression got somber as she looked away from him momentarily. When their eyes met again, she explained. "My mother was wonderful. She knew my strengths and my weaknesses and challenged them both. Writing was my obvious passion, so she would say, 'I want to read about a flower that grew through the snow.' Of course, I wrote more of a children's book about the flower with a weak seed that wouldn't give up, and when it finally bloomed, it was winter when all the other flowers had gone into hiding.

She knew I hated maths at first, so she would challenge that too by asking me to help redesign the old, broken furniture that required the use of it.

The point I'm trying to make is that she was wonderful, and I wanted the girls to have the same. I wanted to be the Mum they never had and hopefully be as good at it as my own was. Building that dummy is not a good example because it was more selfish than you realize. I wanted to beat the hell out of someone and that was the closest I could get. Getting them to join me made me feel it wasn't a horrible act."

Key continued, "But all the girls are artists in their own way. Rachel with food and how she displayed it. Dannie with her drawing and painting, and Sarah with her photographs and sewing. I simply wrote the plays, but we all worked together on the music, Rachel on the props, especially the fake food that looked so real. Dannie designed the sets that we all helped to build and paint while Sara worked on the lighting and stage direction. Each was challenged in both their strengths and weaknesses, and every success they had became another one for me in trying to be the best parent figure I could. The more confident they grew, the more self-worth I gained."

Graduation

It was June first, and Erin stood in front of the mirror admiring her appearance. Her entire ensemble was provided as gifts from her sisters across the pond. The designer dress was from Key and fit her perfectly. *I wonder if she tried it on herself to make sure it would*, she thought. Sara had sent the matching shoes, but it was the jewelry that Dannie sent that Erin probably loved most. She loved designer clothes, but sparkly things always won her over.

Rachel had secured her a hair and nail appointment for that morning at a prestigious solon. They tied her hair up in the back but made it look like she had huge rollers in it. They pinned huge round loops of hair in various directions. It was a style she thought she would want again in the future, maybe for her wedding day.

It was graduation day, which for Erin, meant she was only a week or so away from finally seeing her sister in person. She is hoping, once her sister has returned home, their father will come around. He hasn't agreed to communicate with Key and dismisses any conversation about her. However, Erin is convinced he has finally read her sister's novel because his mood has only gotten more solemn.

Maggie came rushing into Erin's room, "Are you ready?"

"Wow, you look gorgeous!" Erin commented.

"Your sisters have great fashion sense," Maggie replied.

"OUR sisters, according to them. They keep reminding me that blood doesn't matter—only the unconditional love we share does."

"But Key is your actual sister…" Maggie started to reply.

"Do you consider my father any less my father? He's not my blood, Mags."

"Okay, okay, I get it. Sorry. OUR sisters have a great fashion sense."

"Honestly, I think Sara picked out the dress and shoes. My sister prefers very plain, casual clothing. This dress is fitted, and the shoes are sparkly. Every time we've Skyped with them, my sister is in a plain t-shirt and jeans."

"Although, not always in plain jeans. I love the stitched ones."

"What are the stitched ones?" Martha asked as she entered the room.

Maggie answered, very animated. "Whenever they do something for the first time, like sing in public, or once they did an amateur comedy club, they pass around a pair of their jeans to the audience to sign. Then Key stitches over the signatures with different colors to preserve them."

"They always save a small patch of space on the front of one leg to stitch in the date, place, and event. They really turn out looking cool," Erin added.

"That sounds very cool," Martha replied. "Well, we have to get going. You need to get there early and I promised Nora I would take a turn at saving seats for both families.

The morning seemed to fly by. The parents were seated, the students were lined up and the music began for the procession in. Erin hated that her name was alphabetically so far away from Maggie. They had both made friends with just about everyone, so they were still in good company but wanted to celebrate every moment together.

The ceremony began with an introduction from the principal, who did a summary of their four years. He quickly reached the events of Erin finding her sister and how the entire class had come together to celebrate. He then asked Erin to come, front and center before the stage. When she made her way up and stood in front of the stage, the lights went out, and a projection of her sister appeared on a screen over the stage. Everyone clapped but found that it was only a recording.

Key's recorded message began.

Hello! Erin, I just wanted to say how proud I am of my big sis — by about two minutes. I guess you were more anxious than I was to meet the new world.

There are so many things to love about you, Erin. For example, how gullible you always were. I assume you are standing up front, watching this video, completely unaware that the real me is walking up behind you.

The lights immediately go up, and Erin whips around to see her sister Key walking up the aisle in a black robe and colored collars like so many of the teachers wore. The entire student body and parents stand in an uproar of cheers. The two sisters collided in a tight hug. They pulled away momentarily, looked at one another and collided again.

Finally, Key takes Erin's hand and leads her up on stage. The principal hands Key the microphone, and when the room settles down, she turns to Erin. "Every graduation needs one thing. Do you know what that is?"

Erin looked at her with a crooked brow, but just before her sister could answer, she said, "A key speaker?"

"Yes!" Key answered laughter from the audience.

Erin laughed while rolling her eyes.

Then Key turns to the audience, "Isn't my sister beautiful?" Of course, the crowd laughs due to how identical they are, especially today. Key was wearing the same dress, shoes, and jewelry. Sara even did her hair in the same style that Dannie had informed the hairdresser to do for Erin.

"Oh my gosh, they're laughing at you, Erin. That's terrible." The audience giggled again before Key continued, "Never mind them, sis. I think you look fabulous today."

She then looks at Erin again and asks, "Sooo, do you have a boyfriend here?" Three different boys stand up and say in various ways, "I'll be her boyfriend!"

Key takes a step closer to the edge of the stage, "This isn't an auction, fellas." Again, the crowd laughs as the boys put their heads down and retake their seats. Erin shakes her head 'no' as she laughs. "Well, maybe we need to figure out why they laughed at you being called beautiful, and then we can fix the problem."

Erin looks to the ceiling and shakes her head, "Oh my God, stop!"

"Okay, okay, stop being a drama queen."

"You're the drama queen, even going by that name," Erin replied. At that, the student body and many of the parents let out a gasp of surprise. They all knew about the Drama Queen from England who saved their club. It had been in all the papers.

"Wait, seriously?" Key asked, looking at the audience. "A WRITER–also from Willington Boarding school…and you never put the two together?" Key followed with a very animated look of surprise, causing them to laugh again. She then looked back at the principal, "And you're graduating them today, hm?" More laughter ensues when he lifts both hands flat to the ceiling and cocks his head.

Key then turned back to the student body and said, "Before I forget, I have a small favor to ask." As she spoke, Sara ran up to the stage holding a pair of folded jeans. "We're going to put two pairs of jeans out on a table, just outside the school entrance. I would ask that you use the provided pens and sign your name and/or nickname to both. Now be careful, if you don't follow directions and only sign one pair, I'm going to rescind your diploma." They giggled again. She then showed the jeans Sara had brought up and explained. "I will be stitching over your names to preserve them as a gift to my sisters Erin and Maggie."

Erin and Maggie made eye contact and smiled big.

A girl screams from the student body, "I want a pair!" Laughter ensues.

"Are you going to college and if so, what for?" Key asked the girl.

With a voice of defeat, she replied, "No, but I'm hoping to find some classes for design."

"Well, you'll need to pay for those classes, so here is what we'll do. I have invented a machine to save me the hours of stitching and plan to open a business, here in Maine. I'm always looking to partner with a passionate person to oversee the day-to-day operations. Interested?"

"Yes!" she replied, and what everyone suspects were her parents, also gave a cheer.

"Okay, well, I'm a little busy at the moment," laughter starts up again, "so we'll talk later." Key then goes into a more legitimate speech encouraging the students to believe in the doors their current education has opened for them and the doors that will open in the future by what they continue to do for themselves. "You now know I've written plays and one non-fiction novel. What you don't know is I've also written eight other fictional novels." She stops and scans the faces of the students. "Can you guess what I attended University for?"

While most mumbled English or Creative writing, one class clown yelled out, "Business economics!" The students laughed again.

Key waited until the laughter died down before saying, "You think you're funny, huh?" After the kid cocks his head sideways, shrugs his shoulders and smiles, she continues, "Because you would be…correct." The boy's eyes went big. "I have four degrees. Business Economics, Computer Science, Physics and Law. I also have a long list of minors I won't bore you with. My passion, however, is writing and what I learned in all of those classes has improved it. Many of you may expect to get a degree, immediately get a job in that field, and live happily ever after. However, odds are, most of your paths will change as you learn."

"While attending University for one degree, many of you will change your major not just once, but some of you, two, maybe three times as you learn of the vast opportunities out there. And even when you think you have found the right one, you may still take another path once you've graduated. So, what's my point?" Key paused for a moment before saying, "nothing should slow you down or be seen as a failure.

Everything, even when someone says 'no' or 'sorry, we've hired someone else', is not a failure but a learning experience. The experiences will add up until your true path is exposed.

Okay, enough seriousness. Who is having a grad party today? That same boy stood up and said, "I am!"

"Great! What should we bring? Your parents can handle an extra 10 or so surprise guests, right?" While the audience laughs, a woman, obviously his mother, runs up and hands Key an envelope. Key thanks her and opens it. "Well, sorry, Mr. and Mrs. McFeely, it seems you're out of luck. Enjoy your quiet afternoon at home." Again, the crowd laughs while a man stands up and makes animated gestures of protest. Key laughs but then whispers into the microphone, "Stick with us, old man, and we'll see about sneaking you in."

When Key was done, she and Erin made their way back to Erin's seat. She was in the last row with a name like 'Yule', so there were empty seats, and the boy named Ziggler was kind enough to move over one. From that point on, Erin, Maggie and a boy named Ted swept the various awards. Maggie won out over Erin by a slim margin for the top of the class, but if Erin was disappointed, she didn't show it. She howled and cheered louder than everyone for her best friend.

After receiving their diplomas, the students were processed out, and Key walked with Erin to meet up with Sara, Rachel, Dannie, Mike, and Jeff, who were waiting for them in the outer corridor. Erin and Maggie then went and retrieved their purses from a classroom.

Key kept watching the doors in hopes of catching a glimpse of her father, but Erin and Maggie returned first. Erin had bad news. "Da sent me a text. He said he was proud and all that, but that he and Martha have gone home." Erin gave a sad look, "I thought we were all supposed to go to lunch afterward."

"He's avoiding me," Key replied.

"Well, we have that party to go to now, so I guess the day isn't over," Maggie said.

"I'm not going in this nonsense. I need to stop and change into my jeans and t-shirt," Key replied.

"Yeah, me too," Erin said.

"We have to wait until everyone signs the jeans before we go anywhere," Sara added.

For the next hour, students and parents were asking for pictures with all the girls while others lined up to sign the jeans. When the property was finally emptied out, they retrieved the jeans from the table and started out to the cars. When they were about to part ways to the separate vehicles, Key stopped Erin.

"Switch robes with me and tell Maggie what you want to wear today," Key said.

Nora and Maggie both smiled. Erin handed her the robe but was not as sure. "He may never forgive me."

"He'll forgive you. When you go with Sara and them, don't allow her to talk you into something cute and frilly. She has bought me crap like that, and you are welcome to borrow it, keep it even, but you had better bring me jeans and a T-shirt."

"Why don't you just meet us back at your house so you can get changed before we go?"

"Even better. See you in a bit." Key followed Maggie and Nora and asked that Maggie go in with her to get Erin's clothes. "I intend to confront my father straight away and hope to have at least opened communications with him. With any luck, we'll be done by the time you get both Erin's clothing and change yourself. You can meet me out front when you come to pick me up."

Nora dropped them off and wished her luck. When Key and Maggie walked in, Jon was in his office. He hesitated until he heard the door shut behind them. Then he got up and made his way out to give her a hug. Maggie made her way around them and headed up to Erin's room.

As he hugged her, he told her, "I was so proud to see you receiving all those awards. So, so proud, honey."

Key held him stronger than she expected, but when he finally pulled away and looked down at her, he saw the tears in her eyes. "I've missed you, Da."

His tears were instant, and his mouth started to contort. He tried to step back, but she followed him, grabbed him around the waist again and hugged him stronger than before. He put his arms around her again, and his sobs reverberated through them both. She could feel his tears dripping down her head.

Maggie came back down and was touched but felt awkward. She slipped around them again giving Martha and Caitlyn a smile before she headed out to her house. Hearing Maggie go by, Key turned sideways, putting her head on his heart. While still holding him with one arm, she wiped her tears with the other. He did the same.

Key, unaware of Martha and Caitlyn, looked up at him. "Everyone is waiting to go crash that party." He couldn't speak but nodded in agreement. "Afterwards, we're all going back to the house, and I hope you'll join us." This time, he didn't nod. He just pursed his lips to control the quivering, but looked like he was going to lose control of his emotions again. "Sara, Dannie and Rachel want to meet you, but maybe we should meet privately first."

Jon choked out a "yes".

"Okay, I'll call when we're headed back to the house and you can meet, just me, at Mum's grave across the street. Deal?"

He nodded in agreement again.

Key got up on her tippy-toes, and Jon bent down enough to receive a kiss on the cheek. "I love you, Da."

She had started to pull away, but he stopped her and choked out, "I love you too." He tried to smile but still wasn't in control of his emotions, and it looked strange to her. Then he nodded as he let her go.

As Key turned to leave, she noticed Martha and Caitlyn. "Hello," she said while blinking away the tears as quickly as she could.

Martha immediately approached for a quick hug.

Key looked at Caitlyn and said, "There's my fellow ice scratcher. Do you remember me? We met a few years ago, but I had red hair that day."

"I do! I remember!" Caitlyn said with a huge smile.

"Have you kept up on your skating?" Key asked.

"Da still takes me every weekend, and I'm getting better and better."

"Do you own your own skates?"

"Yes, I got some for Christmas."

"Bring them tonight, okay? I have quite a surprise for you when you all come to visit me later."

Caitlyn had a huge smile and nodded in agreement.

With a final smile to her father, she left.

Alexandra's Grave

"Hello?" Martha answered.

"Martha? It's Key."

"Are you headed back to your house now?"

"Yes. Can you let Da know? I'll head over to Mum's grave straight away once we get home."

"He's already there, honey. He left about a half-hour ago."

"Well, that's positive news. I was afraid he would change his mind. Will we be seeing you and Cate?"

"Yes, we'll head over now."

"Don't forget to bring her skates and your own if you have any."

"She already has hers by the door. We'll see you soon, bye."

"Love," Key replied and hung up.

Key jumped out of the car when they pulled up and started over to the graveyard right away.

"Should I come with you?" Erin called after her.

Mike put his arm around Erin and started to maneuver her toward the front door. "I think we should leave them to figure this out. The three of you can talk again another day."

"I'm worried about her," Sara said.

Erin stopped, causing Mike to do the same. "Why?"

"She hasn't had a nap today. She won't be on her best game for this conversation," Sara replied.

Key made her way down the driveway and could see him sitting at her mother's grave, waiting. She had to wait for the lights to change so she could run across all four lanes of the road. Instead of making her way down to the cemetery's entrance, she jumped over the short rock wall that surrounded it. As she got closer, he became aware and started to stand up. They hugged again before Key motioned for them to sit back down in the grass.

A few minutes of silence went by before Key decided to start. "I understand now why you never came after me, so we don't need to talk about that."

"She said you were dead. I swear she sent a death certificate that looked real," Jon said.

"That isn't the part I have problems with, Da. We need to talk about that morning."

Jon got instantly uncomfortable and adjusted the way he was sitting.

"Help me to understand what happened. Why did you make up that lie about Erin having motion sickness?"

Jon took a few deep swallows. "You were so much older than your years. Your Mum and I always said you were six going on 20 or seven going on 30. Erin was a very bright child, but a typical one. I never felt I had to protect you as much as I did her, but I regretted not including you in the lie right away." His voice started to crack. "You have to know I hated seeing you go, and I was kicking myself."

"That's not how I remember it. After you protected Erin, I swear the look you gave me, it was, I can't even describe it, but I knew I wasn't going to be given a choice."

"She wasn't going to stop demanding…she was relentless, and I…" his voice faded.

"So, I was the sacrificial lamb to appease her," Key said in a matter-of-fact manner.

"I didn't want either of you to go. I needed your help here. I swear, I didn't want either of you to go," he choked out, having lost control of his emotions again. "A week, maybe two, and you'd be home."

Key put her hand on her father's shoulder and rubbed it.

"Can you ever forgive me? Oh my God, can you ever…" his sobs took over.

She leaned over and hugged him, "In time. If I can forgive Grandma Izzy, I can forgive you."

His head whipped up to look at her as he wiped his eyes quickly. "Your grandmother? You've…have you spoken to her? You forgave her?"

Key sat back again, *well that was quick*, she thought. "Yes. I've been making regular visits and having it out with her for years."

"SHE THREW YOU AWAY! My daughter, thrown away like…"

"I know what she did; I lived it. We're not here to talk about her. I'm here to make peace with you." Key could see the veins in his neck pulsing. His fists were so tight his knuckles had turned white.

"She was…I should have known not to trust her."

"We're not here to talk about her…"

"I'm not. I'm saying, after everything your Mum told me and what I personally witnessed, I should have done to her what she did to your mother."

"What do you mean?"

"I should have sent her a letter two weeks after the funeral letting her know her daughter was gone. That's what she did to your Mum. The very day you came home from the hospital, she received a letter about her father. She never got to say goodbye." Jon bent almost to the ground with his face in his palms. "Oh Alex, I'm so sorry."

They sat in silence until the sun was almost gone. Finally, Key spoke up in a calm, steady voice. "I'm angry and disappointed, but I don't hate you. I don't hate Grandma Izzy, and I don't hate God for what I suffered. Mum always said, "God works in mysterious ways" and I believe he does."

Key got even quieter, "Sara would have been damaged had I not been there. Dannie and Rachel both often tell me that they would be with Sienna and Julie if I had not been there. If God put me where he thought I was needed most, I should…I should…I don't know what I should be."

They sat in silence for a few more minutes before Key started to stand up. "We need to get back to the house. I promised Caitlyn a surprise."

Jon also started to stand while clearing his throat, "Maybe I should head home."

"No." Key took her father's hand and started walking toward the house. "I have a surprise for you too. It's not an exact replica, but I think you'll get the gist."

When they finally reached the front porch, Key didn't use the front door. Instead, she led her father down the porch to the last door that opened into her wood shop. "This is the part I definitely took liberties with because I like to renew old furniture like Mum used to and needed a space to do it. But thinking of Mum's diaries, can you tell me the theme of this section?" With that, Key slid the barn doors to reveal the courtyard.

Other than a few gasps, Jon said nothing at first. The shops seemed familiar but not quite the same as he remembered. It was the cobble street and front of the apartments that brought back memories. He stopped and just stood in front of them.

"I half expect my brother to come walking out. I still miss him every day."

"I would love to hear all about him. Mum's diaries make him sound like quite the character."

Just then, Sara came through the other side from the kitchen. "Oh, your back. Sorry, I'm just getting Nora another latte, alright?"

"Yes, we'll come out in a bit. He's just looking around," Key replied.

Jon nodded to her before walking into the first hotel door.

Key decided to let him walk through the rooms in private and made her way toward Sara. "I like the way the store looks when the clothing is in there. It doesn't look like it's out of business." As she got closer, she gave Sara a wink to let her know things were going well without having to say it.

"Will you be coming out to the great room?" Sara asked.

Key whispered, "he tried to go home after we spoke, so maybe…"

"Enough said. I'll send Erin out first and we'll follow her after a bit." Sara finished the latte while Key walked back to the middle of the road and waited for her father to finish going through all six rooms.

Just as he exited the last apartment, Erin entered the courtyard. "Da! Did you see all the stores? They're so clever. The clothing store is really just a way for them to store their off-season clothing. The music store is filled with all their own instruments, and they actually know how to play them all."

Jon found her excitement contagious. "This entire thing is amazing. Wow, what a vision. You never could have done this in a normal house with a basement. Basements have posts to hold up the first floor."

"I wonder if that's what this was, the next best thing to a basement," Key said.

"So, you're home for good now, correct? What about the other girls?" Jon said.

"They're also here to stay. Sara will stay as long as I do, but Dannie and Rachel may decide to go back eventually. We applied and received dual citizenship. I convinced America that together, we would bring financial benefit here. The girls finally received official word about six months ago. However, we will all have to go back soon."

"Go back? Why?" Erin asked.

"Because I want to show you Europe," Key said with a smile. "We also need to visit Ireland and see Grandmas Yule and Connolly. You'll need a visa though." Key replied.

"My mothers are still alive?" Jon asked.

"Yes, and I've been reporting to them about your success here. They're very proud. I told them about Caitlyn and sent them pictures of her, so they returned the favor. Have you seen the photo..."

"Yes, yes, that was a wonderful gift to Cate and Erin. Thank you."

"I have their information. I'm afraid your father is gone, so your mothers moved into a smaller home together."

With a froggy voice, he said, "Thank you," again. "I'm a horrible son."

"Not according to them. You should hear how they gush about you. They would love a call from you, though. I'll give you the information tonight before you go."

"What's my surprise?" asked Caitlyn as she led the group out to the courtyard.

"Haha, you'll see. Do you have your skates with you?" Key asked.

"Yes, I'll get'm." Caitlyn turned and ran back toward the kitchen and disappeared.

"We'll need to take a bit of a walk, or we can drive down. We have a few golf carts, but they won't fit all of us," Key told them.

"Let's walk. The weather is perfect tonight, and the moon is bright enough," Rachel said.

They used the same door Key and Jon had walked in through and made their way along the path, past the small cottage, the barn that Frank keeps all his equipment in, and finally, they reached their destination. Key prompted Cate to be the first to walk in.

"Is that an ice rink? It has no walls!" Cate squealed as she ran to the ice.

"We have walls we can put in if you need them," Key told her.

The ice rink didn't have any bleachers, just a few lounge chairs and short side tables. The men allowed Martha and Nora to take the chairs, but Key told Mike and Jeff where to get the folding chairs she had in a closet. Sara and Dannie helped them bring enough out. "I'm sorry, I'm working on additional lounge chairs, but they're still in my shop.

Rachel helped Caitlyn get her laces tight enough. Before Cate stepped on the ice, she asked Key, "Aren't you going to skate with me?"

"I'm not very good with my eyes open, and they would have to be if you're on the ice. Maybe Erin will."

"I don't have any skates," Erin replied.

"You should fit in one of my pairs," Key said before going to get them. There was a dressing room in the far corner, past the exercise bike and ski machine, where Key kept her black, stretch outfits, socks, and skate collection. She had a pair in her hands but yelled back to Maggie, "What size foot are you? Dannie has an extra pair of 37s, and Rachel has a second pair of 38, but I'm afraid that's it."

"What size is a 38?" Maggie replied.

"Oh sorry, that would be an 8 here." Key added.

"Yes, I'm a size 8!" Maggie said in excitement.

Key ducked back into her dressing room and came out with skates for Erin and Maggie with thick socks.

Mike and Jeff also had pairs they had purchased in England and were now putting them on with Danni, Rachel and Sara. Key went and sat next to her Da to watch them.

"Aren't you going to join them?" her Da asked.

"Oh no, I can't while others are on the ice. But I'll get my few hours in later tonight," Key replied. "Oh, blankets." She jumped up and headed back to the closet that had the chairs. She returned with blankets for Martha, Jon, and the Kelleher's. "Is anyone hungry? I could run back up to the house for snacks."

Martha, Nora, and Mr. Kelleher said they were okay, but Jon said, "I'll walk back with you."

He got up and they made their way out.

They were halfway back when Jon asked her, "Are we okay?"

"I love you, Da. I may need time to make peace with everything, but that gets easier the more time I can spend with you."

"Is that what you did with your grandmother, just spend enough time with her?" he asked.

"Sort of. As you now know, I don't mince words or beat around the bush. I'm pretty blunt, which she didn't take well."

They had reached the house, went through the woodshop and courtyard, and entered the kitchen.

"Did she help you financially, to do all of this? You have redone the entire house it seems."

"No. I refused any financial help from her, but I did want our house. I had gotten a lawyer and was suing her for it. She decided to give it to Uncle Bobby, who immediately signed it over to me. And before your imagination goes wild, he said she made sure he would before she did it. It was strange that she wouldn't just give it to me herself."

"How often have you two spoken?" Jon asked.

"I stop in at least once a week now. It's gotten easier over time. As I was saying before, she didn't take my bluntness very well at first and kept walking away and copping out from the conversations. But I kept showing up and was relentless. Eventually, the conversations became more real and much more in-depth. For example, did you know she also has a brilliant memory? She remembers everything she sees and hears as I do."

"Really. No, I had no idea. I always knew your mother had a great memory, but I never knew it came from her mother. Do you think Mum had that talent?"

"Honestly, I don't know for sure. Uncle Bobby doesn't and Mum kept diaries, which I never felt the need to do because of my memory. I wasn't even aware it was something different until I was tested at Willington. The education specialist made a huge fuss over it."

Key pulled out some cheese and handed him a knife. I'll get you a baggy to put them in. She returned with a few sandwich bags for him. She then handed him a pastrami to slice. "I'll get the crackers." As she turned away from him, she said aloud, "V, can you call Dee and ask if she has any wine or beer for the adults?" A voice came back saying, "Yes miss."

"What was that?" Jon asked.

"My house assistant." A few minutes later V told her that Dee had put some in her cabinet behind the kitchen table for just this occasion. She forgot to mention it, so none of it is cold.

"I grew up on warm beer," Jon said and asked where the cabinet was.

Key smiled, "I'll get it. You left some of Mum's wine glasses, so I'll get those too." They filled a few bags with everything, and Key suggested they take the golf cart back.

On the way back, Jon brought up Grandma Izzy again. "So, you have actually forgiven Isabelle, your grandmother?"

"I think I have. She's come a long way since the early visits. She now admits what she did with eye contact and has expressed a lot of remorse. We've had some great talks."

"I don't think I could. Not ever," Jon replied.

"Not trying would be stupid though. If she comes to America…"

"She's coming here? To live?" he asked.

"No, not to live, but I've invited her to come and visit and see what I've done to the house. If she comes, you should at least try to talk it out."

"I'll talk to her when the FBI puts her behind bars for kidnapping."

"Have you called them? Are they looking to go after her?" Key asked in a higher, faster voice.

"Not yet."

Key stopped in front of the ice rink and just sat there while Jon hopped out. He grabbed the bags and waited for her.

"Are you coming in, honey?" he asked.

She was in a dead stare, straight ahead. "I thought when I turned 18, received full control over my finances and could finally own my home outright that my life would be mine to control." Key got out slowly and looked at him, "But you'll never let me have full control, will you?" She didn't wait for an answer, but walked by him and opened the door to go in.

"Kathleen?" he called, but she kept walking. "Kathleen."

She finally stopped just behind Martha, Nora and Michael Kelleher. "I prefer Key, not Kathleen."

He put the bags down on the short table next to Martha, and Key immediately started to unload them, offering wine and beer to them. Then she took out the platter she brought and started setting up the cheese plate. When she was done and had offered some to everyone, she took the seat at the far end, next to Mr. Kelleher.

Mike Visits Jon – Wants To Marry Key

The door bell rang as Martha was fixing the living room. She dusted the last cushion off and walked toward the door to answer. To her surprise, it was Mike Young. "Mike, how are you?"

"I'm good. How are you, Mrs. Yule?

"I'm good. Please come in."

"Is Mr. Yule home?" Mike asked.

"Jon!" she called.

Jon came out of the kitchen. "Batman." Jon reached out his hand.

Mike shook it with a smile and then asked, "Can I speak to you for a moment?"

Jon looked at him with a slight bit of confusion on his face and asked, "In my office?"

Mike smiled and answered, "That'd be great."

"My office is right there. Please," Jon motioned for him to go in. They both sat down in the seats in front of the desk. "How can I help you?"

"I'm having trouble convincing your daughter so far, but I thought I should get your blessing before she finally agrees." Mike took a deep breath, "I want to marry Key."

"But you two are so young."

"I am, but Key has the wisdom of a 90-year-old without dementia." They both chuckled a little before Mike continued. "I can't begin to articulate it properly or make you understand, but I know she is meant to be my wife. I knew it when I met her at eight years old. When I thought she was dead, I dated a little, for short periods, because I couldn't find that again. That instant connection."

"It seems so soon. Let me ask you, why has she been difficult to convince ya think? Jon asked.

"It's not that she doesn't love me the same way. She's told me multiple times that she won't marry anyone else. It's two things, the first being that she can't have children. She's afraid to condemn me to a childless marriage."

"Have you thought that through? No kids, ever?"

"I have. We can either adopt them, or Sara has offered to have them for us. Key won't allow Sara to do it though, because she says pregnancy can ruin a girl's figure, etc."

"What was the second reason?"

"Um…Sex. She's scared she can't please me and says she won't be a wife unless she can be a proper one."

"Then maybe you should wait."

"I will. I'll wait as long as it takes to convince her. I'm here today, so I know I have your blessing for when she agrees."

Jon sat and thought for a moment. *She can handle herself and if she isn't ready, he won't convince her to say yes one second before she is.* "Okay, you have my blessing, son."

"Thank you, sir." Mike stood up, and Jon followed suit. They shook hands once again before he left.

Mike returned to the house and told Sara what he had done.

She just shook her head and rolled her eyes, "It wasn't Jon's blessing you needed," Sara told him.

"Then whose?" he asked.

"Erin's. If Key's mother had been alive, it would have been her, but Key sees Erin as the closest representative of her Mum."

Mike sat down on the couch next to her. "Do you think Key will ever agree?"

"I think she's considering it, but she'll have to know for sure."

"Know what for sure?" he asked.

"If she can be a proper wife." Sara put her laptop down on the coffee table and turned to look at him. "If she were to offer herself to you again, are you prepared?"

"I would go slowly again and, well, make sure she's okay…okay, no, I'm not prepared. I'll admit I'm nervous too knowing what she's been through, but our first and only time seemed to happen very naturally."

"Can I give you a few suggestions?" Sara asked.

"Please," Mike replied, relaxing his shoulders and sinking further into the cushions.

"Always keep a light on. Ghosts tend to appear in the dark. I think it's important she can always see it's you."

"That makes sense, thank you."

"Don't ask her to do anything. Don't motion or encourage her in any way to do anything. Make it all about her."

"That's easy. I've tried to tell her I'm okay with how our first time went. She doesn't need to do more."

"Over time I suspect she'll get braver, but she is never going to believe you are okay with it always being one-way, with you doing everything. What you need to convince her of, is that you are okay with it until she's comfortable doing more."

"Okay. I really appreciate this, Sara. No one knows her like you do." Mike let out a sigh, "but do you think she'll ever be brave enough to try again?"

"I do. As terrified as she may be, she's still the bravest person I know."

"Is she still out?" he asked.

"She found some old couches at the garage sales this morning, and she and Frank went back with the truck to pick them up."

"Where is she going to put more couches?"

"The ice rink."

"Hey! What are you two up to?" Erin asked as she and Maggie came in.

"Not much. Hey, can I talk to you for a minute?" Mike stood up, looking directly at Erin.

"Sure, what's up?" Erin asked.

Mike motioned that they walk toward the kitchen, so Maggie sat down with Sara. Once they got to the kitchen, he pulled out two chairs and then sat in one of them.

"You seem so serious," Erin commented.

"I want to ask Key to marry me."

"I thought you already had…a few times." Erin smiled.

"Yes, I have mentioned it a few times." He smiled back and rolled his eyes. "I'm hoping that one of them eventually wins the day, and she says yes."

"So do I."

"You do? That's great. I was here to ask for your blessing."

"Shouldn't you be getting a blessing from my Da?"

"I did, but your blessing is just as important, if not more important."

Erin smiled and put a hand to her heart. "I appreciate that and love that we're friends today. Even if we were still at odds with one another, I think you still would have had my blessing though."

"I'm also glad we're friends, and I'm fully aware it's only because you've been generous enough to forgive me. I was such a dick to you."

"Yes, you were," Erin said, laughing. "But my sister will straighten you out." Erin wagged her finger at him while they both laughed. "It's amazing how well she has us trained in such a short period of time."

"Trained?"

"Yeah, trained. Maggie and I were talking about it this morning. Okay, for example, if you finish the toilet paper roll and have to exchange it, which way do you put it on?"

"It has to be in the front, so that you can just hit the roll downwards, and the paper unravels."

"Did you ever worry about that before meeting Key?" she asked.

His lips slowly became a smile as he thought about it. "Haha, no, you're right. I don't think I've ever been as neat, as proficient, or as particular about things as I have since Key came home. Her OCD is rubbing off on me."

Mike put his hands on his hips and wagged his finger, "She's sneaky, that one."

"You'll need to adopt or figure out how to get her children. If she can train us this well, without having to yell or nag, imagine how great a mother she would be," Erin mused.

Marry Me – Please!

Jeff and Mike had stopped in to see Mike's parents and were sitting in their house trying to find ways to make Key say yes to his proposal.

"Maybe you should try making her jealous. We have girl friends who would play along." Jeff said.

"Already thought of that, but Sara said that would only backfire," Mike replied.

"How so?" Jeff asked.

"Key would only become more convinced that I could move on and fall in love with someone else. Someone who could give me kids."

Mike's father walked up to them as they were talking.

"What are you two up to today," asked Mike's father.

"Hey Mr. Young. Your son is in a pickle." Jeff answered him. "He's in love with Key and wants to marry her, but she won't agree."

"You're still young…" his father, Markus started.

"I know we're young." Mike looked at his father eye-to-eye. "I also know she's meant to be my wife. And yes, I know none of you understand that."

"Wait, wait, sit back down, son." Mike's father was waving his hand downward at his son while he made his way around the lounge chair and sat down. "I know she is meant to be your wife. What I meant was that you are both still very young. If she needs more time, give it to her."

"In her eyes, it isn't about time though." Mike replied. "She calls herself 'damaged goods' and I need her to know she isn't. She could be a great wife."

"Do you realize you aren't just marrying Key if she says yes?" Jeff asked.

"What do you mean?" Mr. Young asked.

"Sara has made it very clear to me that she's never moving out. I don't know about the others, but Key and Sara will live together forever." Jeff explained.

"All young girls say that with their best friends," said Mr. Young.

"No, for them, it's real. Key has made it clear as well. She says she can't live without her." Mike added.

"So, you wouldn't just be marrying Key. You'll be marrying at least her and Sara. Maybe all of them. Have you thought that through?" His father asked.

"Yes. I'm already living with them all now. I've been living with them since we went to England." Mike looked at his watch again. "Is Mom and Dee coming? I hope Mom isn't getting all dolled up for this."

"You know your mother," Mr. Young said.

Finally, Madison, Mike's mother, and his little sister DeAnne came down.

"Ready?" Mike asked.

"Yes, very excited," DeAnne replied.

"Do you have your skates?" Mike asked.

"Oh yeah!" DeAnne went to the closet.

"Markus, do you have the desert? We can't go empty-handed," Madison asked.

"Yes, it's right here," Mr. Young replied.

Mike's parents took their own car over to the cliff house. Key had invited them for dinner. When they got there, Mike took them to the front door, but there was no one to greet them. He could hear voices in the distance though.

"I love this!" Madison immediately made her way to the back, glass doors to look out to the deck and the water below. "What a beautiful view."

Mike motioned over to the window and pointed down. She looked through and realized what he was pointing at. "That's your beach? Where you two met?"

"Yup."

"How do you get down there?" she asked.

Mike pulled on what looked like a wall and showed that it opened to stairs. "V, where is my future wife?"

"Key is in the courtyard, Michael." V responded.

"What is that?" Madison and DeAnne asked together.

"The house assistant, so be careful what you do and say. The house is wired with cameras too. Okay, you ready to meet my future wife and her sisters?"

They all made their way through the kitchen out to the courtyard. The girls had set up a long table down the middle of the road to fit everyone.

"Hello!" Key saw them and made her way over. "DeAnne!" Key gave her a big hug. DeAnne quickly made her way around Key to look at the stores. "Mr. and Mrs. Young, it is so wonderful to finally meet you, as my true self I mean."

Mrs. Young gave her a quick hug, "I have heard about you forever and now, with your blonde hair and blue eyes, you are exactly as he described you. You have a beautiful home."

Key smiled and then shifted sideways to hug Mr. Young.

"Ahh, the future, Mrs. Young," he said as they pulled out of the hug.

"The what?" Key asked.

"My son's future wife," he replied.

"I don't think you understand what you would be condemning your son to if you help him push that idea." Key's mood visibly changed as she started to turn away and into Mike, who had been standing behind her.

"What's the matter?" Mike asked.

"You convinced your parents to come help work on me," Key replied dryly.

As Mr. Young decided to catch up to his wife and started to make his way around them, he said, "I have never seen my son as confident in anything before you. He didn't have to convince me."

Key let out a loud sigh, looked at Mike and then walked toward the table.

Dannie had made a family-style dinner with beautiful salads, various vegetable bowls, butter, and herb potatoes, and a huge platter of London broil and small dinner rolls. Mr. and Mrs. Young, DeAnne, Jeff, Jessica, Ray, Joe, Erin, Maggie, Sara, Dannie, Rachel, Mike and Key all found and took a seat.

Mr. Young made a point of sitting down at Key's end of the table. Once the food had been passed around and the plates were full, he started the conversation. "My wife and I were fortunate to be blessed with two children. Especially after the doctors told us, we couldn't bear our own."

Key dropped her fork. "They're adopted? Mike and DeAnne are adopted?"

"Mike was—sort of. My sister died in childbirth, and she knew she would. She found out after getting pregnant that she had cancer. She had to make a choice, her life or the baby's."

"Oh my God, she purposely saved Mike's life?" Key asked. "She's a saint."

"Yes. She also knew my wife and I were told we couldn't have children, so she set it up for us to adopt him after birth. She was actually expected to live for at least a while after he was born, but God thought differently." Mr. Young replied.

Key thought for a moment while Sara spoke up. "Did you know before you were married that you couldn't have children or find out later?"

"I was a very sickly child and was told before I met her that my odds weren't good," he answered her.

"Hmmm, so you knew ahead…" Sara started.

Key kicked her under the table.

"Is DeAnne adopted?" Sara asked, ignoring the pain in her shin.

"No. Miracle of miracles, my wife and I were surprised with her so many years later."

Key whispered something under her breath, but only Sara picked it up. When Mike and his father asked what she said, Key just shook her head to dismiss it.

"Key said," and after another kick to her leg, Sara curled her legs away and continued, "that it was because your wife was able to be a proper wife."

"Not at first, but maybe that's why it took so long to figure out we could," Mr. Young replied in a lower voice. "She hated sex. She was a good little Catholic girl and too afraid, to be honest with me."

Mike started laughing, "So, you're saying she's no longer a good little Catholic girl?"

They all giggled, except for Key.

Mike tried to reach over to her, but he watched as her jaw tightened. He felt bad, gave his father a look, and shook his head to stop.

Mr. Young got the hint and changed the subject but found that no matter the topic, Key did not participate.

When dinner was over, Key concentrated on clearing the table, wrapping up the food and loading the dishwasher. Her sisters offered to help after the table was clear, but she insisted they take their guests for a tour and keep an eye on their drinks.

"Key, they're here to meet Princess Kathleen, not us," Dannie retorted.

Key gave her the 'look,' which was enough for Dannie to do as she asked.

Not everything fit in the dishwasher, so she was finishing up the bigger pans in hot, soapy water when Mr. Young came in.

"I'm sorry I made you so uncomfortable. You have been such a gracious hostess, and you have a beautiful home," Mr. Young said.

After standing the pan up to dry on the counter, "I love him," Key replied simply.

"So, do I."

"Then why wouldn't you want him to have better?" Before he could answer, she stopped and turned to him, "You pretend to know why I won't agree. You think it's simple, but your son would be taking on a lot of baggage. A lot of pain, anger, damage he doesn't understand." She turned back and picked the next platter up to scrub it.

He let a minute go by before he spoke again. "I'm not at liberty to tell you all the complications of my own marriage, but I can assure you, it wasn't simple. No marriage is. The difference between my marriage and your relationship with my son seems to be trust."

"Trust?" she asked as she let the water out in the sink.

"We had baggage, but we trusted each other enough to carry it all. We trusted each other to understand, be patient and work through our obstacles. Because we saw them as OUR obstacles." He continued when she didn't reply, "My son trusts you, but do you…"

"I would trust him with my life, that's not it," Key shot back.

"Then what is it?" he asked.

"My baggage is so heavy, so often too heavy even for God and me to carry…" she put her head down.

He pulled her to him and hugged her. "Then don't carry it alone. That's what marriage is."

Key Tries And Accepts

As was tradition, the four sisters and Mike gathered for what they called their 'goodnight' talk. Mike loved this special time, and they started to gather in his room tonight.

Key was the last to arrive, but they saved her a seat beside Mike against the headboard.

"You've been quiet tonight," Dannie noted.

Key just gave a small smile and shrugged her shoulders.

"Well, I think dinner went really well. I like your parents," Sara said, looking at Mike.

"My Mom loved you all playing your instruments. She's a huge music buff." Then he looked over at Key, "I wish you would have sung. I've been bragging to them about you."

Key quietly dismissed it with another pursed-lip smile and one-shoulder shrug.

Mike well remembers when she went quiet tonight. "I'm sorry about my Dad. I didn't mean for him to say so much."

Key didn't even look at them, just down at her hands.

"What did your Dad say? I didn't hear him," Rachel asked.

"He told us about Mike being born to his mother's sister and how they adopted him," Sara started.

"I didn't know that. Is DeAnne adopted too?" Dannie asked.

"No. DeAnne was a miracle baby," Mike replied.

"But why would you apologize about him saying that?" Dannie asked.

Sara giggled a little. "He seemed to be on a mission to convince Key to marry his son."

"I still don't understand why you need convincing. You said yourself, he's the only guy you would trust enough to marry," Rachel said.

Mike smiled. "She did, huh?"

Everyone was looking at Key now.

"I'm too selfish to be a wife," she said quietly.

Everyone disagreed with their own sounds, but it was Mike who spoke up. "Oh please, you are the closest thing to a saint that I know. Everything you do, you do for others."

Key finally looked up at him. "I don't do anything I don't control."

"That's not true," Dannie said. "You didn't like Britney Spears, but you went to her concert for me."

Key turned to Dannie, "Who chose the flights, hotel, car service and bought the seats? And I never said I didn't like her. I said she wasn't one of my favorites."

"But…" Rachel started.

"If you had wanted to live in England, do you think I would have stayed there for you? If Michael were offered his dream job in another state, do you see me following him?" Key asked.

After a short silence, "You don't control us or the things we love to do. I love to cook and decide what we're having for dinner."

"I love photography and videography, and you don't control what I post or use on social media," Sara added.

"You don't understand. What you do, you do in my world, not me in yours. If you went back to England to live, I couldn't stop you and I wouldn't follow. I would visit, but I wouldn't follow." Key looked down at her hands again. "I couldn't be as unselfish as all of you have been."

They all sat in silence again, but this time for a while. Key stared down at her hands as the rest of them stared aimlessly in thought.

Finally, Mike spoke. "Marriage is about giving and doing for the other what they need to be happy. You need control, I can give you that. I can live here or follow you wherever. As for what you give me, I have learned more from you in the past months than I would ever have learned in college. I have done more good in the community both here and in England than I have done my entire life." He took a deep breath and let it out slowly before continuing. "There are Chiefs, and there are Indians. You're a Chief, and I'm proud to be a member of your tribe."

When Key looked up this time, her eyes were watery, but there was a small smile on her lips.

Mike smiled back, leaned over to her and said, "I love you," before kissing her on the forehead. As he leaned back to sit up straight, she followed and cuddled up next to him.

"Looks to me like I have a wedding to plan!" Sara announced with glee.

All three sisters started talking about the details, "Are you going to make her dress, Sara? I know I'm catering it; I already know what I'm making," Rachel declared.

"We'll need to rent tables, chairs, plate settings, tablecloths and…Key what color scheme are you thinking?" Dannie asked.

All three of them looked over at Key who had been quietly watching them. When she didn't answer immediately, they were about to give up, but then she whispered, "Sapphire blue is my favorite."

Izzy Calls Jon

The phone rang at Johathan Yule's house, but the second ring was cut short when Martha walked in the kitchen and answered the phone, "Hello?"

"Hello, may I please speak with Jonathan Yule?" the caller asked.

"May I ask who's calling?"

"Isabelle Harrington…" There was a moment of silence after the name but Martha snapped back and answered, "One moment."

She put the kitchen phone down on the counter and walked to Jon's office by the front door.

"Jon." She whispered.

"What? Why are you whispering?" Jon asked.

"Isabelle Harrington is on the phone, asking for you."

Jon could feel the prickles of heat rising in his face immediately. "I'll take it in here."

Martha made her way back to the kitchen as he picked up the receiver. "Hello?"

"Jonathan, this is Isabelle. I wanted…"

"You want? Is there still something else left for you to take from me? I should hang the fuck up on you right now after all the calls I made that you ignored."

"I know."

There was silence on both ends.

"My call is about Key," Isabelle started again.

"What could you possibly have to say about my daughter now?" he asked.

"She wants Robert and me to visit America to see what she has done with the old house. She is very proud of it. Key has also made me aware that I would be walking into a trap you plan to lay out for me." Isabelle cleared her throat. "I'm not even sure you would have any say or control over this, but since I still intend to go, I wanted to ask that Key be given her moment in the sun first."

"Her moment in the sun?" he asked incredulously. Jon was sitting up with his elbows on his desk. Every muscle in his body was tense, and his face beat red.

"She has been really excited about getting the house done and has been wanting me to see it. I understand she has worked very hard on it, and I want to give her the honor of showing it off to me. Once I've seen it, you can do as you see fit."

"As I see fit? You are too much old woman. You kidnapped my daughter! She was like trash to you to be thrown away to a pedophilic monster, and you want me to let you walk free? You should have been thrown in prison the moment she outed you!"

"No, I'm not asking to walk free. She has told me what you plan to do. I'm simply asking on her behalf…"

"Ten years. For almost TEN years, you allowed me to believe my daughter was dead. What do you have to say to that? Oh my God. Now I'm hearing you two have been talking for YEARS, and you still did not tell me she was alive." His free hand had become a fist as he waited for an answer.

"By then, the damage I caused had been done. Key did not want you to know, fearing you would make her leave. Her reasons should have been clear when you read her book." Isabelle took a deep breath. "Although I gave her my word Jon, I won't use her as an excuse. I admit I was scared. I knew what I had done was a crime, and I was scared of the consequences.

Jon was breathing hard, "You should be."

"Having kept her secret only added more years to my punishment, but Key said she needed to stay with her sisters, who had suffered the same. I gave her my word because I wanted her to heal after everything she had been through. I owed her-"

"What YOU put her through. What you did was pure evil!"

"I know," Isabelle replied.

In order to calm themselves, they both were taking deep breaths, which could be heard clearly through the receiver.

"Has she forgiven you, Jonathan? My plans had been to take them both, not one of them. What I did was evil, but-" Isabelle started.

"Are you blaming me for what you did?" Jon asked in a higher voice.

"I can't blame you for what I did, but she will blame you for what you did. Have you owned up to it yet, or have you made excuses for it?"

"I didn't do anything like throw her away or hand her over to be abused," Jon retorted.

"You could have told me no that morning."

"Oh my God…"

Isabelle took yet another deep breath and let it out slowly. "I will carry my sins, Jon, but if you want her forgiveness, you will need to carry your own." Isabelle waited, but there was no response so she continued. "Everything about Key reminds me of Alexandra. I miss my daughter horribly and regret the pain I caused her before she left."

"Before you exiled her to America," Jon snapped back.

"Yes, before I sent you two off." Isabelle paused and then continued, "spending time with Key now, is both a blessing and a curse. It's like having my daughter back and yet a constant reminder of how I lost her. Having her little clone around after she passed must have been tough."

Another moment of silence.

"If you don't want to give your daughter the chance to show me the house, so be it. When I've made my travel plans, I'm sure you will learn of my arrival, so you can do as you please." She waited a few seconds before finally hanging up.

Jon sat, shaking. Just then, Erin came in the front door.

"Erin?" he called out.

"Yeah, Da, what's up?" Erin turned and made her way into his office.

"Have you spoken to your sister about your grandmother?"

"Yeah." Erin sat in the chair in front of his desk. "I don't think I can forgive her."

"Has Kathleen asked you to?" Jon asked.

"No, she just said I should talk to her. She thinks it would do me some good to have it out with her. Not everyone gets to tell the person who hurt them what they think of them for doing it. Mike did and said…"

"Mike met her?"

"Yeah, while he was in England, he insisted on going with Key to talk to her."

"And what did he think?" Jon finally sat back in his chair, causing it to rock a few times.

"He said she was really honest and remorseful. He hasn't forgiven her either but said he felt a little better after going at her about it."

Jon was calming down and the color in his face was returning to normal. "She's coming to America; did Key tell you that?"

"Yes, although Key told her not to," Erin replied.

Jon just shook his head, "How could she forgive her?"

"Izzy has been honest and remorseful about what she did. And I don't want to start a fight because you walked out on me the first time I brought this up. But Da, you did make up a lie to protect me, and only me."

"I've already explained that to Key. She understands," Jon replied.

"Does she? Key was able to find forgiveness for Grandma Izzy because she was willing to take Key's wrath and eventually stopped with the excuses. My understanding is you haven't."

"Mike said he asked Izzy if she would have fought to take just one of us if you hadn't pushed for Key to go. Izzy couldn't answer him because she wasn't sure. You did not give her any more of a choice than to take Kathleen."

"That's not how I remember it."

"But Key forgets nothing, and it's how she remembers it. Eventually, that's what matters," Erin replied.

Jon & Key

"Hey kiddo, what'cha working on?" Jon asked as he entered Key's woodshop from the courtyard.

Key held up a finger and mouthed the words 'one moment'. He now noticed the earpiece.

"I agree, and I'm so sorry to do this, but my Da just walked in. Can I call you back?" Key listened again for a few seconds, "thank you. Love."

"I'm so sorry to interrupt. I just thought I would stop in on my way home," Jon said.

"It's okay. So, what's up? You, okay?" Key asked.

"I thought we were okay after we talked at your Mum's grave, but Isabelle called and made me feel you hadn't forgiven me and then Erin made me think the same."

"And you thought I had?" Key asked.

Jon just looked at her for a moment. "Yes, I thought you had."

"I'm not going to spare your feelings, Da. Mum left us to you to protect. You knew enough about Izzy to protect Erin. You chose not to protect me and haven't told me why or given me enough reason to think you're really sorry about it."

"I explained that I thought you could handle it. You were more mature for your age."

"You also told me you had a history with her and knew how evil she was. I may have been mature, but how does maturity conquer evil? I was only eight years old, for heaven's sake." Key could feel the heat rising in her cheeks.

"What are you accusing me of?" he asked.

Key shook her head. *He thinks he can twist this into making me feel bad? Amateur move, old man*, she thought. "I'm stating the facts. You are trying to convince one of us that your choices were okay and made sense. I hope it's not me."

"If you don't want to forgive me, then that's between you and God," Jon said with slight frustration in his voice.

"So is your lack of honesty and remorse," Key replied.

"I didn't throw you away. I trusted you with a grandparent."

"A grandparent you said you knew was evil." Key let out a long sigh. "So, let's move on, Da. You want her to take all the blame, even for your decision that morning, but what about after you thought me dead? How many calls did you make to confirm it? How many flowers did you send to my grave? Or did you not have time because you were too busy telling Erin to get over it?"

Jon was flustered. "Well, what about you? When you sued your grandmother for this house, did you sue on behalf of all of us? The memories in this house belong to all of us. She hurt all of us. Did you think of that?"

Key could feel her heartbeat quicken, and her mouth gaped open. After a few quick breaths, she said, "Get out."

"So, you don't like being confronted with facts, is that it?" Jon responded.

"Get OUT!" Key walked over to the door and opened it to the front porch. "You coward! You're delusional! GET OUT!"

As Jon walked out, Key reminded him, "I owe you nothing." She slammed the door behind him. *That son of a...*

"Are you okay?" Mike asked as he and Erin came running in.

"My father is not invited to the wedding." Key looked straight at Erin, "and no one is to tell him when Grandma Izzy is coming."

"What did he say to you?" Erin asked.

"Instead of being honest about the decision he made that morning and thereafter, he wanted to know if he owned part of this house. If I had sued her on behalf of all of us," Key replied. She put the tool she had in her hand on her workbench with a clammer, "I was the only one who was left not knowing where I would get my next pair of shoes. I was the only one who had to accept hand-me-downs from fellow students." Again, she looked straight at Erin, "I lived in a dorm, not a home. This was my first home and so help me God, it will be mine until I die."

"I'm glad you reclaimed this house." Erin watched as Key took another deep breath. "Any chance I could move into the hotel? I don't want to take any chance of saying too much at home, and he's becoming unhinged."

"Yes, Michael and I can help you," Key replied.

"No. I can do it myself. There's no need for you to get in the line of fire. Could Franklin pick me up with the truck when I'm ready?"

"Of course," Key replied and walked near Erin placing her hand on her shoulder. "Erin, I always want you to feel at home here and Maggie is also welcome. If she does, let me know though. I would like to talk to her mother and make sure she knows she's welcome here any time."

The next day, Martha was standing at the door watching Erin collect her clothes that were piled in organized groups on her bed. Her prom queen crown was wrapped in a shirt, as were her cheerleading trophies and awards. The pictures that used to align the inner rim of her mirror were gone.

"Going somewhere?" Martha finally asked, leaning against the door.

Erin was physically startled and whipped around to face her. "Oh my gosh, how long have you been there?"

"Just a minute or so. You look to be packing, honey."

"Yeah, I have really missed my sister and she's offered me to move into one of the hotel rooms. I'm excited to spend more time with her," Erin said before turning back to what she was doing.

"And that is the only reason?" Martha asked as she walked in and sat on Erin's bed.

Erin looked over and locked eyes with her. "Why do you ask?"

"Because I know your father has been a little 'off' lately. He seems obsessed with your grandmother. Have you not noticed?"

She was done boxing the shirts and was closing them up by locking the four sides, rather than taping it. Erin sat down sideways on the bed with one leg off and the other bent under her. "Just thinking about my grandmother makes my skin crawl, but Key is the one that was hurt the most. She suffered much more than we did, and if she can make peace with her, well, then I guess I respect it. I respect my sister, and although I may never forgive Izzy, Key understands and respects that too."

"I wish your father would respect it as well or at least come to grips with it. It seems to be all he talks about anymore." Martha rolled her eyes after the comment.

Erin's shoulders lowered and curled in as if her chest had deflated. "I know. To be honest, it's a big reason for moving out. He really hurt Key when they talked yesterday."

"He did tell me about it, but I would love to hear her side."

"Yeah, I told him he shouldn't assume his actions that morning were forgiven. You kinda had to be there, but he really did seem adamant about getting Grandma to take her that morning. I wish I had realized and done something to stop it."

Martha reached over and touched Erin's hand, "oh honey, it wasn't your fault. You were only eight years old."

"And so wrapped up in being happy that I didn't need to go that I didn't think about her at the time. I didn't think past that moment then, but I didn't want her to go. We didn't always get along, but we loved each other. As soon as she left, I felt so alone and regretted not helping her fight to stay."

Martha gave her a small smile, "I'm sure your sister doesn't hold you responsible."

"We've talked about it and she was hurt though by my silence that morning. My sister may have been more mature at the time, but my Da's insistence she go and then my silence made it appear like I agreed. She thought we both wanted her gone."

Martha sat up straighter, arching her back, "but you told her, didn't you, that you could feel her every emotion and never gave up that she was alive?"

Erin smiled, "Yeah. She was blown away by that. She even said I didn't need forgiveness. She said that just because I was silent, I shouldn't be held accountable for her assumption about why."

"Do you think she'll give your dad another chance? I understand she kicked him out of her house."

"Not sure, but I think he would have to prove he deserves it. What did he tell you why she kicked him out?" Erin asked.

"Just that she got angry when he tried to confront her with some facts, but he didn't get specific."

"The 'facts' that he refers to are his own facts. He actually asked Key if she had sued our grandmother for the house on behalf of all of us. Can you imagine? The very idea that he would threaten her ownership of it makes me sick. He has a home. I always had a home. Key grew up knowing her school would be kicking her out at 18. She needed a home and used her intelligence to get the one she wanted, and I'm glad she did. That house means a lot to us, and I love that she has restored it and owns it."

"So, you are going to sneak out while your dad's at work today? Do you think that's the answer?" Martha asked.

"I'm only packing and getting my things out while he's at work. I'll be here to tell him myself when he gets home. I wasn't lying when I said I was excited to spend more time with my sister."

"Okay, then what can I do?" Martha asked as she stood up.

The two of them worked for an hour and quickly packed up her belongings before they called Frank to bring the truck. Martha also insisted on following them over and helped her unpack until she had to leave to pick Caitlyn up.

When Jon returned home that evening, Erin had not yet returned.

Jon came into the kitchen and gave Martha a little kiss on her cheek. "Why only three plates for dinner?"

Just then, the front door opened, and Erin came in. "Hi!"

Martha didn't realize her shoulders were up by her ears until they dropped down to a normal position. "Hi honey," she replied.

Jon sat on a stool at the kitchen counter and leafed through the day's mail. "Do you have plans tonight?"

Erin stopped, put her fingers on the counter and asked, "Why do you ask?"

"Because I noticed only three plates are set for dinner," he replied.

"I'll be eating at Key's, but I need to talk to you. Do you want to go to your office or the TV room?" Erin asked.

"We can talk in my office; I need to take these bills in any way." He stood up and started to follow Erin out of the kitchen. "This sounds serious. Are you okay?"

"I'm great, Da." When they finally reached his office, Erin didn't sit down. "I've moved out. I'm going to be…"

"You what?" he asked with a crooked brow, slapping the bills down on his desk.

"I moved out." Erin finally took a seat in front of his desk. "Key offered me to move in with her so we could spend more time together."

Jon had also sat down and picked up the mail again, tapping the desk with it. "When she gets your grandmother here, Key will probably invite her to stay there too. Have you thought about that?

Living in the same house with your grandmother?" Jon started tapping the envelopes faster and harder on the desk.

"I have actually. Key said I should talk to her and I'm sort of anxious to do so. Unfortunately, it doesn't sound like I'll get an opportunity anytime soon."

"Why? Is she scared?" Jon asked.

"No. Something about Uncle Bobby having to get a procedure before they come. Bobby wants to come with her." Erin avoided his gaze when she made up the procedure thing, but figured she wasn't lying about her uncle wanting to come.

Martha had just approached the office door, motioning to Jon that dinner was ready.

Jon finally put the mail down and sat back. "Well, I think I would like to talk it out with Isabelle too, so let me know when they set a date to come, okay?"

Martha heard Erin reply, "Sure, Da. Well, I have to go. They're expecting me for dinner."

Jon made his way around the desk, dragging his fingers across the edge until he left toward the kitchen. Erin was following him out when Martha shook her head to stop. Once Jon made his way down the hall and into the kitchen, Martha whispered to Erin, "Is your grandmother really coming? When?"

"Sorry Martha, but I wouldn't tell you even if I knew. I wouldn't want to put you in that position," Erin whispered back.

FBI

Key hears the doorbell as she is reading in the great room, she asks V who it is. V describes that there are two men at the door in dark suits. She walks to the door, confused about what it is about and answers it to discover two tall figures awaiting her at the doorstep.

"Hello, Miss Yule. I'm Agent Harbaugh, and this is Agent Roberts from the FBI. May we talk?"

"What is it in regard to?" Key asked.

"May we come in?" the agent asked.

"No, but I can come out." Key stepped out on the front porch and motioned for them to take seats. "Now, what are you here to talk about?"

"We understand you were kidnapped as a child…" the agent started.

Key cut him off quickly with a giggle while she answered, "Uh, no, I wasn't."

"Sorry, are we talking to Kathleen or Erin?" he asked.

"Kathleen. I grew up in England. My sister, Erin, grew up here in Maine. Does that help?"

"We were under the impression you grew up in England because you were kidnapped by your grandmother. Your book…"

"I went with my grandmother because my father insisted I should go. He didn't give either of us, myself or my grandmother, much of a choice in the matter. It turned out my grandmother wasn't prepared to raise me, so she sent me to one of the best boarding schools in England. If you read my book, you understand the unfortunate nature of that decision."

"Have you been in contact with her since that decision?" the agent asked in a tone of disbelief.

"Yes. I speak to her every few days."

"And your father? Do the two of you speak often?"

"I had to trick him into finally speaking to me when I first returned. Unfortunately, after a brief time of communication, I had to cut it off."

"And why was that?" Agent Roberts asked.

"He became obsessed with my grandmother, wanting to blame her for the morning he sent me off. He then started asking if he owned part of my home." Key crossed her legs and leaned forward a little. "He became toxic, and I thought it best to remove him from my environment until he seeks help."

Key's cell phone rang, and she saw it was Grandma Izzy calling. Key answered it and put it on speaker, "Grandma, how are you?"

"I'm lovely, but we aren't sure which airport to fly into when we come."

"I told you already that Sara was making the arrangements. She'll send you the tickets."

"Hello, this is Agent Roberts with the FBI. Are you Isabelle Harrington?"

"Yes. Key, what's going on?" Izzy asked.

"Grandma…"

"Mrs. Harrington, we were speaking with your granddaughter about how she went to live in England," Agent Harbaugh said quickly.

"You don't need to answer…" Key tried.

"You mean when her father insisted that I take her after my daughter, Alexandra, passed away?" Izzy asked.

"So, he insisted you take only one of the twin girls?" Agent Roberts asked.

"Yes. I thought it strange, but I also knew he had a lot to handle. My daughter home-schooled the girls and never held a job while in

America. Key was also a gifted child, and finding the right programs for her would have been extra work. If you know anything about my granddaughter, Key, you know that she was well past the twelfth grade at eight years old."

Key interjected, "the boarding school my grandmother sent me to opened up the opportunity for me to attend a university. By seventeen, I acquired four degrees, became a best-selling author, and started up three different businesses in England."

"But your book was not kind to your grandmother. You wrote about the car ride to the airport…" Agent Harbaugh started.

Key was about to answer, but Grandma Izzy responded faster. "Yes, I was horrible to her. I'm embarrassed to admit I did not handle my daughter's death well. I also was not prepared to raise a young child. Actually, if I'm being completely honest, I didn't handle my daughter's life well even before she got cancer. I…"

"That's enough. Grandma, I'll call you back, okay?" Key asked.

"Alright honey," Izzy replied.

"One last question, if I could." The agent looked at Key and continued, "has the girl's father contacted you since you took Kathleen that morning, or did you contact him in any way?" Agent Harbaugh asked.

"Yes, to both. He called a few times immediately after but never answered when I called back. Of course, that could have just been a timing issue. I believe there is a five-hour difference between us. I finally wrote him a letter to let him know where Key was. I assumed that's what his calls were about. Months later he called again but this time left more specific messages about wanting to purchase the house."

"Thank you, Mrs. Harrington," Agent Roberts said.

After Key hung up, she focused back on the agents. "I have things to do, so if there's nothing else…"

"When will your grandmother be coming in?" Agent Roberts asked.

"In time for my wedding," Key answered.

"Could you be more specific? We will want to speak to her while she is here," Agent Roberts replied.

"Why?" Key asked.

"Kidnapping is a federal crime, and we need to be sure," he replied.

"Wouldn't I know…" Key started when the front door opened.

Erin and Maggie came out. "Hey, we're going to run to the store. Do you need anything?" Erin asked.

"No, thanks," Key replied.

Agent Roberts stood up, "are you Erin Yule?"

"Yes."

"Hello, I'm Agent Roberts, and this is Agent Harbaugh. We would like to talk to you about your grandmother, Isabelle Harrington."

"Why? You can talk to her when she comes," Erin replied.

"Do you speak with her often?" Agent Harbaugh asked.

"No, but looking forward to it. I haven't seen her since the day my Da sent my sister off with her."

"We understand your grandmother sent a death certificate to convince you that your sister was dead." Agent Roberts added.

"So, my Da told me. I never saw it though," Erin replied.

"You didn't believe she had been kidnapped then?" Agent Roberts asked.

"No, and I didn't believe my Da when he said she was dead," Erin replied dryly.

"I can attest to that. Erin kept trying to talk to her dad about calling England and he kept shutting her down. He would get furious at any mention of her sister," Maggie added.

"How long have you known the family?" Agent Roberts asked Maggie.

"Since Erin's first day of third grade. We've been best friends ever since," Maggie replied.

"Your name?"

"Maggie Kelleher. I live across the street and up a house from Erin's family. By the way, Erin's stepmother, Martha Yule, can attest to what I'm saying. The subject came up the night the Yule's got engaged. Mr. Yule got very angry, but Martha smoothed out their tempers."

"Thank you, Ms. Kelleher," Agent Harbaugh said as they made their way off the porch. "We may be back with additional questions, but thank you for your time today."

Key nodded in acknowledgment and then entered the house. Sara and Michael were waiting just inside the great room. A live picture of the porch was on the TV screen, and they could hear the cars pulling off. Mike had a sympathetic look, but Sara had an awry one.

Sara and Key locked eyes. "You did all of that, didn't you?" Key asked.

Sara gave her a closed-lip smile.

"Even having Grandma Izzy call?" Key asked again.

Sara's smile grew, turning into a grin.

"Well, thank you for knowing enough not to send Michael out. Although I'm sure my Da will give them his name, and they'll be back." Key finally turned her attention to Michael with a frown.

"Michael said he shouldn't go out, but why?" Sara asked.

"Because he was there when my grandmother's letter arrived. Until he tells them that, it's only my Da's word that it ever existed."

Michael stepped closer to them, "but I'm sure he still has it. I doubt he would throw something like that away."

Key looked down and then peeked up at Sara, who was doing the same to her.

"What are you two not telling me?" Michael asked.

Key finally looked at him, "according to Erin, he was tearing his office apart looking for it and never found it. He told her it had never left his office, yet he and Martha went through every single piece of paper in the room and found nothing."

"Do you think Erin took it?" Michael asked.

Key and Sara answered in unison, "no."

Mike stood and kept looking back and forth between the two. "There is still something you aren't telling me."

"Some things are best left unsaid," Key replied.

Ringggg. It was Michael's cell phone, he answered it and started speaking, "Mom? What's up?" He immediately closed his eyes and said, "It's okay, Mom, you didn't do anything wrong. Thanks for letting me know." After another moment, "I'll explain later, but no, I'm not in any trouble."

Key knew as soon as he looked at her. "Oh my God, they're coming back already?"

"Yeah. My Mom told them I was here," Michael replied. "Shit! Why did I have to pick that dam thing up?" He put his hands in his pockets and just shook his head while looking at the floor.

"Don't stress it, love. They still don't have it no matter what you remember seeing," Key told him. She stepped over and put her arms around his waist. "Please don't stress it. What happens, happens."

Key had him sit down to relax before the knock on the door came. "I would prefer you speak to them outside, if that's okay."

"Yeah," Mike answered her.

When they arrived, Mike answered the door and stepped out.

"Mr. Young, I'm Agent Roberts, and this is Agent Harbaugh. We would like to ask you about the morning Kathleen Yule left for England."

Michael motioned for them to take a seat on the porch again before taking one himself. "I was ten years old back then, but I'll help however I can."

"Were you there when Kathleen was told to go with her grandmother that morning?" agent Roberts asked.

"No, not in the house. It was my birthday, and I came to ask if Kathleen could come to my party. I had promised my friends they would finally meet a real princess. So again, I was ten years old, and her dad called them princess…"

"And you thought she really was, I understand. Did you come to the front door before or after she had gone?" Agent Roberts asked.

"At first, I came the same way I always did, down the hill to their beach. When I got down to the sand, Kathleen came out in her nightgown, crying and screaming, "save me, Batman". It's what she called me because I had introduced myself as Batman two years earlier. I didn't realize she thought it was my real name."

Mike could tell they weren't interested in the antidotes by the sighs they let out. "Anyway, I knew from the looks of her that she wasn't going to be able to come and my friends would never let me hear the end of it, so I got upset. I looked down, and when I kicked the sand out of frustration, it ended up in her face. She was wiping her eyes and choking on it. It was horrible. Her Dad came out after her and sounded angry. I panicked and ran up the hill."

"Did you ever enter the house after that day?"

"I entered the house that same day. After watching Kathleen and some old lady walking out to a black car and Mr. Yule putting suitcases in the trunk, I was curious. I walked around to the front and knocked. Mr. Yule invited me in and gave me a picture I found on his floor." Michael then pulled out his wallet and showed him the picture of him and Key.

"What did he tell you about Kathleen or where she was going?" Roberts asked.

"He said she had left with her grandmother to England. I asked when she would be back, but he didn't know."

"He said he didn't know?"

"Correct. So, after a week of being grounded for messing up my new suit, I kept going back to ask every day."

"How many days did you go back to ask? Do you remember?"

"It was at least another two weeks before he got something in the mail with a return address from England," Michael answered. *Dammit, why did I offer that?*

"Do you know what it was?" Agent Harbaugh asked.

"A page he had to unfold, so it was at least 8 ½ by 11". Mr. Yule immediately started to say, "Not my Kathleen. I didn't mean this," or something like that. He was saying it so loudly I kept looking around for Erin, but she never appeared. Then he fell to his knees and curled his head to the floor. He must have said something that made it really clear she was dead though. I had lost my grandmother, so I knew what death was, and I freaked out and ran."

"So, you never read or touched the letter?" Agent Roberts asked.

"Oh, I may have picked it up and put it on the table. I think he dropped it when he went down, but don't quote me on that." *I need to get them past that moment,* he thought. "The next time I saw the Yules was the day of the memorial, where Erin told me she wasn't dead. It was a very confusing time because I had just sat through a memorial for her. I also wasn't a huge fan of Erin's at the time. She and Kathleen didn't get along as kids, and Erin didn't like me since I was friends with her sister."

"So, you never read or saw a death certificate with Kathleen's name on it?" Agent Roberts asked again.

"A death certificate?" Mike asked and just let the question hang there.

The agents just stared for a few moments but finally relented. "Thank you, Mr. Young. If we have additional questions, should we reach you here in the future?"

"Yes, sir," Mike replied.

Mike stood and watched them leave, thinking to himself; *Mr. Yule never saw me read anything. Right or wrong, no one can prove what I saw that day.* He walked back into the house and his future wife was smiling and ran to hug him, but he stopped her. "Why are you so confident he can't show them the death certificate?"

Her eyes got big, but she said nothing.

"Key, you are the one always talking about honesty. Why not now? Why are you so confident he can't produce it or that they don't already have it?" He asked again.

"Because it no longer exists. I made sure of it." Key took a step back with reddened cheeks.

"I assume your grandmother is just as confident?"

She just nodded in the affirmative before quietly being completely honest. "I gave them to her to destroy. I watched her burn them."

"What if I had told them I'd read it?" Michael asked with a crooked brow, his hands now crossed in front of his chest.

"Then I would have told her not to come and left it to God's will. I told you 'it is what it is' and never asked you to do anything."

"You know your father is looking like a fool to the FBI, right?"

She looked to be in deep thought but didn't answer him.

His arms dropped back down to his sides. "You're lashing out at him. You're lashing out like your grandmother would. How are you diff-"

Key's eyes instantly teared up and one escaped her eye while her breathing became erratic. "That was…that was never the intent," she choked out.

Mike stepped closer to her, "Let's not make a habit of it, okay?"

With a nod in the affirmative, Key broke down into full sobs against Mike's chest while he embraced her.

Wedding Plans

"A few months doesn't give me much time. What are you thinking for a dress?" Sara asked.

"You know me, I like simple. Nothing too glittery. Any chance I could wear…" Key started.

"No."

"You don't even know what I was going to ask," Key whined.

"Pants. You wanted to know if I could somehow create a look with shorts or pants rather than just a dress, and the answer is no. You will wear a traditional white dress, Key."

"But…" Key started again.

"Don't start with me about not being a virgin. If you don't want to wear a veil over your face, fine, but you will wear a white dress and a veil at least on the back. Period."

"Fine, but I'm not wearing shoes," Key said.

"Well, for pictures…" Sara started.

"Period," Key snapped back. "It's a beach wedding. If I can't wear shoes in the sand, then I won't wear them at all."

"Okay, fine, but now I'm rethinking your hair. Pinning it up will look out of place with a slip dress and no shoes. I see the front pulled up in strands, weaved like a basket, but the length will be left down."

"What should the boys wear? Tuxedos won't work," Key said, looking at her with a curious look on her face.

"A light khaki for Mike and a slightly darker version for his ushers. And yes, no shoes either."

"And the girls?" Key asked.

"Slip dresses, but t-length, each with a tint of color," Sara answered.

"Miss Key, there is a Nora Kelleher at the front door," said the house assistant.

"V, let her in, please."

Sara and Key made their way downstairs to greet her. "Hello Mrs. Kelleher."

"Sorry, I think I beat them here. Maggie said they were on their way home," Nora replied.

"Can I get you something to drink?" Key asked, motioning her to take a seat.

"Oh no, don't fuss."

"Well, I'm about to fuss over myself and get something, so why don't you follow me in case you change your mind," Key laughed.

Key had just poured the three of them a glass of sweet tea as Erin and Maggie walked into the house. Both of them were carrying multiple bags in each hand.

"Are we going back to the women's shelter this week?" Erin asked.

"Tomorrow, why? What did you get?" Key asked.

"Baby stuff!" Maggie said. "We went to a pop-up sale, and they were practically giving this stuff away. The sale was almost over, so I think they didn't want to carry it all back home."

"Maggie was smart enough to tell them we were going to donate it to the shelter, and their already low prices dropped even further," Erin added.

"We have more in the car," Maggie said just as Mike and Jeff also came in.

"We should clean this stuff up the best we can, so just drop bottles and stuff on the kitchen table," Key said, standing up before turning to Mike and Jeff. "Can you finish unloading Maggie's car? I would like to talk to Maggie for a moment."

"Sure," the guys responded.

Key had a very serious look on her face when she addressed Maggie. "Erin may have told you that the two of us didn't get along when we were little. She was everything that irritated me." This caused them all to giggle, and Key winked at her sister. "She played with dolls. She loved being a fashionista with her frilly dresses and shiny shoes and had no fondness for her school lessons."

Maggie nodded in agreement with a huge smile.

"When I left and was roomed with Sara, she was all those things, but they didn't bother me anymore. They were the very things that endeared Sara to me. I missed my sister."

"I can't say for sure, but the things that seemed to bother Erin about me, I see in you. Yet, here you are – like sisters as well."

"I know she missed you," Maggie replied.

Key smiled and then asked, "Would you consider being a bride's maid at my wedding?"

"I would be honored." Maggie and Erin shared smiles with one another.

"Thank you." Key and Maggie hugged. When they pulled away from each other, Key continued, "Please don't mistake her love for you, or mine for Sara. Sara is my sister in her own right, as you are for Erin in yours. Neither of you were replacements but simply reminders of what we'd lost. So, thank you, Maggie. I'm happy to know all our sisters will be together on my big day."

Mrs. Kelleher, realizing she had not asked Erin, said, "Well, I'm sure both girls would be honored to be bride's maids. They-"

"No," Key replied, cutting her off. "Erin can't be a bride's maid," she scoffed.

As Erin took a step back, Key reached to grab her hand and pulled her closer. "You have bigger shoes to fill, but you are the only one who can."

Everyone's faces, except for Sara's, became crooked, and the room went silent.

Key turned to face Erin more directly, lifting her other hand, which Erin took. Key's eyes started to fill with tears while she choked down the emotion. "You…you know when you get married, Da is the obvious choice to walk you down the aisle. You also know he would never have been the obvious choice for me, if…" She had to stop to swallow the emotion again.

Erin knew what she was trying to say, "You would have wanted Mum to do it." Key's head nodded up and down slowly, and now both were emotional.

Finally, after clearing her throat a few times, Key regained her voice. "You are the closest to my memory of her. I see her in you and feel she's never closer than when you're here. You are the only one who can fill her shoes for me that day. Will you walk me down the aisle?"

Erin couldn't speak but nodded her head furiously as she embraced her sister.

Make It Right

Erin answered the door and it was Martha with Caitlyn, she greeted them inviting them in.

"Hi Caitlyn." Erin gave her a big hug. "Hey Martha. I have my room set up; do you want to come see it?" Erin asked.

"We would love to. Is Key home today?" Martha asked.

"Today was their day to serve at the House of Hope, but they should be back soon."

"Why aren't you there? Don't you normally volunteer with them?"

"We decided to divide and conquer. There were two groups that had issues finding enough volunteers for their commitment dates, so we split the family into two to fill both."

"Well, I stopped in, hoping to speak to both of you," Martha said.

"About what?" Erin asked as they walked into the kitchen.

"Your father knows Mike and Key are engaged."

"Does he know the FBI stopped in on us?"

"That's how he knows. They came back and told him there didn't seem to be a case against your grandmother and then mentioned that she was invited to the wedding this summer."

"I hate being in the middle of all this," Erin said with a frown. Just then, the front door opened. "Hey Key, Da knows you two are engaged."

"How?" Key, Sara and Mike asked in unison.

"Those agents told him," Erin replied.

Key dropped the bag she was holding and leaned up against the wall.

"Although I'm a little upset that Caitlyn and I weren't invited, I do have some good news to add. They came back to inform him that they didn't believe there was a case," Martha said.

Key stood up, off the wall, "Martha, I'm sorry, it's my fault you weren't told. Sara and I were putting together a plan to kidnap the two of you that morning."

"That's sweet, I guess, but I wouldn't have attended without my husband. I really wish you two could work this out for all our sakes," Martha said.

Key let out a long sigh, "Fair enough." She turned to Mike, "could you drive me over?"

"Oh, he's at work, honey," Martha interjected.

"Good, he'll be less likely to cause a scene there." Key headed back out the door, and Mike followed.

"What are you going to say to him?" Mike asked when they got in the car.

"I'm not sure, but it's time I make this right," Key replied, shaking her head. She stared out the window the rest of the ride until he pulled up in front of the building where Jon worked.

"Should I come-" Mike started to say before Key cut him off with a wave of her hand.

"No. I'll call you when it's over." Key didn't look back once she was out of the car and swung the door shut. She entered the building and headed straight for the receptionist.

"Hi Erin," said the young brunette behind the front desk.

"Sorry, no, I'm her sister, Key. And you are?" Key held out her hand.

"I'm Nancy. Oh my God, I was so hoping to meet you. I watch your skating videos constantly. It's crazy what you can do."

Key smiled at the compliment. "Thanks. Is my Da available?"

"Let me check." The young girl picked up the receiver of her phone and pushed some buttons. "Yes, Mr. Yule has a visitor. Is it alright if I send her back?" She waited a moment, "His daughter. Okay, thank you." She hung up and looked back at Key, "His office is room 105. Straight back. His assistant, Agnes, will meet you."

"Thank you," Key replied before heading down the hall.

An older woman who reminded Key of Mother Goose, looked to be waiting for her when she reached room 105.

"Erin, it's so good to see you, dear," Agnes greeted her.

"Hello, Agnes. I'm Erin's sister, Key. It's very nice to meet you."

"Oh, my heavens, I was wondering when we would finally meet you. You and Erin truly are identical, aren't you? Your sister still has a bit of her English accent, but not like yours, dear."

Key smiled and stood there waiting. Agnes just kept looking her over, putting her hand to her heart, shaking her head in wonder.

"Is my father available?" Key finally asked.

"Oh, yes, sorry." Agnes turned and did a light knock on his office door before opening it. "Your daughter is here."

"Thank you, send her in," Key heard him say.

Agnes stepped aside, and Key walked past her. The room looked lived in, with pictures, awards and nick-nacks filling the bookshelves and windowsills. There was a small, round table with four chairs around it and then two more chairs directly in front of his more formal desk.

Jon peeked up quickly but was typing something that stole his focus. "I'll be right with you, honey." He finished his typing and did a quick re-read before hitting a button and giving her his full attention. "To what do I owe the honor of this? You haven't visited me at the office in years."

"Actually, I have never visited you at the office. It's very nice though." Key gave him a few seconds to adjust before continuing, "am I interrupting?"

"No, no, sit down." He motioned with one hand to the seat in front of him. "I'm even more surprised to see you since you kicked me out of your house."

"Yes, my house, good for you," Key said with a wry smile.

He didn't reply. His jaw tightened as he sat back and crossed his arms in front of him.

"I was curious about something and thought I would stop by to ask," Key started.

"And what is it you were curious about?" Jon asked.

"If you love me."

"So, you came to start a fight. You came to my place of business…"

"No, I came to ask if you loved me. Can you not answer it?"

"You know the answer to that."

"Do I? Then why would I feel the need to ask?"

Jon was visibly angry and sat without saying a word.

"You say you thought I was dead, but when you found out I wasn't, you didn't call, come to England, and you avoided me at Erin's graduation. I had to trick you into talking to me at all. So, I'm asking you, do you love me?"

"You know I love you, but I know you don't love me. You seem hell-bent on hating me for the past."

Key leaned forward in the chair. "If I hated you, I would not have bothered to trick you into talking to me. I would not have bothered trying to make peace with our past. I would not have allowed you to get away with the excuses you fed me the first time we talked. And I would not be here now."

"Excuses? I told you-" he tried speaking but was interjected by Key.

"That I was more mature, I know. You thought I could handle it, I know. However, when Grandma was asked if she would have settled for taking only me, given a choice, she honestly wasn't sure. She wanted both of us, but you took charge and insisted I go."

Jon was about to protest, but Key talked over him again. "I remember it like it was yesterday. I wasn't the only one who didn't have a choice that morning. I remember her arguing for both Erin and me and you ignoring her while you cleaned me up, packed my things and pushed me out."

"She was unrelenting-" he started.

"Don't go there. You cut her off cold on Erin's behalf with that lie about motion sickness."

"What do you want from me, for Christ's sake?" Jon asked loudly.

Key sat calmly for a moment, just staring at him. When she began again, she spoke more slowly, "The truth. No matter how hard you think it will be to say it or for me to hear it. Tell me if there was a reason you didn't want me around."

Jon uncrossed his arms and laid them on the arms of his chair. He started rocking it slowly while in a daze. His eyes closed for about three full seconds. Finally, his eyes opened, and he spoke somberly, "Do you remember when the nurses came to take care of your Mum?"

Key nodded yes.

"Your mother would call for you when she needed something, the nurses would go to you to notify medication changes, and I would find out later. Even Erin looked to you first. I felt useless." Jon looked down at his lap and was blinking his eyes quickly.

His head shook from side to side. "I seemed to have no say in the house. I had to keep going to work and I would come home to a meal you had cooked, to a house you had cleaned, wearing clothes you had washed. The nurses would go on and on about how you kept up Erin's home-schooling and would bring them coffee."

Jon finally looked up at Key, with tears flowing down his cheeks. "I think the last straw was you taking my place in your Mum's bed at night. You would crawl up and fit in that hospital bed with her, and it was you who felt her last moments." Jon's breathing became faster until they turned into full sobs.

Key immediately got up, made her way around the desk and sat in his lap, hugging him. "I'm sorry, Da. I'm so sorry."

At hearing her words, he embraced her until he slowly regained control of his emotions.

They sat quietly for some time before Key spoke again. "I would have resented you in the same way if it had been the other way around." Her eyes blurred in thought, "I did what I needed to in order to survive her last year and no, I didn't think about the effect on you. I'm sorry."

When Jon loosened his embrace, Key sat up a bit. He found a kinder face, looking back before he wiped his eyes and looked down again.

"Da? I need to hear you say it. I know it may seem like I'm torturing you, but I need to hear you say the truth. You didn't want me there. Even if it was getting rid of me for a few weeks, you didn't want me there."

Jon looked up again, and his face contorted. The tears fell more readily as he choked out, "I didn't want you there." He shook his head from left to right, "I'm so sorry. I never thought you wouldn't come back. It's easy to say I regret it now, but..."

Key embraced him again while she spoke. "Peace is coming easily because I can honestly understand what you were feeling. Had it been the other way around, I would have been angry and wanted to get away from you. I probably would have volunteered to go."

Jon rolled his eyes at the idea but said nothing.

She pulled away to look at him eye to eye, "So, we need never speak of this again." Key kissed his cheek and sat back on his lap to lay her head on his chest. They sat quietly, even listening to his phone ring over and over, going unanswered.

Finally, Key slipped herself off his lap and stood up. She was looking down at him with a red face. "Now it's my turn to confess."

Jon looked up, blinking heavily to regain his focus.

"Erin's graduation wasn't the first time I had been in your house or seen your office." Key started to breathe quick, short breaths. "I entered knowing-"

"That we would believe you were Erin." Jon interrupted her to say.

"Yes." Key felt the shame rise in her throat. "And I took-"

"Oh my God, YOU took the folder!" Jon now stood up and looked down at her. "Why?"

"I wanted the power to decide."

"The power to decide what? If she should be held accountable?" Jon scoffed.

"Yes, I suppose-" Key started while Jon sat back in his seat. "Da, can I ask you a question?"

"Sure," he scoffed again.

"Did you believe she was capable of throwing me away when you handed me over?"

"NO!" Jon looked surprised.

"So, you shouldn't be held responsible for what she did, correct?"

"Correct."

"Well, Izzy never thought the monster was capable of what he did-"

Jon cut her off again, "But that's the least of it, she threw you away-"

"The LEAST of it?" Key replied with wide eyes.

"No, sorry, that's not what I meant, honey-"

"Here's my point, Da." Key said in a stern voice. "Yes, she threw me away, but think about it. If he hadn't been the monster he was, I would have figured out that my letters weren't getting to you and found another way. So, at worst, I would have spent some time at a prestigious boarding school, got professionally tested and enrolled in a university. Bu-"

"And I would have come and gotten you in a heartbeat," Jon said.

"Yes. You would have come, and she probably would have been held responsible right away, but more importantly, I wouldn't have been much worse for the wear."

"But he was a monster, and you were there because of her."

Key sighed heavily. "Take a step back, Da. Why was I with her again?"

Jon just put his head back down and sank further into the cushion of the chair.

"You agreed that you shouldn't be held accountable for what she did. So, it's only fair you not hold her accountable for what the monster did." Key's shoulders sunk forward. "I'm trying to make peace with all of it, each step of what happened, in my own way. I need you to respect that even if you don't agree with it." Key gave one last, "please Da."

Jon let out a long sigh and just stared at her. He shook his head slowly a few times and, after another deep breath, replied, "I'll try."

Key cupped his face in her hands, "I'm sorry for asking if you loved me. I've always known the truth. I swear I've never doubted it."

I have never understood this kid, Jon thought.

After another deep breath, Key said, "I have one more thing-"

"More?" Jon broke a smile that Key matched. They both giggled a little.

"Yes, well, Michael asked me to marry him, and I accepted. I would love it if you, Martha, and Caitlyn were there."

"Of course we'll be there." Jon's smile got wider.

"That's not all," Key said quickly. "I have something difficult to explain." She took a moment and broke eye contact before looking at him again and said slowly, "I've asked Erin to walk me down the aisle."

"Is it because of our fight, or…" Jon asked in confusion.

"No, no. If Mum had been alive, I would have had her do it. She and I had the same bond you and Erin have. I hope you understand."

"I won't lie, although a little disappointed, I think I do understand." He gave her a sideways smile and a wink.

"Thank you, Da." She returned the smile, "I would still love to do a father-daughter dance."

"I hope so, I would love that too." Jon looked at his watch, "is it 5:00 o'clock yet? I'm exhausted."

Wedding Day

"I'll get it," said Mike's mother, Madison. She answered the front door to see Jon, "Hello, Jon, come on in. Oh, I like the sandals."

"Hahaha, thanks. I have to say, this is the most comfortable outfit I've ever worn to a wedding," Jon replied.

"The men are in Mike's room. It's the door to the left after the stairwell. I guess it's time I get dressed too."

"Thanks." Jon walked past her and found Mike, Mike's father, Jeff, Ray and Joe. Mike was the only one who stood out with a white button-up shirt, sleeves rolled up, and the same casual cargo pants in light khaki. The others were all in a light shade of brown cargo pants with pastel shirt colors to match the ladies. Jon found he was the only one with footwear on and his pant legs and shirt sleeves not yet rolled up.

"Hey, Mr. Yule. You look great," Mike said, greeting him with a handshake.

Jon shook his hand and reached up with his left to squeeze Mike's shoulder. "I really appreciate you inviting me to be a groomsman. It means a lot to be a part of this today."

"Well, you were there from the start, so-" Mike started.

"I'm ready!" DeAnne announced as she entered.

All the gentlemen turned to look at her and started making adoring sounds.

DeAnne was asked to be a flower girl with Jon's daughter, Caitlyn. She was in a sundress with a pastel flower pattern of pink, yellow and brown. Her hair was down but with long curls.

"You look beautiful, Dee," Mike said further adding, "alright, well, If Mom has her dress on, we should be heading over."

"Hold it taunt, Rachel!" Sara lamented. She was weaving just the top of Key's hair like a basket might look while the length was still in big, hanging curlers. She needed to recruit both Rachel and Dannie to hold strands while working on it.

"Erin, come hold these, I'm tired of being yelled at," Rachel said.

Erin walked over, giggling and slowly took the strands from her. Maggie was curling Mike's friend Jessica's hair, and Rachel greeted Martha and Caitlyn as they entered the room. "Oh Caitlyn, you look fabulous, love. You too, Martha."

"Thank you," Martha replied. "You all look wonderful." She made her way until she saw an empty chair. "Hello, I'm Martha Yule," she offered the old woman sitting in the chair next to it.

"Hello, I'm Isabelle, their grandmother."

Martha froze for a moment before sitting down very slowly.

"You're Jon's wife? And is that his daughter, Caitlyn?" Isabelle asked.

Martha nodded at first and then gave a quick glance before answering, "Yes."

Isabelle could see how stiff Martha was sitting and addressed her one more time, "I'm sorry, I understand your loyalty to your husband, so I won't bother you with further conversation, but your daughter is beautiful. She looks just like him." Isabelle got up and walked over to the girls. "I'm going to go down and get water. Is anyone in need of one?"

"Yes," said Jessica. "Thank you."

Isabelle made her way out of the room and started down the stairs. She had just reached the bottom when Mike and the guys were coming in. She walked a little quicker in hopes of not being noticed, but Mike immediately turned toward the kitchen and walked behind her.

Once they reached the kitchen, Mike whispered, "Izzy, if he starts anything, please come to me. I would like to resolve it as quietly as I can without upsetting my bride today."

"If he starts anything, I'll tell you about it tomorrow," she replied. Isabelle kept walking into the courtyard, past the tables decorated in blue sapphire cloths and wildflower centerpieces, until she reached the café. She waited until the caterer moved out of the way of the refrigerator before opening it to grab a few water bottles. Once she had them, she turned and found Mike had followed her.

She gave him a simple smile, "Today is your day, please don't stress me. You have beautiful weather, a lot of friends and family coming and most importantly, a gorgeous bride upstairs." Isabelle put both waters in one hand to pat him gently on the chest before she made her way around him to head back.

As Isabelle exited the kitchen, she saw her son Bobby at the glass doors, looking out to the patio and speaking to Jon. She quickened her pace to get back upstairs.

"It's good to see you. You were so young when we met. I think it was the day I married Alex," Jon said.

"It was," Bobby replied with a nod.

"So, did you ever marry?" Jon asked Bobby.

"I did. I married a widow, but it didn't work out. We only lasted a few years before she left me. I understand you remarried and had a daughter. What is her name?" Bobby asked.

"Caitlyn. She's here somewhere, I saw my wife's car outside," Jon replied while making a quick scan of the room. "I assume you didn't come alone, so where is the old bat?"

Bobby gave him a frown before answering, "My mother is upstairs with Key. Good to see you, Jon." He started to walk away, but Jon grabbed his arm.

"You can't expect me to just forgive and forget everything overnight," Jon said.

"But you expect I should?" Bobby answered before yanking his arm out of Jon's grip and turning to face him again. "My mother wasn't alone in the decisions. Key has made that abundantly clear."

Jon started to object, but Bobby continued, "Here is what I expect: I expect all of us to be civil for Key and Michael's day and anyone who can't be unselfish enough, should go home. Key worked for years to make peace with the hell she suffered. She can't forget a second of it and she had no control over the decisions that caused it. So, I think respecting her wishes and being civil for one day is the very least we can do." Bobby turned and walked off before Jon could respond.

The house assistant, V, announced, "There are two guests approaching the front door."

Bobby had made his way to that side of the room, so he answered it. "Claire, Jarred! Come in, come in."

Claire hugged Bobby before Jarred shook his hand.

"They're upstairs, I'll take you up." Bobby led them to the staircase and up to the master suite at the top.

"Oh my, this place is gorgeous," Claire commented as they ascended the stairs.

Bobby tapped his knuckles on the door, "Are you decent in there?"

Sara opened the door with a huge smile, "Yes, we're decent." She stood aside and invited them in.

When they entered, Key had just gotten her dress on and was looking at herself in the mirror. She gave a confused look at Bobby and his guests.

Bobby approached with a huge grin. "I'm sure your mother's diaries talked a lot about her best friend, did she not?"

Key's confusion turned into a huge open-mouthed smile, "Yes, she wrote often of her best friend Claire and her fiancé, Jarred. Are you…"

Claire had tears in her eyes. "Oh, my goodness, it's like Alexandra is here, standing in front of me, having never aged." She put her hands up and covered her mouth. "You're a little replica."

Just as Claire stepped closer to hug Key, Erin stepped into her view.

"Oh my God, two replicas!" Claire hugged them both. When she pulled away, she turned and introduced them to her husband.

"Did you both know our father, Erin?" Erin asked after being introduced to Jarred.

"Oh, yes. He was quite the character that one. Oddly, I kept trying to convince your Mum to drop Erin and go for Jonathan. He seemed a bit more stable, but she was so smitten," Claire replied.

Looking at Key, she asked, "I know you're a writer, but did you know your Mum was?"

"Grandma Izzy gave me her old stories. I don't think she continued to make them up once she came to America, or at least I didn't find any. She just kept very detailed diaries," Key replied.

"Well, I figured you may need something borrowed. I would like it back because it is very dear to me, but I brought it for the two of you to enjoy." Claire handed her a little pile of paper, tied with frayed ribbon down one side to make a book. The title on the front said, 'Love Everlasting'. "Your mother wrote it for us as a wedding gift."

"Thank you! This means a lot Claire. I'll read it before you leave." Key then looked at Bobby, "and thank you for thinking to invite them. They are a great gift. Claire played such an integral part in Mum's life."

Bobby and Claire both looked at one another before Claire let on, "he wasn't the one that tracked me down. It seems you've had quite the effect on your grandmother and her need to make peace with the past."

Key looked over at Isabelle and received a wink and a grin.

Key took Erin's hand, "Mum really is here today. She's everywhere; do you feel her?"

Erin hugged her sister, "she is."

Izzy had gotten up, grabbed a small box with a bow and stepped over to Key. "Since you have something borrowed, I got you something blue. I hope they match your rings."

Key untied the bow and opened the box to find a beautiful blue sapphire and diamond necklace with matching earrings. "They are too beautiful."

"I have to be honest about them. They were new about 19 years ago when I purchased them for your mother. Her favorite was also blue sapphire, and she was due to officially graduate-"

"These were her graduation gift," Key finished her thought. After Isabelle nodded in the affirmative, Key said, "thank you, grandma, I love them."

Isabelle turned to Erin, "I thought you might also appreciate some of your mother's jewelry. I brought everything she left behind and what would have been left to her. The two of you can figure out who keeps what."

Erin gave her an awkward smile, but Key thanked her for the kindness.

"Well, you now have something borrowed and something blue, so let's go see your something new," Sara sang. "It's from all your sisters, but it's downstairs."

"Then let's go!" Key started for the door, but the older women, Claire, Martha and Isabelle, all protested.

Claire stood in the way of the door, "but your fiancé is probably down there. He'll see you."

The girls all started giggling, when Key finally said, "I don't believe in those old superstitions."

"But your fiancé does. That's why he stayed at his mother's last night," Isabelle said.

"Fine. I've got this." Sara walked out of the room and yelled down, getting everyone's attention. "Mike, go to the courtyard and make sure it's ready for the reception."

"I've already checked, they're-" Mike started.

"Your bride is about to come out. We want to show her the something new," Sara said.

With a nod of understanding, Mike immediately made his way toward the kitchen. Once he was out of sight, Sara turned and said, "come on, he's gone."

Martha whispered to Caitlyn that it was from her as well, putting a little pep in her step to follow them out. Key followed Sara out and saw it immediately.

"Oh, my goodness. When? How?" Key lifted the front of her dress a bit and started down the stairs to see it up close. "It has everyone! The entire family! Oh my God, even Mum, Da and Da-Erin."

There had always been a picture that scrolled up when they wanted to use the TV. Today, the picture had been replaced by a montage of painted faces that represent everyone in the family. The collage of images included her grandparents from Ireland, both grandmothers and grandfather Yule. Isabelle and William Harrington were there with Uncle Bobby and her mother, Alexandra. Both her fathers, Jon and Erin, with Jon's new wife Martha and Caitlyn. Sara had even thought enough to add Maggie, Jessica, and all her sisters. Sara also had Jeff, Ray, and Joey in the mix, with Michael and Key in the middle.

They all gathered in front of it, while Key took it all in. "This is fantastic, thank you all." She started hugging all her sisters, one by one.

"Have you gotten something old yet?" Jon asked from behind them.

Key let go of Dannie and turned to focus on him. The girls stood aside so he could step up.

"Before your father left, he asked me to hold on to something that meant a lot to him. My father had given him this as a gift, and Erin was very proud of it." Jon started to pull it out of his pocket as he continued, "He asked that I hold onto it so it wouldn't be stolen when he went for training." He handed Key the old watch.

Key looked at it carefully, "I really feel like Mum and your brother Erin are here with us." She looked back up at him and gave him a tight hug. "Thank you, Da. I love you."

When they pulled away, he asked, "So, you have something new and something old, but…"

"Mum's best friend, Claire gave me something borrowed. It's a story Mum wrote for them as a wedding gift. I also…"

"Claire? Is she still with Jarred? Your Mum was devastated not to be with her on her wedding day." He gazed up like he could see the memory better on the ceiling, "I remember…" Jon was saying when Claire stepped up and patted him on the chest.

"Yes, Jarred and I are still together! Why would you doubt it?" Claire stood in front of him and then leaned in for a hug.

"Claire! Oh, it's been forever. You look fabulous." Jon reached out to shake with Jarred, "Good to see ya ole'man."

"I haven't seen you since, well…" Jarred started.

"Erin's funeral," Jon said.

"Otherwise known as your wretched wedding day," Claire added.

"That was my fault," Isabelle said. Everyone in the room seemed to freeze. "My daughter, they both, were doing something so brave and as usual, I made it ugly."

"I shouldn't have brought it up. I'm sorry," Claire said, taking a quick glance back at Isabelle and then looking down.

The room went silent. Isabelle's head was looking down while Jon's stare burned holes in her.

Key lightly touched the front of her father's chest, "An ugly start, but a beautiful love affair." She then turned to look at everyone, "Despite everything, they fell in love and raised both Erin and me as if we had been planned all along."

Key felt a familiar hand come around her waist from behind and pull her closer. When she looked up and back in surprise, Michael bent down and gave her a kiss. "If rough starts are a sign of a good future, then we're solid."

Key giggled with a nod of agreement before turning to face them all. "I only knew 'of' some of you from my mother's diaries." She looked at Claire and Uncle Bobby with a smile. "By some, I was disappointed and felt tormented. The need to rebuild and restore a few of you…" Key gave Danni and Rachel a quick wink…" and to reunite with others or just take the time to get to know the rest. In the end, family is not something you give up on, and I never did. Family is something you build not with bloodlines," she reached for her father's hand, "but with unconditional love and a willingness to forgive. Only love endures all things to allow forgiveness in the end."

They all looked to be in deep thought when Key continued. "I hope you'll all love me through my worst and always find forgiveness in your hearts. We are family, and I need and love you all."

Key and the girls stood looking out the glass doors. There were white chairs with sapphire-colored sashes on them, aligned on both the left and right of an aisle down the middle. The chairs were filled with family and friends from both America and Europe, none wearing shoes. Most of the women wore sun dresses while the men wore long shorts with nice collared golf shirts or button-up shirts with their sleeves rolled.

Jeff, Ray and Joey had come down the hill and walked directly toward the glass doors.

Sara slid the door open to greet them. Jeff immediately turned his back toward the house and held out his bent arm.

"Thank you," Isabelle said as she took it and allowed herself to be led to a seat at the front.

Ray did the same to escort Mike's mother, while Jon Yule followed suit to escort Martha.

Once the women were in their seats, the guys ran back up the cement steps.

A few minutes later, Father Reissman made his way down the steps to stand in the middle of two large vases filled with wildflowers. Although he was in his usual catholic robes, it was plainly obvious he too, went without shoes for the event.

It was time. Mike and his groomsmen made their way down the steps to stand at the Priest's left side. Jeff stood proudly as the best man, followed by Ray, Joey, Uncle Bobby, and Mr. Yule.

The glass doors opened to the tune of This Is The Day. Caitlyn and DeAnne made their way out, dropping rose petals as they walked. Shortly after, Maggie started out, followed by Jessica, Dannie, Rachel, and finally, after a quick hug with Key, the maid of honor, Sara.

The music stopped when Sara reached the Priest.

Everyone stood up, awaiting the bride, while the three-piece quartet started to play J.S. Bach's Arioso from Cantata 156.

Erin started to move but stopped when she felt Key squeeze her hand. She wondered if her sister was nervous and said, "You are truly home, Key, and your future is just down that aisle."

After another quick squeeze of their hands and a smile between them, Erin stepped out, and Key followed but stopped as her feet felt the sand.

Locking eyes with her future husband, she screamed, "Batman, save meee!"

About the Author

Kathleen Howell Young's happy place was always in a daydream. Now, she is ready to share one of them in her first novel, *Love Endures All Things*. Born in Texas, raised in Delaware as the baby of six kids who loved having that captive audience. She married her husband in 1991 and had the three children he promised her: two boys and a girl. She juggled a family while working in the same IT Department at a beautiful museum she hopes to retire from someday.